Ruth Gogoll

Forbidden Passion

Ruth Gogoll

Forbidden Passion

Translated from the German by
Susan Way

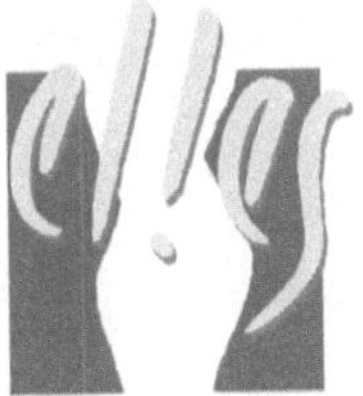

édition el!es
www.elles-books.com
Translation by Susan Way
Edited by Jill Bailin

Cover illustration:
© -Misha – Fotolia.com
ISBN 978-3-941598-09-6

1

Tiny letters danced across the screen in front of Kim's eyes. Exhausted, she rubbed at her eyelids. Working at a computer for hours at a stretch wasn't exactly restful. But when she could work no more, she went to one particular Internet site, where she could relax a little. There were stories there that she read again and again.

Very special stories. From woman to woman.

Slowly, Kim let herself slip into the tale. The woman with the chestnut brown hair sank back on the couch, and the other woman leaned over her –

"Ms. Wolff?"

Kim spun around. Her boss stood in the doorway. Silky chestnut brown hair fell across her shoulders, shiny and seductive. Kim swallowed.

"Are you working on something urgent?" her boss asked. "Or could you come see me right now?"

"I can . . . come," Kim managed with an effort. That was certainly true. She probably could've, almost.

Sonja Kantner, department head and object of Kim's restless dreams, glanced briefly at Kim's computer screen, but she was too far away, the screen stood at too sharp an angle, and the letters were too small. Kim thanked all the goddesses in heaven for that.

"Let me just save this." Kim felt heat rising to her face. She hoped she hadn't turned beet red. Lucky for her that she didn't usually suffer that fate.

"Fine, do that." Sonja Kantner nodded, then turned away.

Kim watched her luscious backside disappear from the doorway. Did she have to be so attractive? It was a daily torture.

Six Weeks Earlier

Six weeks ago Kim had seen her new boss for the first time, in the conference room at Sonja's introduction to the company. Kim had nearly fainted. She immediately began working out a plan for how, "for reasons of strategic importance to the company," she could move the department head's office – normally immediately adjacent to her own – to the other end of the hall, or better yet, to another floor. Or even better still, to another building.

After relating a few of his new department head's career highlights, the CEO gave the floor to Kim's new boss. "Why don't you start by introducing yourself, Mrs. Kantner?"

He stepped back, and Sonja Kantner stepped forward. She repeated, in slightly different terms, what he'd already said about her work history, but Kim wasn't interested in all that. What interested her was something Sonja Kantner had said right at the start: married, no children.

"Yet," she added with a charming smile.

She'd guessed right. Kim almost sighed when she received confirmation of what she'd already known anyhow. Sonja Kantner was straight, and solidly so. But what good would it have been, even if things were otherwise? Kim brooded some more over her plan to ship her off to another building. Maybe over in Eichhalde. Didn't they have branch offices in other countries than Germany, too? Couldn't Sonja be assigned overseas?

Kim knew one thing, at least: She wouldn't be able to stand having her new boss so close to her for long, every day, almost every minute. Or perhaps Kim would get used to her and the attraction would fade with time? Kim examined Sonja Kantner's body once more from head to toe as she spoke. No. No, the chances of that were exceedingly slim. The opposite was more likely to occur.

The assembly started to break up, and Kim was about to leave when the CEO waved in her direction. “Ms. Wolff? Would you come over here, please?”

Kim took a deep breath and squared her shoulders. Courage! She walked over to the two of them, and he introduced her with a smile. “This, Sonja, will be your closest coworker, Kim Wolff. Kim, I’d like to formally introduce you to Sonja Kantner.”

Sonja smiled and extended her hand to Kim. Kim would rather not have touched her, but she could hardly be rude, after all. Sonja’s hand was soft and warm. Once they actually touched, Kim would have preferred never to let go, so it was left to Sonja to draw back after the appropriate interval, which she did.

“I’m glad to meet you, Kim. I hope we’ll work well together.”

Work together? Kim thought, but aloud she responded with what was expected of her: “I hope so, too, and I’m looking forward to our association as well.” She smiled in a way that she hoped came across as confident. The tingling that had slowly spread from her hand throughout her entire body somewhat hindered her ability to be precise in her reactions.

“You’ll take Sonja on a tour of the company and show her everything, won’t you, Kim?” her CEO surmised, in a tone of friendly command.

Kim tried not to gulp. “Yes,” she replied, the effort required to control her voice making it sound very soft. “Of course. I’ll show her everything.” If only that were possible! What Kim would have liked to show her . . .!

Sonja laughed. “But not until tomorrow! Today, I still have to tour the executive floor.”

The CEO melted at her charming smile just as Kim had, only he was permitted to let it show; Kim wasn’t. One day’s reprieve! At least she had that!

“Then until tomorrow.” Sonja smiled at Kim once more. “What time will you get in?”

Kim forced out an answer. “At eight.”

“Good.” Sonja smiled. “I’ll be here at seven.”

"This really wasn't necessary, Kim." Mrs. Kantner greeted her, beaming.

Already in such a good mood this early in the morning – this was going to be something! When had she gotten up? Kim had been punctual, but Sonja was already sitting at the desk when Kim entered her office.

She came over to Kim and extended her hand. "Good morning," she said when she'd reached Kim, and her eyes delved into Kim's with an irresistible gaze.

She probably had no idea what effect that had on Kim . . . what effect she herself had on Kim –

"You could just as well have come in at eight," Sonja continued. "I know I get on everyone's nerves by being such an early riser. But I like to catch up on things in peace and quiet first thing in the morning. When there's no one here yet. Otherwise there are some things I'd never get to." Her laugh was enormously likeable.

She'd only just started. What was there for her to catch up on? Kim nudged herself into an understanding smile and withdrew her hand, which Sonja was still holding. "You're right about that," she agreed. "Although I prefer to do it in the evening, when everyone else is gone."

Sonja Kantner laughed once more and went back to her desk. "To each her own." She turned to face Kim. "How late do you stay at the office in the evenings?"

"Sometimes until ten. But I usually don't come in until –" Kim broke off. Perhaps she shouldn't reveal to her new boss what time she normally came in in the morning.

Sonja smiled. She was too clever to be led so easily astray. "You don't normally come in at seven or eight, do you?"

Kim sighed. "No," she admitted. "But I'll change that, of course," she added hastily. "If you're here at seven, I will be, too."

"That won't be necessary. As I said: I know I get on everyone's nerves by being such an early bird, but I don't demand it of anyone else." Sonja kept smiling. "Although by ten o'clock in the evening, I'm usually in bed. So we ought to agree on some time in between."

In bed? Kim looked at her. How seductive must she look lying in bed, if she was already this attractive during the day? She was sure to have wonderful negligees for nighttime . . . and if she wore nothing at all . . .?

"What's the earliest you can be here?" Sonja was paging through a file on her desk, something her predecessor must've left behind.

Kim had to tear herself away from her un-businesslike thoughts. "Eight-thirty?" she suggested. She could probably manage that, just about.

Sonja looked up. "Fine." She smiled once more in that unbelievably likeable, almost loving way. "And if it's more like nine sometimes, that's not a problem. I suspect that was the time you really wanted to suggest, am I right?"

She must've graduated from a great many leadership seminars, to be this good. "Yes," Kim admitted.

"We'll thrash it out together eventually!" Sonja laughed. "Will you show me around now?"

Thrash it out together – what a nice image, Kim thought for a moment. Then the two of them left the office for the tour.

And they really had thrashed things out together, so to speak. Working with Sonja was a pleasure. What Kim found less enjoyable was the physical proximity that usually went with it, and which Sonja showed no inclination to limit. She leaned over Kim's chair when she stood behind her and Kim had to show her something on the computer screen. When they met at a conference table to discuss something, she sat very close to Kim so they could study the same papers. Again and again, she smiled when they talked – always purely business, of course – and brushed casually against Kim's arm, raising goosebumps that were visible for miles – or would be, if Kim hadn't made a habit of wearing long-sleeved blouses to work.

Straight women! It never occurred to them that women might also be receptive to such temptation. In that respect, only men existed for them. Kim was already dreading the approach of summer. Her T-shirts and short-sleeved blouses would have to rot in her closet, and she would sweat like hell. But she still preferred that to letting Sonja Kantner see how she felt.

On the other hand, Kim also yearned for that physical closeness. To a certain extent, it was sweet torture whenever her boss called her over or approached her to work . . . when she was so dreadfully close, and yet Kim couldn't come any closer.

Never would Kim have dared to touch her the way Sonja carelessly touched Kim, just brushing her arm like that.

Kim would've exploded – on the spot.

▫▫■▫▫

Kim brought herself back to the present. *I should go over there*, she thought. *She'll be wondering where I am.*

She entered Sonja's office and was greeted with a smile, as always. "Let's sit there." Sonja indicated the conference table.

Oh, no, not that again! Kim had barely managed to calm down after being surprised by Sonja at her computer screen so uncomfortably – but Sonja was completely unaware of that. For her, all of this was innocent. She was straight, after all.

Kim lowered herself into a nearby chair and waited for her boss to sit down next to her, but she didn't. She sat down on the opposite side of the table and placed a prospectus in front of Kim.

Kim picked it up and looked inside. "You're going to this seminar?" *Thank the Goddess! A couple of days of peace!*

"Yes, and I'd like you to come along."

So much for the relaxation. "Me?" Kim asked, astonished. "This is a management seminar." She looked at Sonja. "Do you need someone to take minutes?"

"No." Sonja shook her head. "I don't want you to take minutes. I want you to take part in the seminar, just like I will."

"But I . . . I'm not a manager," Kim marveled rather feebly.

Sonja Kantner leaned forward and looked at Kim with that intense gaze that Kim could barely endure. "But you could become a manager." She leaned back again. "In my opinion, you are considerably under-challenged in your current position. You have many other qualities than those you're putting to use here. And I wish to foster them. Once you've completed this seminar, you'll meet all of the prerequisites for a promotion. You could be a manager by the fall."

Other qualities? What did Sonja Kantner mean by that? Had she noticed that . . .? Did she want to get rid of Kim? Kim cast a furtive glance at her boss. No, she seemed as friendly and competent as ever. "By the fall?" Kim asked, taken aback.

"Yes, it can't happen any sooner. Promotions are only announced once a year."

"I know."

"And? What do you say?" Sonja asked with an inviting smile. "Will you come along?"

"If you want . . ." Kim replied vaguely. This was her boss. If she said Kim had to, then Kim had to.

"No, no!" Sonja shook her head. "I don't want to force you into anything. You're welcome to say no. But I think this would be a great opportunity for you, wouldn't it?" She gave Kim a questioning look.

"Yes. Yes, it certainly would be," Kim admitted.

Kim's misgivings were not of a professional nature. She was more than happy to have the chance at a promotion. That would certainly have more money attached to it. But at a seminar like this, they'd be even closer than they were here in the office. And there would be no blessed end of the day at which they'd part ways and go home.

Kim knew about these seminar hotels, too. There was never anything nearby. That meant conference attendees sat in the bar in the evening with other seminar participants, because there was nothing else to do but have a drink and gab away. All small talk, and normally not a problem, aside from the inevitable boredom, but if Sonja were there, she and Kim would probably tend to concentrate on one another because they didn't know anyone else. Until well past midnight, probably, when it was finally time to go to sleep.

Fine. Kim would at least have those few hours alone in her hotel room to recover from her, from her constant gaze, from her uninterrupted presence.

Sonja was still watching Kim, waiting for her answer. She was probably wondering why Kim would hesitate at all. Anyone else would surely have agreed right away, and with excitement.

Kim nodded. “Sure. I’m looking forward to it.” She gave Sonja the most enthusiastic smile she could muster, to make her forget her hesitation.

“Lovely.” Sonja stood up. “Are you finished with the report that we talked about this morning?” she asked as she went back to her desk; she was obviously already thinking about something else.

“Almost. The meeting with the project group took longer than expected. I haven’t quite had time to finish it up.” And because of the little excursion Kim had needed to make on the Internet . . . But Sonja Kantner certainly didn’t need to know about that.

“When, then?” her boss asked succinctly. She was exceptionally efficient when it came to work.

“In an hour,” Kim promised.

Her boss nodded. “Bring it to me as soon as you’re done, please.” She sat down, and with that, Kim was dismissed.

Kim glanced down at the prospectus one more time as she stood up. “Should I reserve the rooms?”

Sonja looked up briefly. “No, I’ll take care of that. It’s included with the registration. I need to talk to them about something else anyway.” She went back to reviewing her files.

Kim nodded, left the office, and stopped at the coffee vending machine. She needed something to get over that shock. Unfortunately, the company management hadn’t seen fit to provide stronger drinks for such occasions. Hard liquor would’ve been just the thing right now. Kim did know of a colleague or two who were guaranteed to have a bottle hidden in their desks, but she didn’t really want to go so far as to ask.

The seminar took place a week and a half later.

The drive took just under two hours. Kim and Sonja chatted about in-house business, appointments for the following week, when they'd be back, and other organizational matters. Kim became more and more aware of Sonja's proximity while her boss drove and talked at the same time, developing entire concepts as she spoke. Kim's job was primarily to listen. She could observe Sonja Kantner the entire time in complete innocence.

Sonja's car was a large one, but Kim pressed herself inconspicuously against the outside edge anyway, into the door. The broad automatic transmission console in the center did separate them, but it wasn't enough to keep her from feeling Sonja's body heat with increasing intensity and smelling her perfume. Her scent was familiar to Kim, but was intensified by the closeness of the car. It unleashed indecent fantasies in her mind. Kim imagined how Sonja would smell when she was aroused, when she lay in bed and spread her legs –

"Do you think we can do it that way?" Sonja glanced briefly over at Kim.

Kim hadn't been listening. "Yes. Yes, sure. Certainly," she answered quickly. She'd find out eventually what it was her boss had been referring to.

Sonja turned her attention away from Kim and back to the road. Ten minutes later, they had arrived and headed for the reception desk. Sonja took care of everything while Kim looked around and waited for the concierge to hand her the room key.

When Sonja had finished, she turned around and dangled the plastic keycard in front of Kim's face. "Would you like to . . ." she inquired with an inviting smile.

"Is that my key?" Kim asked in return. She was rather surprised. Normally, the concierge only gave them out individually, and each guest had to sign something first.

"Ours," Sonja Kantner replied, similarly slightly surprised. "I explained all that in the car earlier. The registration was too last-minute. They only had one more room available. And the other participants are all men. So they put us two girls together." She laughed at her own joke, referring to grown women as 'girls'. "Earlier, in the car, you said it was fine. Or would you rather room with someone else –?" She broke off, even more confused than before.

With a man? Oh, no, definitely not! In that case, I'd rather stay with you. Although Kim didn't find that prospect exactly enticing. That is, she *did* find it enticing – but *that* was hardly open for debate. So she wouldn't even get to recover alone in her room at night. Even then, *she* would be there.

Why, oh why hadn't Kim paid attention in the car earlier? But what difference would it have made? If there weren't any more rooms . . .

"No, of course not," Kim assured her. "That's all fine. I'd just forgotten about it."

They took their things to the room, and Kim looked at the double bed with considerable worry. It was wide, as always in this sort of hotel, but Kim feared it would not be wide enough. Sonja was going to lie down next to her, Kim would hear her breathing, smell her, feel her warmth . . .

Kim put her bag in the closet and went to the door. "I'm going to go down now." *At least five minutes. Please! Please, let her stay here!*

Sonja Kantner nodded. "I'm going to unpack a few things. Then I'll catch up."

Exhaling, Kim left the room and shut the door behind her. She walked slowly down the stairs. She needed air. She couldn't have endured the elevator again. *Her* scent was sure to remain in there from moments ago, when they'd ridden up together. Once downstairs, Kim crossed the small entrance hall to the exit and stepped out onto the driveway.

The landscape, into which someone had so audaciously disturbed nature to erect this hotel, was gorgeous. Nothing but mountains all around, green meadows; in the middle distance, a cow mooed. Presumably on one of the nearby alpine pastures. It could've been really nice, relaxing, recuperative . . . but it wasn't. For that, Kim would've needed more distance from *her* – at least at night.

Well, then. Kim sighed. She would just have to deal with it, at least for these three days. Those, too, would pass, they'd drive back, and nothing would have happened. Nothing would have changed between the two of them. That seemed certain.

Kim looked at her watch. Too late to go for a walk – the seminar was about to begin. When Kim entered the lobby, Sonja was just coming down the stairs. She, too, had passed on the elevator, but – in Kim's estimation – more likely out of concern for her figure than because of Kim's beguiling scent. Kim wanted to sigh again right then.

Sonja was heading toward Kim. "Isn't there any sort of a reception?" she asked, smiling.

"Yes. Yes, sure there is. Over there in the lobby." Kim had to swallow. "Coffee and croissants."

"They could think up something new once in a while." Sonja sighed a little and turned in the direction Kim had indicated.

Kim followed her. They received two pin-on nametags and a slim folder of handouts. There were place cards arranged on the tables, with their seat assignments. Kim stopped. She saw her own name, but not Sonja's.

Sonja went around to the other side of the U-shaped arrangement of tables. "Ah, here!" She smiled and held up her place card.

Kim tried not to show her relief too plainly. She *wouldn't* have to sit next to her all day long! Saved! At least during the day. Nights would be another story ... What luck that someone seemed to have distributed the name cards randomly, and not according to company affiliation.

After they'd found their places and set down their folders, they went out and joined the male participants. Sonja paid not the slightest attention to the way their tongues all hung out as soon as they saw her. She would've had to accept ten cups of coffee and at least as many croissants at once in order to satisfy all the offers she received. Graciously, she honored an elderly gentleman by choosing him to be her coffee carrier.

Kim and Sonja stood at one of the tall bistro tables and awaited his return.

"Men!" Sonja said. "Can't live with them, can't live without them!" She laughed once more.

Well, I seriously doubt the latter, Kim thought. But her boss didn't know any different. "But you're married," Kim said. Since she'd been with the company, they'd never talked about Sonja's husband, but then, they rarely exchanged a word regarding their private lives.

"Yes," Sonja replied, exceptionally tersely, but then turned a captivating smile on her returning attendant, who was trying desperately to balance two coffee cups and two croissants with his two ungraceful man-hands. At home, his wife probably did that sort of thing, but on the other hand, she probably wasn't twenty-five years younger than he was, and she probably didn't look like Sonja Kantner.

"Thank you," Sonja said when he finally arrived. Not much coffee was left in the sloshed-over cups. She took one from him and placed it in front of Kim, so that he could hand her the second with a gallant gesture.

They'd barely tasted their croissants when a man of about forty entered the room – a man who was obviously attractive to straight women, which Kim immediately became aware of by noticing Sonja's gaze. She watched him with noticeable interest. On top of that, in contrast to her coffee-beau, he was much more age-appropriate. She was thirty-five, as Kim knew from her personnel file.

The newcomer introduced himself as Klaus, their seminar leader, and asked everyone to gather in the conference room. He did a double take when Sonja Kantner walked past him, and she smiled when she noticed it. The two of them had yet to say a single word to one another, and yet things were already well underway.

Kim would gladly have traded places with him.

During the seminar day, Kim watched the tension build between the two of them. Perhaps she'd be sleeping alone in their room tonight, after all. Jealously, she observed her boss when Sonja turned her attention to the course leader, gave him a charming smile, or asked him a question.

Kim tried to stop paying attention, but she couldn't. Sonja was sitting across from her, and sometimes a friendly smile would come Kim's way as well, when she happened to glance in her direction. But it was nothing compared to the ones she gave *him*. Kim's jealousy swelled.

She's my boss, damn it, not my friend – and definitely not my lover. Unfortunately. Kim tried to tell herself that over and over again, so that she could at least partially follow the seminar. But when Kim looked at Klaus, she saw how fixated he was on Sonja, so Kim's eyes wandered back over to Sonja, and Kim noticed her interest in him. It was endless . . . and hellish.

After the end of the seminar day, they all gathered in the bar. Klaus fetched two champagne flutes. He came over to the table with them and placed one in front of Sonja. He knew what women liked. Reluctantly, the others made room for him, so that Klaus could sit next to her. They clinked glasses, gazing deep into one another's eyes; after a moment, Klaus forced himself to look away and toasted everyone else at the table.

Klaus made sure that Sonja's glass was never empty, and she became ever more buoyant. She liked to laugh, even in the office, but this evening, her laughter took on a new quality. She was flirting with Klaus and he with her.

Kim observed them, and everything she saw felt like a stab to her heart. Her insides shriveled. *I ought to go to bed*, she thought, *and spare myself this sight.*

But she couldn't. It was like an addiction, needing to look at Sonja, to enjoy her laugh, even if it wasn't really meant for Kim, and her presence.

When she got up later to go to the toilet, she heard a muffled sound in the hallway, around the next corner. She followed the sound and saw – her boss.

Klaus had already pushed Sonja's skirt halfway up and was pressing her against the wall. They were kissing, and she was moaning and pressing into him just as much as he was into her.

Oh, no, I really don't need this! Kim turned away, but at that moment, she heard Sonja's voice.

"Klaus ... Klaus," she sighed, aroused. But then her tone changed. "No, Klaus, please don't."

He didn't stop. "Oh, come on," he coaxed, kissing her again, which Kim saw as she spied on them from around the corner. "What's the matter?"

"I'm married," she replied, slightly breathless.

"So am I." He laughed, his voice hoarse with arousal. "But your husband isn't here and neither is my wife. So what's the problem?" He kissed her again, and she did absolutely nothing to fend him off – until he reached under her skirt again.

"Don't, Klaus." She held his wrist firmly. "Not like that, and not here. I don't like that."

"Where, then?" he asked.

"It'll have to be your room. I'm sharing my room with my colleague."

"Yes, right," he remembered. He let her go. "Let's make it not too obvious," he suggested. This clearly wasn't the first time he was doing this sort of thing at one of his seminars. "I'll go first, and you come later. 125."

That must be his room number. Did his wife know how he amused himself when he was away from home?

He turned around, and Kim had to disappear quickly when he came toward her. She was nearly seated back at the table when he turned up. A while later Sonja appeared, and not two minutes after that, Klaus was suddenly terribly tired and yawning. "I'm going to sleep," he announced. "That was pretty tiring today." He rapped twice on the table. "Good night."

A general nodding and murmuring answered him, and three of the others joined him.

Sonja waited a couple of minutes, and then she stood up likewise. "It's getting to be that time for me, too." She looked in Kim's direction. "But you're welcome to stay here," she offered.

How big of you! But Kim knew why she was doing it. She nodded. "Yes," she said. "I'm not tired yet." Kim followed her with her eyes as she left the bar. Lucky Klaus . . .

Kim didn't get back to their room until close to two, but Sonja still wasn't there yet. She selected a side of the bed and lay down. The alcohol, which she'd consumed in more abundance than usual out of desperation, helped her fall asleep. Nonetheless, she perceived that some time later, her boss lay down cautiously beside her.

Kim lay there, stiff as a board, but as much as she tried, she could not ignore Sonja Kantner's presence, her warmth, her scent, all of which stole over Kim like a seductive mist. With considerable effort, including the counting of sheep, Kim finally managed to fall back into a restless sleep, but it was unavoidable: she dreamed of Sonja. Of the two of them. Kim caressed her, massaged her breast, and brushed her nipple with her thumb. Next to her, Sonja sighed. Kim awoke with a start. It was already daylight outside. Her hand lay on her boss's breast, and Sonja sighed again. Quickly, Kim drew her hand back, before her boss could wake up.

Kim got out of bed hastily and stumbled into the shower. She couldn't bear lying next to Sonja any longer, and it was probably almost time for breakfast, anyhow. She grew queasy at the thought. After all that alcohol, food had definitely lost its appeal. But the hotel was also likely to have a couple of Alka-Seltzers on hand, she assumed.

She went downstairs and asked a waitress for the relief-inducing pills. The prompt fulfillment of her wish indicated that Kim probably wasn't the only one requesting them for breakfast. She had a cup of coffee, as well, and sat down to wait for the medicine to work. It took a while, but then her headache improved. She even started to feel hungry.

She went to get herself something from the buffet. Shortly after she returned to her table, another seminar participant appeared. He looked dreadful. He still seemed to be staggering as he approached Kim and sat down at her table.

"You look chipper this morning," he remarked with a reluctant grimace, glancing at her half-empty plate.

Kim waved to the waitress. "Bring this gentleman the same thing you brought me earlier," she requested.

The waitress nodded and disappeared. A moment later, she came back and set a glass of murky liquid in front of him.

"What's that?" he asked skeptically.

"Drink it, it'll make you feel better," Kim promised. "It worked for me."

He drained the glass, and after Kim had finished her breakfast, it appeared that her colleague was finally enjoying the beneficial effect of the analgesic, too. "Man, what a night!" he groaned, head propped up by both hands. Then he grinned. "Did you sleep well, you two gals?" he asked sneakily.

"Don't even try it. I'm not telling you anything," Kim warned him.

Of course, he wanted to know whether Sonja had been there at all. Their little stealth maneuver hadn't fooled anyone. Everyone had noticed the coinciding departure times.

"Aha. So she wasn't there."

"No 'aha'," Kim replied, irritated. "Of course she was there."

Why was she defending her boss? There was no reason she should do that. After all, Sonja was an adult who could do whatever she wanted. Kim wasn't responsible for her reputation. If she wanted to spread her legs for Klaus and everyone else knew it that was no one's business but her own.

"These married singles," he was still grinning at her. "They just don't get it. I prefer to stay single, *period*." He looked at Kim with interest. "And you're single, too, aren't you?"

Kim looked back at him. What should she tell him? The truth? "Yes, I am," she answered, taking the last sip of her coffee. "I'm single."

"Not in a relationship, not married?" he asked again to be sure, and he glanced briefly at her ring finger. But nothing sparkled there.

"Neither, nor," Kim confirmed.

"I like you." He gazed deep into her eyes. "A lot." He laughed. "I've never met a woman who can hold her liquor the way you do!"

Kim shook her head. "If that's the only reason . . ." She stood up.

When she reached the entrance to the breakfast room, she almost crashed into Sonja.

The waitress came out of the kitchen at the same moment. "Alka-Seltzer?" she asked sympathetically, giving Sonja the once-over.

Kim nodded, as her boss didn't seem able to do so for herself. The waitress disappeared once more. This had become a sort of ritual.

Kim was about to continue on her way, but Sonja grabbed her arm. "I need to speak to you, Kim," she said with some effort. She might not have had as much to drink as Kim, but she'd had plenty. Her head must be buzzing like a swarm of bees.

"The seminar is about to begin." What did she want? To confess? She could spare herself that. Her private life was, after all, absolutely none of Kim's business, which, to Kim's regret, she made clear by her behavior time and again.

Sonja peered closely at Kim. "Can I rely on your discretion?" she asked with a slightly hoarse voice. She was obviously still somewhat the worse for wear.

Kim looked into her agonized face – possibly more agonized by the effects of the alcohol than by her infidelity, but that, too, was none of her business – and nodded. "Of course." She glanced toward the colleague with whom she'd shared a table earlier. "I told him you'd been in our room all night."

"Thank you," her boss said. "You know that I'm married –"

Kim interrupted her quickly. "I know." She couldn't stand it anymore. She simply left her boss standing there and walked away.

It was at least reassuring that Sonja seemed not to have noticed Kim's faux pas in bed this morning. That would have been far too embarrassing: so many forced confessions at once – and coming from both sides. Kim could only hope that the remaining three days would pass without further incident.

Perhaps the friendly waitress might have a couple of sleeping pills, too. Kim would have to ask her.

During the day, Klaus and Sonja restrained themselves astonishingly well. No more flirtatious glances, no more questions, and his attention now seemed rather more evenly divided among the other participants, and even on Kim. What a Casanova! He actually winked at her!

But that was probably just her imagination. Yesterday, they'd all been drunk, and today, they all had hangovers – including those two. His winking was probably nothing more than eyelid twitching due to overexertion. Or had something happened? In his room? Sonja seemed to barely acknowledge him, and during the breaks they sat as far apart as possible. Even at lunch, they chose seats at opposite ends of the long table.

But then, perhaps, they were sure to be plagued by guilty consciences – married as they were. It was possible that Kim had judged him too harshly. Maybe he wasn't such a rogue. Nor did Kim know whether this was something *she* typically did when she was away from home. Kim wouldn't have thought, thus far, that Sonja was the type. But a woman as attractive as Sonja was would of course be offered constant temptations. Many men would try to pursue something with her. And apparently, some of them succeeded.

Sonja had never spoken of her husband, nor had he ever called, at least when Kim was within earshot. There was no photo on Sonja's desk. But that didn't necessarily mean anything. Perhaps she just valued her privacy.

That evening in the bar, Kim continued to observe Sonja and Klaus. Indeed, Klaus conversed ostentatiously with men only, and Sonja talked with everyone but Klaus.

Kim shrugged. Straight people and their silly games. His and hers both. Well, it was nothing important for Kim, at any rate. For her, it changed nothing.

She watched Sonja as much as possible without staring openly. *She is simply unbelievably beautiful*, she thought. When she tossed back her hair, it looked as though thousands of tiny feathers were lifted into the air and then reassembled into a cascade of satin. The dark red sheen of her chestnut brown hair seemed to glow when light fell upon it. Like highly polished, wonderfully fine-grained wood. Her eyes, her lips, her forehead when she furrowed it thoughtfully and then laughed a moment later, so that the tiny wrinkles around her eyes radiated in all directions – everything about her was perfect.

She had a small dimple on her chin that was visible only when it was lit from a certain angle and she happened to be turning her head. It looked sweet, and Kim always tried to sit in the right position to be able to see it. The entirety of the woman was simply ravishing.

I have got to stop doing this! Kim squared her shoulders and forced herself to look in the other direction. *She is ravishing, yes – ravishingly heterosexual!* It made no sense whatsoever to become attached to a woman like that, or to even waste time thinking about it. Sonja was quite suitable as an object of sexual fantasy, but not for anything real. That was simply out of the question.

Two more nights, it's just two more nights … She'd already managed one night; she'd get through the rest somehow, too.

She couldn't stare at the bar forever. She turned her head and –

her gaze landed directly in line with Sonja's eyes. Apparently, her boss had been watching her.

"Are you bored?" Sonja asked.

"Oh ... hm ... no, not really –" Kim was utterly confounded by the silky gaze of those gold-brown eyes. Never before had they been so close to her and looked at her so directly.

"It's not exactly exciting, I know, but I never promised it would be. You just need the certificate for the promotion." She raised her eyebrows in slight apology. "Maybe I should've warned you."

"Hm ... no ... I –" *Where was this going?* Kim cleared her throat. "I do know about these seminars, not necessarily as a participant, but I've taken minutes or been in charge of the logistics for them now and again."

"I know." Sonja smiled. "I'm familiar with your personnel file."

Oh, that smile ... Damn it! "Of course." Kim attempted to respond around the frog now stuck in her throat.

Sonja sighed. "Business life is sometimes really dull. Unfortunately, it's unavoidable. One simply has to make the best of it. Seminars like this aren't exactly my thing, but the topic of this one comes up so rarely in other seminars, it just had to be."

Kim lifted her hands. "I have absolutely no objections. The seminar's been quite interesting so far." *In one respect, anyway*, she continued in her thoughts.

"I'm glad to hear that." Sonja went on smiling, and Kim didn't know where she ought to look, so as not to seem impolite. Those lips ... she could already feel their silky softness, as though she were touching them. *Think about something else!*

"I think I'll turn in a bit earlier tonight. It's pretty tiring, listening so closely all day long." Kim yawned behind a raised hand and stood up.

"I'll join you." Sonja stood up as well.

Must you?

"Sonja, can I talk to you for a minute?" Klaus was leaning in their direction.

Sonja hesitated imperceptibly, but then she nodded. "Of course."

Klaus stood and pointed at two armchairs in a corner of the foyer. "There?"

He and Sonja went over to the conversation nook. A smirk, which Kim unfortunately could not join in on, traveled contagiously through the assembled ranks. She left the bar. On the way to her room, her Alka-Seltzer companion caught up with her.

"Think something's still going on between those two?" he asked, grinning.

"Nothing's going on," Kim answered sharply.

"Good grief, aren't you a mother hen! You'd never know it to look at you." He laughed. "She's your boss, not your daughter. You don't have to guard her virtue." He laughed again. "I think she's way beyond that. Seems to be quite the hot little number."

Kim shot him a withering glare.

"Oh, excuse me!" He lifted his hands in the air. "Didn't mean it like that. The lady is highly attractive, I wanted to say."

Kim remained silent.

"Other ladies, too, though." He tilted his head to one side. "You, for example."

"You don't say."

"And I mean that, seriously." He remained standing close to her, even while she was holding the keycard in her hand to open the door. "You're much more attractive than she is – in your way."

"In my way? What way is that, then?" Kim had to chuckle. What questionable compliments her colleague was dishing out!

"You're just . . . well . . . nicer," he replied vaguely. "I just like you."

"Because I happen to be the only woman other than Mrs. Kantner at this seminar?" Kim could no longer suppress her smirk. "The selection isn't that large, you must admit." She stuck the keycard into the slit in the door. There was a *pling* and the light above the slit switched to green.

"I admit it. But even if there were more women here –"

"You'd fall in love with me on the spot?" Kim laughed. "Oh, sure, I believe that." She opened the door.

Her colleague took a step toward her, putting one foot inside her room. "You're not as cold as she is," he whispered excitedly. "That one's like a block of ice, the pure Sahara."

"A block of ice in the Sahara would presumably melt," Kim said, amused but also annoyed. "And earlier, you claimed she was hot." *What kind of conversation am I having here?* she thought, irritated.

"Well, yeah, in a way, but –" He squirmed.

"But she's out of your league. Is that what you're trying to say?" Kim shook her head. "And you don't think I am?" She gave him a stony look. "Then be aware, my friend, I play in a completely different league than she does. And most definitely not in yours."

He just looked at her, dumbfounded and uncomprehending.

Kim pushed his foot out of the way with hers, entered her room, and shut the door behind her. *Good grief!*

A minute later, there was a knock at the door. Kim didn't imagine it would be her erstwhile admirer and opened it. She was right. She let her boss inside.

"Pardon me," Sonja said, a little embarrassed. "I didn't mean to . . . but I have to sleep somewhere, too, after all."

She looked outrageously sweet, standing there like that. Why couldn't Kim just kiss her right now?

"Did you want to go with him?" Sonja asked her. "I really didn't mean to stop you –"

How touchingly concerned she was about Kim's sex life! If only she were so concerned in the *right* way . . .

"No. You didn't stop me from doing anything. Don't worry." Kim went to the bed and took her nightshirt out from under the pillow.

"Men can certainly be awful sometimes," Sonja remarked suddenly, and rather bitterly, it seemed.

What on earth had Klaus done to her last night? She certainly hadn't been sounding like this beforehand.

Could Kim ask her about it? Hardly. This was none of her business. Sonja wasn't her friend, she was her boss. They had no personal relationship whatsoever, as much as Kim regretted it. That didn't change the facts.

"You said it," Kim agreed with her and went into the bathroom.

When she returned and lay down on the bed, Sonja was getting ready to take her turn in the bathroom. She stripped down, completely naked, and walked past Kim, clad only in her birthday suit.

Kim held her breath. Her body was – oh, God, she was starting to feel awfully warm . . . Her body was a work of art. Kim had, of course, touched Sonja's breast once already, but the rest as well . . . she was truly beautiful – and insanely desirable. Though what Klaus had helped himself to last night, Kim couldn't have.

Kim rolled over and curled up under her blanket. A pathetic substitute for Sonja's skin, which Kim yearned for; for Sonja's caress, which Kim would never be permitted to experience except when she accidentally brushed her arm; for Sonja's kiss, which Kim longed for.

And Kim wanted more from Sonja than that. She wanted to hear the same sounds that she'd granted Klaus, the sighing and the moaning. Kim wanted Sonja to whisper her name the way she'd whispered Klaus's. Ah, she was crazy. None of this would ever happen, and Kim knew it.

Sonja came out of the bathroom – still naked – and slipped on a negligee when she'd reached her side of the bed. Kim briefly shut her eyes in order to calm herself down. It was an extravagant item. Didn't she have anything simpler? Just for a trip to a seminar? But perhaps she'd been planning to amuse herself here. And had come prepared.

Sonja lay down. "Would it bother you if I watch television?" She pulled the blanket up. "I'm not actually tired yet. I just wanted to get away from those . . . men." She pronounced the last word with a certain degree of contempt. "But if you want to go to sleep –"

"No, that's fine," Kim answered immediately. "I'm not tired yet, either."

Sonja smiled a little. "Lovely." She got up to get the remote control.

"Why don't you grab something out of the minibar, too, and a couple packages of nuts or chips. I know there are some around here somewhere." Kim grinned crookedly. "They say you're not supposed to eat anything after you brush your teeth, but as far as I'm concerned, snacking just goes with watching TV."

Sonja nodded. "Yes, for me, too. Even though my mother made such an effort to teach me proper tooth brushing." She was grinning now, as well.

She brought the snacks back with her, and she plumped up her pillow so she could prop it behind her back.

Like an old married couple, Kim thought.

Sonja turned on the television and they agreed on a Woody Allen comedy, a real one, not one of his dark ones with the undertones of misery.

It was delightful. They sat in bed, nibbling on chips and peanuts, drinking cola and wine – who cared if those went together? – and laughed themselves silly at Woody Allen's jokes. Now and then, when Sonja wasn't looking, Kim glanced over at her and enjoyed watching her laughing, relaxed profile. What a wonderful woman.

When the movie ended, they talked about it a little, laughed anew over a couple of very funny scenes, and settled down to sleep.

Sonja extinguished the light on her side of the bed. So did Kim on hers. Kim heard Sonja fall asleep; her breathing grew deeper, calmer. She murmured just a little as she finally sank all the way under.

Kim desired her, would have loved to touch her, but at the same time, she simply enjoyed her presence, even now, as she slept. It was nice to have Sonja there, lying next to her, after they had laughed and gotten along so well together. All of that was a large part of what Kim wished for in a woman.

The rest – well, that would never happen, and that was for the best. Kim sighed. She could no longer fend off the clutches of sleep, as the sandman paid her a visit and gave her a clear order to shut down her mental apparatus for the night.

She sank into a dream very similar to the one she had the night before, except that this time her boss looked even more seductive, because Kim could now incorporate the view of Sonja's naked body, which had been forced upon her, into her dream sequences.

Kim awoke to the sound of someone crying. At first, she thought her senses were deceiving her, that it was a remnant of her dream (although no one in the dream had been crying, rather the opposite). But then she realized that the noises coming from the other side of the bed were real. Kim leaned over and touched Sonja's averted shoulder. Pale moonlight shone brightly on her back.

She didn't seem to be awake; she was still sleeping. But she was crying – clearly, she was crying in her sleep. What should Kim do?

Wake her? Maybe she'd be embarrassed to realize that Kim had been a witness to whatever unhappiness that was. But Kim couldn't just leave her to cry like that. Sonja began to sob. It was heartrending.

"Sonja . . ." Kim shook her shoulder very cautiously. "Sonja, please, wake up."

With a great spasm, Sonja suddenly threw herself onto Kim's breast. "Hold me!" She sobbed. "Please, hold me tight!"

She seemed to be talking in her sleep. Nonetheless, Kim did what she was asked and held Sonja in her arms. She stroked Sonja's back soothingly and let her cry. Sonja slowly calmed down; the sobbing became softer, and the pauses between sobs, during which she breathed deeply, became longer.

It seemed that she had fallen into a deep sleep on Kim's breast. Well – to tell the truth, Kim really had nothing against that. Actually, it was turning her on; the way Sonja lay in her arms like that, her breath brushing against her skin . . . Kim could feel that Sonja was just exactly as soft as she'd imagined.

Kim raised her hand and brushed it very carefully across Sonja's face, with just one finger and very, very softly, so that she wouldn't wake up. Oh, it was wonderful! What Kim wouldn't have given to be allowed to go on caressing her. Not just her face, her whole body, her breasts, her belly, her thighs, and then between them –

Something suddenly changed about Sonja's posture; she froze in Kim's arms and seemed not to breathe any more – she had woken up.

Kim quickly pulled her hand away, and Sonja's eyes flew open. She noticed where she lay. Within a flash she withdrew to her own side of the bed. "What . . . what happened?" she asked, shaken.

"Nothing," Kim reassured her. She reached toward the light switch. Perhaps with a little illumination this all wouldn't feel quite so intimate.

"Don't," Sonja said. "Please don't."

Kim let her hand drop and stared at her boss through the dimly lit darkness. She couldn't see much, but shimmering reflections formed in Sonja's eyes whenever she moved.

But she hardly moved at all. She just sat there trembling. Kim didn't see but rather felt Sonja's trembling. She was obviously waiting for something, a reaction from Kim, or to finally wake up from her bad dream. But it was no longer a dream.

"What happened?" Sonja asked once more, this time more firmly and with a more alert-sounding voice, but in spite of that, she still sounded deeply shaken.

"You were crying in your sleep, and then you ... sought protection from me, and I held you. Then you woke up," Kim explained to her, as soothingly as possible.

"I ... I'm sorry." Sonja sounded deeply ashamed. "Please, forgive me for burdening you like that. I don't know how that could've happened. Please forgive me."

"You had a bad dream. That happens to everyone from time to time."

Sonja let out a desperate laugh. "But not everyone responds to it by throwing herself into another woman's arms! Especially when she's a woman herself." She straightened up a bit more. "I must sincerely apologize to you. That surely couldn't have been ... pleasant for you."

Kim felt sorry for her. It wasn't fair. Sonja thought it had been terribly uncomfortable for her, and all the while, Kim had enjoyed it. In fact, Kim really regretted that Sonja had woken up. "I wouldn't say that," Kim replied honestly. She wanted no more deception. "I'm used to it."

From the darkness, only silence answered her. Then, after a while: "How ... how do you mean that?" Sonja gave a somewhat nervous laugh. "Do people often soothe themselves at your breast?"

"Not so much that," Kim admitted. "Although – it's happened once or twice, of course. But what I meant is that I'm used to holding a woman in my arms."

Sonja got up and went to the bathroom, where she turned on the light. The glow that appeared from the doorway made their bedroom no longer so dark. But it wasn't proper light, either. She obviously wanted to avoid that for now. Her face was still in the shadows. "That means ...?"

She knew what it meant, Kim assumed, or else she wouldn't have gotten out of bed so fast. "Since I'm neither a nurse nor a social worker, it means exactly what I said: I'm not interested in men, but in women." *Women like you*, Kim would have liked to add, but that probably would've been much too shocking.

Sonja folded her hands and went over to the little living room suite that stood in one corner of the room, two armchairs and one tiny loveseat. She lowered herself into one of the armchairs.

In her flimsy negligee! Kim thought, concerned. *She ought to put something on.*

"You're going to catch a cold. Wouldn't you rather get under the covers?"

Sonja's head shot up. No, she obviously did not want that . . .

Kim didn't know what to say. Really, nothing had happened. And so the room filled with silence.

It took some time before Sonja spoke again. "The situation is somewhat . . . strange for me," she remarked coolly. "You'll forgive me if I don't quite know how I ought to react." Her voice sounded expressionless.

Somehow Kim had to take the tension out of the situation. She laughed. "Well, you know, the situation is kind of strange for me, too. Never before have I been in bed with a woman I have such a formal relationship with . . . and who, on top of that, is my boss."

Sonja looked at her, and again, said nothing. Kim had to end this. Clearly, her boss had a huge problem with her, and evidently some internal struggle, some big problem with herself, as well – whatever it was that caused her to cry in her sleep. If she didn't want to talk about that, she was well within her rights. But then Kim couldn't help her, either.

"You're going to freeze to death." Kim stood up. "Please, get back into bed. I'll sleep on the couch."

Sonja looked over at the tiny piece of furniture. "You'd have to be a Lilliputian for that," she remarked dryly and got up. "No, stay where you are! I'm being silly. I guess it's all just been a bit too much for me these last few days. But you shouldn't have to suffer for that. You're right. The bed is big enough for both of us, after all."

Something she said resonated with Kim: *I guess it's all just been a bit too much for me these last few days.* What did she mean by that?

Why wouldn't she speak her mind? Would that be so terrible? What had happened? But she obviously didn't want to talk about it.

She got back into bed, and Kim lay down again too. When Sonja crept under her blanket without looking over at Kim, Kim got up to turn off the bathroom light. Maybe Sonja had left it on intentionally, to keep Kim at more of a distance. But if that was the case, she ought to have said something. She didn't.

When Kim slid into her side of the bed once and for all, she noticed that Sonja had scooted over all the way to the far edge. If she moved just an inch further, she'd fall onto the floor.

My God, she must be afraid of me! What did straight women really think of lesbians? That they had nothing better to do than pounce on unwilling partners? That's how it looked, anyway.

But Kim didn't have to concern herself with what was going on in Sonja's mind. She lay down in the middle of the mattress and rolled over.

If Sonja wanted to sleep that uncomfortably – she was welcome to do so.

But Kim certainly wasn't about to ruin her own good night's sleep.

When Kim awoke, her boss was already gone. At breakfast, Kim assumed. She probably wanted to avoid any more all-too-private situations. Which was fine with Kim. She showered and headed to breakfast herself.

Sonja was there, sitting alone at a table. It was still quite early. The others didn't seem to be up yet.

Kim went to the buffet, served herself and was about to head for a different table. Sitting down with her boss would've felt too intrusive. Sonja certainly wouldn't welcome that, Kim was sure.

But when Kim started in the opposite direction, Sonja called her name.

Kim went over to her, but didn't sit down. "Good morning."

"Good morning." Sonja considered Kim, standing before her.

"Please, sit down with me. Let's have breakfast together."

Kim raised her eyebrows. She hadn't expected this. But since her boss wanted her to, Kim sat down across from her. The waitress brought the coffee that Kim had already ordered when she'd first walked into the room.

For a while, they sat across the table from each other in silence. Sonja was eating nothing, just drinking tea. Kim was hungry and bit heartily into her roll. The silent breakfast wasn't exactly pleasant for her, but she certainly wasn't going to starve on that account.

At last, Sonja cleared her throat. "I have to apologize to you again. I behaved very stupidly last night. Please forgive me – I didn't mean to insult you."

Kim shook her head. "You didn't insult me. Don't worry about it. Nothing happened."

"Oh, yes!" Sonja let out a dry laugh and leaned back. "A great deal happened!" She gave Kim a peculiar look. "Maybe not for you, but for me it did. You have to consider, I've never . . . I've never lain on a woman's breast before, except my mother's."

"And you'd hardly remember that." Kim chuckled.

Her boss laughed, a bit more relaxed now. "True." She considered Kim again with the same odd expression. "You . . . you've always been with women?"

Kim nodded. "Yes. Exclusively." She spread butter on the other half of the roll and waited for what would come next.

"And you were never . . . I mean –" Sonja broke off. This was clearly embarrassing for her. "Excuse me," she pleaded again. "I'm pestering you with my questions. None of this is any of my business, after all."

Kim put her roll down and gave Sonja a friendly look. "There's really nothing to it, though. For me, it's completely normal. And to answer your question: I've never been with a man." She laughed, amused. "Except during my teenage years. Then everyone thinks they have to be like everyone else and wants to give it a try. But I quickly found out that men were not for me."

"How –?" Sonja began to ask another question, but then dropped it right away. She shook her head, apparently at herself. "I'm dreadful," she said then. "Usually I'm not this nosy. I have no idea what's going on." She laughed, a bit embarrassed.

I could tell you what's going on, Kim thought, mildly amused. *You're interested. Maybe you're not as straight as you think.*

"What would you like to know?" Kim encouraged her. "You can ask me anything. I have absolutely no problem with it. Honestly."

Sonja considered Kim once more, this time even more intently. *Ooh, she should be careful where she points that look!* "If it's so normal to you, then why didn't you ever tell me about it?"

"Did *you* ever tell me that you're straight?" Kim asked, rather smugly, in return.

Sonja laughed in surprise. "No, of course not. That's just –" This time she broke off, because she'd obviously hit on a realization.

"That's just normal, you were about to say?" Kim inquired, still somewhat amused. "You see, it is for me, too. So why do I need to talk about it all the time?"

"You're right." Her boss sat there, bewildered. "I never thought about it like that."

"I believe you," Kim remarked with an amused twist of her mouth. "Straight women never stop to think about that sort of thing."

"Straight women!" Sonja spat out the phrase as if it were a derogatory term. Then she laughed again, rather nervously. "Even that –" she continued. "That you differentiate it like that. That's completely strange to me. For me, before, it was always just men or women. And that was it."

Now Kim had to allow herself a mocking little smile. "There's a great deal more to it. The selection you've encountered so far is pretty incomplete."

"Is it?" Again, Sonja gave Kim a funny look, as if something more was going on behind it. "Oh, God, what a disgrace I've made of myself now," she remarked then, in the beautifully dry way Kim liked about her so much.

"You haven't done anything of the sort," Kim appeased her obligingly. "How were you to know? Considering it's completely irrelevant to your life."

"You're very gracious. But it's just as embarrassing. I feel like a little kid."

At that moment, two more seminar participants came in and

joined their table, having served themselves at the buffet. That ended the conversation, since neither Sonja nor Kim wished to continue it in the men's presence. They agreed on that without having to say a word.

But Kim noticed something interesting after the two others joined them: Sonja was suddenly auditing her reactions to the men. As soon as one of them did or said something, Kim could see the wheels start to turn. Every time. A simple compliment that Sonja would previously have acknowledged with a modest, automatic smile now caused her to marvel. Several times she leaned back and watched the men as though she'd never before beheld such beings, as though the entire species had suddenly become strange to her. Probably, things were occurring to her that she'd never given a thought to before.

She shouldn't concern herself with this so much, Kim thought with an internal sigh. *It will only confuse her*. She shuddered a little at the thought that they were going to have to spend one more night together in the same room, in the same bed. It would be weird – now that everything was out in the open. After they'd talked about it.

Granted, Kim had not told Sonja that she desired her, nor how much – and she would keep that to herself. That would definitely be too much for a woman like Sonja – but everything else Kim had told her was presumably enough to put Sonja a bit off her stride. That was quite clear.

Kim was glad when the seminar finally began and they could go their separate ways. Poor Klaus! Today, Sonja watched him with completely different eyes than yesterday or the day before. She practically murdered him with her looks. He no longer had any idea where he ought to look, and he seemed to become more and more anxious. At lunchtime he excused himself to take care of some other business. Kim grinned. He wanted to escape Sonja's piercing gaze, at least for an hour.

But the afternoon passed as well, and Kim and Sonja retired to their room early after dinner.

"I'd really like to go for a walk," Kim said. "This area is so beautiful, and I haven't gotten to see any of it. Would you like to come with me?"

Sonja shook her head. "I'll read a little. I could use the relaxation."

Hm. And to think of all the relaxing things Kim could show her . . . She grinned to herself and put on her sturdy walking shoes.

Kim walked for longer than she had expected. She was glad that she'd accepted a flashlight from the concierge; it had gotten so late by the time she got back that she'd have been stumbling around in the dark, otherwise. And when she got to the room, Sonja was already lying in bed, asleep.

Kim smiled and studied Sonja briefly . . . she was so adorable . . . then went quietly into the bathroom and showered. She had barely gotten horizontal herself when she, too, was asleep. The walk and the fresh air had been the best possible soporific.

This time, Kim didn't wake to crying, but to a touch – a touch on her breast! She could hardly comprehend it. Should she pinch herself to check that it wasn't a dream?

But no – it wasn't a dream. A hand lay on her breast, caressing it cautiously, almost fearfully. Questing, it stroked over it and slid – probably accidentally – over the nipple, which immediately stood erect to meet it. The hand paused suddenly, and Kim had to bite her lip to keep from moaning.

But why bite her lip, after all? *She* had started this. "That's very nice, what you're doing there," Kim whispered.

Sonja immediately pulled her hand back and placed a little more distance between herself and Kim. "I beg your pardon," she said, abashed. And then once more, "I'm sorry, I don't know what . . . what came over me."

Kim sat up slightly. "You want to try this, don't you?" she asked gently.

Sonja turned her head toward Kim, and Kim saw only the reflections in her eyes. "I don't know," she replied. "I truly don't know. It's so . . . your breast, it's so soft . . . so wonderfully soft." Her voice sounded amazed.

Kim laughed. "Yes, that's the case with women. Yours, too, you know."

"Yes, exactly," Sonja said. "But that never occurred to me before.

I never knew how . . . how nice it feels."

Kim slid over toward her. "There are many other things between two women that feel nice," she said softly. "Very nice." She bent down over Sonja and kissed her very softly. Her hand sought Sonja's breast and stroked it, just as gently and carefully as Sonja had been with her.

Sonja didn't try to stop her, but she didn't do anything else, either. She simply lay there, still, and let Kim proceed. Kim noticed, though, that Sonja's breath had become very shallow. She wouldn't permit herself to become aroused.

Kim kissed her tenderly again, although Sonja wasn't kissing her back. Kim hoped she would, and ran her hand down along Sonja's body, seeking the hem of her negligee and pushing it up.

"Oh, no, no!" Sonja suddenly gasped, pulling away from Kim's mouth. "No, I can't do that. Please –"

Kim let her hand rest where it was, and looked at Sonja. "You don't have to do anything you don't want," she assured her. "I'll follow your lead entirely."

"I . . . I can't," Sonja said in a very quiet, stifled voice. "I don't think I can. This is so strange."

Kim withdrew her hand from beneath the negligee and placed it on Sonja's breast. "Is this better?"

"That's –" Sonja broke off. "Yes," she said then. "Better." But her breathing was still shallow with fear.

Kim leaned down to whisper into Sonja's ear. "Don't you want me to caress you? I won't do anything to hurt you. I promise. Don't be afraid." She sat up, waiting for an answer.

Sonja turned away from her and stared at the door. Sonja's movement had dislodged Kim's hand from her breast, and Kim's hand lay loosely by her side. Kim looked at Sonja's back quietly, giving Sonja time to sort out her thoughts.

Sonja said nothing for quite a while. "I . . . I yearn to be caressed," she said in a whisper Kim could barely understand, "but whenever I've thought about it, it's always been a man who ought to be doing it, not a woman."

"So you don't want that from me." Kim gave Sonja's shoulder one more tender caress and then withdrew again to her side of the bed.

Alright then. She couldn't force her, nor would she want to. Kim's whole body was in an uproar. She desired Sonja. She wanted her. She was totally crazy about her. But that didn't mean anything at all. That was her problem, not Sonja's.

"No." Barely above a breath had this one word come from Sonja's side. "No, I *do* want it. But I'm afraid."

"What are you afraid of?" Kim bent over Sonja and gently stroked her hair. "What could happen?"

"I ... I don't know. I feel so uncomfortable with unfamiliar things." Sonja's voice was still very soft.

"You're a control freak!" Kim laughed. "I've noticed that at work." She leaned farther over Sonja's shoulder and whispered in her ear. "But this has nothing to do with work. You don't have to control anything. On the contrary. Just let yourself go."

"That ... I can't do that." Sonja turned to face Kim, scooting away from her at the same time. "I've never ... it's not my style –" She pushed herself up in bed until she was sitting up, and pulled the blanket up to her chin. "I'm not exactly the spontaneous type."

"You mean you and Klaus had that planned in advance?" Kim asked too quickly, before she could think about what she was saying. "Oh! I'm sorry." She looked away from Sonja. "That's none of my business."

"Indeed, it isn't." Sonja's voice now sounded cool and composed. "But if you really want to know: no, we hadn't."

"You mean, you're not the spontaneous type with women, but you are with men. Is that what you were trying to tell me?" Kim noticed how much it was riling her up inside to be having this conversation.

"I didn't mean anything by that. You forced me to answer." Sonja seemed to be entirely herself again. No more sign of uncertainty or fear.

"Ah." Kim stared at her. "Just like I was probably about to try to force you into having sex, is that it? If something were to happen, it would be all my fault; you have nothing to do with it, do you?" *It's always the same with these silly straight bitches!* "I'm sorry." Kim stood up and started to get dressed. She was now in dire need of some fresh air. "I'm sorry that I'm not what you need," she apologized once more. *Especially since you're exactly what I need!* It was quite the cross to bear.

Kim picked up her pants and pulled them on.

"What are you doing?" Sonja asked, irritated.

"I'm going," Kim replied. "I won't molest you any more." *Although she was actually the one molesting me tonight ...* "Then you can sleep in peace. And if you want, I won't come back until it's time to leave. You'll still drive me back, won't you?" She turned on a light to search for her shirt.

Sonja stared at Kim, not making a sound. What if Sonja wouldn't drive her back? Kim wondered. In that case she would have to ask the concierge about other transportation options.

"And it goes without saying," Kim said when she'd finally found her shirt and was pulling it on, "that I will behave formally and respectfully to you in every way, as befits our professional relationship. I'm sorry to have forgotten myself in that way."

"Why are you so offended all of a sudden?" Sonja asked astonished.

"I'm not offended!" Kim bridled. "I'm just ... When you touched me it ... it unleashed something in me. I understand that it's not the same for you, but I am attracted to women, and you are a very desirable woman. And that is why I better leave now, so –"

She can kiss my ass! Why am I telling her all this? None of this is any of her business whatsoever!

"You find me desirable?" Sonja asked with interest.

Oh, my gosh! "Yes." She had to get out of here! "I think you know well enough what you look like. And you can hardly have missed the men's reactions to you."

"Yes –" Sonja replied, very slowly, "the men's. But apparently I missed yours."

Kim went to the door. "Sure. You're not interested in my reaction."

"Stop!" It sounded like an order.

Kim froze with the doorknob in her hand.

"You're not getting away from me like that! I'm still your supervisor."

"I'll resign as soon as we get back," Kim responded with a stony stare at the door. "Don't worry."

Kim heard Sonja get out of bed behind her and come toward her. Why couldn't she just let her go? She felt Sonja's breath on her ear.

"I don't want you to resign," she whispered. "And I don't want you to leave, either." She wrapped her arms around Kim and held her firmly.

"Ah – and what *do* you want, then, Mrs. Kantner?" Kim snapped.

"Please, stop it," Sonja said with a quiet voice. "Stop treating me that way."

Kim felt Sonja against her back, her breasts, her warmth, her closeness. It was so wonderful – and so terrible. "I can't stay," Kim forced the words out from between tight lips. "I want to sleep with you, but you don't want that, and of course I respect that. If that's the way it is, I can't change it, but then there's no way I can stay. I can't stand being so close to you, but so far apart at the same time. Do you have any idea what I'm talking about?"

"Of course I do," Sonja answered, still softly. "But . . . but I never said that I don't want it."

Kim turned around in surprise, making Sonja loosen her grip. "Yes you did!" she protested, gaping at Sonja, who stood directly before her.

"I'm not very spontaneous with these things, is what I said, and that really isn't the same thing," Sonja defended herself.

Kim continued to gape. "You said all your fantasies revolve around men. There's no room for a woman in that."

"Men are the only thing I know," Sonja said earnestly. "What else should my fantasies revolve around? Perhaps I forgot to mention it, but not only am I not very spontaneous, I'm not very imaginative, either. My fantasies are nothing but . . . memories. I can't remember something that never happened."

"You've never even dreamed about a woman?"

"No." Sonja shook her head with regret. "Not yet."

"Well, then, that's the way it is." Kim sighed. "I'll go."

She started to turn around again, but Sonja wouldn't let her. She embraced Kim and pressed herself against her, so that Kim stumbled back into the door. "No," she said, "you won't." She sought Kim's eyes. "That I'm a little afraid of something new and strange, is something you'll just have to accept. And that I have too little imagination to picture something unknown, that I have no experience with, is . . . well, okay, I admit that's my fault. But have you always known everything in advance? Before you slept with a woman for the first time, did you know what it would be like?"

"I had imagined it," Kim said.

"And was that a pleasant imagination for you?" Sonja asked.

"Oh, yes." Kim laughed. "Very pleasant."

"And then, when it happened . . . was it . . . just as pleasant?" Her voice went very soft toward the end.

"No!" Kim laughed. "It was very, very different from what I had imagined." She shook her head in fond recollection. "But nice . . . yes, it was nice. Different, but good."

"Then you have the advantage over me in that respect. I can't imagine much before . . . before it happens. And nice . . . no, it wasn't nice, either." Sonja gave Kim an almost pleading look. "This time will be . . . nice, won't it?"

"Sonja, I –" How could she resist those pleading eyes? Kim wrapped her arms around her. "I just don't want you to do something that you'll regret later," she said softly.

Sonja began to smile. "I think I'm old enough to decide that for myself."

And what about Klaus? You obviously regretted that, and very quickly so, Kim thought, but she didn't say it out loud.

"Earlier, you claimed that you're not what I need," Sonja went on, "but I think the opposite is the case: I need you. In fact, I need you very much."

She leaned toward Kim and offered her lips for a kiss. Apparently, she didn't want to be entirely responsible for that kiss. She closed her eyes and waited for Kim, who realized that holding back now would be insane. And Kim couldn't wait any longer, anyway. She wrapped her arms even tighter around Sonja and enjoyed the sensation as she went very soft and sank into her. Kim ran one hand over her neck, caressing her hair and pulling her even closer.

She kissed Sonja tenderly, opening her lips with her tongue and thrusting cautiously inside. Sonja sighed as Kim explored her mouth, caressing the inside and then tugging at her lips as she withdrew.

Sonja opened her eyes and looked at her. “What was that?” she asked, astonished.

“A kiss?” Kim suggested, equally astonished. *What kind of question was that?*

“A kiss,” Sonja repeated, still amazed.

“Pardon me if I didn’t meet with your liking,” Kim added, rather piqued.

“That . . . that’s not it.” Sonja caressed Kim’s face briefly, almost in passing, still seeming taken aback. She turned around and sat on the edge of the bed.

“Should I go?” Apparently, Sonja was extremely confused. This couldn’t end well.

Sonja looked up. “No. No, not at all,” she contradicted firmly. “Please . . . please don’t be annoyed by my behavior. It’s all so new to me. You probably think I’m quite odd.”

Kim went over and knelt before her. “I understand that this isn’t easy for you.” She looked up at Sonja’s withdrawn expression.

Sonja’s gaze turned outward once more, sought Kim’s eyes, then considered her entire face as if it were an exotic landscape she was seeing for the first time. She said nothing, but pulled her negligee off, and lay down completely naked.

Kim held her breath for a moment in the face of this matter-of-factness. Her loins constricted with desire, and she saw Sonja’s abdomen trembling with excitement. Her nipples stood erect and seemed to beckon. Her body was overwhelming to Kim once more, just as it had been the night before, when Sonja walked naked to the bathroom. Still, she was breathing as shallowly as she had the first time Kim tried to touch her. She was afraid.

Kim sat down next to her on the bed. The sight of Sonja’s body had left her utterly speechless, but now she had to say something. “You’d better cover up,” she remarked lovingly, “or you’ll freeze.” She pulled the blanket up over Sonja’s body and gazed at her.

Sonja’s expression was becoming increasingly confused. Kim realized that this didn’t seem like a good idea. She should have left.

Sonja stretched out an arm from beneath the blanket and reached for Kim, wrapping it around her neck and pulling her down. Her lips touched Kim’s, and this time, Kim also felt Sonja’s tongue searching for hers. Kim answered her, and they played a little together, letting their tongues slide in and out, caressing one another's lips.

Sonja began to sigh and pulled Kim even closer, until Kim let one hand slip beneath the blanket to touch her. Only her belly, but still, Sonja froze. Then Kim felt her slowly open her thighs.

Kim swallowed. "Sonja . . ."

Kim quickly took off her shirt, but she got no farther than that, because Sonja had reached for her breast. With an expression of amazement, she observed and stroked it. Then she cradled both of Kim's breasts in her hands. Her fingers caressed the skin until they reached the nipples, which stood erect, and Kim moaned.

Sonja paused.

"Oh, please, keep going," Kim begged her. Her voice sounded raw in her own ears. "That feels so good."

"I don't know what to do," Sonja replied, quiet and ashamed.

Kim bent down over her. "Take me in your mouth," she asked, with an even huskier voice. "Please." She laughed a little. "And then, try to remember what you did with your mother when you were a little baby." She would surely have been an adorable baby, Kim thought to herself, and a sweet little girl.

"I can't remember that." Sonja laughed, too. "I already told you that." But nonetheless, she took one of Kim's nipples in her mouth and sucked on it, as if she might remember.

Kim moaned even deeper. Although she wasn't completely undressed yet, she pushed herself all the way on top of Sonja. She couldn't help it.

Sonja pampered her breasts with tongue and lips as though she'd always known how. She seemed to like increasing Kim's arousal, and she enjoyed letting it recede again as well. She drove Kim so crazy that Kim could hardly stand it. Gasping, she let herself fall onto her back next to Sonja.

"Will you undress me?" Kim asked, still fighting for breath. "I don't think I can manage this by myself anymore."

Sonja bent over her for a moment and looked into her eyes. She smiled softly. "That bad?"

"Oh, yes!" Kim gave her a mischievous grin. "Just you wait!

You're up next. Then you'll see what I mean."

A shudder ran through Sonja's body. Her smile vanished. She placed a hand on Kim's pants and stroked gently while she stared at Kim's breasts. After some time, she tore herself away from that view and let her eyes sink lower, onto Kim's belly. Her hands began to unfasten Kim's pants. Then they slipped inside. "Oh, my God . . ."

Kim clenched her jaw. Sonja's fingers lay precisely on top of her center, and it had felt like an electric shock when she'd touched her. Her hand still lay on the same spot, motionless. Then she began to caress Kim between her legs, with the fabric of her panties as a delicate barrier.

Kim could've screamed. "Weren't you going to undress me?" she asked her voice very tight. Her loins were blazing at just that gentle touch.

"Oh – yeah." Sonja laughed softly. "I'd almost forgotten. It was so surprising –"

"It's fine." Kim undressed herself quickly.

"Are you mad?" Sonja asked cautiously, because Kim had pushed her aside a bit roughly in the process.

"No." Kim turned back to her. "I'm not mad. I'm wild for you, and I want you now – right now." She turned Sonja onto her back and, in one rapid movement, lay on top of her. Sonja immediately spread her legs and wrapped them around her hips. "You're expecting the wrong thing." Kim laughed a little. "But we can start that way, if you want."

Sonja turned her head to the side. Kim bent forward and kissed her on the throat. Sonja trembled beneath her lips. "I'm sorry," Kim whispered. "I shouldn't have said that. It just slipped out."

Kim ran her lips along Sonja's neck until she could feel Sonja's skin prickling there in tiny goosebumps. Sonja's breathing became heavier.

Kim let herself sink down onto Sonja until their breasts touched. Sonja held her breath and lay completely still. After a while, a deep sigh erupted from her throat. "That's wonderful," she whispered.

Kim felt a tingling everywhere on her body. She let her lips caress the length of Sonja's throat once more; the softness of Sonja's skin overcame her anew. She felt the nipples jutting hard into her flesh, and at the same time, she felt her own equally stiff nipples sinking into Sonja's softness. It was such a heavenly feeling. This alone would've made it all worthwhile. But Kim wanted more.

Her lips glided down from Sonja's neck; she could see the blood pulsing wildly in her veins. It already looked a bit frantic, although Kim could see little evidence of Sonja's untamed arousal elsewhere. Kim sought her averted mouth, and as she neared it, Sonja turned toward her longingly and sighed once more. Her lips were already partially open, and Kim thrust inside and kissed her, carefully at first, until she could no longer control herself. Kim took possession of Sonja's mouth entirely. It was so sweet, so soft, so inviting. Wildly, Kim thrust into her, and moaned aloud as she felt lightning strike her loins.

Sonja raised her hands to the nape of Kim's neck and buried them in her hair. She caressed Kim's hairline with tender fingers, then suddenly, she moaned as she lifted her hips up, shoving them against Kim's belly, trying to thrust upwards again and again.

Her arousal grew, and Kim thrust back until Sonja moaned again, almost desperate. Her movements became faster, stronger; she clutched at Kim's back until the pain bored through Kim and she almost had to cry out from that, too. Her fingernails weren't *that* short, after all ... Then Sonja let go and fell back onto the sheets, tossing and turning, her head rolling from one side to the other.

Kim slid down a little and took one of Sonja's nipples into her mouth, flicking across it with her tongue.

"Oh, no, no!" Sonja cried out sharply, although aware of her location and the proximity of the other hotel guests, she remembered to try to muffle her cries. But this time, she didn't really mean *no,* as she had earlier. Once more, she thrust upward with her hips, but Kim held her down on the mattress, with another plan in mind.

Sonja's legs let go of Kim's hips when Kim increased the pressure and she could no longer hold them. Kim teased her breasts some more, first one, then the other, then back to the first again. Sonja moaned. She sighed. She writhed. She was losing control. She was beautiful to watch. Kim was thrilled to sense Sonja's arousal as it continued to mount.

Kim abandoned Sonja's breasts with a final caress – they were so wonderful, it was hard to part from them – then slid deeper, kissing Sonja's warm, supple skin, enjoying the pulsing beneath it, the thumping heartbeat that was transmitted to Kim's lips.

Slowly Kim arrived at Sonja's navel and flicked her tongue inside; Sonja jumped, moaned, and sighed. Kim glided lower, touching the edge of her groin; Sonja cried out anew, quietly, stifled, tormented. Once again, Kim ran her tongue across the silky skin just above the junction of Sonja's thighs.

"What are you doing . . . what are you doing . . .?" Sonja murmured, still rolling her head from one side to the other without interruption. Her hips jerked as though they wanted to escape from Kim, as though they could no longer stand this.

"Don't you like it?" Kim teased her gently.

Sonja let out a deep sigh as Kim left her in peace for a moment, sparing her from the stimulation. Kim ran a very leisurely hand up over Sonja's hips, touching her belly, but not her breasts or her groin, where she was so sensitive.

Sonja's breathing subsided a little, became more even. "It's wonderful," she whispered, "so . . . gentle."

Kim pulled herself up to eye level once more and looked at Sonja. Her face, beautiful as it was, but also so expressive, touched her deeply. Kim felt herself wanting more from Sonja than just this night, than just sex. She wanted *Sonja* – she wanted the woman, all of her, she wanted to fall asleep and wake up with her, to hear her affectionate laugh as they lay in bed together and cuddled or told each other stories, to sit in front of the television and snack on nuts as they'd already done. Kim wanted to hold her in her arms and feel her, soak up her warmth, appreciate her closeness, not just today, not just here in this hotel where they'd forgotten time and space and their professional relationship.

Kim sighed. Delicately, she lowered her lips to Sonja's and touched them with the merest breath of a kiss, just a loving gesture, not meant to arouse, but to touch her in a different way.

"What is it?" Sonja stroked her hair just as lovingly and tenderly as Kim had just kissed her. She caressed her, and Kim sighed anew.

"Nothing," Kim said. "It's nothing." She was about to slide back down Sonja's body and continue where she'd left off, but Sonja stopped her.

Intent, she considered Kim's face. "Yes, something's up with you."

"No, nothing in particular," Kim assured her. She smiled down at Sonja. "I just want to make you happy; I want you to enjoy this, to not be afraid anymore, to never forget this night."

Sonja was still caressing Kim's hair gently, watching her. "I won't," she said softly. "Ever."

Kim let her hand glide down onto Sonja's belly, and then lower, between her thighs. Sonja gasped when Kim reached her wetness at last, brushing across it without diving in.

"Yes," Sonja breathed softly, even quieter than before. She shut her eyes, and when Kim increased the pressure of her fingers, Sonja pressed her head into the pillow, tensed her body, and arched her back slightly upward. "Mhm," she sighed through closed lips, as if she didn't want to reveal too much of her feelings.

Kim was torn. She wanted to go down between Sonja's legs, but at the same time, she wanted to watch her – to watch the first time that Sonja came in the arms of a woman. She wanted to know how she looked doing that. She decided to do both, one after the other.

She caressed Sonja some more, and she could feel Sonja's tension increase as Kim spread her wetness around with her fingers, still gently, without too much pressure. Kim avoided touching her inner labia, although she could feel how swollen they had become, but instead just ran along the outside, then along her inner thighs, until Sonja sighed with increasing arousal and began again to move, to press her hips toward Kim, trying to catch her hand in order to get satisfaction at last.

But Kim wouldn't let her get too close. Again and again, she dodged. Sonja's sighs grew more hectic, less patient. "Come," she murmured, "come on . . ."

Kim wrapped her free arm around Sonja's shoulders so that she could lie directly on top of her. She slid just one finger between the swollen, wet lips, entering only briefly, then withdrawing.

Sonja moaned deeply, aroused at first, but soon disappointed. "Please . . ." she breathed, "please . . ."

The next time, Kim entered her with two fingers, and Sonja moaned even more deeply. "Yes!"

Kim sought the sensitive spot just inside the entrance and rubbed a little as she continued to slip her fingers gently in and out, still only a short distance. Sonja could no longer hold her hips still, but shifted back and forth, thrust upward. When Kim increased the pressure slightly, Sonja almost wrenched herself away, her motions were so intense.

"Oh ... oh ... oh ..." Sonja sighed and moaned without pause. When Kim touched her thumb to Sonja's pearl, the last "Oh ...!" turned into an "Oh, God!" Sonja cried out, louder than before; she'd forgotten her surroundings and was now simply giving herself over to her lust. And to Kim.

Suddenly, she whispered her name. At last. "Kim ... Kim ... oh, Kim, what are you doing to me?" It seemed she could hardly speak.

Kim took a deep breath to curb her own excitement for a bit longer; this moment belonged to Sonja alone. Kim had heard what she had wanted to hear. She pressed her thumb on the top of Sonja's pearl, and on the inside she pressed her fingers against it, then moved both together, faster and faster, rubbing, gliding, until Sonja could barely breathe between moans, until her breath caught and her hips thrust wildly and uncontrollably into the air; she pressed higher and higher, her back arched, her body feverishly tensed in anticipation of that moment of ultimate release.

She froze. "Aaaah!" she burst out at length, then once more, softer and longer, "Ohhhh, yeah ..." as she sank back onto Kim's arm, falling against her and burying her face in her breast as she had once before; not crying this time, but instead fully awake, and intentionally.

She gasped, struggled for breath, and calmed herself only slowly. Kim brushed a kiss on Sonja's hair and caressed her softly, her back, her side, her thigh, her bottom, very gently. When Kim noticed Sonja returning to reality, she allowed herself to sink back down a little, and smiled at her.

Sonja opened her eyes. "Oh, my God."

"That intense?" Kim asked, smiling.

Sonja nodded, said nothing, and rolled onto her back, away from

Kim; her ribcage was still heaving to meet her demand for oxygen.

Kim took the opportunity to slide down her body, between her legs, pressing them apart and lifting them up –

"Oh, no!" Sonja cried out in apparently genuine horror. "No, no, please don't . . .!"

"Why not?" Kim asked, astonished. Sonja had been enjoying herself a moment ago. What was wrong all of a sudden?

"I . . . I . . . don't, please . . ." was all Sonja could repeat, still not quite mistress of her own lung capacity, and now also agitated by something that Kim didn't understand.

Kim let go of Sonja's legs and straightened up between them, kneeling. "It feels good," she said convincingly and slightly confused, "you'll see. Even better than what I just did. And you liked that, didn't you?"

Sonja took a deep breath. "Yes, I liked it," she affirmed softly. "But that . . . I can't do that."

"Why not?" Kim lay down next to her so she could see her face, which wore a slightly fearful expression, as it had earlier.

Sonja turned her head away. She didn't want Kim to read her emotions. "I . . . I just can't do that," she explained in an even softer voice. "Not . . . not now, not the first time. I never do that the first time." She hesitated. "Let's just go to sleep," she said then. "That was enough." She turned her whole body away from Kim, her back like the insurmountable Great Wall of China.

Kim smiled to herself. *Oh, no!* She wasn't getting away that easily. The night was young, and regardless of what *Sonja* wanted, Kim herself still had a few wishes that needed fulfillment. This liaison was not going to be that one-sided.

"Is that an order, Mrs. Kantner?" Kim asked, almost laughing.

"You're being silly," Sonja said, but her voice sounded . . . well . . . not quite as fierce as she'd acted.

"You are my supervisor," Kim reminded her. "If you issue me an instruction, I am required to follow it."

"But not in bed!" Sonja contradicted irritably. She turned back toward Kim, to glare reluctantly at her.

"No?" Kim razzed her. "I'm glad to hear it." She leaned over Sonja and kissed her.

At first, Sonja withheld a response, pinching her lips together and trying not to allow herself to be kissed. But as Kim caressed her gently and tenderly, Sonja's body with her hand, and Sonja's lips with her tongue, she finally surrendered and opened up to let Kim in.

"You're impossible," she sighed when Kim let her go. "What have I gotten myself into?" But the gaze she directed toward Kim seemed more affectionate than chastising.

"I don't know." Kim grinned. "A woman?"

Sonja let her gaze wander across Kim's body. "Yes, that's for sure." She lifted her hand and brushed it across Kim's face. "Please, don't be mad at me," she pleaded. "I just can't do that. I'm sorry. Is it something you really want?" She was now looking rather shyly at Kim again. In a way Kim had only seen here, in bed. At the office, she was certainly never like that.

Kim sighed. "I do," she said. "I find that's the most enjoyable thing two women can do together in bed. Don't you think?"

Sonja laughed, a bit confused. "You're asking me? I don't know what two women can do together in bed. I lack any experience in that matter. Did you forget already?"

Kim leaned over her again. "Almost." She smiled. "You were so good, no one would guess."

Sonja leaned back and considered Kim. "It's odd to hear something like that coming from a woman!"

"What?" Kim furrowed her brow.

"That I'm good in bed." Sonja made a face.

"I didn't mean to insult you," Kim apologized. "It was supposed to be a compliment."

"Yes. Yes, it probably always is." Sonja sighed, somewhat resigned.

Kim placed her hand on her heart. "I hereby swear never to mention it again, on my honor," she pledged earnestly, if still grinning a bit.

"You're being silly again." The corners of Sonja's mouth twitched. "I never noticed that about you at the office."

"At the office I work. I have no reason to be silly there. Besides which, I wasn't being silly just now. I meant it very seriously."

"Something else I'd never noticed about you before," Sonja said. "You tend to exaggerate."

"If I tell you that you're a beautiful woman, would you call that an exaggeration, too?" Kim asked softly, bending over Sonja and kissing her tenderly.

Sonja returned the kiss cautiously and then disengaged herself from Kim. "I'm not going to answer that. But it does confirm my impression."

Kim considered Sonja's face and felt warmth flooding her. "You're the most beautiful woman in the world," she said softly. "You have beautiful eyes, a beautiful nose, a beautiful mouth . . ." She touched Sonja's lips softly with her own and then withdrew again.

Sonja's eyes wandered across Kim's face, seeming to pause in one place or another, before moving on. Suddenly, Sonja threw her arms around Kim and pulled her tight. Their kiss became ever sweeter. When the tips of their tongues met, they both sighed at the same time. Sonja's soft, smooth, silky mouth pampered Kim with unbelievable sensations, and Kim felt the wetness that had already been collecting between her legs for hours suddenly increase, felt strokes of lightning rekindle the fire that had smoldered in her belly the whole time.

Kim moaned and pressed herself against Sonja's thigh, trying to clamp it between her own legs so she could finally reach the end. She rubbed against her and felt the first little waves approach when Sonja pushed her away and rolled on top of her, turning her onto her back.

Kim gasped as the stimulation disappeared from between her legs. "Please, Sonja, let me come," she begged. "I can't stand much more of this . . ."

Sonja leaned down and looked at Kim.

"I won't demand anything more of you afterward, I promise," Kim assured her pleadingly. She wondered if Sonja was afraid that Kim would try to talk her into doing something she didn't want to do.

Sonja lowered her lips onto Kim's breast and began to indulge the hard, swollen nipple. Kim moaned, deep and loud. She didn't care who might be sleeping next door! They were leaving the next day, anyway. Kim reached for Sonja, trying to hold onto her, trying to caress her, but Sonja dodged and slid lower.

Her hand caressed Kim's belly, her groin, so that Kim tossed and gasped for breath. Then she felt her way cautiously between her legs. She touched Kim's labia and paused.

"Sonja, Sonja . . ." Kim whispered. "Please . . ."

Sonja's hand sought and found the entrance, one finger slipped inside, and Kim lifted herself, moaning, to meet her. Sonja shifted a bit lower. With an effort, Kim raised her head from the pillow enough to see Sonja staring between her legs as if she were looking at the eighth wonder of the world.

"Sonja, please . . ." Kim attempted to squeeze Sonja's finger, and indeed she could feel it inside her, but she wanted more.

Sonja looked up into Kim's face, then pulled her finger out and thrust inside Kim once more with a deep, hard thrust. Then again, and again, and again – steady, rhythmic. As if she was trying to imitate a man. Kim groaned every time Sonja thrust into her because it almost hurt. And it didn't arouse her.

"That's . . . not . . . how . . . it goes," Kim tried to instruct her between her hard, forceful thrusts.

Sonja stopped and lowered her mouth onto Kim.

"Oh, no, Sonja!" Kim protested in horror. Sonja was truly throwing her from one sensation to the next. Like a roller coaster ride. "You said you don't like that. It's fine if you . . . with your hand . . ." Kim tried to close her legs, but Sonja knelt between them. "Please . . . I don't want you to do anything you don't want."

Sonja raised her head and looked up at Kim. "This is different," she said, already bending over again. "I've always done this."

She touched Kim with her mouth, and Kim moaned aloud. It was so glorious. "Maybe you won't like it," she still managed to protest weakly. She lacked the strength to do more, since Sonja's tongue was already moving across her labia and exploring every fold and curve. Kim moaned again. "Oh, Sonja . . ." she whispered. Any further desire to stop her completely left Kim's mind.

Sonja directed her attention to every single place that she could reach with her tongue. Then she slid it inside Kim. A soft, warm feeling filled Kim up and left her sighing endlessly.

"Am I doing this right?" Sonja asked now and then, to which Kim could only manage a laboriously whispered, "Yes."

Her lips closed around Kim's pearl and pressed together. Kim moaned and raised her hips up against Sonja, whereupon she began the whole sequence again. Her tongue joined in and met the center. Kim cried out. There was no stopping now. Sonja licked around the edges of her pearl, then across it, again and again, and Kim came in long, unending waves, during which she pressed a pillow over her face to keep from being too loud. Even so, she could probably still be heard very well from next door.

Kim lay there, gasping, and was close to suffocating under the pillow when Sonja picked it up and peered cheekily underneath. Kim fought fiercely for breath. "You're a natural," she panted, exhausted.

Sonja smiled, placing the pillow to one side and stretching out on top of it. "Thank you, but it's not really that hard," she replied graciously. "I'd imagined it would be more complicated than that. I'm surprised, myself."

"More complicated?"

"Well, you know, I thought . . . actually, I couldn't picture it at all. When you've only known one way for twenty years, you think there is no other way," Sonja admitted, a bit embarrassed. She smiled as she turned her head to face Kim. "I never had any comparison before now, you know."

"What would you have done if you had?" Kim asked.

"Oh, I don't know," Sonja answered thoughtfully. "It's possible that it wouldn't have made any difference at all."

Kim withdrew. *In that case this won't make any difference, either.* Sonja had absolutely no need to repeat this experience. Did she really expect anything else? She should have known better!

Sonja turned back to Kim, smiling with her gorgeous eyes as if to refute Kim's conclusion. "Aside from which, that wouldn't be very fair, would it?" She winked. "I've slept with . . . let's see . . . a few men, and only with one woman. That's hardly enough material for a fair comparison."

And she wasn't likely to want to even out that imbalance, either,

Kim assumed. She seized upon a courage born of despair. Even if in just one night she couldn't offset all of Sonja's experiences with men, Kim could try to increase the weight on one side of the scales, at least a bit.

She slid her arms around Sonja and pulled her close.

Sonja's eyes looked searchingly at her face, serious again now, and seemed unable to decide what should happen next.

But Kim had already decided. She wanted to make the most of this night, the only, the last – the first.

Kim drew close and saw Sonja close her eyes before she kissed her.

When she woke up, Kim again found herself alone in the large double bed.

She glanced at the clock. Oh, boy – she had overslept! She smiled. No wonder, after last night. What time had they finally fallen asleep? She didn't know. She only knew that Sonja had been insatiable, that she'd surprised Kim again and again with new ideas, and that time had vanished from her consciousness entirely.

Kim jumped out of bed. She might not have slept much, but the exercise she'd gotten last night had apparently paid off and toughened her body. She laughed out loud. She felt wonderfully happy, as though she were floating on cloud nine.

A quick shower and she was on her way downstairs. Breakfast was, in fact, over, and she didn't feel like she could eat anything, anyway. She felt as satisfied as if she'd just eaten a five-course banquet. She quickly grabbed a cup of coffee and raced to the seminar room.

When she opened the door, everyone turned to look at her. She was the last arrival. She nodded apologetically to Klaus – if only he'd known why she was late! – and took a seat. She sought Sonja's face. Sonja gave her a serious look and turned her attention back to Klaus, who was moderating the closing discussion.

When it was over, Klaus distributed a certificate to each seminar attendee that confirmed their participation. Everyone said their goodbyes and headed quickly for their parked cars, scattering like a startled herd of cattle.

Sonja came up to Kim with one of the older seminar participants at her side. "Matthias is riding back with us. He needs to get to the airport." She avoided Kim's gaze.

Too bad. They wouldn't be alone on the drive back. But at least they were driving together. "Fine," Kim said. "Shall we go pack?"

"I'm already done," Sonja said. "My things are in the car."

Another surprise – not even a few minutes alone in the room together. Kim cleared her throat. "I'll go get mine. It will take me just a few minutes."

"We'll wait outside," Sonja said and walked with Matthias to the parking lot.

Kim sprinted up the stairs and hastily threw her things into her overnight bag. Not two minutes later she was in the parking lot too.

Sonja and Matthias were already sitting in the car, Sonja in the driver's seat and Matthew next to her. Kim stowed her overnight bag in the trunk and climbed into the back seat. Sonja only interrupted her conversation with Matthias briefly to start the car. She paid no attention to Kim.

Well, all right, in Matthias' presence she could hardly do otherwise, Kim thought. It wasn't particularly pleasant, but she'd endure it.

Sitting in the back, Kim felt rather cut off. She could follow the conversation between Sonja and Matthias, but it was difficult to actually participate. They talked about the seminar, about other seminars, about their career histories. Really, though – as Kim observed from behind – Matthias was just enjoying sitting next to Sonja. He cast glances at her that clearly reflected his interest.

Sonja, on the other hand, seemed interested only in the conversation. What else would she want with a man like Matthias, who was at least twenty years older than she?

Kim wondered how the drive might've gone if she hadn't been there – or if *he* hadn't been there. She yearned to touch Sonja, to at least be able to speak to her, to look into her eyes. But the only topic she'd be able to use for that purpose was the seminar. Everything else was taboo now.

Sonja looked in the rearview mirror to answer Kim after she'd asked a question, and for one brief moment, their glances met in the mirror, lingered, then darted quickly away as Sonja turned her attention back to the road.

What was it that she'd just read in Sonja's eyes? Kim allowed herself to sink back into the leather upholstery to ponder that. Sonja's gaze had seemed not tender, not questioning, just . . . thoughtful. Perhaps that was the right word. Thoughtful, as was certainly appropriate after everything that had happened. Or thoughtful in response to a situation that made Sonja uncomfortable.

Did she offer Matthias a ride so that she wouldn't have to be alone with Kim? Kim was annoyed with herself for not having woken up earlier, for not having awakened Sonja with a kiss. Then she wouldn't have been able to withdraw so easily.

She would simply have to wait until they were alone. The drive passed calmly and uneventfully, with the conversation petering out after a while, as they all seemed rather tired from the seminar. Kim dozed off for a bit in the back seat. When she awoke, they were at the airport, and Matthias was getting out of the car.

"Goodbye." He reached Sonja his hand. "Thank you very much for the ride."

"My pleasure." Sonja nodded to him.

Matthias waved a quick farewell to Kim and went into the terminal building.

Kim was going to get out and sit in the front seat, but Sonja was already pulling away from the curb and driving onward. "Sonja?" Kim asked cautiously.

"Where should I drop you off?" Sonja replied. "Do you want to go to the office, or would you prefer downtown?"

The office building was only a five-minute walk from the center of downtown.

"Well, really, it's still working hours," Kim said.

"Officially, the seminar lasts until this evening. It's all paid for. You can spend the rest of the day however you like."

"Are you going to the office?" Kim asked.

"No."

"Oh." Kim was surprised. Sonja usually worked round the clock, it seemed. "So I have your official permission as my supervisor?" Kim grinned a little.

"Yes. I'll sign off on the hours." Sonja was far from grinning. Her voice sounded impersonal and serious.

"I . . . Sonja . . ." Kim swallowed. "I was actually hoping to talk to you."

"We can talk on Monday," Sonja said. "At the office. I don't have time right now."

"You can drop me off wherever you want." Kim resigned. "Office or downtown, it doesn't matter." A stone lay in her stomach. The morning's high spirits were long gone.

"Office, then." Sonja said nothing further, just drove until she turned into the driveway of the office building. She stopped, but didn't get out.

Irritated Kim got her overnight bag out of the trunk and went around to the driver's side. It was obvious that she couldn't, right here in front of their office building, bid Sonja goodbye with a kiss, but neither could she just –

Sonja took the decision out of her hands. Barely was Kim standing next to the driver's door when Sonja pulled back out of the driveway and turned down the street.

A minute later she was out of sight.

Kim drove home, thinking about Sonja's behavior on the way. She couldn't have made it clearer that she didn't want to talk. She'd been hot last night, and now she was as cold as a block of ice. Maybe that was her usual M.O. The thing with Klaus had gone similarly, after all.

Kim sighed. Yesterday she'd told herself that there would only be the one night, no more, but this morning when she'd woken up – somehow, she had hoped that her prediction wouldn't come true.

Sonja had been so ... sweet last night, so tender, but also so abandoned and passionate – Kim wished for a sequel.

Was she in love? She thought about it. She couldn't say. Her hormones were screaming too loudly.

Sex. Was it just sex?

Kim took a deep breath. In any case, it was obvious that her body wanted that. Just at the thought of Sonja, she began to tingle all over. That had been the case with a number of women before, and it had had nothing to do with love. She had her confirmation.

When she got back to her apartment, she unpacked her overnight bag and started a load of wash. Some housework was in order; she'd neglected it a bit lately.

In the kitchen, her gaze fell on the large calendar on the wall.

Oh, yes, tonight was the women's café, and tomorrow the dance; it was the first weekend of the month. Not a bad idea, to distract herself.

Where was the best place to hide a grain of sand? On the beach.

And where was the best place to hide a grain of sand named Sonja? In a sea of women that washed across the sand and covered everything.

"Guess who?"

Two hands covered Kim's eyes from behind.

"Andrea, Carla, Melanie, Sophie –" Kim grinned.

"What, you know so many women you can't tell them apart anymore?" a disappointed voice complained. The face that belonged to it pushed its way into Kim's field of view.

"Wait, what's your name again? I'll think of it in a second." Kim furrowed her brows mightily, as if she had to concentrate very hard.

"You're impossible." Jennifer laughed and sat down at Kim's table. "You're here early. You don't usually come until later."

"I didn't have to work so late today."

"Ah," Jennifer replied. "Well, it's about time you started paying more attention to having fun and not just work."

"Oh, it's not that bad. True, I usually come later, but I do come."

"You don't say ..." Jennifer propped her chin in her hand and gave an impish look.

"Yes, that too," Kim said defiantly. "I'm well taken care of, thank you for asking."

"Anyone special?"

"N-no."

"So, still playing the same old game of musical chairs." Jennifer grinned.

"As do you. Otherwise we probably would've become the couple of the century."

"One night is nice, too. Ours was anyway." Jennifer smiled in fond recollection.

"Yeah." Kim didn't smile. She was thinking about a different night than Jennifer was.

"We just weren't meant for each other," Jennifer said. "Instead, we're best friends now. That's worth something, too."

"Sure."

Jennifer frowned. "You're acting a little weird. Is something wrong?"

Kim shook her head. "I guess I'm still tired. I was away at a seminar the last few days and just got back today."

"Interesting seminar?"

"In part." *Not so much the days, but the nights*, Kim thought. "It was purely professional. A management seminar. My boss wants to promote me, so to get the promotion I had to do one of these."

"Your boss wants to promote you and sent you to a management seminar?" Jennifer nodded in appreciation. "Sounds good."

"Well, yeah ..." Kim hesitated. "It's okay."

"Sounds like you're not exactly scrambling for the promotion."

Kim shrugged. "I have no idea what it involves." *And Sonja's office will then presumably be miles away from mine*, she thought.

"But you'll make more money?" Jennifer looked inquisitive.

"Of course." Kim nodded. "That, I will."

"Most people would be satisfied with that, but apparently not you."

"No." Kim wanted to drop the subject. "No, I am, really."

"Really." Jennifer looked askance at Kim. "Honey, we maybe only had the one night, but since then, we've had a lot of days together. Don't tell me that nothing's wrong. We've known each other too long for that."

"It's nothing ... It was just – as it happened, my boss and I had the same room at the seminar."

"Oh, wow!" Jennifer's nose grew an inch out of sheer curiosity. "Double bed?"

"Yes." Kim was wishing she'd left. Why had she even mentioned this?

"How old is she?" Jennifer asked. "Was it worthwhile?"

"The seminar was good."

"A-ha." Jennifer leaned back, grinning. "You don't want to talk about it. So it must've been very good."

"She's my boss!" Kim replied angrily.

"Who doesn't want to do it with the boss now and then? It happens a lot." Jennifer propped her elbows on the table and leaned forward. "Oh, come on. How was she?"

"She's married, straight as an arrow and a pain in the ass," Kim said. "Satisfied?"

"And your point is? What does she look like?"

Fantastic, Kim thought. "Normal. You know."

"Oh-ho-ho," Jennifer said. "If you're being that secretive, there's something behind it."

"Not really." Kim sighed. "Yes, she looks good, but ... as you said, she is my boss, so –" She left the rest hanging in the air.

"So she's out of the question?" Jennifer shook her head. "You were in bed next to her and felt nothing?"

A tingle shot through Kim's body and left her with goosebumps.

Jennifer saw the small shudder. "So you did!" she said triumphantly. "You had sex with her!"

"Sex doesn't mean anything," Kim said defensively. "We're a good example of that."

"Oh, it meant something to me. It just doesn't have anything to do with love. Let's not confuse the two. *Now* I love you – as a good friend; back then, it was all just hormones."

"And for her, it was the same way, presumably." Kim sighed. That was the only explanation, when she really thought about it. Without a doubt, Sonja was a very passionate woman, and perhaps she really couldn't last three days without sex. So she'd gotten herself what she needed.

"But not for you?"

"Maybe," Kim replied.

"But you're not sure?" Jennifer wouldn't let it go.

"I liked her a lot even before the seminar." Kim took a deep breath. "She's only been with our company for a few weeks, and just seeing her has made me have trouble concentrating on my work."

"Major hormonal crisis." Jennifer grinned.

"Yes, exactly." Kim nodded. "That's probably what it is. She just looks damn good – and is very charming."

"Bring her along sometime." Jennifer grinned even more. "She sounds interesting."

"I don't think –" Kim broke off. "Like I said, she's married," she finished.

"Now that is definitely not an obstacle." Jennifer turned around partway and gestured into the room. "There are at least half a dozen of 'straight' married women back there." She smirked. "One of them is pretty steamy. It does sometimes have its advantages that men don't understand anything about sex with women. They're absolutely starved, I can tell you." Once again a cheeky grin stole over her face.

"I know," Kim said, rather aggrieved. She was gradually beginning to understand that she and Jennifer were talking about different things. She desired Sonja – without a doubt. But that night when Sonja had lain on her breast and cried, that was something else. That had nothing to do with sex. She had just wanted to protect Sonja, to hold and comfort her. Sonja was simply a very special woman.

"I think I'll bring the menu out." Jennifer rose. "Maybe one of those creatures will find something she likes." She was really grinning shamelessly. The *menu* she meant was, of course, herself.

Kim nodded and followed Jennifer with her eyes as she joined a woman who was standing rather shyly in a corner. Jennifer's menu seemed to suit her tastes – after just two minutes, Jennifer was touching her arm, they were both laughing, and the reticent woman was starting to thaw.

"All alone, young lady?"

Kim turned her gaze from Jennifer and her latest conquest toward the woman sitting down at her table. *Were people really still using that trite old come-on?* Kim thought, amazed.

The other woman considered Kim's face. "Was that your girlfriend?" She glanced briefly into the corner where Jennifer was now proceeding with a physical onslaught. She was kissing her new acquaintance and feeling around her body with interest while the woman pressed against her.

"No," Kim said. "Well, yes," she corrected immediately. "We're friends, but not –"

A broad smile spread across the new woman's face. "I'm glad to hear that. I don't enjoy trouble with jealous partners."

"Neither do I. Which is why I don't have one." What difference did it make? Should she deny herself all contacts just because there was one woman who . . . who . . . whatever.

"Wonderful." The woman's smile grew. "I've been watching you for a while now. I like you." Her hand rose, and she stroked Kim's cheek with one finger. "Interested?" She looked inquiring.

Kim considered her more closely. The touch of her hand hadn't triggered much in Kim, and aside from that, she wasn't exactly her type. But what was the difference, really? As Jennifer had said: It wasn't about love, just about sex. She pursed her lips. "Maybe."

"My name's Jo."

"Kim." Kim nodded.

"Okay, Kim. Would you like something to drink?"

"No, thanks. Instead, let's . . ."

"Hmm, you're on the fast squad." Jo was delighted. "Shall we go to the back?"

"Yeah." Kim stood up.

Jo followed her, and they took themselves into the back room of the café, the Darkroom.

Kim let Jo go first, who opened the door for Kim with a broad grin. Kim hesitated for a moment – the Darkroom wasn't exactly her territory, she usually preferred a bed, although she had made use of it once or twice before. She entered, and Jo shut the door behind her, holding onto Kim's arm so as not to lose her in the dark.

Jo pressed her against the wall. Kim felt her hot breath on her face. "You are so hot," Jo whispered excited. "So incredibly sexy . . ." Her tongue swept across Kim's cheek and then snaked its way into her ear.

Kim didn't like that at all. Jo, of course, couldn't see Kim's grimace. "Hurry up," Kim whispered in the darkness. She decided she didn't want this stranger in her presence any longer than necessary.

Jo gave a throaty laugh. "You didn't look like that type at all, sweetie. But I like that even better." Her hands ran down along Kim's body and sought her waistband. With practiced fingers, she quickly opened button and zipper.

Kim waited for the usual arousal, or at least a fraction of it, but Jo's hands, pushing her pants and panties down over her hips, left her cold. "Take my breasts," she whispered to Jo. That usually helped.

Jo, who had been caressing her backside with enthusiasm, let her hands wander higher, and pushed up Kim's T-shirt. She gasped when she touched Kim's breasts, caressed their feminine curves. "Hm, nice . . ." Jo found a nipple with each thumb and rubbed them.

Although Kim still wasn't aroused, her nipples reacted of their own accord. They went hard.

"Yeah, baby, come on!" Jo whispered hoarsely. She bent down and licked across one nipple, took it into her mouth, licked some more, sucked.

What's going on? Kim thought. *Why am I not feeling anything?* This had never happened to her before. When she wanted to be in the mood, she always could. Sure, Jo wasn't someone she wanted to get to know better, but that didn't have anything to do with sex. Jo was making an effort and doing all the right things. But it did nothing for Kim.

She let out a frustrated sigh, which Jo misinterpreted. "Yeah, baby, let yourself go, enjoy it," she murmured.

Sonja! Damn it, it was Sonja! She was blocking all of Kim's responses. Although she couldn't see anything in the dark, Kim knew that Jo wasn't Sonja. She could hear it and feel it. But that shouldn't make any difference at all! What did one woman have to do with the other? Sonja wasn't here, but Jo was, and she was making a considerable effort to win Kim over with her sexual arts.

Sonja, on the other hand ... Sonja was now at home with her husband ... who without any doubt had awaited her hungrily after her absence ... and just this moment those two were probably doing exactly what Kim and Jo were also trying to do. Sonja would be in bed with him, she'd spread her legs –

Kim moaned, then reached for Jo's head with both hands, pulled it up, and sought her mouth. Their lips met forcefully. Kim thrust into Jo's mouth, and Jo's tongue immediately thrust vigorously back.

"Oh baby, baby ..." Jo murmured, after they'd separated from that highly violent kiss. "I knew you'd be good." Jo breathed heavily. Her hand slid down along Kim's side and sought the way between her legs. She pushed Kim's thighs farther apart and tried to enter between her labia. "Don't you want this?" she asked confused.

Kim could feel how dry she was. "Sure."

"Ah." Jo nodded understandingly, although Kim felt the movement more than she saw it. "Then we'll do this differently. I once had a girlfriend with the same problem." She slid down Kim's body and knelt before her.

Kim felt Jo's hair brush the insides of her thighs; she spread Kim's legs even wider in order to fit her face between them. Kim leaned her head back against the wall and stared at the ceiling – if she could've seen it in the darkness. *Quick*, she thought. *Hopefully it'll at least work this way*. She was already feeling burned out and empty, and her patience was exhausted.

The tip of Jo's tongue tapped against Kim's pearl, rubbed it, licked it.

Kim felt nothing. *This can't be happening!* She simply couldn't comprehend it, and she didn't want to keep thinking about it, either. "I can't, Jo, I'm sorry," she burst out, pushing Jo's upper body aside, pulling her pants up and her T-shirt down, groping her way quickly toward the exit.

When she opened the door, she almost crashed into Jennifer and her evening's conquest. Jennifer stopped short for a moment, then grinned. She pushed the other woman into the Darkroom, turned around and whispered "Your zipper," then disappeared behind the closing door.

Kim reached awkwardly for her zipper and pulled it up. She'd just plain overlooked that in the commotion. Another first. Today, things were happening to her that had never happened before. It was like a slapstick comedy, but unfortunately, she wasn't the audience – she was in the middle of it, the leading lady.

Buster Keaton wasn't a role she'd ever envisioned for herself, and she didn't like it.

Quickly, she left the café and went home.

Late the next morning the telephone rang.

"Hey, how about breakfast at the women's café?" Jennifer asked, clearly good humored. "I don't know if the Darkroom will be open this early, though." Her impudent grin crept right through the phone line.

"I don't think I'd be comfortable at the women's café today," Kim replied reluctantly.

"Oh, you didn't have a good time?" Jennifer asked astonished. "Well, I'm not complaining about my date." Now her grin hung like a poster on the wall.

"Then just go with her. I'm sure she'd be glad to."

"She's long gone, back home to her three-legger," Jennifer remarked cheerfully. "She didn't even want to spend the night with me."

"I'm sorry," Kim said.

"I'm not." Jennifer took a deep breath and yawned. "Good thing there's the Darkroom. She was hot; probably because she liked it that no one was looking. But afterwards, I certainly enjoyed recovering in my own bed by myself. I don't need all that 'Will we see each other again?' and 'Do you love me?' junk. You know –"

"Yes, I know. But at least you didn't drag me into the Darkroom."

"That should tell you how much I already treasured you, even back then." Jennifer laughed. "I thought the bed was more appropriate."

"Thanks," Kim said. "How incredibly gracious of you."

"You got that right. So, what about brunch? My stomach's growling."

"I don't know . . ." Kim was undecided. "Actually . . . actually, I'd rather stay home today." It was possible, after all, that Jo would also go to breakfast at the women's café, and then Kim would've had to explain some things. She wanted to spare herself that. Besides, she really didn't feel like being around people, even if they weren't Jo.

"Why are you so unsociable today?" Jennifer asked puzzled. "You're not usually like this."

"I'm just not myself today. It's not a big deal."

"Fine – if that's what you want. But you're definitely coming to the dance tonight – promise?"

Kim groaned. "Do I have to?"

"Yep. It's got to be one or the other," Jennifer said determinedly. "I'm not letting you waste away in your hovel, not when the dance only happens once a month. I can't do that to my best friend."

"Thank you for your concern," Kim said sarcastically. "You just want me to see whoever it is you're going to cart off today. Do you even have room for any more notches on your bedpost?"

"I have a metal bed frame, as you know," Jennifer replied with dignity. "Besides which – who are you to talk? How many notches do you have now?"

"Not as many as you, I am sure." Kim laughed. "All right, fine – you twisted my arm, I'll come tonight. But if you just disappear straight into the Darkroom and I don't even see you, it'll be the last time."

"Likewise. Ms. Came-out-the-Darkroom-door-still-hot-yesterday."

"Hardly hot." Kim answered automatically, without thinking about it.

"Your fly was open!" Jennifer reminded her. "So you two weren't just playing Scrabble in there."

"It's much too dark for that in there, as you know perfectly well."

"I am getting terribly curious about all this," Jennifer said. "If you don't come tonight, I'm coming to you. I want to hear the rest. Right now, I'm insanely hungry; it's impairing my ability to concentrate."

Kim sighed. "See you tonight, then."

"You bet!" Jennifer called into the receiver and hung up.

All afternoon Kim thought about avoiding the dance, but since she'd promised Jennifer, and also because she was hungry for distraction, she went after all.

And what was bound to happen, happened: even before she saw Jennifer from afar, Jo crossed her path.

"Sweetie, what happened yesterday? Why did you run away? Did I do something wrong?"

"No, of course not." Kim frowned and tried to find Jennifer over Jo's shoulder. "You didn't do anything wrong."

"So what happened then?"

"Nothing." Kim sighed, annoyed. "It has nothing to do with you."

"Do you have a problem?" Jo asked concerned. "I mean, I know that there are some women who . . . women who can't . . . well . . . can't."

Kim stared at her. What kind of crazy conclusions was Jo drawing about her? It came as such a surprise, she couldn't speak.

"Kim! Here!"

Jennifer! Kim exhaled with relief. "No," she said quickly. "I'm not one of those women. Like I said: It wasn't about you. It was just bad timing." She walked past Jo with long strides to reach Jennifer.

"Well?" Jennifer asked impishly. "Got a woman lined up for afterwards?"

"Pfft!" Kim lowered herself onto the barstool next to Jennifer's.

"We met yesterday, that's all." She ordered a beer from the woman behind the counter.

"Oh, she was the one you –" Jennifer looked around, trying to locate Jo. "Doesn't look half bad," she said when she got a look at her. "Was she some kind of pervert? Is that why you're mad at her?"

"I'm not mad at her." Kim sipped at her beer. "She's completely harmless. No perversions."

"But something sure spoiled your mood," Jennifer said. "I've never seen you like this. What was it? What did she do – or not do?"

"Nothing." Kim was getting annoyed. "Neither, nor. She just did completely normal things . . . or she tried, anyway."

"Tried?" Jennifer was suddenly alert. "What does that mean? I thought you two –"

"We did. I mean, we would have, if I hadn't . . . left beforehand." Kim now took a large swallow of her beer and another one right after it.

"You left *beforehand*?" Jennifer's expression was one of utter amazement. "I mean, I understand leaving *afterward*, but before?" She knit her eyebrows. "There must've been a reason. I can't think of any off the top of my head, but you must've had one." She gave Kim an encouraging look.

"I . . . I . . . She just wasn't turning me on," Kim said furiously. "It happens."

"It happens to *some* women," Jennifer said, "but I never thought that either of us would be among them."

"Well, then, you're all on your own, now, aren't you?" Kim replied insolently, finishing her beer and ordering a new one.

"I hope you two aren't fighting because of me?" A new voice joined them.

Kim stared at Jo, who was suddenly standing next to her. "Of course not."

"Since Kim is guaranteed not to introduce us . . . I'm Jennifer." Jennifer glanced at Kim out of the corner of her eye and winked at Jo.

"Jo. I don't know why," she went on, "but something scared her off yesterday, and she doesn't want to tell me what."

"Me neither. So we have the same problem." Jennifer gave Jo a stern look. "What did you do to her?"

Jo raised both hands in a conciliatory gesture. "Nothing, I swear. At least, nothing unusual," she added grinning.

"If you two are just going to amuse yourselves," Kim said poisonously. "That's not what I came here for."

"You promised to tell me the whole story," Jennifer complained. "I haven't seen a bit of it. You keep dodging behind mysterious intimations. That isn't like you at all. What's up with you all of a sudden?"

"Um . . . did you two used to have a thing together?" Jo asked cautiously. "Because if you did, then I think I'd better go."

"No, no, stay, it's fine." Jennifer was in her element. "It was a long time ago." She smiled at Kim. "One wonderful night. And since then, we've been friends, without any further obligations. So don't worry."

"Are you sure?" Jo remained unconvinced. "Kim said something like that yesterday, but the way you two behave . . ."

"Don't give it a second thought," Jennifer said. "We always act this way. But we still don't sleep with each other. That's probably why we've stayed friends for so long." She chuckled.

"Yeah, sometimes, that's better than –" Jo looked from Jennifer to Kim and back again. "You had a wonderful night?"

"Oh, God!" Kim groaned. "Are we done yet?"

"Yes, we did," Jennifer answered nonetheless with a look at Kim. "And I still remember it fondly." Her lips curled expressively.

"Too bad." Jo sighed. "I would've liked to have had that, too." She looked at Kim.

"I'm leaving. Go ahead. Keep swapping stories about me." Kim slid off her barstool.

"Come on, don't be so sensitive. I really don't know what's going on with you," Jennifer said. "You know, Kim, you need to relax. How about a threesome?" She looked at Jo. "So we all get something out of it." She laughed.

"You're off your rocker!" Kim scolded. "Both of you. I should never have come here in the first place. Have fun."

She turned around, but was restrained by Jo's arm. "I'm sorry.

Maybe we went a little too far, but I didn't know you'd take it so seriously." Jo let go of her arm, and her apologetic expression soothed Kim.

"It's all right. I . . . maybe I overreacted a little." Kim ran a helpless hand through her hair.

"I think this has to do with her new boss," Jennifer said to Jo. "She slept with her in a double bed . . . at a seminar." She raised her eyebrows meaningfully.

"Thank you for your discretion," Kim snapped. "I thought you two were going to behave yourselves."

"We are," Jennifer said. "But I think Jo has a right to know why you're not yourself at the moment. She's getting the complete wrong impression of you."

"If you're going to make me . . ." Kim sighed in resignation and slid back onto the barstool. "But really, that's none of anybody's business."

"In the lesbian scene, everything is everyone's business." Jennifer grinned. "You know that."

"A little more consideration from time to time would be nice," Kim said.

"Okay, you're right." Jennifer nodded. "But how are we supposed to do that – when everyone knows everyone else?"

"I didn't know you two yet," Jo said, "but then, I haven't been in the city long."

"That's the only reason you didn't know us. That, and when someone doesn't bring her new flame along." Jennifer looked at Kim.

"She's not –" Kim took a deep breath. "Why can't you just leave me in peace?"

"Dance with me." Jo smiled. "Then I'll leave you in peace. I accept that we're not meant for each other – even though I'd hoped otherwise – but I'd still like to know you better." She turned to face Jennifer. "And you, too. No sex, but friendship – that would be something completely new for me." She laughed.

That laugh took Kim by surprise. And all of a sudden she found Jo quite likeable. "I'm really sorry, Jo," she said. "But I'd be happy to dance with you."

“Then I’ll have a look around for a dance partner, too,” Jennifer said. “Now that a few more women have come in besides just the youngsters who’ve been here all night. You can’t do much with them.”

“All self-serving declarations.” Kim winked at Jo. “She has the highest virgin-rate in the entire city.”

“Well, yeah, in a pinch . . .” Jennifer grumbled and disappeared.

“You two are funny,” Jo said, as she and Kim walked toward the dance floor. “You act like an old married couple, and yet –” She started moving to the music.

“And yet, we don’t have sex?” Kim shook her head smiling. “Yeah, sometimes I find it strange, too, but I like it. Sex isn’t everything.”

“Wisely spoken, young lady.” Jo laughed. “If I’d known that in advance . . .”

“You still would’ve come on to me.” Kim chuckled. “That’s just how you are.”

“As I said, I’m new in town,” Jo defended herself. “How else am I supposed to make contacts, when I don’t know anybody?”

“And then afterward, you know everybody,” Kim replied with a sigh. “And everyone’s already had a thing with everybody else.”

Jo shrugged. “What am I supposed to do? There are only so many of us. And we don’t even all come to the dances and other events. We’re all just on the search for true love, really.”

“Are we?” Kim frowned dubiously.

“More or less. Aren’t you?”

Kim didn’t answer.

“No answer is also an answer.” Jo grinned.

Kim didn’t get home until close to six o’clock Sunday morning, so she spent most of the day asleep in bed. She’d so overexerted herself on the dance floor that she needed to recover. She hadn’t danced that intensely in a long time, and when she woke, she had the muscle cramps to prove it.

This is another way to compensate, she thought, *if it doesn't work out in the Darkroom*. It was all still a puzzle to her. But the whole time she was dancing, she hadn't had to think about Sonja – or at least, not often. If she hadn't overexerted herself like that, she might've just brooded and brooded.

Sonja surely hadn't done that, Kim thought. She was certain that Sonja had resumed her normal life, and on Monday, they'd sit in their adjacent offices, as if nothing had ever happened.

▫▫■▫▫

Monday morning, Kim found Sonja already working, as usual. As if nothing had happened – as predicted.

"Good morning," Kim said, making an effort to keep her tone neutral. That was difficult for her, since Sonja was looking great and making Kim's heart pound. How much she would've liked to take her in her arms, to caress her shiny, silky-soft hair . . .

As if nothing had happened . . .! Ha! Kim became aware that she'd been kidding herself. A great deal had happened, and she could no longer push that to the back of her mind. She didn't want that. She didn't want to subject herself to this torment, but neither could she defend herself against it. Why did it have to be Sonja, and not some random woman from the dance, with whom she could easily have avoided further encounters?

Sonja didn't respond to Kim's greeting. She sat behind her desk deliberating and watched her. Then she stood up. "Since you work so late into the evening so often, I figure that you aren't in a committed relationship. Most men –" She broke off. "Most people," she corrected herself, "don't much like it when their wife comes home so late."

What was that supposed to mean? A lump formed in Kim's throat, and even though she found Sonja's particular comment irritating, the sound of her voice sent hot shivers through Kim's body.

She nodded her confirmation, because she couldn't speak.

"I'm afraid that I can't –" Sonja began rather hesitantly. "I mean, I *am* in a committed relationship. I'm married."

Ah, that was it! She was trying to tell Kim that she could forget about the prospect of having her as her girlfriend. Kim felt her stomach cramping, even though she'd been expecting this. How could it be otherwise?

"I know that, Sonja." She tried to sound as composed as possible. "I've known that since the first day, when you introduced yourself in the conference room." *Which is precisely why I never should have started anything with her*, she thought. *Why do I always have to be so dumb?*

Sonja grimaced, almost painfully. "Perhaps we shouldn't try to continue any kind of personal relationship – just keep it professional," she said. "I'm sorry that I ever started that. It was my mistake."

Kim went to the door and shut it. As she did, Sonja watched her warily. What did she think? That Kim was going to try to rape her this early morning?

"We slept together," Kim said in a muted voice, and Sonja grimaced again. "So we absolutely have a personal relationship. And I'm afraid I can't just forget that. Can you?"

She observed Sonja, and it nearly tore her heart from her chest. Sonja appeared to be so distant; she might as well have been on the moon.

Sonja waved it away. "You're right. That's silly. But – well, we shouldn't take any hint of a personal relationship outside of this room. Publicly, we have to look as though everything is completely and entirely professional between us, and *only* professional. Are you prepared to accept that?"

Kim nodded. "Of course." Nervously she cleared her throat. "I think it would be appropriate for you to tell me what you're going to do now." *Because I don't know*, she thought. *But I have an inkling.* She thought it would be best for her to share her inkling out loud; then perhaps the issue could be dealt with quickly. "Should I clear out my desk right now, or are you going to grant me a reprieve?" she asked.

Sonja looked her up and down. She ran a pensive hand across her chin and left it there as she continued to observe Kim. "Good question."

I knew it! Kim tried to remain calm, even though she felt like she was dying to escape.

After a very long pause, allowing Kim to grow even more nervous, Sonja continued. "I've never gotten involved with a coworker." Then she laughed dryly. "Let alone a female coworker! It only causes problems. I've always kept my professional and personal lives separate. Always." Again she paused. "I'm going to push your promotion through as a high priority," she said then. "So maybe you'll be able to move into your new office a bit sooner. Would you be in agreement with that?"

Kim nodded. She was feeling a little confused. So Sonja didn't want to fire her? For a second, she wondered if she ought to resign. But then she might never see Sonja again.

Sonja gestured in such a way as to indicate they'd reached the end of their conversation, but then gave Kim a reprieve. "Or do you still have questions?" she asked.

Questions? Thousands! But Sonja wouldn't want to answer a single one of them. So Kim slowly shook her head no.

"Well, then . . ." Sonja sat down again.

Kim left her office, and a minute later, for the first time since they'd started working together, Sonja shut the connecting door between their two rooms.

The following weeks passed so coolly between them that Kim felt like she'd landed in an ice chest. No more side-by-side conversations, no more accidental touches, no laughter coming from Sonja's office.

It was so apparent that Sonja found the idea of any mention of the seminar so abhorrent that Kim refrained from bringing it up, even though that demanded exceptional self-control of her. Seeing Sonja every day was bad enough. Their relationship had been reduced to supervisor – employee. Period.

It pierced Kim to the very bone every time she saw Sonja. She felt the yearning as much as she had on the first day, and she couldn't prevent herself from envisioning Sonja the way she'd been then, on that one night, the only night.

But nights like that seemed to mean nothing to Sonja, Kim thought. She'd spent one with Klaus, and afterwards looked daggers at him. So Kim should count herself lucky that Sonja wasn't doing the same thing with her.

One morning, Sonja called her into her office. "Your promotion has come through," she said businesslike. "Property management will have your new office set up in just a few days. They'll let you know when you can move in."

"That fast?" Kim felt a slight quiver inside. "I thought it wasn't until fall –"

"There was an open Team Leader position that needed to be filled quickly," Sonja said coolly. "And so I suggested you."

"I . . . thank you," Kim stammered.

"I did tell you I was going to push through your promotion as a high priority," Sonja continued, still objective and firm. "That's what I did."

"I . . . yes . . . which location?" Kim felt incapable of forming a complete sentence. In the next few days! At least the agony of giving Sonja a wide berth would be over, but what would come next?

"The Service Team on Michelbergring. Or doesn't that suit you?"

Michelbergring. That was on the other end of the city. Kim almost laughed. At the start, she had wondered how she could move Sonja's office as far away as possible, so that she wouldn't have to be so close to her, and now Sonja was doing just that to her.

"Yes . . . yes, of course." She cleared her throat. "That's fine with me."

"The new salary and other details are things you had best discuss with the personnel office," Sonja said. "They have all the files." She looked down to read something on her desk, and when Kim didn't reply at all, Sonja looked up. "Is there anything else?"

Kim slowly shook her head. "No," she said softly. *I'm afraid not*, she amended in her thoughts. *I'm afraid there's absolutely nothing else.*

Two days later, Kim got the news from property management that her new office was ready. Sonja had probably once again applied pressure to make things go faster than normal. After her own experiences with property management, Kim had figured on closer to a week.

She knocked hesitantly on Sonja's office door. It still seemed strange that the door should be closed; until recently Sonja's open door policy had always been in effect.

"Come in!"

Kim opened the door and entered the room. "My new office is ready."

"Ah." Sonja raised her eyebrows, apparently pleased.

She won't miss me, Kim thought.

"You can go right on over. If you like."

No, I don't like. "Sure. I'll do that. But –" Kim hesitated. "My successor – shouldn't I stay to orient her?"

"I'll take care of that. She's coming next week. Until then I'll manage on my own." Sonja smiled a little. For the first time in a long time.

She's glad to finally be getting rid of me, Kim thought. "Good," she said. "If you have any questions or if you need anything, you can always call me, of course."

"I doubt that will be necessary. Your filing system is quite easy to follow."

She's going to avoid contacting me at all costs, Kim thought. "Who . . . who will be taking over my position?"

"A Ms. Mayrhofer," Sonja said. "You don't know her. She just moved here recently from Munich."

Kim nodded. She really couldn't draw things out any longer. "I'll go, then."

"See you later." Sonja returned to the files on her desk.

Hardly – not if you can avoid it, Kim thought. Sonja didn't even offer to shake her hand in parting. She wouldn't even grant Kim that one small touch.

Kim sighed and left Sonja's office.

Over on Michelbergring her new team awaited her with curiosity. Kim didn't know any of the team members, since the two office buildings were so geographically distant that the employees never encountered one another. She was greeted by her new department manager, an older, jovial-looking man, and introduced to all the others.

The large company that Kim worked for manufactured electronics, and it was her team's job to handle all the customer inquiries that came in by e-mail, letter, fax, or phone. Not an easy job – the customers weren't very friendly, since their devices had usually caused them a great deal of aggravation before they reached the point of calling.

Until now Kim had worked mostly in the background and rarely had contact with customers; now, she was on the front lines. She sensed that the members of her team were professionals. They spoke calmly with the customers when they were upset, and usually, the problems that existed with their products could be solved without a great deal of trouble or expense.

The first day flew by, and Kim had no time to think about Sonja. Kim stayed at the office until almost midnight, trying to get a complete overview of her new responsibilities. All of a sudden, it was her role to give instructions to others, and she couldn't do that if her employees understood far more about the work at hand than she did herself. Of course, she had a basic understanding of the whole process, but in direct contact with customers, practice sometimes looked rather different than the theory.

She finally felt like she'd achieved some insight and leaned back with a sigh. The next morning she'd ask her team members to acquaint her with more of the details. *It's not so easy being the boss*, Kim thought.

Boss – keyword – Sonja . . . the chain of associations in her mind arose unbidden.

Well, now it was over for good. *But it's best that way*, she thought annoyed. *Obviously Sonja felt like everything that happened between us meant nothing. I should be glad that I don't have to see her anymore . . . that I don't have to be constantly reminded of it all by her presence.*

But she wasn't glad. That was the problem.

For Kim the whole next week was a wild roller coaster ride through one sixteen-hour day after another. She hadn't imagined it would be that taxing. But her team was good, and the collaboration was fun.

Her telephone rang from morning 'til evening; the call coming in must be at least the tenth one today. She picked up.

"Ms. Wolff? This is Johanna Mayrhofer. I'm Mrs. Kantner's new assistant."

Kim's fingers tensed around the receiver. "Yes?" she asked as calmly as possible.

"Mrs. Kantner isn't in the building today, and she left me with an assignment, but I can't find the necessary documents. Do you possibly have the time to help me?"

"What is it that you need?" Kim felt herself relax. Sonja wasn't in the building; that meant she wasn't standing behind Ms. Mayrhofer right now, looking at her, listening to her, brushing against her arm . . . Kim shuddered as though just that were happening to *her* at that moment.

Meanwhile, Ms. Mayrhofer explained what she was looking for.

"I transferred that to offsite storage," Kim said, once she understood the situation. "The paperwork, I mean. But you'll find everything on my . . . your PC. Look it up under the year in question. I set up several subfolders within that folder. You'll see where it is right away."

"I'm glad to hear that," a grateful Ms. Mayrhofer said. "Because Mrs. Kantner expects this assignment to be finished when she gets back."

"She always does." Kim smiled a bit. "You can call me anytime you have questions, no problem."

Ms. Mayrhofer thanked her, and they hung up.

Kim had almost forgotten the call an hour later, when Ms. Mayrhofer rang once again. "Something awful has happened," she said. "Your PC . . . I mean, my PC . . . nothing's working anymore. I can't get at the documents."

"Sometimes it helps to shut the whole thing down and restart it," Kim said.

"Could you hold on while I try that?" The computer was in a slightly awkward spot under the desk; only muffled noises were audible for a moment, then her voice came back on the line. "Nothing. No dice."

"There is a backup." Kim thought it over. "But if the computer is defective, the IT department won't be able to reload it that fast. I'll run the printed documents over to you; they're in storage in this building, and I was planning to come over and eat in the cafeteria anyway."

"That's awfully nice of you," Ms. Mayrhofer said. "Maybe we could have lunch together. I'd like to ask you a few procedural questions – about how Mrs. Kantner likes things done. She's so rarely in the office, and she only tells me the most essential things."

I could describe to you in great detail how Mrs. Kantner likes things, Kim thought, and she had to smile for a moment. Then she got serious again – that had been inappropriate and unnecessary, she thought. Old news. "I'll come to your office. I'll be there in half an hour."

It gave Kim a peculiar feeling to enter the building and trace the path to her previous workplace. Everything was still very familiar; she'd walked this way every day for years, but now she no longer belonged here.

Her heart began to pound when, all the way at the end of the hall, she saw the open door to her former office – and behind that, Sonja's.

Oh, stop that nonsense! She called herself to order. *Behave yourself!*

Sonja wasn't there, after all; Ms. Mayrhofer had said so.

She went in and saw only two feet behind the open drawer of a large filing cabinet. The cabinet was over six feet tall and completely concealed the rest of the person. "Ms. Mayrhofer?"

The feet moved. A woman appeared. The smile on her face froze. "Ms. Wolff?" she asked startled.

Kim froze likewise. "You?" she finally managed surprised.

"Yeah." Jo grinned.

"You're my replacement?" Kim still couldn't grasp it.

"Seems that way. That's quite a coincidence."

"Indeed." Kim was only slowly recovering.

Jo came over to Kim. "Don't worry. As they say: Our common past will have no influence on our present cooperation." She grinned even more.

"You're nuts," Kim said. "What past?"

"Hey, if it'd been up to me . . ."

"Here are the documents." Kim handed Jo a large envelope. "You'll find your way around them easily."

"I'm sure." Jo nodded and accepted the envelope. "Before your PC quit working I could tell that you set everything up quite logically. Folders, subfolders and descriptive filenames – it really wasn't hard to figure out at all. I've certainly seen a lot worse."

"I hate having to search for things. That's why I make such an effort to keep everything in order."

"Me, too. There's just no reason to waste time on pointless searching."

"Exactly. I didn't know we had so much in common."

"Maybe that's why things didn't work out."

"I'd be very grateful if you would forget about the whole thing." Kim grimaced with embarrassment.

"I'd rather not. You were very sweet." Jo simply couldn't hold back another grin. "Even though I wish it could've ended differently."

"Then we'd better not have lunch together. Because I do not wish to hear another single word about the subject."

Jo pantomimed zipping her mouth shut. "Locked and barred. Not one single word. Completely forgotten. I don't even remember what we were talking about."

"That's good." Kim smiled. "Because I'm hungry."

"Me, too." Jo set the envelope on the desk. "Let's go."

At lunch they discussed a number of questions related to the new job that Jo had in store for Kim. When they got to the coffee, Jo was back to more personal topics.

"So you really slept in a double bed with Mrs. Kantner?" she asked rather mischievously. "Or is that topic also taboo?"

"Actually, it is." *More than anything else*, Kim thought. *In fact, I'd prefer a conversation about the Darkroom.*

"She looks terrific," Jo continued unperturbed. "She's not my type, though. But that you . . . and she . . . somehow, I can't imagine it. That she would be open to something like that."

She isn't. Not really, Kim thought. "You'll be sorry if you breathe the slightest word about this to her," she warned. "And anyway, it was nothing." At least, that's what one of the participants seemed to think.

"I will be very careful not to breathe a word to her. I like this job. I was glad to find something so soon after moving here."

"Then everything's fine."

"I'll see her through somewhat different eyes from now on, though," Jo said. "I won't be able to help it. Considering that because of her, you –"

Kim arched her eyebrows.

". . . got a promotion," Jo went on quickly. "And so I have your job now. That should be something to celebrate. What do you think?"

"I have no objection to that," Kim said.

"Then I'll call Jennifer."

"You'll call Jennifer?" The second surprise of the day. Kim looked astonished.

"Well, yeah, Jennifer and I . . . we've been seeing a lot of each other," Jo said a bit bashfully.

"Jennifer and you?" Kim hadn't expected that.

"Yeah . . . I know . . . we're the one-night-stand ladies . . . but –"

"I'm glad." Kim smiled. "Honestly, I'm glad to hear it."

"You are?" Jo asked uncertainly.

"Yes." Kim nodded in confirmation. "I like both of you, and if the two of you like each other, so much the better."

"And we both like you." Jo grinned. "We'll turn into the *Infernal Trio*."

"I should hope not!" Kim laughed. "I don't actually feel all that devilish. A completely normal friendship is enough for me."

"*Normal* might be difficult, but friendship is okay." Jo chuckled.

"Good." Kim smiled. "Then go ahead and call Jennifer. Let me know what you two decide." She looked at her watch. "I have to get back. My lunch hour is over. And if you have any more questions about work, you know you just have to call."

"I may do that a little more often now. Now that I know who my predecessor *Ms. Wolff* is."

Kim laughed, and they left the cafeteria together.

"Ms. Mayrhofer? Would you bring me the analysis?"

Sonja swooshed past Jo on the way to her desk.

Jo jumped up. She reached for the report she'd put together. "Here," she said, laying the pages on the table in front of Sonja. "It almost didn't happen, but Ms. Wolff helped me." She just couldn't stop herself from saying so.

"Ms. . . . Wolff?" Sonja froze. "She was here?"

"Yes." Jo pressed her lips together to keep from grinning. Her boss seemed rather shaken by the mention of Kim's name. "I called her. Unfortunately, my PC, which of course used to be Ms. Wolff's PC, decided to crash today. The IT department made another one available for me to use right away, but it only has the standard applications on it; the files were on the frozen computer. Luckily, Ms. Wolff had also printed out the documents, and she brought them over to me."

Sonja took a while before she said, "I see." She glanced briefly at the pages Jo had placed in front of her. "These look good," she said. "Thank you."

"You're welcome, my pleasure." Jo returned to her own desk quickly so that Sonja wouldn't see the expression on her face.

Something definitely happened, she thought. *No matter how much Kim claims it was nothing.*

Sonja sat at her desk and laid her head in her hands. She was exhausted. Lately her days had consisted primarily of fieldwork. She was rarely in her office. The company's upper management was planning a reorganization, and she was supposed to lay the groundwork for it. It was a back-breaking task.

Which might be a very good thing, she thought. *Not having time to think about things.*

She went to a filing cabinet and took out a folder. As she returned to her desk, the telephone rang. She picked it up. When she heard who the caller was, her face hardened. "Why are you calling?" she asked. "I asked you –"

"I know what you asked, dear wife," her husband's voice said, "but I need you."

"I can't right now." Sonja's voice was cool. "I have a lot of work to do."

"Have you forgotten what we agreed on?"

Sonja's shoulders fell. "No," she said quietly. "I can never forget that."

"It's all good, then," her husband said.

"Uwe . . . please . . . I have to work."

"Then you'll come home late again, and I won't even see you. That seems to be your standard operating procedure lately. I'm sure you'll be able to spare a few minutes for your *husband*."

"What are you trying to say?"

"You know perfectly well," he said. "And it's all okay, too – as long as you stick to our agreement."

"I am sticking to it. I have –"

"You have a husband," he interrupted her harshly. "That's all you have – and ever will have."

Sonja shut her eyes briefly. "I know."

"So – do you have a few minutes?" His voice sounded self-assured.

"Yes," Sonja replied quietly.

▫▫▫▫▫

"**M**ust I really?" Kim furrowed her brow.

"You're a manager, so I'm afraid it's required," Rolf Winkelmann, her new department head, said. "I'm not exactly thrilled about it either. I've been going to these things for years. There's nothing we can do about it. It's a total waste of time."

"You said it." Kim sighed. "Shall we drive over together?"

"Yes." He nodded. "That'd be best. In half an hour."

Kim returned to her office. She was annoyed. Meetings had never been her favorite activity, and this one seemed particularly pointless to her; the whole afternoon would be lost. She reached for the chart she'd been working on and compared a couple of values. Customer satisfaction was in an entirely acceptable range, the numbers said, but there was still room for improvement. That, at least, she could bring up at the meeting. If she got the chance. Most meetings consisted of nothing but *blah, blah, blah.*

A half hour later, Rolf knocked on her door. "Shall we?"

At the conference center, on the way to the elevator, they met up with a number of managers Kim had only ever seen from a distance during all the years she'd worked there. Rolf greeted every one with a handshake, introducing Kim to each as his new team leader.

That dog and pony show eventually came to an end, thank God. Since the elevator could only hold a limited number of people at once, Rolf let the most senior managers go first. "Best that way," he said to Kim with a wink. "It's all the same to me whether I get there first or last, but not to some of those guys."

Kim made a face.

"You'll get used to it," he assured her in a fatherly manner. "Believe me. Supposedly, we live in a democracy in which all people are equal, but some are still more equal than others." He laughed.

The elevator doors opened again, and Kim and Rolf got on.

"Sonja! Nice to see you!" Rolf called out enthusiastically. "You've been hard to pin down lately."

"I've been on the road a lot." Sonja smiled slightly. "The reorganization."

"I know," Rolf said. "A pretty mess."

"Hello, Kim," Sonja said, turning to Kim. Her voice sounded polite and reserved, and her smile vanished.

Kim just stood there, practically in shock. Sonja's face had appeared in front of her eyes when the elevator doors had opened, but Kim had taken it for a dream; this wasn't the first time she'd seen Sonja without her actually being there. But this time it was no dream.

She swallowed. "Good afternoon, Sonja," she finally managed halfway civilized. She tried to suppress the trembling that seized her.

"Now, I still don't know why you ever let me have Kim." Rolf laughed. "Didn't it make your heart ache, as good as she is?"

Sonja seemed to hesitate for a moment. "That's exactly why she deserved the promotion."

Kim felt like she was standing on an auction block.

"No doubt," her new boss said. "I'm glad to have her." He looked over at Kim with a broad grin. "Since you've been here, I only have half as much work to do."

The elevator stopped, and Kim, who felt like she was about to faint from Sonja's scent and presence, stepped out quickly.

This hadn't occurred to her before. A meeting of the management would always entail a meeting with Sonja. And these meetings happened at least once a month. She took a deep breath. If she could find out the dates far enough in advance, maybe she could schedule a vacation or call in sick.

Sonja was also extremely uncomfortable having to be in the same room with Kim. As soon as they left the elevator Sonja went all the way over to the opposite end of the room, as far away as possible, and greeted some fellow managers standing there.

That suits me just fine, Kim thought. *Please, go ahead, keep me at arm's length.* Granted, they now had an hours-long meeting before them, during which they couldn't avoid one another.

Rolf chose a different part of the room for his territory, and Kim joined him with a relieved sigh. At his side she felt protected to some degree. He brought her into the discussion, introduced her to the other members of the leadership ranks, and new colleagues asked about her new position.

Thus, she had to concentrate on the answers she was giving, and Sonja's presence was thankfully forced into the background. When the meeting began, their seats in the large conference room were as far apart as befitted their relations.

Kim tried to avoid Sonja's gaze, sometimes by staring at the conference agenda in front of her or writing something completely meaningless on a pad of paper. The meeting whooshed past her, but that was no great loss. As both she and her new boss had expected, the whole thing was a waste of time; self-adulation on the parts of the various departments, a scrap over budget allocations, and an exchange of constantly repeated phrases. Kim was amazed that it was possible to run a business like this. But apparently, it was possible, since the company wasn't doing too badly.

Something was said about her, as well – Rolf Winkelmann praised her in the highest terms and practically nominated her as his successor.

Kim was so surprised that all she could do was stare at him.

"I second that," a clear voice announced from the other side of the conference room – Sonja's voice. "I let Ms. Wolff go with regret, for the good of the company. She was always an able and reliable employee, but vastly underchallenged in her role as my assistant. She's capable of much more – as she has now proven."

I proved it to you, too – in a different respect, Kim thought. *But you weren't interested.* She was amazed at Sonja's openly pronounced praise. This must be how she had pushed for Kim's promotion, as well. She truly could separate the personal from the professional; Kim had to give her that. If Sonja had insisted on Kim's dismissal with the same vehemence, no one could possibly have countered it.

Kim sought Sonja's gaze, and for a brief moment their eyes engaged each other, before Sonja turned her face away from her and looked, unmoved, in a completely different direction. *She doesn't look good*, Kim thought. *But that can't have anything to do with me. She's probably just working too much.* Still, she recalled that exactly that had always tended to excite Sonja – it spurred on to ever more work, which she enjoyed doing and which brought her satisfaction. Which conjured forth her laugh that could fill an entire room with sensuous joy.

Maybe I showed her that there's another kind of satisfaction, Kim thought. *And she misses it now.*

No, that's crap! She doesn't miss anything! Why should she? She's married. She has sex whenever she wants. She never said that it wasn't fun for her.

Maybe she didn't always get exactly what she had in mind. With Klaus, it seemed to have gone that way, but surely, there would be some compensation for that.

Me, for instance. Kim sighed. Probably that was all it had been. Klaus caused a certain balance to teeter that had to be brought back into equilibrium, and here was this little assistant who wanted nothing more dearly than –

Kim stopped, and her teeth clenched. That's how it had been, exactly like that.

She looked at Sonja, whose face was turned away as she listened attentively to someone's contribution, unaffected, focused. In contrast to Kim, she seemed genuinely interested in the contents of her colleague's speech.

She's just like that. She's only interested in her work, and in between, she needs some recreation, that's all.

Kim locked up all the chambers of her heart and waited for the end of the meeting.

When it was finally adjourned, everyone picked up their papers without any great hurry, conversing with one another or rising to go. Kim looked for Sonja.

But Sonja had disappeared.

"You two are definitely a pair of odd birds," Kim said with a laugh as Jo and Jennifer led her blindfolded into Jennifer's living room.

"Hey, come on. It took long enough," Jennifer replied. "Jo and I couldn't agree, but eventually I just had to put my foot down."

"Yeah, sure." Jo sounded good humored. "You put your foot down."

Jennifer hesitated, considering her answer. But then she reached for the cloth around Kim's head and untied the knots. "And now – kindly be delighted. Surprise!" She ripped the cloth from Kim's eyes.

I hate surprise parties, Kim mused, but so many beaming faces met her gaze that it chased away all traces of displeasure. "You really are crazy. All of you." She had no way to oppose this roomful of good cheer and had to laugh once again.

"That's the meaning of life," Jennifer said. "What's the point in always running around stressed out?"

"This causes stress, too," Kim objected.

"But positive stress," Jo said, "and that's healthy."

"I read otherwise recently," Kim said.

"You read too much," Jennifer replied nonchalantly. "I've always said so. So, are you happy, or not?"

"Yes, I'm happy." Kim smiled at Jennifer. "Thank you."

"Not at all," Jennifer said. "It was getting to be high time for a party anyway. The women's dance just doesn't come around often enough."

"You can say that again," Jo agreed. "Hey, girls, turn up the stereo!"

The music blared from the loudspeakers much too loudly, grating and howling. A second later, the volume was turned down a bit, and the women in attendance began to dance.

"We have a couple of presents for you," Jennifer said. "From us and a few of the others."

"You didn't have to do that," Kim said. "What for?"

"Because, of course, we're expecting presents from you in return." Jo laughed. "The next time."

"When you get promoted?" Kim asked.

"Oh, no, no!" Jo lifted her hands as if to ward off such misfortune at all costs. "Not me! Sappho forbid! I have enough work to do already!"

Kim grinned. "Too much work? Do you need an assistant?"

"Do you want to come back?" Jo asked with a wink.

"No." Kim became serious. "I'm doing pretty well in my new spot."

"Me, too, actually," Jo said, "but that Kantner –" She broke off. "Sorry, I wasn't going to mention her."

"Go ahead," Kim said, her face dispassionate. "That doesn't concern me anymore."

"If you say so," Jo replied doubtfully.

Jennifer chimed in. "Jo tells me Kantner's been getting edgier by the day. She blows up at every little thing."

"She looks pretty stressed out," Jo added.

"I know," Kim said automatically.

"You saw her?" Jennifer and Jo gaped at her simultaneously.

"At the managers' meeting." Kim cleared her throat. "We didn't speak."

"Hmm," Jennifer murmured. "But obviously you got a really good look at her."

"That was unavoidable," Kim retorted. "We were in the same room for hours."

Jennifer opened her mouth as if to say something, but changed her mind and shut her mouth again.

"After her husband calls, she is always absolutely intolerable." Jo sighed. "Then I really have to watch my ass around her. I feel like I have to be walking on eggshells, and even that doesn't always help."

"Her husband?" Kim raised her eyebrows in astonishment. "He calls her?"

"Oh, yeah!" Jo rolled her eyes. "And he calls her a lot more often than he used to."

"The whole time I was there, he never called once."

"Lucky you." Jo sighed again. "He seems to really upset her. On top of everything she already has to do for the company. Sometimes, I feel sorry for her, but then again – sometimes she can really be a bitch, you know."

"I'm sorry about that, Jo," Kim said.

"Nothing *you* can do about it." Jo took a deep breath. "You're not her husband, after all."

Jennifer's eyes widened.

"Oh, damn." Jo frowned in embarrassment. "Sorry, I didn't mean to say that. I didn't want –"

"It's fine." Kim waved it away. "You're right. What you said only reflects the facts."

She didn't know what to call the feeling that was gripping her just now. Sonja was unhappy, that was obvious. And she had also been unhappy back when she'd cried in Kim's arms. Was this the same unhappiness or a new one? Had her husband been the reason back then, too? For everything? For Klaus? For . . . Kim?

"Forget about it." Jo rested a hand on Kim's arm. "Hey, look over there, the blonde. Fresh meat. You like her?"

Automatically Kim followed Jo's gaze and saw the young blonde swaying across the improvised dance floor like an angel. It didn't stir anything in her. The girl was cute, sure, but that was it.

"Not interested?" Jo looked inquiringly at her.

"I could've told you that right away." Jennifer shrugged. "Or would you say that she could compete with Mrs. Kantner?"

"Well . . ." Jo watched the blonde with interest.

"Please, stop," Kim said softly.

"Sorry," Jennifer said abashed. "You're still pining for her?"

"I'm not pining for her –" Kim flared, but then her voice became quieter again. "It's just that . . . she really didn't look good at the meeting."

"Which is no longer your concern," Jennifer added. "Nor was it ever, really. I'm sorry to have to put it that way, but it seems to me like you're losing touch with reality, Kim."

"You two brought it up," Kim defended herself.

"Just don't get your hopes up," Jennifer warned. "She might be in the middle of a marital crisis, but that certainly doesn't mean that you can come in like a knight in shining armor and rescue her. Maybe she doesn't even want to be rescued. And if she does, it's not by you."

"I didn't want to –" Kim protested.

"Oh, yes you did. I know that look." Jennifer sighed. "And I know the feeling. They're always so enticingly helpless, these ladies. But she doesn't want your help. She wants a man. When will you finally understand that?"

"I've understood that for a long time," Kim said softly. "Believe me." She looked at Jennifer. "She has a man – and not just one. I don't think she's missing anything in that department."

"Not just one?" Jo looked at her in astonishment. "You mean she's having an affair? That's why her husband is freaking out?"

"She's not having –" Kim took a deep breath. "I have no idea whether or not she's having an affair. But back at that seminar, she wasn't just with me –" She broke off.

"Wow!" Jo gasped and whistled between her teeth. "I never would've guessed that of her. To me, she's always seemed a little . . . stuffy." She gave Kim an apologetic look. "Sorry."

"What for?" Kim said. "I think we ought to change the subject. It's not very polite to talk about people behind their backs."

"Maybe not polite, but interesting," Jennifer said. "I've heard so much about this woman already, first from you and then from Jo – I'd really like to see her sometime."

"Sure, you can do that. Just come visit me for lunch at work." Jo grinned, and Jennifer grinned back.

"You will not do that!" Kim raised her voice.

"What did I just say?" Jennifer shook her head. "She keeps sticking up for her."

Kim made a face. "Leave her alone, please. If she's really not doing so well . . ."

"We're not going to do anything do her," Jennifer said. "I just want to have a look at her. Mostly thanks to you. Jo doesn't much like her, after all."

"She's not a circus attraction!" Kim was furious.

"I think we'll have to skip lunch, darling." Jennifer lifted her hands placatingly. "Or else Kim is going to kill me."

"I think you're right." Jo grinned. "Calm down, Kim, we're not going to do anything, did you hear?"

"I . . . I'm sorry," Kim said. "I . . . I . . . I know that none of this is my concern, you're right."

"Obviously, it's very much your concern." Jennifer sighed. "Kim, this is not good for you . . ."

"But I don't want . . . I mean . . . I know she's married . . . and that she . . . prefers men." Kim's expression was agonized. "But sometimes . . . when I think about her . . ."

"You had a passionate night, I understand that," Jennifer said. "That sort of thing sticks in the mind, whether you want it to or not."

"Unfortunately." *Then again, maybe not*, Kim thought. "Maybe I just need to talk to her again –"

"Are you nuts?" Jennifer punched her painfully on the arm. "Do you want to start the whole thing over from the beginning? Keep your distance from her, that's the only thing you can do."

"Ow! That hurt!"

"Not as much as it will if you see her and talk to her and get yourself all worked up again," Jennifer warned. "I can promise you that."

"Jenny's right. And you know it." Jo looked sympathetically at Kim. "We've all been through this at one time or another. It'll pass. Eventually."

"You, too?" Kim looked at Jo, who nodded. Kim looked at Jennifer. "But you haven't."

"Oh, sure," Jennifer said. "Before we met. We're all susceptible to it. But like Jo said: It'll pass. Eventually."

"Eventually," Kim repeated pensively.

"I know it's hard to remember that while it's happening, but one morning, you'll wake up and not think about her first thing. It's always like that," Jennifer said. "You know I'm telling the truth."

"If you say so . . ." Kim replied slowly.

Jo laughed. "You don't believe it – now. But just wait."

"How long?" Kim frowned.

"Oh, come on." Jennifer picked up her hand and squeezed it. "Nobody can answer that. But you can count on it."

"Okay, fine." Kim sighed. "I'll keep my distance from her. Promise."

"Well . . ." Jennifer's voice sounded skeptical. "Can we take that to the bank?"

"Yes." Kim nodded vigorously. "I'll call in sick the next time there's a managers' meeting. Or plead an appointment out of town. There's nothing about these meetings to miss, anyway."

"Do that." Jennifer began to grin eagerly. "And now, open your presents."

▫▫▪▫▫

"If you don't go home right now, I'm throwing you out," Rolf said, laughing as he leaned into Kim's office. "It's eleven o'clock at night!"

"You're still here, too, Rolf," Kim replied with a smile.

Rolf and Kim had found out that they worked very well together and enjoyed each other's presence at the office.

"I'm an old man. I'm allowed. You're a young woman. You ought to have other plans on a Friday night."

"But I don't." Kim was still smiling. "And the work doesn't do itself."

"No, hardworking Kim does it." Rolf came over and pressed the button that shut her computer down. "No matter what you were doing just now, it can't possibly be that important."

"I was right in the middle of the statistics –" Kim started to object, but Rolf interrupted her.

"Whatever statistics they were, they can wait until Monday. Go home." He tugged her chair out from under her so that she had to stand up.

"Rolf!" Kim laughed.

"Don't 'Rolf' me, and you're leaving now. That's final. I'm only trying to protect the interests of the company. They can barely afford your overtime pay anymore. And I'm accountable for that."

"The interests of the company." Kim chuckled. "Right."

"That's how it is." Rolf's confirmation was assisted by the jolly little wrinkles around his eyes, which twinkled so much that a person could hardly take his words seriously.

"Well, then, I'd better ... before I bankrupt the company ..." Kim reached for her jacket.

"That's very considerate of you, as far as the company's concerned. Would you give me a ride to the main parking garage? My car is over there."

"Ah, not quite so altruistic, after all."

"I never claimed to be. You know I'm notorious for taking advantage of my employees." The twinkling in Rolf's eyes increased another degree.

"Yes, I hear about it every day. You're quite the dreaded slave-driver."

"I should think so. That's how it's got to be." He grinned. "Let's go."

"Ah, I almost forgot," he said, when they'd arrived at the main building and Kim was about to drop him off. "I have something for you in my car. My wife asked me to give it to you. Would you come down with me for a second? If I show up with it at home, all hell will break loose."

"Hey, now, Margit's not that bad." Kim laughed. "You just like to say so."

"You're not married to her." Rolf sighed. "It seems that she's quasi-adopted you, and now she wants to mother you from sun-up to sundown."

"A cake?" Kim asked apprehensively.

"I was trying not to have to say so. I don't want to have to eat the thing myself. That's what's in store for me if I bring it home again. That, plus a tongue-lashing." He grimaced comically.

"Poor Rolf. All right, fine, I'll come get the cake. I don't want you to suffer unnecessarily."

"That's kind of you," Rolf said gratefully, and they took the elevator to the underground garage.

Rolf handed the cake to Kim, wished her a nice weekend and put his seatbelt on.

She watched his brake lights get smaller as he drove off.

She considered the cake. Should she just leave it there? Unfortunately, Margit was not much of a cook. She seemed not to know it; she was always trying to please others with her cooking and baking arts. By now, when Kim brought anything made by Margit home, Kim's friends refused to touch it. She sighed. Perhaps she could find a homeless shelter or any other place where people would be glad to have it.

She walked back to the elevator. The heavy steel door between the garage and the hallway offered some resistance when she tried to pull it open with just one hand. Suddenly, the resistance lessened. Someone was pushing from the inside. The door opened.

Sonja was suddenly standing in front of her.

Kim nearly dropped the cake, and Sonja didn't move, as though struck by lightning.

"Hm-hmm." Kim cleared her throat. Her head was spinning. "Sonja." She cleared her throat again. "How are you?"

Sonja said nothing, but even in the pallid light of the parking garage Kim could see that the dark rings beneath her eyes had grown deeper.

Kim raised the cake in the air. "Want some cake?" She forced a laugh. "I just got one as a present."

"Now?" Sonja seemed to awaken. "In the middle of the night?"

"My boss's wife –" Kim began.

"Ah, Margit," Sonja said. "I understand."

"Has she given you cakes, too?" Kim was grateful for this innocuous topic of conversation, even though it wasn't likely to last long.

"Yes," Sonja said. "She seems to do that to everyone."

"I think so, too."

They fell silent and looked at one another.

Kim felt the yearning overwhelm her. If it hadn't been for the cake, if she'd had both hands free . . .

"Sonja, I –" She raised a hand as if to caress Sonja's cheek; it was like a magnet, drawing her close.

Sonja interrupted her with a movement. "Don't, Kim . . ."

"Yes." Kim let the hand drop. "Are you not feeling well?" Intently, she examined Sonja's face. "You look tired."

"It's nearly midnight," Sonja said coolly. "How else should I look besides tired? You can't be doing much better."

"It's all right. I can recuperate over the weekend, after all." Kim looked at Sonja, who still hadn't moved, and made up her mind. "I need to talk to you."

"There's nothing to talk about," Sonja replied forbiddingly.

"Yes, there is." Kim set the cake down on the ground.

Sonja stared at her. "What?" Her face was a solid mask.

"I just want to talk." Kim looked at her and saw the wariness in her eyes. What was she afraid of? "We should've talked a long time ago."

"No. Everything is fine the way it is."

"You look like you're on the brink of collapse," Kim countered concerned, "and you call that fine?"

"That's none of your business," Sonja said sharply. "Besides which, I *am* fine. It's been a rough week, that's all. A few hours of sleep –"

"Do you get that at home – with your husband?" Kim asked.

"Ah, that's what this is about." Sonja seemed to relax. "You're jealous." Apparently, this was a familiar situation for her, something she knew how to deal with. "May I remind you that I'm married?" Her voice sounded smug.

"You don't need to remind me of that. I've never forgotten. But there are apparently a variety of ways of being married. For some people, it appears to include having affairs." Sonja had wrapped herself in so much armor; Kim didn't know how she'd be able to crack it.

"We did not have an 'affair,'" Sonja said dismissively.

"That may be true. But they say you're having one now. Is that why you're so exhausted?"

"Excuse me?" Sonja glared at Kim.

"Your affair. Does it take a lot of energy? Are you going to see him now?" Kim could feel things spinning out of her control.

"That's ridiculous," Sonja said coldly. "Let me through." She attempted to take a step forward, but couldn't get past Kim through the narrow doorway.

"I'm sorry." Kim looked at the floor. "That's not what I wanted. I honestly just wanted to talk to you."

"That's what appointments are for," Sonja said, even colder than before.

"Yeah, sure," Kim replied, disappointed. "In your office."

"Better there than in the parking garage," Sonja countered angrily.

"Sonja . . . my God . . . I . . ." Kim could no longer contain herself. All her feelings overwhelmed her at once. She pushed Sonja up against the wall and stared into her face. "Sonja . . . Sonja, I . . ."

Sonja's gaze was icy. Kim no longer knew what to do. She felt so helpless. She leaned forward and pressed her lips against Sonja's.

Sonja didn't open her lips. Kim tried again, and at some point,

Sonja relented, but she didn't let go of her briefcase. She kept it in her hand until Kim released her.

"Are you happy now?" she asked, just as cold as before. Her voice practically clinked like ice cubes. "Or do I need to get undressed, too?" She looked Kim up and down. "Just talk. Of course," she said scornfully.

Kim stepped back. She thought she remembered Sonja going soft beneath her kiss, but she wasn't sure whether or not she'd only imagined that.

"Forgive me. I . . . you're . . . you're so wonderful. I miss you." Her voice sounded tender.

"There's nothing to miss," Sonja said, still cold. "It was nothing."

"Nothing?" Kim stared at her. "You call that night in the hotel nothing?"

"Exactly." Sonja was acting like an iceberg that continued to freeze even colder and harder. "I've experienced nights like that often, and they never mean anything once they're over."

"For me, it's not over," Kim said tenderly. She yearned so badly to be able to take Sonja in her arms now, as she'd done then. "I'd very much like it not to be over."

"But it is. Over and done with. One night means nothing." Sonja turned away and pressed the remote to unlock her car. A beep came from the middle distance, and her car's lights flashed.

"It was your only night with a woman. Doesn't that make it different?"

Sonja didn't answer. She stared impassively at her car.

"That night means a great deal to me," Kim said softly. "*You* mean a great deal to me, Sonja."

Sonja started to walk toward her car.

"I love you, Sonja," Kim said.

Sonja jerked to a halt and spun around. "Are you insane?" she hissed. "Saying something like that to me?" She paused a moment, not speaking, collecting herself. "I'm still your superior," she said, slightly calmer.

"What kind of difference does that make? Does that mean you're no longer a desirable woman? Does it mean you're not the woman I love?"

Sonja frowned disdainfully. "Who you love makes no difference to me whatsoever. Just leave me alone about it." She turned and walked to her car.

"Are you ashamed of yourself? Are you ashamed because you slept with a woman and liked it?"

Sonja turned back once more. "What makes you think I liked it?" she asked contemptuously.

Kim laughed sadly. "I'm not a man, Sonja. I know perfectly well that you did. You can't fool me. But if you want to try to fool yourself . . ." She shrugged.

Sonja glared at her angrily again. She left without another word. Her footsteps echoed through the underground garage, the car door slammed, and the engine started.

In a moment she would drive past Kim.

When she did, there was no expression on her face.

Kim got the impression that had she thrown herself in front of Sonja's car, she would have kept right on driving.

After Kim had finished up the statistics on Monday morning that she'd only half finished on Friday, she leaned back in her chair and gazed out the window.

Over the weekend, she'd experienced a feeling of shame about her behavior toward Sonja. She had hurt her; of that, she was convinced.

Certainly, Sonja had done the same to her. She had rebuffed her and pushed her away, but perhaps that was just in reaction to Kim's method of approach. Kim had simply kissed her, hadn't respected the boundaries that Sonja had drawn around herself, had crossed them without permission.

Kim sighed and reached for the telephone. She needed to apologize.

"Kim, can you help me?"

One of her coworkers stood in the doorway.

"What's up?" Kim looked at her inquisitively.

"A customer. He just won't calm down. He absolutely insists on talking to the boss."

Kim nodded. "Okay, put him through."

A moment later the phone rang. Kim steeled herself and picked it up. Right away, a barrage of imprecations rained down on her, before she could even say a word.

Then she finally managed to cut in. "You're absolutely right."

The customer had been about to launch into another string of abuse, but then he fell silent, perplexed.

"That model is very prone to error," Kim went on, "as we have already determined most unfortunately. It's being taken off the market."

"Fat lot of good that does me," the customer replied, still furious. "I already bought it."

"I understand that you're frustrated. I would be, too, in your situation. Unfortunately, all I can do is ask you to return the device. You'll get your money back."

"And my nerves?" the customer asked rather loudly.

"Valerian," Kim said. "You'll receive a free year's supply from us."

The line went still, and then a laugh broke loose from it so loudly that it prompted Kim to hold the receiver even farther away from her ear than she already had.

"You're terrific." The man could barely calm himself. "What's your name?"

"Wolff."

"Well, then, Ms. Wolff, send me the valerian and I'll send you the machine." He laughed some more. "I can't believe it! You're really all right! I'm going to have to tell my wife about this!"

"I'm happy that I'm able to help you," Kim said. "Have a nice day."

"Thanks, thanks." The man was still laughing. "You, too." He hung up.

Kim's colleague came in. "Valerian?" She chuckled. "Where did you come up with that idea?"

"Doesn't that always help?" Kim arched an eyebrow. "By the way, do you happen to know what expense category to count that under?"

Her colleague laughed. "Ask Rolf. I'm afraid that question has never come up before."

"I'm afraid so, too."

Her colleague left, still laughing.

I could use a little valerian myself about now, Kim thought, picking up the telephone one more time. *Maybe more than a little.* She hesitated for a moment before she dialed Sonja's number. Her heart was pounding in her throat.

It rang twice. Then she heard, "Mayrhofer?"

She swallowed. A fat frog in her throat was preventing her from speaking.

"Ah, Kim." Jo apparently recognized the number on her caller ID. "Is it time for lunch already?"

"No, I . . . I actually wanted to speak to Sonja," she managed with an effort.

Jo sighed. "Haven't you had enough of her yet?" She took a deep breath. "She just left. Won't be back in today. Her phone calls are being redirected to me."

Damn. Did that idiot have to call right then? A minute earlier and I would've caught her.

"Kim, be sensible," Jo went on persuasively. "You promised to keep your distance from her."

"I am keeping my distance – I'm clear on the other side of town," Kim replied peevishly. "Isn't that far enough?"

"Quit splitting hairs," Jo said. "You promised us."

"I . . . I need to apologize to her," Kim said sheepishly. "There's no way around it. I offended her."

"You offended her? How did you do that when you two never even see each other? Or did you –?" Jo broke off, suspicious.

"We ran into each other – by coincidence – in the parking garage on Friday night. That's all."

"And you had nothing better to do than to go and offend her?" Jo chided.

"Not exactly . . . I –" Kim ran a hand through her hair. "I told her that I love her," she whispered very quietly.

"You did *what?*" Jo was presumably shaking her head. "Have you lost your mind? What did you think that would accomplish?"

"Nothing. I didn't think it would accomplish anything. But it's the truth. I've been fighting it all along, but right then, when she was standing there right in front of me, it finally became clear to me."

"Oh, my God!" Jo moaned. "You really aren't attached to your job, are you?"

"This has nothing to do with my job."

"She sponsored you, Kim. It was because of her that you got your team leader position. How fast do you think that could turn around and go the other way?"

"She wouldn't do a thing like that," Kim said with conviction. "She can keep personal and professional issues separate."

"Can she?" Jo wasn't so convinced. "Well, if you think so. She was especially charming again today. I'm glad she has things to do outside the building."

"What do you have against her, Jo? She was always downright nice in the office."

"To you, maybe." Jo sighed. "I've almost never experienced her like that. She's already mad when she gets here, and over the course of the day, it just gets worse."

"She comes in later than you do?" Kim asked, astonished.

"Oh, yeah, never before nine. Sometimes not until ten. And of course, I'm always glad when she has off-site appointments and doesn't come in at all."

Something in Sonja's life must have gotten seriously mixed up, Kim thought. When a person changed her habits that much, something was wrong. Something significant. "I never knew her to come in any later than seven, usually even earlier."

"Seven?" Jo laughed. "Good heavens!"

"Yeah. When I worked for her, she was always the first one in in the morning," Kim said thoughtfully. She chewed at her lower lip. Originally, she'd just wanted to apologize to Sonja, but that thought had now receded into the background. She was worried. Even though she had no right to be. She sighed.

Jo had heard the sigh. "Get her out of your head. She's no good for you. She's a cold, straight bloodless harpy, that's all. She and her husband can go off and scratch each other's eyes out. Leave it alone."

Kim took a deep breath. "Yes, it has nothing to do with me. You're right."

"Then why does it seem like you mean the opposite of what you're saying?"

"I mean exactly what I'm saying," Kim asserted. "It's none of my business what she does. But I still need to apologize to her. Because what *I* do *is* my business."

"You're incorrigible." Jo moaned. "Will you ever learn? What else does she have to do to you?"

"She didn't do anything to me," Kim said softly. "I did something to her."

"Good grief, what horrible thing did you do?"

Kim didn't answer.

"Do what you have to do. At any rate, you won't reach her anymore today."

"Where is she?" Kim asked.

"Oh, no!" Jo was obviously shaking her head, to the point that her hair rustled against the receiver. "I'm not telling you that. You'll just jump right up and drive over there."

"So it's not that far away?"

"My lips are sealed. You'll get nothing out of me."

"I can already imagine where she is," Kim said. "I read the reports on the state of the reorganization, too, you know."

"Kim, please ..." Jo resorted to pleading. "Don't. She's no good for you. She's no good for anybody."

"She is ... Jo, you don't understand. She's very different from how you've gotten to know her. She can be very different, really." Kim closed her eyes, and it was as if she could smell Sonja's scent, just as she did back then –

"In bed?" Jo pursed her lips audibly. "You know perfectly well that that doesn't count. That's not everyday life. That's always an exceptional circumstance."

"But she was ... she was like that in the office, too, before we ... I mean ... what you're experiencing with her now, I never experienced. She was always nice, friendly, competent." Kim was confused.

"She's still competent," Jo said. "Very much so. She can run circles around any man. But nice . . . friendly . . . that must've been somebody else. Calling her a dragon would be too kind."

Something isn't right here, Kim thought. *If she treats me like that – okay, but other people, too? Jo never did anything to her.* "I have to see her," she said decisively. "I'm sorry, Jo, but I can't keep my promise."

She heard Jo groan again before she replaced the receiver.

She pulled out the latest internal report. There was a photo of Sonja in it, which was why she'd filed it away in her bottom drawer. The status of the reorganization project Sonja was leading was described in it, and she was praised for her success with the project.

For the first time, Kim looked closely at the photo of Sonja. It was an old photo, probably dating back to when she was hired. Sonja was smiling and looked not the slightest bit strained or worn out. It made the difference between then and Sonja's current condition even more apparent to Kim. The woman she'd met in the parking garage on Friday could've been the grandmother of the woman pictured in this photo. Or at the very least her embittered older sister. And that had all happened in a couple of weeks.

Kim considered the photo once more, examining every inch of Sonja's face. Sonja's eyes beamed out from the picture; she was artfully made up and the photo was perfectly lit. She looked just great.

And that's how I met her, Kim thought. *Exactly like this. Beautiful, impressive, charming.* She could hardly tear herself away from Sonja's image, but she had to. The real woman needed her support; she couldn't prove her love to a photograph.

And if she doesn't want your support?

It was almost Jennifer's voice, she heard in her head.

She was always very proud of being able to accomplish everything alone. And your love? You heard what she thinks about that.

"She was horribly exhausted," Kim said aloud, as if the Jennifer in her head had spoken directly to her. "She couldn't think clearly anymore."

Are you sure?

Kim growled. She stood up and left her office. "I'm going out to Eichhalde; they're having service problems there," she called to her colleague, the same one who'd helplessly relinquished the furious customer to her earlier.

"Eichhalde?" the woman asked back. "We don't have a service point out there."

But the door had already shut behind Kim.

The Eichhalde building was the company's oldest. The company's founder had once established its first offices there, and immediately next door sat the original production hall, no longer in use. The best thing would have been to abandon the office building entirely, since it was nowhere near up to modern standards, and the production hall ought to have been razed, but the company's founder was attached to his beginnings and had strictly forbidden any such sort of demolition. The building was to continue to be used productively, but not changed in its essence. A difficult, if not insoluble, exercise during any reorganization.

Kim knew that management's opinion was completely different from the company's founder's. They would've liked nothing better than to tear down the old buildings, since they just cost money and didn't bring any in. One of Sonja's assignments was to find a compromise between these two extremes. How she was supposed to do that was a mystery to Kim. The two positions were basically irreconcilable.

She drove into a courtyard and stopped in front of the old hall. It looked ramshackle indeed. There were almost no windows left, mostly empty frames with a few sharp-edged glass fragments around the edges. Scorch marks on walls, doors, and some of the windows didn't exactly inspire confidence. Time and again, homeless people had moved in, lit fires, and set parts of the building ablaze.

Too bad they never quite managed to burn the whole hall down, Kim thought. *Then Sonja would have one less thing to worry about.*

Where could she be? Kim looked around. From one end of the building to the other, there was nothing to see, or at least no human being. In the office building next door, a few windows were open; people were working in there. Apparently there was no air conditioning, as in the modern buildings, which was why the windows could still be opened.

No one would jump at the chance to work there, given how uncomfortable it was, but still, the founder insisted on its use. If perhaps not the hall, then at least the office building, as old as it may be.

There wasn't much even Sonja could do to rescue the hall, so she must be in the office building.

Kim headed in that direction. She pushed open the antique wooden door, whose hinges squeaked a bit, and entered. It smelled musty; apparently even the open windows couldn't change that. The foundation itself seemed to be damp.

An ancient wooden staircase spiraled upward from the foyer. There was no elevator. To her right she saw a door standing open. She approached it.

"Good afternoon, I'm Kim Wolff," she introduced herself to the surprised employee sitting at a tremendously nostalgic desk in the office behind the door. "Service team leader at Michelbergring."

The employee just gave her a questioning look.

"We were wondering if we might not be able to move over here in the course of the reorganization," Kim ad-libbed. "So I wanted to have a look at the building."

"The service team? Here?" The employee stared at her in bewilderment. "Over here, the fuses blow every time the refrigerator kicks on."

"Fuses can be replaced," Kim replied nonchalantly. "May I have a look around?"

"Do you have your company ID?" the employee asked. "I mean . . ." She laughed. "There's not much to worry about here, of course, old papers at the most, files from the beginning of time, but –"

"Of course." Kim pulled out her ID card.

The employee nodded. "Your colleagues have been here for a while already. On the second floor."

A shiver ran through Kim's body. She could only mean Sonja. Kim nodded. "Thanks."

She left the office and looked up the stairs. Should she really dare? What if Sonja chased her out of the building? But how would she? She was evidently not alone. She wouldn't show any such weakness in front of others.

Kim set one foot on the staircase and hesitated again. Then she nudged herself onward and started upstairs. As she approached the topmost landing, she heard a murmur of voices. The closer she came to the landing, the clearer it became. She took the last step and peered around the corner.

A small group stood at the far end of the hallway. Sonja was nowhere to be seen.

She couldn't just keep standing here. One of the men had noticed her and was looking in her direction, startled. She quickened her pace and walked over to the group.

Just before she reached them, Sonja stepped out of a door on the left side of the hall. Her head was lowered; she was studying a blueprint.

"Pardon me," she said absently, because she'd almost walked into Kim without recognizing her.

"I beg *your* pardon, Mrs. Kantner," Kim replied with emphasis.

Sonja froze, but then forced herself to look up. "Ms. Wolff," she said flatly. "What are you doing here?"

"We might perhaps wish to move the service team over here from Michelbergring," Kim repeated her fabrication, which now almost sounded like the truth to her. "So I wanted to have a look at the building."

"Don't you like it on Michelbergring?" Sonja asked, her voice still flat. Like a robot playing back a prerecorded text.

"Oh, sure, sure," Kim assured her easily, "but of course, it doesn't have the same ..." she cleared her throat, "nostalgic charm."

Sonja could no longer maintain her pillar-of-salt demeanor. "Ms. Wolff used to be my assistant," she introduced Kim to the men. "Now she leads the service team at Michelbergring."

"Ah, you're the one," one of the men said. "Wolfgang Schäfer. I've heard only good things about you. You've brought a breath of fresh air to the service department." He offered her his hand.

"I think Mr. Winkelmann had a good handle on things before, too," Kim said with a smile, shaking Mr. Schäfer's hand.

"Rolf is an old soldier who's fought too many campaigns," another man said. "They needed some fresh blood in there." He reached out his hand to her as well. "Jürgen Niederkreuz."

Next the other two men introduced themselves to her. "You really want to do this to yourselves?" Wolfgang Schäfer asked. "With all your high-tech equipment?"

"Well, you know, I thought ..." Kim found herself skidding slightly out of control. "Precisely that would be the attraction."

"No doubt." Wolfgang Schäfer raised his eyebrows. "That would require a real pioneer spirit. This thing isn't a reorganization, it's a suicide mission." He looked at Sonja. "I don't envy you, Mrs. Kantner."

In earlier days – not so very long ago, in fact – Sonja would've reacted to such a statement with her delightful laugh and said that she loved a challenge, but at the moment, she said nothing. She simply remained silent.

"The idea isn't really all that new." Kim couldn't bear seeing Sonja so lacking in drive. "Old buildings that are restored so that only the façade remains. Everything inside gets gutted and outfitted with the latest technology."

"Puh!" Jürgen Niederkreuz folded his arms across his chest. "I don't suppose you happen to have brought the cost estimates for that with you?"

"That would far exceed the budget set for the reorganization project," Sonja interjected, still relatively detached.

Wolfgang Schäfer laughed. "That would blow any budget!"

Kim raised her hands. "I didn't say it was a solution I could imagine here. It was just an idea I read about somewhere."

"It's not a terrible idea, at least in principle," one of the two men, who had yet to participate in the conversation, said. "No one's proposed it so far. We've mostly been looking for ways to convince the owner to tear down the whole thing."

"Because every other solution is too expensive," Jürgen Niederkreuz said. "It's obvious."

"Forget the idea." Kim was starting to feel embarrassed. "I didn't mean to intrude on your work."

"It's really not such a bad idea." Sonja's voice sounded ruminating, not indifferent as before. "One would just have to modify the implementation." She took the blueprints, she still held in her hand, back into the office on the left. "We can forget about all this." She tossed the blueprints onto a desk. "We have to start over from the beginning."

"If you think you can pull this off . . ." Jürgen Niederkreuz stood there with his arms crossed once more, clearly signaling that he doubted Sonja's abilities in that respect.

"Would you really move over here?" Sonja looked at Kim.

Oh no! What had she gotten herself into? It was just a spontaneous idea, and now she couldn't escape it.

"I still have to discuss this with my team. It was more of a . . . well, we've thought about it." Kim wished she could mop the sweat from her brow.

"It wouldn't happen overnight in any case," Sonja said. "I'm sure the renovations would take months. And first, we'd have to get the okay for it."

Oh, my goodness! How on earth am I going to sell this to my team? And Rolf? Hot and cold shivers were running up and down Kim's spine, because she didn't doubt for one second that Sonja would achieve whatever she set out to do.

"I think we can conclude our meeting for today," Sonja said at that moment. "This is a completely new situation. I need to think it over." She now seemed very reminiscent of the earlier Sonja, the Sonja that Kim had so much enjoyed working with.

The men nodded. "Let us know when you're ready to proceed," Wolfgang Schäfer said. "I'm very curious to hear what you come back with."

Me too, Kim thought, her heart fluttering. *Where is this going to lead?*

"Would you stay for a moment, Ms. Wolff?" Sonja asked in her usual efficient manner as the men headed off toward the stairs.

"Umm . . . yes," Kim stammered, taken by surprise.

Sonja bent over the desk and allowed some time to pass. Then she turned around.

"Why are you here?" She crossed her arms over her chest. "None of this has anything to do with your work."

Kim swallowed. "No, I . . . to be honest . . . I wanted . . ." She swallowed again. "I wanted to . . . apologize to you."

Sonja arched her eyebrows. "Apologize." She fell silent for a moment. "For what?" she asked then.

"Have I wronged you in so many ways?" Kim let out a nervous laugh. Then she became serious again. "For Friday. It wasn't right of me to . . . None of it was right. I . . ." She wrung her hands. "I'm sorry, terribly sorry. Your private life is none of my business, and I had absolutely no right –" She broke off and examined Sonja's withdrawn expression. "I didn't want to hurt you," she said softly. "That wasn't my intent."

Sonja examined Kim's face as well. Her eyes seemed to be searching for something there. "Good," she said after a while. "Apology accepted." She turned back to the desk.

Kim was so surprised by Sonja's reaction, she almost fell over. "Ah . . . um . . . that's it? You're simply going to accept my apology?"

"What else am I supposed to do?" Sonja straightened up. "Shoot you?"

"You could . . . well, you could rebuke me, for instance," Kim said, taken aback.

"I don't have time for that sort of thing. I have work to do. And because of you I now have to throw out this entire concept and develop a new one."

"I . . . Sonja . . . really . . . I didn't mean –" So many disconcerting shivers were running through Kim's body right now, she couldn't even count them. "I mean . . . the service team . . . they don't even know . . . they don't want to move." Now it was out.

"I know," Sonja said.

"You . . . kn-know?" Kim stuttered. She almost collapsed.

"The idea is simply too good to scrap. I'm very grateful to you for it. We were stuck in a dead end before you arrived. We weren't getting anywhere. And men –" Sonja broke off, then had second thoughts. "Men have no imagination, anyway," she concluded.

"So my team doesn't have to move?" Kim asked cautiously.

"Your team or another one – that doesn't really matter. The idea isn't tied to a single team."

Kim exhaled with relief.

"That's what you get for making things up that aren't true," Sonja said rather ambiguously.

"Yes." Kim took another deep breath. "You're right. Thank you. I'll never do it again."

"You will. That's the way you are."

"But why . . . how did you know –"

"That it wasn't true?" Sonja looked at her. "The situation is not new to me."

Kim frowned. "What . . . situation?"

Sonja sighed. "Let's leave it at that," she said tiredly. "I just knew." She ran a hand across her eyes.

Kim's concern, which had temporarily retreated into the background in all the commotion, reawakened. Sonja looked no better today than she had on Friday, perhaps even worse. True, she'd just found her energy again briefly, but her basic condition seemed to resemble that of the production hall outside: nearing collapse.

"Now that I've caused you so much trouble again," she said guiltily, "can I make up for it somehow? Can I help you?"

"Do you want your old job back?" Sonja asked, still tired. "I don't think Ms. Mayrhofer is very happy with me."

"That . . . that . . . She just doesn't know you very well," Kim replied evasively.

A hint of a smile crept into the corners of Sonja's mouth. "If you're one thing, you're loyal. But that isn't necessary. She has every reason to complain about me. I don't treat her very well."

"Why? What's the reason? Our work together always went so smoothly. I mean, until we . . . but even afterward . . ." Once again sharp twinges of embarrassment went shooting down Kim's limbs.

"A great deal has changed since then," Sonja said. "A very great deal."

"Is it because . . ." Kim swallowed. "Is it because of me? Then, please, don't take it out on Jo. I'll volunteer for that."

"Jo?" Sonja looked at her. "Is she a particular friend of yours?"

Kim sighed. "Jo and I know each other, that's all. I met her shortly before she took over my job. Meanwhile we've become good friends, but that's all."

"And she's also –?" Sonja asked hesitantly.

"Seeing as you're her boss, I can hardly answer that," Kim replied. "You'd better ask her yourself."

"That's enough for me."

"Please ... Sonja ..." Kim interlaced her fingers rather tensely. "This won't have any effect on your work together, will it?"

"As poorly as I've been treating her lately? I hardly think so," Sonja replied with a trace of the dry humor she had previously exemplified. "Unless, of course, she –" She broke off.

"Unless she tries to drag you into bed, like I did?" Kim asked stiffly. "Don't worry, she won't do that. You're not her type."

"Oh." Sonja walked around the desk and stood on the other side. "I'm not?"

"No." Kim had to laugh, because Sonja looked genuinely disappointed, or at least confused. "I know people usually throw themselves at your feet, but Jo ... Jo is the exception that proves the rule. I hope you're not too disappointed."

Sonja didn't answer right away. "No," she said then. "I'm not disappointed. That would be ridiculous."

"Because you're not attracted to women?" Kim asked. "Yes, indeed, that would be ridiculous."

"Are we back on that subject again?" Sonja asked clearly exhausted. "Please ..." She sat down and rested her forehead in her hands. "Please ... not ... today," she said, quiet and halting.

"Sonja ..." Kim immediately regretted what she had said. She went around the desk and crouched down next to her. "Sonja ..." she repeated. "You're not feeling well. Why won't you admit that? Go home. Get some sleep. You look dreadful, like you're about to fall right over."

"Oh, thanks." Sonja raised her head. "I love compliments."

"I did commit myself to telling the truth." Kim smirked gently. "That's what you get out of it."

"Yes, true." Sonja's voice sounded dead, as if it rose from a grave. "That's what I get."

"Are you not sleeping well?" Kim asked. "Or just not enough? Do you have too much work? What's going on?"

"Oh, I . . . it's fine." Sonja lifted her head, but her eyelids didn't follow. She looked as though she were already asleep.

"You're practically falling asleep in your chair. Should I take you home? I'm not letting you drive like this."

"No!" Sonja's eyelids flew open again. "Not home."

What was that about? Kim hesitated. "But you need to sleep," she said. "Seriously, Sonja. You're about to keel over. I could take you to my house," she suggested.

Sonja squinted at her from one eye, skeptical.

"Not what you're thinking." Kim laughed. "I'll go to my office. You can sleep in my bed. Or on my couch, if you'd rather. I won't be there."

"I . . . I don't want . . ." Sonja murmured. She was nearly asleep already.

"So before you fall asleep completely here, we're going to my place." Kim stood up. "Come on." She placed her hand on Sonja's shoulder. "Get up. My car is right outside the door. You can come back for yours tomorrow."

Sonja rose slowly, as though her arms and legs each weighed a ton. "I . . . can . . . drive," she said laboriously.

"Sure. You look like it." Kim laughed. "No, I'll drive. No ifs, ands, or buts. This isn't a matter of company hierarchy anymore, just common sense."

Remarkably, Sonja said nothing further, but followed Kim downstairs. She got a few things out of her car – all very slowly – and then sat down next to Kim.

Kim drove away. They hadn't even made it off of company property before Sonja was asleep.

My God, she must be exhausted, Kim thought. *How has she managed for this long? And why didn't she want to go home?* She shook her head. She wasn't likely to find out the answer to that any time soon.

But she had accomplished one thing, today, at least: She had spoken to Sonja, and in fact Sonja had even spoken to her. She had apologized, and they hadn't fought. That by itself was something.

When they reached her apartment building, she was sorry to have to wake Sonja. She parked right out front and watched Sonja's sleeping face for a little while longer.

Truly, I love her, she thought amazed. *It's not just hormones. Why did it take me so long to realize that?* Perhaps because Sonja had been so dismissive. That rejection had caused Kim other kind of worries.

Kim sighed. "Sonja ..." Softly she brushed against Sonja's cheek. "Wake up. We're here."

Sonja's mouth twitched, but she didn't wake up. Kim touched her face one more time. "You're so sweet . . ." she whispered. "My sweetheart ..." Even if Sonja wasn't that in real life, in Kim's dreams Sonja was her sweetheart, and while Sonja slept, Kim could imagine whatever she wanted to. "Wake up," she whispered again, brushing a kiss across Sonja's sleep-softened lips.

I shouldn't have done that, she thought. *What if she'd woken up?* She cleared her throat. "Sonja," she said a bit louder than before. "We're here. We're in front of my apartment building."

Sonja's eyelids twitched, and slowly, she raised them. "Hmm?" She still hadn't quite made it back to reality.

"We're at my house, or at least in front of it. Come on, let's go in."

Sonja turned her head, still half asleep. "You live here?"

"If you don't like it, then just don't look too closely," Kim said. "Unfortunately, you and I are in different income brackets. I can't afford a big house."

"That's not what I meant," Sonja said, now a bit more awake. "It was just an innocent question."

"Sorry. I've been a little sensitive lately." *Not least on account of you*, Kim added mentally.

Sonja got out. "I like the building. There's a garden."

"Which doesn't belong to my apartment, however. I live upstairs." Kim pointed upward. "All the way upstairs."

"That's fine, too. I wasn't planning to move in." Sonja smiled slightly.

Too bad, Kim thought. But of course, this was just about getting Sonja some sleep. Sonja's smile, even just a hint of one, distracted her. It was difficult for her to escape its radiance. "There's no elevator," she added. "I forgot to mention that."

"I usually take the stairs, anyway," Sonja said. "Even when there is an elevator."

"I know. No problem then." Kim shut off the car and led Sonja up to the top floor into her tiny penthouse.

"It's small, but it's mine," she said as they entered the apartment. She pointed ahead of her. "Bathroom, kitchen to the left, and over there bedroom and living room. That's it."

"Entirely sufficient." Sonja yawned. "Excuse me."

"I'd say it's unnecessary to ask if you want a cup of coffee." Kim chuckled. She pushed open the door to the bedroom. "You can sleep here. Or in the living room on the couch. Whichever you prefer."

Sonja went over and glanced into the bedroom. "The bed looks comfortable."

Kim laughed softly. "Would you like to render an opinion of the couch, as well?" she asked. "I'll have to pull it out first."

"If it doesn't bother you that I'm sleeping in your bed . . ." Sonja said.

"No, that doesn't bother me." Kim chuckled again. *You're welcome to do any time you want*, she thought.

Sonja looked at her.

How I would love to stay here with you, Kim thought. "I'll go, then. Make yourself comfortable. You know where everything is. Get some sleep." She sensed how her hand wanted to rise and caress Sonja's face. She had to fight it with all her strength. "Good night." She grinned.

Sonja smiled tiredly. "It's in the morning."

"That doesn't matter." Kim lifted a hand, but then just waved at her. "See you later."

She left the apartment quickly and pulled the door shut behind her.

She ran down the stairs until she stood in front of the main door. She leaned against it. She really couldn't have lasted much longer in Sonja's presence, looking at her bedroom eyes. As haggard as Sonja appeared, she was still seductive. And standing right next to the bed . . .

Kim took a deep breath and sighed. Soon Sonja would lie in bed and sleep . . . In *her* bed. But alone. Kim sighed again. That was all of it. Sonja, the straight woman, and Kim, the lesbian – those two did not add up to a couple; that was the way of the world.

When Kim came home that evening, she thought that Sonja was still there. Her scent still hung in the air.

Remembering that Sonja was sleeping in her bed at home had made it tough for Kim to concentrate on her work all day.

A peculiar situation. They hadn't seen each other for weeks, and then suddenly, everything had happened so very fast. Not quite the way Kim would have wished for things to work out, but still . . .

Kim entered the bedroom. The bed was neatly made, all the covers smoothed out and tucked in. Kim didn't normally bother, but she would almost have bet that Sonja valued such things.

She sniffed. *Oh, God.* She was going to have to put new sheets on; otherwise, she would never be able to rest tonight, with Sonja's scent in her nose, as though she were lying right there.

The telephone rang. Kim jumped, but didn't move. The ringing didn't stop.

She answered in a husky voice.

"What did you do with Mrs. Kantner today?" Jo began, clearly in a good mood. "You saw her, didn't you?"

It wasn't Sonja. And why should it be her after all? Kim swallowed, then cleared her throat. "Yes. I saw her."

"Even though I was against it this morning, I happen to be very grateful to you at the moment." Jo laughed. "She's like a whole new person." When Kim didn't answer, she continued. "You slept with her, didn't you? She was totally relaxed when she came into the office this afternoon."

"Oh my God, Jo," Kim scolded. "You really do only think about one thing."

"Well, in connection with you and her, it's the obvious thing," Jo said, unperturbed. "And? How was it?"

"It wasn't anything," Kim said, annoyed. "She was horribly overtired, and so I offered her my bed –"

"Oh, cool!" Jo seemed practically to be dancing on the table. "Not a new ploy, but it still seems to work. Even with straight witches like this one. Do you win over a lot of women with that line?"

"*She* slept in my bed," Kim emphasized. "I wasn't there. I sat in my office and worked."

"Yes, of course," Jo said sarcastically.

"You don't need to be so sarcastic. That's the truth. I brought her to my apartment, and then I left. *Before* she undressed."

"Well, undressing isn't necessarily required."

"Get it through your thick skull already," Kim said sharply. "I told you exactly what happened. And that was all of it." She sighed. "Although I would've been happy to have had it otherwise."

"Okay, I believe you," Jo said. "She didn't want to?"

"Could we please change the subject, Jo? She's your boss."

"Now, please . . ." Jo objected, indignant. "And what did *you* do with her when she was *your* boss? I'd say a little small talk ought to be allowed."

"Apparently, she hasn't been able to sleep well lately," Kim said. "I think that's why she's been so irritable. Now that she's finally gotten some sleep, you can see the difference."

"I still have my doubts about whether just *sleep* achieved that."

"For your sake I'm going to have surveillance cameras installed in my bedroom, so you'll finally believe me," Kim said. "But honestly you can feel free to think what you want. Just don't you dare breathe a word of it to her!"

"Don't worry. This afternoon, I thought I'd been transported to paradise. I don't want to go and blow that." Jo paused briefly. "Is she going to be *sleeping* at your house often from now on?" she asked smugly.

"Didn't I ask you to change the subject?" Kim frowned.

"Well, I just thought. Maybe then I can look forward to a few more pleasant afternoons like today. That'd be nice."

"I hardly think so," Kim said. "I think this was an exception. She was really totally exhausted. I was afraid she was going to collapse."

"Well, you should've seen her this afternoon. Absolutely bright-eyed and bushy-tailed, I'm telling you. As if she'd had her pick of mood enhancers from the pharmacy."

Too bad I couldn't see how well she was doing, Kim thought. "Oh, by the way, Jo," she teased. "Since you don't seem to value the privacy of others at all, I'm sure you won't mind her knowing that you and I –"

"You told her *that?*" Jo interrupted her loudly.

Kim smirked. "Actually, I didn't tell her anything. She just drew the correct conclusion when I told her that we knew each other."

"Oh, hell!" Jo groaned. "Did you have to?"

"It is what it is," Kim said. "Some things are simply unavoidable. But she assured me that it wouldn't affect your work together. Or maybe – as you've already noticed – the effect will only be positive."

"You never know with straight girls," Jo said skeptically. "They change their minds every five seconds."

"We'll have to live with that. Although I don't believe she'll do that. If she does, you can have my job."

"You're very confident of her. And you're sure nothing happened between you two at your place this morning . . .?"

"I am simply not going to answer that anymore."

"Well, fine," Jo said. "I'm supposed to say hi from Jenny and ask you if you'll come over for dinner tomorrow. She's cooking. With a little help from me. I found out that she hardly knows the difference between an apple and a tomato." She laughed.

"That's true!" Kim laughed, too. "This is the first time she's ever invited me over to eat." She cleared her throat. "Coincidentally I do have this cake . . ."

"From your boss's wife?" Jo asked right away. "Forget it. Not even Jenny is that bad of a cook."

"Probably," Kim said. "Then I'll see you tomorrow. I'm looking forward to it."

She hung up and glanced toward the bedroom. Some bed-making was in order. And airing.

Otherwise she wasn't likely to sleep well tonight.

Chaos reigned when Kim arrived at her office the next morning. Everyone was running around like chickens with their heads cut off.

"What's going on?" Kim asked one of the staff.

"Rolf." The woman sobbed. "He had a heart attack. They just

took him to the hospital. They don't know whether he's going to make it." She sobbed even louder.

Kim's throat cinched tight. She couldn't respond. Clearly shaken she walked into her office and sat down.

Rolf. She hadn't known him for long, but he was already almost like a father to her. Her own father was long dead, and Rolf and his wife Margit had immediately clasped her to their bosoms. They had no children of their own and treated Kim like a daughter. And now?

She pulled herself together. "Which hospital –" But she was in her office, talking to herself. She stood up and went out. "Does anyone know which hospital they took Rolf to?" she asked loudly.

The babble of voices quieted down. She repeated her question.

"Antonius Hospital," someone stated.

The phone on Kim's desk rang. No one felt like providing technical support or answering customer inquiries right now, but it had to be done. Kim went to her desk and picked up.

"Thank you," Sonja's smooth, warm voice said. "I slept wonderfully in your bed."

Kim had to reorient herself. It was all a bit much for this early in the morning.

"My pleasure. I'm sorry, but I can't talk right now, Sonja. Rolf had a heart attack. I have to go to the hospital."

"Rolf?" Sonja sounded horrified. "Oh, no!"

"Yes, unfortunately so," Kim confirmed. "I can't leave Margit waiting there all by herself. They . . . the paramedics didn't know whether he was going to make it."

"No," Sonja repeated, shaken. "Not Rolf."

"I can hardly believe it, either. I wasn't here when it happened. I just got in," Kim explained. "I'll let you know later what I find out. I have to leave." She hung up without saying goodbye.

Kim arrived at the hospital at the same time as Margit stepped out of a taxi. She was white as a sheet.

"Margit." Kim approached her and took her by the arm. "I'm so sorry."

"Forty-two years." Margit's pale lips trembled. "We'll be married forty-two years next month."

"And you're going to celebrate that anniversary together," Kim said confidently. "I know you will."

"Where . . .?" Margit looked around, bewildered. "Where is he?"

"Let's go and find out." Kim supported Margit by the arm, and together, they went inside the hospital.

The clerk at the reception informed them that the doctors in the ER had managed to stabilize Rolf. He was currently transferred to the intensive care unit.

Kim got Margit a coffee. The two of them headed to the IC floor and sat down in the waiting area. After a while a nurse walked past.

Kim jumped up. "What's his condition?"

The nurse stopped, clearly confused. "What?"

"Rolf Winkelmann. How is he?" Kim asked.

"I'm just coming on duty," the nurse said. "I'm afraid I can't give you any information. Are you relatives?"

"This is his wife." Kim indicated Margit.

The nurse nodded. "I'll find out." She kept walking.

"How long have we been here?" Margit's voice sounded as though she were suppressing a sob. "I've lost all sense of time."

"Half an hour. Not very long."

"It feels like an eternity," Margit said softly.

Kim wrapped an arm around Margit's shoulders. "He'll get well again. He's got to."

"Rolf was always so strong," Margit whispered. "He rarely ever gets sick. A cold from time to time, but nothing serious. I never thought he –"

"Just wait." Kim squeezed her shoulder comfortingly. "We don't know anything yet."

"Mrs. Winkelmann?" A nurse they hadn't seen before was coming toward them. "You can see your husband now. But only briefly. He's still sedated."

"He . . . he's alive?" Kim stammered.

"Yes." The nurse nodded. "Because he was brought here immediately, his chances are good. But only the doctor can tell you anything definitive."

Kim supported Margit, who could barely walk on her own, and

they went inside.

Rolf lay in a bed surrounded by hoses, wires, and machines that pumped and hissed and beeped. A monitor showed his heartbeats.

Kim exhaled with relief. *His heart is beating. That's the most important thing.* She pulled up a chair for Margit and helped her sit down.

Margit stared at Rolf's face, half hidden by the oxygen tubing. She sought his hand, took it in hers, and simply held it tightly.

Kim remained standing next to her, observing Rolf's shallow but even breathing under the blanket. *He's alive,* was all she could think. *He's alive.*

After a while, the nurse came in. "I need you to go now. There's nothing you can do for him at the moment, in any case. He won't wake up for the next few hours. It'd be best if you check back tomorrow."

"This afternoon," Kim said. "I'll call this afternoon."

The nurse nodded.

Kim laid a hand on Margit's shoulder. "Come, Margit, I'll take you home. You can't stay here."

Margit seemed not to hear her.

Kim leaned down to her. "Come," she repeated. "You need to rest."

"He looks so small. But he isn't really this small."

Kim patted her shoulder. "It just looks that way now. When he's well again, he'll be just as big as he was before." She grabbed the arm of Margit's chair. "Give me your hand. I'll put the chair back."

That seemed to pull Margit out of her lethargy somewhat. "I can do it . . ." She stood up and swayed. Quickly Kim braced her and let the chair be. That had been a diversionary tactic in any case, to bring Margit back to the real world.

She drove Margit home, made her some tea, put her in bed, and at her request, gave her a sleeping pill.

"Call me when you wake up." She set the telephone next to Margit on the nightstand.

Margit nodded sleepily. The sleeping pill seemed to already be taking effect.

After Margit had fallen asleep, Kim drove back to the office.

She called Sonja.

“I’m sorry I cut you off like that this morning,” she said. “I just got back from the hospital.”

“How is Rolf?” Sonja asked.

“He’s alive.” Kim ran a hand through her hair. “I drove Margit home and helped her to bed. She’s sleeping now. Rolf is sleeping, too. He’s in intensive care. They’ll be able to say more this afternoon. Maybe then I can talk to a doctor. There wasn’t one available when I was there.”

“Thank God!” Sonja exhaled with audible relief. “He’s alive.”

“Margit was horribly shocked. She says he’s never been seriously ill a day in his life. This is the first time. They’ve been married forty-two years.”

“Yes, I know. That’s a long time.” Sonja cleared her throat. “Should you and I go get something to eat? Then you can tell me more.”

Kim didn’t know what to say at first. She was surprised by Sonja’s suggestion. “Yes.” She looked at the clock. “It’s almost noon. I didn’t even realize that.”

“Understandable. But I’m a creature of habit. I get hungry promptly at twelve o’clock.” Sonja laughed lightly.

“I don’t get up as early as you do. But I’ll join you nonetheless.” Kim was still surprised at Sonja’s open approach. “I can’t be there for another half hour, though; I have to drive over from here first.”

“I’ll meet you in front of the cafeteria.” Sonja hung up.

Kim just sat there for a moment, feeling slightly overwhelmed. First the crisis with Rolf, and now Sonja in such a convivial mood – Kim was feeling thoroughly discombobulated.

But she was glad. She felt her desire to see Sonja grow. There was a tingling . . .

But we’ve gotten past that, haven’t we? an internal voice asked.

You know she’s not expecting the same things you are, don’t you? She associates nothing with this invitation but lunch – and perhaps a good conversation.

“I know.” Kim sighed. But still. She had missed Sonja, had gone without her beauty and presence for so long, that any encounter was a reason to celebrate.

Sonja was waiting for her outside the cafeteria entrance. She smiled as Kim approached.

"You look rested." Indeed, Sonja looked miles better than she had yesterday. "Amazing, what a little sleep can accomplish . . ."

"Oh, yes." Sonja smiled even more. Kim didn't know where she ought to look. That smile could drive her right over the edge. "I slept superbly in your apartment. It's so calm and peaceful there."

Kim laughed. "When the neighbors' children are in school! It can get pretty loud on the weekends."

"I probably wouldn't even have noticed. I slept like a log."

"I'm glad." Kim smiled. "That was the point, after all."

"Shall we go in?" Sonja went ahead toward the executive cafeteria, and Kim followed her. Kim didn't typically eat there, because she spent her lunch break with the rest of her team. The rank-and-file cafeteria had to suffice for them.

The executive lunchroom was a separate area that operated more like a restaurant, with table service by a waitress.

They sat down at a table, and the waitress came over with a large bottle of water.

"Thank you," Sonja said. Obviously, that was her usual lunchtime beverage, and the waitress knew that. "What would you like to drink?" Sonja asked. "Water as the only beverage isn't to every man's taste."

Kim chuckled. "Or every woman's either. At lunchtime, definitely something non-alcoholic. Otherwise we can forget about getting any work done in the afternoon." She addressed the waitress: "Orange juice. Freshly squeezed, if possible."

"Of course." The waitress disappeared.

"Perhaps now I can finish thanking you." Sonja smiled. "The way I wanted to this morning."

"Not necessary. It was nothing special."

"No, I think it was." Sonja gave her a curious look. "Yes, indeed," she added, reaffirming.

Kim laughed rather stiffly. "You're welcome back anytime."

Sonja looked at her anew, and there was something in her eyes that Kim couldn't decipher. "I hardly think so," she declined the invitation. "But yesterday . . . yesterday, I was very glad about it."

"That's what Jo told me." Kim laughed. "And I was very happy to hear that you were feeling much better in the afternoon than you were in the morning."

"Those jungle drums. Why do I even need to tell you anything? You already know it all." Sonja looked rather wary.

"Just that you were doing better in the afternoon," Kim qualified quickly. "Jo didn't tell my any more than that. She was very taken with you."

"I thought I wasn't her type?"

"Oh, why did I ever tell you that?" Kim groaned. "I shouldn't have. It doesn't mean a thing."

"No, it doesn't," Sonja agreed. "It was pleasant for me, too, yesterday afternoon, *not* to feel like Ms. Mayrhofer hates me for once."

"She doesn't hate you!" Kim looked appalled.

"No?" Sonja arched her brows. "I had that impression."

"No, no." Kim shook her head. "You're her boss, and she wants her work to meet with your approval, that's all. If you're not happy, she's not happy, either. That's completely normal."

"Presumably." Sonja stared out the window.

"Your orange juice." The waitress set a large glass in front of Kim.

"Thanks." Kim picked up the menu, a little leaflet printed by the in-house printer. "I'll have the spaghetti." The food in the executive lunchroom was no different than that available to the rest of the staff. It was just presented more appealingly and in more attractive surroundings.

"The usual salad for you, Mrs. Kantner?" the server asked.

"Yes." Sonja nodded.

"Ah, salad," Kim said. "I never even thought of that. It's not on the menu."

"There's always salad," Sonja said absently.

"You're much more health-conscious than I am." Kim laughed.

"If I ate what was on the menu, I'd probably have to buy some new clothes pretty soon."

"Oh, I'd say . . . a few more ounces . . . do you really think that would be so terrible?" This was not a good subject to be on. It made Kim start thinking about what she could do with those few ounces. She felt rather warm. "You're really quite . . . slender." She tried to keep her swallow unnoticeable.

"Thank you. But that's the hard work. And lately, I haven't had much opportunity to eat in peace."

"The reorganization project?"

"Yes." Sonja stretched the word a little and looked at Kim. "It's lots of work."

And your husband? Kim wanted to ask. *Does he keep you from eating, too, perhaps?* Obviously, Sonja's answer had been incomplete. But it would be better to avoid any insinuations, as much as possible.

The waitress returned with their lunch and set the plates down in front of them, as well as bottles of oil and vinegar for Sonja. Apparently, she didn't like premade dressings.

While Sonja poured her salad dressing, Kim observed her out of the corner of her eye. Why had Sonja invited her to lunch? Well, okay, less "invited" than taken along, but that wasn't important. She must've had a reason.

"And you think Rolf is going to get better soon?" Sonja asked suddenly.

Aha, she was changing the subject. "I don't know." Kim shrugged. "I hope so. For his sake and for Margit's. Of course, she's deeply shaken. When you've been married for that long . . ."

"Yes. It must be awful." Sonja picked up a fork and started to eat.

"I think a person gets very used to being with a partner over such a long time. It must be hard to imagine living without him."

"Probably." Sonja's attention stayed focused on her salad.

Probably? Sonja had been married for a few years by now. Really, she ought to have experienced the same thing herself. Even if she and her husband weren't getting along well now, at some point . . . at some point, they must've loved each other.

Kim tried to make herself drop the subject. In any case, it wasn't one she wanted to spend much time thinking about.

"Margit is devastated," Kim said, "and I'm sure Rolf would've been, too, if she had been the one to have the heart attack. Even if she's not a very good cook."

"That's not what matters," Sonja mused. She seemed to be pondering something.

"No, certainly not." Kim laughed once more. "In that case, Rolf would've gotten a divorce long ago!"

Sonja turned her head toward her. "A divorce isn't always that easy."

"But not Rolf and Margit! They're the couple of the century, if not the whole millennium. They still love each other, you can see it in everything they do, how they are with each other."

"Yes, they treat each other very lovingly." Sonja's voice sounded as if she were quoting a newspaper article. Stating a fact that had nothing to do with her whatsoever.

"People should always treat each other like that," Kim said. "Those two are excellent role models."

"What if he dies?" Sonja asked abruptly. "What will she do then?"

"That would be terrible!" At this thought Kim got a heavy feeling in her stomach. How must Margit feel?

"Yes, that would be terrible," Sonja repeated. "To live with one person for so long, who suddenly isn't there anymore – Margit's whole life is built around Rolf. And all at once to be alone. Old and alone. How can she adapt? How could she get used to that? She's too old to start fresh at anything. The best part of her life is behind her."

"Sonja!" Kim stared at her, aghast. "You're predicting Rolf's death?"

"Oh, no." Sonja appeared to wake from a dream. "No." She laid her fork aside. "Nothing is farther from my mind. I hope he gets well again. And that he lives a long, long time. Together with Margit."

"Yes." Kim took a breath. Sonja had described the scenario after Rolf's death so realistically; it felt like it had already happened.

"I'm sorry," Sonja said. "I guess I'm not quite up to snuff yet. A few hours of sleep weren't enough, after all."

"Couldn't you sleep last night? Sleep disturbances can be awful. I'm glad that I don't have that problem."

"Sleep disturbances . . . Yes, awful. It's hard to catch up."

"Have you seen a doctor about it?" Kim asked. "Isn't there anything that will help?"

"A doctor?" Sonja looked at her as though that were a completely absurd idea.

"Well, you know, when it persists like this … There must be a reason for it."

"A reason." Sonja looked out the window again. Then she turned her gaze back to Kim. "Yes, there must be a reason."

"I'm sorry, I didn't mean to grill you," Kim said. "Am I getting too personal? I mean, sleep disturbances … lots of people suffer from those. There are plenty of ways and means –"

"Of course," Sonja interrupted her. "There are ways and means of remedying sleep disturbances. You're quite right. You weren't getting too personal. I'm just … well, like I said, not quite up to snuff."

"I have some vitamins in my office. Do you want to try that?"

Sonja's lips curled into a semblance of a smile. "No, thanks." She waved to the waitress. "My coffee, please."

The waitress nodded and looked inquiringly at Kim.

"Yes, me too, please." When the waitress had gone, Kim went on. "I read in the company newsletter that the reorganization project is supposed to be finished soon. I'm sure you'll have some quiet again after that's over."

"If they don't find something else for me to do." Sonja looked at Kim with her head tilted. "And if a certain colleague hadn't made suggestions that just set the whole thing on its ear."

"I'm sorry. I didn't mean to do that. It was just a spontaneous idea. You don't have to incorporate it."

"Yes, I do. It's too good. I'm annoyed with myself for not coming up with it first."

"You were probably just too tired." Kim smiled. "I can't think in that state, either."

"Yes, I was probably just too tired," Sonja confirmed. But it sounded like she didn't really believe it.

"Sonja, I –" Kim gazed up at the ceiling, then started over. "Sonja, I … I'm so glad that we can talk to each other again."

The coffee arrived.

Sonja didn't answer, but waited until the waitress had left. She dropped two tablets of sweetener into her coffee and stirred them around.

"If you … if you don't want to talk about it, I understand," Kim said, abashed. "I accept it. It's just . . . I wanted to tell you that."

Sonja wrapped her hands around her coffee cup, peering into the cup as though she sought an answer there. Then she raised her head. "When I said yesterday that I'm familiar with the situation, I meant exactly that. It's not the first time that . . ." she hesitated, ". . . someone," she continued, "believed he had a claim on me because of . . ." she hesitated again, ". . . an indulgence I had granted him. But one thing has nothing to do with the other. I believe I've made that clear already."

Kim looked at her, and she wished so dearly to be able to touch her, if only to show Sonja that she didn't need to worry about Kim or be afraid of her. That she could trust her. "You have. I accept it. But unfortunately, it doesn't change anything about my feelings for you, and I also have to come to terms with that. But I won't burden you anymore, you can count on that. I'll never mention it again."

Sonja silently considered Kim's face. "Can you do that? Come to terms with it?" she asked after a while.

Kim almost had to laugh. "Oh, lesbians are used to having to come to terms with our feelings for straight women. That's a situation that *I'm* familiar with."

"Is that so." Sonja leaned back as though she were astonished. "Does it happen so often?"

"The ratio is nine to one. I think that says it all."

"I never thought about it that way. That means that almost every woman you fall in love with is . . . well, like me?"

Now Kim really had to laugh. "No. It's not quite that bad. Most of the women I get to know well are lesbians. And by the way –" she leaned in closer, "not one of them so far has been like you."

"Kim, please . . ." Sonja made a face. "What did you just promise me?"

"Something else," Kim said. "You're unique. I'm sure I can still say that."

"Ow." Again, Sonja grimaced. "Can't you . . . cut back a little on that, on that sort of comment? I really can't deal with that, and . . . well, we were going to –"

"All right. You needn't be afraid. That was the last time I'll say something like that. Now you know." Kim smiled crookedly.

Sonja frowned. “What I don’t know is whether I’m up to it. I thought I – the situation was simply untenable. I didn’t want that.”

“Neither did I,” Kim said gently. “Now it’s much better.” She laughed. “We should eat together more often!”

“We can,” Sonja said, completely unexpectedly. “When I’m in the building at lunchtime, I have no objection.”

Kim looked at her. “Are you sure?”

“Why not?” Sonja shrugged. “I hate talking about work during lunch. These are the only few minutes of the day I have for myself. That’s why I don’t like to eat with colleagues – they usually can’t talk about anything *but* work.” She smiled. “Except for Rolf. He was always different. A family man.”

Kim sighed. “I think the fact that he and Margit don’t have any children was a great sadness to them. They always wanted some.”

“Yes.” Sonja’s expression hardened. She glanced at the clock. “I have to get back. Do you want to meet at the same time tomorrow, outside the cafeteria?” She stood up to leave.

Even though Sonja had said she’d be happy to have lunch with Kim again, Kim was still very much taken by surprise. She just sat there. “Sure. If you want.”

“See you tomorrow, then.” Sonja turned around, and a moment later she was out of sight.

Kim shook her head. Sonja’s departure felt like a cold shower that tingled pleasantly at the same time. She made promises – perhaps these, too, were only promises Kim imagined – that were hedged with stinging prickles. The prickles, on the other hand, appeared so soft, so silky, that they made a person want to pet them.

If I do that, will I get stabbed? Kim wondered. *Or will she retract those stingers?*

In the ensuing days Kim and Sonja saw each other every day, usually for lunch. It became a regular habit.

Work was a taboo subject between them, as was everything that had happened in the hotel, but they found a number of other subjects they could talk about. Music, literature, movies, and even food. And of course, Rolf’s convalescence, which was proceeding slowly, but positively.

"I'm so glad that he can stand up again now," Kim said. "A couple of days ago, I couldn't imagine it."

"I saw him yesterday afternoon," Sonja replied. "He really looks good. He's already telling jokes again."

"Then we must've just missed each other when we were there," Kim marveled. "If you'd said something, we could've gone together."

"I was just in the neighborhood. It was a spur-of-the-moment decision."

Spur-of-the-moment? Sonja? Hadn't she denied that categorically? "Hmm," Kim said. "Margit is still very worried. Did you see her?"

"Yes. She's at the hospital practically all day."

"Rolf's heart attack was such a huge shock, and all this convalescence ... She won't get over it quickly, even though he's doing so much better."

"Well, he'll have to watch out." Sonja grinned. "Margit announced she's going to bake him a cake soon."

Kim had to laugh. "Good grief! That'd be grounds for a second heart attack."

"Hopefully not." But Sonja smiled, too. Neither of them meant it seriously.

"Well, maybe his heart attack did have its good side," Kim said. "Rolf has been spared Margit's cooking for several days."

"That's a harsh cure. Just to avoid eating her cooking."

"Her cooking is gruesome." Kim made a face. "I don't know what she puts in there."

"I do. Concrete and a ton of sugar."

Kim laughed again. "That describes it perfectly!"

Sonja poked at her salad. "I finished the new concept for the project."

Kim looked up. Talking about work? Wasn't that taboo?

"I was wondering –" She looked up, then back at her salad, took a little dressing, and stirred it into the lettuce. "I was wondering if I might be able to requisition you as a collaborator on the project. Not full time. Just as much as you can fit in alongside your other work. You have to fill in for Rolf now, after all."

Kim was speechless.

"It was your idea in the first place," Sonja said, almost apologetically. "I thought perhaps you ought to be involved in the implementation as well."

"I . . . I'd be thrilled," Kim finally managed to say, amazed. "I'm sure we could make it work. I could probably be available ten percent of the time, maybe. Or twenty. I've been acting in Rolf's stead all along, really, and the team is functioning well. They can get along without me for a day now and then."

"I thought so, too. Good. It's settled. I'll make the request."

"Then I'll finally get out into the fresh air once in awhile," Kim said with a chuckle.

"There is such a thing as too much fresh air, too." Sonja sighed. "Constantly out of the office and on the road, that's really not my thing. But it's necessary. Next week, all that starts up again for me, now that I have the concept ready."

"Then you can still rest up over the weekend." Kim smiled. "Gather your strength." It was Friday; the cafeteria had been half empty when they arrived, since many people chose to go home early on Fridays rather than eat lunch at work.

"Yes." Sonja answered very tersely. "Next week is going to be hard."

"If you like, I could start on Monday, even if the requisition hasn't gone through yet. I'm sure that would be fine."

"That would be great, if you have the time. I don't think it'll be a problem, either. The reorganization has top priority. I generally get everything I want."

"I had that impression myself . . ." Kim smiled crookedly again.

"Kim." Sonja gave her a stern look. "Must I remind you . . .?"

"No, you mustn't. I didn't mean it that way. I meant the project, of course."

"Yes." Sonja was still looking at her very gravely. "And that's how I understood it."

Kim would gladly have gazed into her eyes for longer, but Sonja averted her face and studied the salt shaker on a neighboring table.

Why does she do that? Kim thought. *First, she pushes me away as a colleague, and now she's pulling me back. Our lunches – fine, that's one thing. But working together again, all day long? Even if it's not every day?*

She truly couldn't make sense of Sonja's behavior. On the one hand, she seemed to want distance, but on the other hand, she seemed to be taking advantage of every opportunity to spend more time together.

That Friday was a work day for Kim like any other. She didn't go in early, as many of her colleagues did; rather, she stayed late. It was dark when she left the building and drove home.

She'd found a parking place which wasn't always so easy to do, since most of her neighbors came home earlier than she did. She was walking along the sidewalk to her apartment building when she stopped short.

She knew that car. She went up to it and looked in the side window.

"Sonja?"

Sonja rolled the window down. "You're getting home really late."

"Uh . . . yeah." Kim didn't know what to say. "I always do."

"I . . ." Sonja hesitated. "I need to talk to you."

"Here? In the car?" Kim was confused.

"No, I. . . let's go upstairs." Sonja closed the window and got out of the car.

Kim looked at her, astonished. Sonja walked ahead to the door and waited for her. Kim practically had to pinch herself in order to get out of her amazed mode and into a walking mode. She was still incredibly surprised.

They climbed the stairs in silence. Kim unlocked the door and let Sonja in.

"Would you like –" She started to offer Sonja a cup of coffee, even though it was probably a bit late for that.

Sonja wrapped her arms around Kim's neck and kissed her. "You have to be clear that this can never be more than an affair," she said as she let go of Kim. "I'm married, and I'm always going to be married. Always. Do you understand?"

Kim still felt Sonja's lips against her own. The kiss had been sweet, but not passionate. Kim hadn't been able to react at all.

"I . . . Sonja . . . what's this about?" she asked, perplexed.

"Don't you want this?" Sonja asked in return. "Haven't you wanted it all along?"

"Yes," Kim admitted. "Of course I do." She hesitated slightly. "Actually, no. To be honest, I don't. I never wanted an affair. That's . . . well, it doesn't usually bode well as a starting point."

"I can't offer you anything else." Sonja hesitated. "I just thought, because . . ." She looked at the floor. ". . . because you showed so much interest, that maybe you . . . But if I was mistaken, I apologize. Please forgive me."

Kim shook her head slightly. "You weren't mistaken in regards to my . . . interest. I told you that I love you. A person can hardly have more interest than that."

"I . . . Kim . . ." Sonja looked up. "I can't forbid you to . . . love me, but please don't say that to me. Never again. It . . . I can't give you what you expect in return."

"You mean you don't love me?" A cold hand clenched around Kim's heart. But what had she expected?

"I –" Sonja wrung her hands. "I can't answer that. However, I thought . . . well, I thought it could work without that."

"Without that?" Kim just wanted to shake her head. "Without love, you mean? At least as far as you are concerned?" She looked solemnly at Sonja. "That means you're offering me a purely sexual relationship, did I understand that correctly? Without love and without obligations."

"I . . . I'm married," Sonja repeated quietly. "I have an obligation that I can't ignore."

"A marriage doesn't have to be forever. Unless, of course, you believe the Catholic church, which I don't. Do you?"

"No." Sonja shook her head slowly. "I don't." She took a step backwards. "But my marriage isn't up for debate here – and definitely not for disposition. If you make it contingent upon that, then I'm sorry."

"Why are you here?" Kim asked. "What did you have in mind?"

"You know my powers of imagination aren't very keen," Sonja replied rather dryly. "I was working from my experience."

"Your experience with . . . men? Did it ever occur to you that a woman might react differently?"

"To be honest, no. Until now –" Sonja broke off.

"Until now, you've never had this problem with a woman, I know," Kim said, just as dryly as Sonja before. "And the men – did it always work out with them? After offering a no-strings-attached affair, each and every one just went for it?"

"That sounds like I jump from one affair to the next. It's not like that."

"In any case, they obviously didn't turn down your . . . indulgences, as you call it, or else you wouldn't have assumed that it would work the same with me."

"Yes, for God's sake!" Sonja raised her voice angrily. "They didn't turn me down. Why should they? Or do you find me so unattractive? I certainly had a different impression earlier."

"Which was absolutely correct," Kim said calmly. "I find you *very* attractive."

"No man demands love in order to have sex," Sonja said coolly. "They don't need it."

"But I need it," Kim said. "At least with you. There have been women where it was different, but you . . . you're very special to me. I wish you could feel the same way about me."

"It *is* something special. If for no other reason than you're a woman and because I've never –" Sonja collected herself. "But if it won't work, then it won't work. I always insisted you had to hold yourself back, and now you're doing exactly what I demanded of you. I can't blame you for that. It was my mistake."

"It wasn't a . . . mistake. A misunderstanding, perhaps, but not a mistake. I mean . . ." Kim ran a hand through her hair. "I mean, I would be very happy if we . . . if we were to get together. I –" She looked at Sonja. "I yearn for you. I dream about you. You're everything I wish for."

Sonja examined her face. "Why can't it work, then?" she asked softly. "Let's give it a try." Again she wrapped an arm around Kim's neck and pulled her close. "I yearn for you, too," she whispered.

Her lips rested gently against Kim's, and Kim was reminded of how she had kissed Sonja in the car that time, while Sonja slept. That hadn't been fair, either. She had taken advantage of the situation. How could she reproach her for this now?

And aside from that – her body showed her the way. It reacted to Sonja's touch, to Sonja's kiss. It wanted more.

She leaned forward and ran her tongue cautiously over Sonja's lips.

Sonja sighed. She opened her lips wider to grant Kim entry.

Kim explored Sonja's mouth and in the touching she experienced sweetness like a river that flowed warmly through her entire body. She wrapped her arms around Sonja, pulled her closer and felt how Sonja's softness sent her reeling. Every sensible thought in her brain vanished.

"Sonja . . ." Kim whispered again and again. "Sonja . . ."

Sonja pressed against her, closer and closer. Her hands ran up and down Kim's back, gliding under her shirt and caressing her bare skin.

Kim moaned. Her hands sought Sonja's bottom, then wandered lower and pushed up her skirt.

"No." Sonja stopped caressing Kim. "Please don't."

For a second, a memory flickered in Kim's mind and vanished again. "What's wrong?" she whispered, brushing Sonja's cheek with her lips. She could feel Sonja's skin glowing.

"I . . . Wait. Not like that," Sonja answered haltingly. "I'd like to . . . shower first."

Kim took a deep breath and let her go. "Of course. However you like." She smiled. "That's probably a good idea. It's been a long day. May I shower with you?"

Sonja looked at her. The corners of her mouth twitched. "Why not?"

Kim followed her to the bathroom. On the way Sonja let her suit jacket fall to the floor and started opening the buttons of her blouse. When they had arrived at the bath, she pulled down the zipper of her skirt and slipped out. Now she stood in front of Kim in just her panties and a bra.

Kim couldn't hold back; she embraced Sonja from behind and kissed the nape of her neck. "You're wonderful," she whispered in her ear. "You're simply wonderful."

Sonja pressed briefly up to her. "Take your clothes off. Or did you want to get in the shower dressed?"

Kim laughed. "No." She let Sonja go and undressed quickly, while Sonja, naked by now, stepped into the shower.

Sonja turned on the water. It ran over her body as if she were the Venus de Milo arising from the flood.

Kim gazed at her like a never-before-seen uncharted wonder of the world. She was so beautiful, so unbelievably beautiful. Her chestnut brown hair fell across her bare shoulders as if it meant to weave a cape for her.

"Come on." Sonja smiled gently. "I didn't think I'd have to invite you twice."

Kim felt awkward. She pulled herself together. "Me neither." She joined Sonja in the shower.

The water pattered on her back as Sonja slid back slightly. It was warm, but not warm enough to compete with the heat welling up in Kim's body.

Sonja reached a hand out to her. "Will you lather me up?"

Kim stared at her hand with the soap bar, then looked up and felt overwhelmed by Sonja's naked beauty. "I don't know if I can," she said hoarsely.

"Try. Or should I start with you –?"

Kim reached for the soap. "No, let me." If Sonja had touched her right then, she didn't know what would've happened.

Sonja turned around, and Kim ran the soap over Sonja's shoulders, her back, her arms; at her waist, she slid to the front, over Sonja's belly and up to her breasts. Then she dropped the soap. She glided with just her hands over Sonja's body, spreading the lather.

Sonja began to writhe under her touch and sighed softly. She leaned back, to draw closer to Kim, spreading the soap through her movements across Kim's breasts and belly.

Kim felt the arousal growing more and more in the painfully taut tips of her breasts. "Sonja," she whispered.

Her hands encircled the soft curves of Sonja's breasts, lifting them gently, appreciating the weight, then letting them slowly sink down again, wandering higher and feeling the hard little gems at their centers pressing back against the palms of her hands.

Sonja moaned and pressed herself more into Kim. Her bottom pushed against Kim's thighs, leaving no more space between them.

"Kim . . ." Her whisper was no more than a breath in the steam.

Kim slid up and down over Sonja's nipples; the soap made it possible to stimulate those small peaks uninterrupted. Just the surface, nothing more.

"Oh, God!" Sonja moaned loudly.

She was pressing so hard into Kim that Kim stumbled backward into the wall. She held Sonja tight and kept rubbing just her nipples, while Sonja's bottom gyrated in her lap.

"Kim . . . Kim . . ." Sonja's voice trembled. "Please . . . please . . ."

"Please what?" Kim whispered in her ear. She nibbled at her earlobe and let it go again.

"Please . . . please . . ." Sonja repeated, helpless.

"All right, my darling." Kim let one hand rest on Sonja's breast, still running the thumb over the nipple, and let the other hand wander lower on Sonja's body. She enjoyed every inch of the way, because she could feel Sonja's skin pulsing as if a tiny power plant were humming away inside her.

Sonja separated her thighs as Kim reached the triangle at their tops, opening the way for her.

Kim felt Sonja's folds beneath her hand and placed her fingers there, softly touching the topmost edge of her labia.

Sonja moaned in agony, resting her head back against Kim's shoulder. "You're driving me . . . crazy," she breathed laboriously. Her thighs were trembling.

"That's what I want," Kim whispered back. "You're so beautiful when you're crazy." She kissed Sonja on the nape of her neck, bit her tenderly there, and at the same time, slipped one finger into the opening between her legs.

Sonja cried out softly.

Kim could feel how wet Sonja was. That wasn't from the shower. Between her thighs, she was wide open, and her labia seemed to keep swelling more beneath Kim's fingers. Kim's belly tugged yearningly at her; she wanted to make love to Sonja until she finally understood what love was. But that was hopeless.

For a moment, reality took over. What did she think she was doing? What had she gotten herself into? Was this at all what she wanted?

Then Sonja sighed again and hot lightning shot through Kim's legs. She could no longer think, only feel. "You are so sweet."

Her fingers thrust deeper and deeper into Sonja. Sonja only moaned, thrusting her hips downward to take more of Kim into her. "Come . . ." she whispered. "Come . . ."

Kim let go of Sonja's breast and encircled her waist, since she was afraid Sonja would soon be unable to hold herself up as her movements grew ever wilder. With her thumb she sought Sonja's pearl. Sonja moaned. "Yes!" she cried. She froze in place for just a moment, and then began to writhe in Kim's arms ever more passionately.

Kim concentrated on the little knob, which grew larger and harder.

"Oh . . . yeah . . . come . . . yeah . . ." Sonja moaned, writhing out of control. "Good . . . good . . . come on . . . good . . ." Her voice was raw, aroused to the extreme.

Kim held her tight; Sonja was so slick with lather that she kept sliding out of Kim's embrace, but she managed to hold her.

"Oh . . . now . . ." Sonja moaned. "Now!"

Kim's thumb danced wildly across Sonja's pearl; her fingers thrust into her more and more, deeper and deeper.

"Yeahhh!" Sonja went stiff, gasped, panted for air. Her breath caught. A moment later, it resumed. Her breathing was even and labored; thoroughly exhausted.

Kim felt her go very limp in her arms. Sonja slipped out of Kim's arm, down to the shower floor.

Kim sat down next to her.

Sonja was breathing heavily. "Oh my God!"

"Nice?" Kim smiled.

Sonja opened her eyes, which she'd had closed for some time now. "Nice?" She smiled wanly. "You have to ask?"

"Asking never hurts." Kim grinned.

"I would have to be a very good actress to fake that," Sonja said. "And I'm not."

"Have you . . ." Kim cleared her throat. "Have you done that before: faked it?"

"Yeah, sure." Sonja seemed utterly unfazed. "Every woman has.

Sometimes it's all you can do." She looked at Kim. "Granted, it doesn't take that much effort." She curled her lips into a disparaging smile. "All men need is a little moan. Then they think it's over."

"Phew!" Kim exhaled. "I didn't really want to know that much." She stood up and offered Sonja her hand.

"Why did you ask, then?" Sonja allowed Kim to pull her up.

"You're right." Kim sighed. "It just seems so odd to me –"

"You mean, you've never . . .?"

"No." Kim shook her head. "It's really never been necessary." She laughed. "I can hardly imagine it."

"You mean, between women, it . . . always works?"

"I don't know why it shouldn't," Kim said. "If you're responsive to your partner's wishes . . ." She thought of Jo and her experience in the Darkroom. Perhaps she ought to retract her statement? No, that had been something different. And she hadn't faked anything. She'd simply left.

"If you're responsive to your partner's wishes . . ." Sonja repeated thoughtfully. She looked at Kim. "Then what are your wishes right now?" She smiled a bit cheekily.

"Um . . . I . . . Just rest," Kim replied, taken by surprise. "There's no rush."

"I know what you want." Sonja pressed Kim against the wall and knelt before her.

"Sonja . . . you don't have to. . ." Kim protested weakly.

But Sonja was already pushing her thighs apart and diving into Kim's paradise with her tongue.

Kim moaned. She grabbed onto the shower handle to hold herself up. Her knees were already weakening. In her loins a wildfire was raging, that had only smoldered as long as it was Sonja's turn, and now broke loose unchecked at just that first touch.

"You . . ." she whispered weakly.

Sonja firmly encircled her thighs and thrust inside Kim with her tongue so that Kim thought a snake was entering her. Sonja was very adept at these things, she remembered that from the first time.

"Oh, Sonja . . ."

Sonja's tongue became harder, then softer again, sliding out and, like a gentle palm frond, brushing every spot between Kim's legs, which in turn swelled to meet her and awaited her touch.

Kim felt her thighs start to tremble, her whole belly, her whole body. Weakness overtook her arms; she had to tense them to hold on again. Her nipples were practically leaping out of her skin, aching with desire.

At that moment Sonja thrust inside her with several fingers.

Kim was nearly lifted right off the ground. "Oh, yes!" she moaned. The tugging of her loins strengthened into a spasm. "Yes. . . yes. . . yes. . ." She tried to meet Sonja as much as she could. Since she had to stand, that wasn't so easy.

The wildfire spread, consuming everything, driving the heat to unspeakable heights. Suddenly, Kim felt Sonja squeeze her pearl with her lips as her tongue flicked across it faster and faster.

Like lightning, the feeling shot through her body; she jerked and writhed as if she could not escape. She felt caught in an orgasm that didn't want to end. Her hands clenched around the shower handle, holding her upright; without that, she certainly couldn't have supported herself.

She felt caught up in eternity. The orgasm simply did not stop, its waves flooding her entire body, taking possession of her, not letting her go.

Finally . . . sometime . . . days later? . . . she was able to escape, let out a cry of satisfaction, and collapse.

Sonja sat down next to her and waited for her to open her eyes.

"Oh, baby . . ." Kim still breathed very heavily. "That was intense."

"Hmm." Sonja's hand rested on Kim's breast, caressing it.

Kim could feel that her nipples were just as hard as they'd been earlier, and Sonja's finger, gliding softly over them, chased hot thunderbolts through her body.

"Give me . . . a minute," Kim stammered, still recovering from her first orgasm.

"I don't have much time." Sonja's mouth sank to Kim's breast, and Kim moaned.

Sonja pampered her breasts and, at the same time, thrust in between her legs, where it was still glowing hot.

"Just wait," Kim moaned. She reached for Sonja and entered her.

Sonja's bottom twitched, writhed on Kim's fingers, rode them, while Sonja kissed Kim's breasts and her fingers filled Kim completely.

They drove each other higher and higher toward a climax and came simultaneously.

Kim gasped; Sonja sank down on top of her and lay on her breast, panting likewise for breath.

"I think maybe we should get out of the shower eventually," Kim said after a while. She laughed lightly. "Or at least turn off the water!"

"Why?" Sonja said. "I still want a real shower."

"Do you?" Kim grinned at her. "I thought you must be wet enough."

Sonja pursed her lips. "That's exactly why."

"Fine, then." Kim stood up. "I'm going to the bedroom. You can follow when you're done."

She stepped out of the shower, casting one appreciative glance back at Sonja's naked, glistening body, and shut the door. Through the frosted glass, she saw Sonja's blurred form shimmer like a work of art. She was moving, but her precise motions were difficult to discern.

Sometimes she had the same feeling about Sonja as a person. Kim shook her head. They still didn't really know one another – that was why. She knew nothing of Sonja's innermost feelings, and Sonja didn't know everything about her. That would change once they'd been together longer.

She dried herself off, went over to the bedroom, and lay down on the bed. It was somewhat unusual for her to lie in her own bed and wait for the woman with whom she was going to spend the night. But it increased the suspense. Despite everything that had already happened today, she still lusted for Sonja, and she recalled that the night in the hotel had left no wish unfulfilled. She was looking forward to repeating that.

She heard the shower door being pushed open. Excitement danced across her skin, her insides. Soon, she would come.

It took a while, then she heard the hairdryer, then she heard footsteps in the hallway that kept pausing. What was Sonja doing out there?

All of a sudden, she stood in the doorway. She was dressed. Only the buttons on her suit jacket remained open; otherwise, she looked neat as a pin, as if on her way to the office.

"I'm leaving," she announced.

"You're . . . leaving?" Kim stared at her, startled.

"I never said I was going to spend the night here."

Kim was speechless.

"I have to be at the office early in the morning," Sonja went on. "So it's better if I get some sleep tonight. You know how insufferable I am otherwise."

"Yes . . . I know," Kim stuttered.

"Shall we see each other tomorrow?" Sonja looked at her watch. "Same time?"

"I . . . Sonja . . ." Kim tried to collect herself. "Why aren't you staying? You could sleep here, too."

"I hardly think so." Sonja pursed her lips mockingly. "It's better this way. You can sleep in; you don't have to work tomorrow, after all. But I still have to get some things ready for Monday. I might even need to go into the office for a while on Sunday."

"You're a workaholic."

"Sometimes," Sonja said. "But that doesn't mean we can't see each other. At some point, I always stop working, and then I'll have time for you." She smiled enchantingly.

Kim couldn't resist that smile, which always robbed her of all sense and reason. Sonja's words seemed absurd to her, but she couldn't think of any response.

"Then I'll see you tomorrow." Sonja hesitated. "It was really lovely," she added and turned around. A moment later the apartment door shut behind her.

Kim lay motionless in the bed and stared at the empty doorframe in which Sonja had stood a moment before.

So *this* was what she understood by *an affair*.

Kim had thought she'd had her share of affairs before, but apparently she was mistaken. This here was a classic affair – they met for sex, and then left – or at least one of them left.

It took her a while to recover from the surprise. She shook her head. No. No, this couldn't go this way. Certainly not on a regular basis. When Sonja returned, she'd have to talk to her about it. Before they . . . before they did anything else.

She rolled over and pulled the blanket up over herself. It didn't even have Sonja's scent. It just smelled like soap. No trace of Sonja's enchanting scent, which had all flowed down the shower drain.

Kim sighed. A woman like Sonja was quite a challenge, and Kim didn't know whether or not she felt up to it. Sonja's reactions left her baffled. And full of desire. She yearned for her whenever she thought of her. Now even more, after fresh experiences had churned everything up again.

She thought about Sonja standing naked in the shower, water flowing over her, beading up like raindrops, with a smile on her face that was a promise in itself. Sonja was an enchanting woman, like her scent, enchanting and sweet, seductive, attractive.

Kim took a deep breath. Tomorrow . . . tomorrow they'd have to talk.

Suddenly, she felt dreadfully tired and fell asleep.

"If you didn't want to play mini golf with us, you should've just said so."

A reproachful voice tore Kim away from her thoughts.

"Sorry." She woke up. "Is it my turn?"

"It has been for hours." Jennifer frowned disapprovingly. "Why do we have to wait for you on every single hole?"

"I . . . I'm not quite on top of things today, pardon me," Kim apologized.

"I can tell you're not quite on top of things," Jennifer said. "Or to put it better: not at all on top of anything. What's going on?"

"Nothing. I just didn't sleep well." Kim put her ball down and sighted on the hole it was supposed to go into.

"Going to bed earlier helps sometimes." Jo smirked. "Of course, only if you go alone."

"I did go to bed early, and I was alone," Kim replied inattentively. Just as inattentively she hit the ball, and it rolled wide of the hole. She walked over to give it a second stroke. "I woke up in the middle of the night because I went to bed too early, and then I couldn't get back to sleep again." She placed the putter next to the ball and knit her brows, trying to estimate the distance. "I just feel kind of mushy." She gave the ball a tap and it rolled on, but lost its momentum. It stopped quite a ways from the target.

"Shall I show you how this works?" Jennifer stood behind the ball, cast a quick glance at the hole, which lay at the top of a small rise, took a swing, and *presto!* The ball was in the cup. "Three!" she called to Jo, who held the scorecard and a pencil in her hand.

"You can't do that," Kim said. "That was mine."

"Doesn't matter. Who cares, anyway?" Jennifer looked at Kim. "Are you sure you were alone last night?"

"Yes, I was." Kim lifted her chin stubbornly. "Completely alone."

"Hmm." Jennifer strolled over toward the next tee. "How's Mrs. Kantner doing?" she asked with pointed innocence.

"Ask Jo," Kim replied. "She sees her more often than I do."

"Are you sure?" Jennifer looked back at her, her head tilted askance.

"I've had lunch with her a few times," Kim admitted grudgingly. "In the cafeteria."

"I heard about that," Jennifer said. "Not from you, though."

"Jo's a more reliable messenger anyway," Kim scolded. "What do you need me for?"

"To find out a little more than what Jo knows." Jennifer putted her ball in and then took the scorecard from Jo.

"Mrs. Kantner has been in an exceptionally good mood lately." Jo fixed her gaze on the goal, which lay around a corner. "Remarkably."

"I suggested she see a doctor . . . for her sleep disturbances," Kim said. "Maybe she did."

"I'd know about that. I would've made the appointment for her," Jo said. "But I didn't."

"She's fully capable of operating a telephone," Kim said rather mockingly. "Even when she has a secretary."

"You don't say," Jo murmured as her ball bounced around the corner and rolled toward the hole.

"Hole-in-one!" Jennifer cheered. "You got a hole-in-one, sweetie, super!"

"Against the two of you I don't have a chance anyway," Kim said. "Why do I even play with you?"

"Because you like to lose so much." Jennifer winked. "Or maybe it's because you used to play better?"

"I haven't played in a long time," Kim defended herself. "I have to get the hang of it again first."

"You have three holes left. We're already on number fifteen," Jo said. "Ever since she slept in your apartment," she changed the subject abruptly, "allegedly alone. Ever since then, she's been like this."

"She *was* alone!" Kim flared. "Just ask my team. I was in the office all day."

"I already checked that. It's true."

"You checked?" Kim gaped at her.

"Well, you know, that sweet young thing who works for you." Jo grinned. "She's really cute."

"Did you tell me about this?" Jennifer asked.

"I was going to, love," Jo said. "This just happened yesterday."

Jennifer gave her a skeptical look.

"Ah, my little bear!" Jo hugged her, laughing. "There's really no reason to be jealous, you can be sure of that. Do you know what she told me about the whole time? Her boyfriend. How great he is, how sweet he is, everything he does ..." She exhaled. "I'm telling you, that was plenty boring. I could hardly get my questions about Kim in edgewise."

"You quizzed her? About me?" Kim was still in shock.

"Believe me, she had no idea I was doing it," Jo said. "Her be-all and end-all is her stallion. That's the only thing she's interested in."

"Babsie," Kim said.

"Yes, exactly." Jo nodded. "And she might as well be called Barbie. That's what she looks like, anyhow."

"And you think that's cute?" Jennifer asked, indignant.

"But darling . . ." Jo took Jennifer into her arms and kissed her right in the middle of the golf course. "No other woman can ever be as cute as you, you know that." She looked deep into Jennifer's eyes.

Kim had to chuckle. "I'm discovering a whole new side to you, Jennifer," she teased. "A feminine one."

"Oh, go on." Jennifer looked at the ground. "I'm the same as I've always been." She pointed to the scorecard. "It's your turn."

Kim stood at the tee and tried to concentrate on her stroke, but she couldn't. Sonja's face – and not just her face – kept forcing itself into her field of view. She glanced at her watch surreptitiously. Two more hours, if Sonja came at the same time as yesterday. But then, yesterday she'd been waiting for Kim, so she'd probably be there earlier today.

"Are you daydreaming?" Jo nudged her. "Again?"

Kim straightened up and took her swing. The ball flew way out of bounds and into the lawn.

"You love the extremes." Jo laughed. "It's all or nothing with you!"

Kim shrugged. "Today just isn't my day."

"Looks that way." Jennifer put the next ball down and conveyed it into the hole with one stroke.

This time Jo cheered. "That's your fourth hole-in-one today. I think I'm going to have to watch out for you more next time."

"Or else practice more." Jennifer grinned.

"I like to practice with you." Jo grinned back, pinching Jennifer's backside. "Today, right now."

"But darling, what will people think?" Jennifer countered in pretend prudishness.

"That we have the best sex in the city." Jo kissed Jennifer once more. "Every day."

"We do have that." Jennifer grinned.

"What was that again?" Kim asked, smirking. "Just friends? No sex?"

"Yeah." Jo shrugged. "What can I say? That was my firm intent . . . until I got to know Jenny better."

"That's how it goes sometimes. I never wanted a committed relationship. It was way too tiring for me. But with Jo, it's – well – it's still tiring, but in a different way." Jennifer was grinning from ear to ear.

She hit the next ball down a complicated green that couldn't be completed in one stroke. Even Jo needed one more stroke, and Kim gave up after seven.

Kim looked at her watch again as Jennifer disposed of the next hole. She was getting more and more nervous. This was all taking longer than she'd thought it would.

Jennifer putted, then Jo, then it was Kim's turn. She missed the hole on her first stroke and also on her second. By the third, she was already so nervous she could barely see the goal anymore. She swung randomly – and got it right in the hole.

"That wasn't too bad," Jennifer said. "You're finally getting there."

On the last hole she could no longer concentrate at all. She swung her club right over the ball, not hitting it.

"Now . . ." Jo said. "You're not that much of a beginner. What are you doing?"

"I'm losing," Kim said. "I have been since the first hole. You're both miles ahead of me. So what's the point? Let's call it quits."

"Okay, fine." Jo wrote it down. "Seven."

"It wouldn't have been any less than that anyhow." Kim smiled uncertainly.

"How about we go out for a drink?" Jennifer asked. "Sort of get tuned up for Saturday night?"

"I have to . . ." Kim yawned behind her hand. ". . . get home. Catch up on the sleep I lost last night."

"Already?" Jo looked amazed.

Kim didn't want to let her nervousness show. Good grief, it was getting later and later! What if Sonja was already there? What if she waited just a little while but then left, because she thought Kim –

"I have to," she repeated. "Enjoy your Saturday night."

She waved at the two of them, who gaped after her, astonished.

Sonja wasn't there when she got home, and she breathed a slight sigh of relief that she'd arrived first. Why was this so important to her? Yesterday, Sonja had waited, after all.

What was she even waiting for? To be able to tell Sonja that this wouldn't work?

She *had* to tell her that. Sonja had told her quite precisely what *she* wanted, and it wasn't remotely what Kim wanted.

The night before, she had woken up in the middle of the night. Tossing and turning, she had fantasized about Sonja; Sonja coming home to her husband; Sonja greeting him; how he'd hug her, undress her . . .

They were estranged. They no longer slept together.

How do you know that? Straight women always say that men want to sleep with them most when they've just had a fight. Maybe they do that – every time. And they fight constantly . . .

Damn! Kim pressed her hands over her ears, as if that would block out the thoughts in her head.

At that moment, the doorbell rang.

Kim startled, closed her eyes briefly, then went to the door. She pressed the button to open the door to the building, left the apartment door standing open, and walked over to the living room.

Not in the hall, and definitely not in the bedroom. It's more neutral in the living room.

"Kim?" Sonja had quickly come up the stairway. She was probably peering through the crack that the apartment door left standing open, and wondering at it.

"Here," Kim called loudly. "In the living room."

A second later Sonja stepped through the door. "Here you are," she said with a smile.

"Yes." Kim looked at her, and her heart wanted to go to her. She held on tight to the sides of her armchair.

"Did I disturb you? Were you reading?"

The book Kim had been reading some time ago still lay open next to her.

"No." Kim shook her head. "You didn't disturb me. I was waiting for you."

"I couldn't come earlier," Sonja said apologetically. "The project just has too many rough edges, and I keep tripping over all of them."

"You're not late. I just got here myself. I was playing miniature golf with Jennifer and Jo."

"Miniature golf." Sonja chuckled. "I haven't done that in a long time." She approached Kim and stood in front of her. "Maybe I ought to."

"Maybe." Kim laid her head back and looked at Sonja. Now, with her standing so close, she could smell her, and it was almost impossible not to desire her. Not almost – it *was* impossible.

Sonja suddenly sat down on Kim's lap.

Kim gasped for air. Sonja's nearness took her breath away.

"What are you waiting for?" Sonja asked quietly, stroking one finger across Kim's lips. "I'm here." She bent down and kissed Kim with gentle grace, not passionately, but with the promise of seduction.

Kim closed her eyes; she felt very warm, and Sonja's scent made her dizzy. "Sonja," she whispered. "I have to . . ."

"Shh." Sonja placed a finger on her lips, not to caress them this time, but to shut them. "You don't have to say anything. Talk is superfluous." She kissed Kim again. This time her tongue entered Kim's mouth and caressed her lips from the inside.

Kim felt the tickling spread down to her nipples. She couldn't help herself. It was simply too good . . . and Sonja was too near . . . and everything else was unimportant.

"Come." Sonja jumped up. "Today, I'd like something more comfortable than the shower!" She laughed and pulled off her jacket. "How about a bed?" She leaned down to Kim. "*Your* bed . . ." she breathed seductively. Her eyes flashed.

She planted one more quick kiss on Kim's lips, then straightened up again and left the room.

It was as though Kim were in a trance. She stood up and followed Sonja. As she stepped into the bedroom, she saw Sonja unbuttoning the cuffs of her blouse – she'd already unfastened the other buttons – and slipping the blouse off.

Her lace-trimmed bra was a different one than yesterday's. Everything she wore was different from yesterday. She never wore the same things to the office two days in a row, not the same suit, not the same jacket. She was very particular about such things.

She gazed at Kim and her eyes flickered. "Undress me," she whispered. "I want you to undress me."

Kim, as if in a trance, approached her. She stopped and considered Sonja's face, her eyes. She felt magically drawn to her. She unhooked Sonja's bra, slid her hands underneath, and pulled it off.

Sonja's breasts bobbed slightly when they were no longer contained. Kim ran her hands over them, caressing them. Sonja leaned her head back and sighed.

Kim sought the nipples. They were already hard. She leaned down and took one in her mouth, caressing it with her tongue.

"Mmm . . ." Sonja's sighs grew louder.

Kim switched to the other nipple, caressing it, and at the same time let her hands slide down to the waistband of Sonja's skirt. She opened the zipper and slid her hands under the fabric, then slipped the skirt over Sonja's hips.

It fell to the floor. Kim caressed Sonja's hips, then glided farther around to her bottom.

"Wait!" Sonja breathed heavily. She reached for Kim's chest and unbuttoned her shirt. "I want to see you." She pushed the shirt quickly off of Kim's shoulders and pulled her T-shirt up over her head. "Oh, God," she whispered. "Oh my God . . ." She took Kim's breasts in her hands and looked at them as though she'd never seen such wonders before.

Kim caressed her bottom, and Sonja closed her eyes, caressing Kim's breasts just as Kim caressed her bottom. Her hips slowly began to move. She inhaled deeply.

Kim slid her hands inside the lacy underpants that matched Sonja's bra, and slowly pushed that tiny bit of fabric down over her hips.

Sonja opened her eyes and groped for Kim's waistband, unbuttoning her pants and pulling down the zipper. Her hand slipped inside and underneath Kim's panties.

Kim felt Sonja touch her and bit her lip. She pushed Sonja's panties farther down and slid one hand between her legs.

Sonja was already wet. She must've been wet already, before she got there; everything about her was engorged and open.

"What were you doing at the office today?" Kim laughed softly.

"Thinking about you," Sonja whispered hoarsely. "The whole time."

Kim began to caress Sonja, running her finger back and forth over Sonja's pearl, and at the same time, Sonja slid over hers. Their breathing seemed to take on the same rhythm as the pace of their fingers. Kim felt the first signs approaching. "Sonja ..." she moaned.

They went faster, each helping the other.

"Come ... yes ..." Sonja moaned as well.

Both climaxed together. Thoroughly out of breath, they fell onto the bed and laid for a while side by side.

Sonja stirred first. "That was silly. We could've just been lying down from the start."

Kim laughed. "Yes, but we didn't do that." She freed herself from her pants. "But now we're lying down." She pushed herself on top of Sonja. Sonja's eyes were dark and wide, their golden shimmer almost gone. She sought Sonja's lips with her own and kissed her tenderly. "Hi," she said with a smile. "It's nice that you're here."

Sonja smiled back. "I'm glad, too. I've been looking forward to it all day."

"I noticed!" Kim laughed once more.

"Was I that bad?" Sonja asked, suddenly unsettled. "I mean, don't you like it when –?"

"Oh, sure, I like it." Kim kissed her gently on the mouth. "I like it very much when a woman is excited. So much that she can hardly wait. That's nice. And afterwards, there's always plenty of time left, too."

Sonja considered Kim's face, hovering above her, smiling. "You don't think it's ... well ... depraved?"

"Depraved?" Kim shook her head, still smiling. "Where would you ever get that idea? What could possibly be depraved about your arousal?"

"I ... well ... I just wanted to know."

"Do you feel depraved?" Kim asked, chuckling. "Is that what you'd like me to think? In that case, I find you very depraved, quite dreadfully depraved, Madam Department Manager." She poked Sonja on the nose.

"Oh, leave the title in the office." Sonja made a disconcerted grimace. "That really doesn't belong here."

"I'm just practicing. If we're going to start working together on Monday, I have to make sure to address you professionally and respectfully."

"Yes, but you don't have to call me Madam Department Manager," Sonja said. "First names are fine. I do that with some of the other managers, too, after all."

"Including the ones you've slept with?" Kim teased.

"Oh, please . . ." Sonja gave her a chastising look. "I call Rolf by his first name!"

"Yes, that's true. Rolf's certainly in the clear."

"But I might not be?" Sonja asked, indignant.

Kim grabbed Sonja's wrists and pushed them up high. She held them there, above her head, and looked into her eyes. "You are under suspicion of being the most seductive woman in the world," she said softly. "No one can resist you when you set out to get them." She leaned down and kissed Sonja full on the mouth.

Sonja tried to evade Kim, who kept holding her firmly. "I never set out to get anybody. Never."

Kim thought about the looks she'd given Klaus, as far back as their first encounter. "Hmm."

"If that's what you think, then did I set out to seduce you, too?" Sonja asked. "Even though I didn't know it was a possibility?"

"Well, maybe not," Kim admitted. "Or was that intentional, when you walked past me stark naked?" She brushed a kiss across Sonja's nose.

"Of course not. Among women . . . I mean, women like . . . me . . ." Sonja fell silent.

"Straight women." Kim let herself slide off to Sonja's side. "Straight women think nothing of it when a woman dances around naked right underneath their nose. It doesn't turn them on. That's perfectly obvious." She was sobered.

"I . . . back then . . ." Sonja propped herself up on her elbows and looked down at her. "Back then, I truly didn't think anything of it. It never crossed my mind. Now . . . things are different."

"Really?" Kim looked up at her, and that gorgeous face was simply everything that she wanted. She couldn't imagine anything nicer.

"Things . . . things have changed a lot since then. A whole lot."

"What are you talking about, for instance?" Kim asked. "Have you stopped sleeping with your husband?"

Sonja stared at her. "What does that have to do with it?" she asked, irritated.

"Well, if you're no longer attracted to men . . . that would tend to have consequences for him, don't you think? Is that why you fight so much?"

Sonja lay back and scooted a little distance away from Kim. "My marriage is not up for discussion between us," she remarked coolly. "I've told you that before."

"But maybe it should be." Kim sat up in the bed. "What is this that we're doing here, Sonja? What do you call an affair? Does it mean I can't ask you any questions? That your life has nothing to do with mine, except when we're actually together for a couple of hours in bed?"

Sonja's jaws clenched. "I . . . It would be good if we could limit it to that."

"Would it?" Kim spun herself around with a furious jolt that shook the whole bed. "It would be good?" She stared at the ceiling. "Have I ever told you that I don't care for restrictions?"

They fell silent for a time.

"It . . . it isn't easy for me, Kim," Sonja said, suddenly quiet. "Don't demand too much of me . . . please."

Kim turned her head toward Sonja. "I'm not asking you for anything more than you're asking me for. And that's a lot."

"I know." Sonja took a deep breath. "I know that." She turned toward Kim. "Kim . . . I . . . give me a little time, please." Her eyes surveyed Kim's face. "It's not always so obvious to me what I'm asking of you. You're . . . I'm not familiar with this. It's different."

Kim looked at her seriously. "Will you sleep here tonight?"

Sonja closed her eyes, as if tormented. "No," she said when she opened them again. "I'm not going to sleep here, ever."

Ever, Kim repeated in her mind. She clenched her teeth. "Because your husband is waiting for you," she forced out between them. "And you –" She stood up. "Then you better go to him now. So he doesn't have to lie there all alone in your marriage bed."

Sonja shut her eyes again and only opened them again after quite a while. "Yeah." She stood up as well. "I need to take a shower." She looked at Kim. "May I?"

Kim nodded. But as Sonja walked by her, Kim's arm suddenly shot out as if of its own accord and held her firmly. "So he doesn't smell me on you? Is that it? You have to wash off anything that smells of me? Or can't you stand it yourself?"

Sonja stared at her and said nothing.

"Do you sleep with him?" The tension in Kim's body grew. Her fingers dug into Sonja's arm. Sonja grimaced with pain, but remained silent. "Are you going to sleep with him right now, when you go home?" Kim repeated.

"He's my husband. That's none of your business."

"It's none of my business." Kim's jaws were clenched so firmly that her cheekbones stood out sharply. "Your marriage is none of my business. Good thing you keep emphasizing that; otherwise, I might forget completely." She reached for Sonja's second arm with her other hand and turned her to face her. "But I can't forget it. I see pictures in my mind . . . how he touches you . . . and what he does to you." She took a deep breath. "What does he do to you, Sonja?"

"We're married," Sonja replied forbiddingly.

"So you sleep together, right?" Kim could no longer control herself. The tension inside her was becoming unbearable. She shoved Sonja onto the bed and lay on top of her. "*This* is what he does to you, right?" She stared down from above into Sonja's tight-lipped face. "He lies on top of you, he penetrates you, he ejaculates into you. And what do you do then? Do you go . . . take a shower?" Kim's voice was trembling with tension just as much as her hands were, which held Sonja still.

Sonja didn't stir, but lay there, unmoving. "Let me go." Her voice was cold as ice. "Immediately."

"Sonja . . ." Kim leaned down and pressed a kiss onto Sonja's cold, closed lips. "I yearn for you so much. I want so much . . ."

"To rape me?" Sonja asked coldly. "That's what you're doing right now."

Kim gaped at her as though she were only just coming to her senses. She rolled down off of Sonja and laid a hand on her forehead. "Forgive me," she whispered. "Please, forgive me."

Sonja stood up without a word and went into the bathroom. Kim heard the water running, then heard it shut off. Sonja came back into the bedroom, a towel wrapped tightly around herself.

Kim sat up. "I'm sorry," she said, ashamed. "That's not what I wanted."

Sonja picked up her belongings and left the room again, as wordlessly as she had the first time.

Kim grabbed her bathrobe and threw it on. Sonja was standing in the bathroom, getting dressed. Kim stood in the doorway.

"Sonja . . . please . . ." She raised her hands helplessly. "It will never happen again, I swear. And I'll never ask again. I promise."

"And how have you kept the promises you made so far?" Sonja countered disparagingly, with only a brief glance at Kim as she continued to get dressed.

"I know it was wrong. I was so . . ."

"Jealous," Sonja said. "We've been there before. In the parking garage. Almost the same situation. You'll never learn. You can't control yourself."

Kim considered her for a while, then turned away. "Maybe I really can't. Not with you."

"What's so special about me?" Sonja had finished dressing and stepped out of the bathroom. "You've been with plenty of women before, if I understand correctly. Did you treat all of them this way?"

"No." Kim turned around and surveyed Sonja's face. Tenderness welled up in her.

"Oh, so then I alone have that pleasure," Sonja said sarcastically. "What an honor. The only woman you constantly feel obliged to rape. What luck." She let out a hollow sound.

"You're right. You have every right to berate me."

"It does me no good to berate you." Sonja went into the living room to retrieve her jacket.

Kim remained standing and waited for her to come back.

"The only thing that'll do any good," Sonja continued, "is simply to cut off any contact between us. I never should've started it up again."

"Maybe that would've been better," Kim said.

"Yes, maybe it would've." Sonja gave Kim a grave look. "But I thought ... when you let me sleep here ... well." She cut herself off. "It was nothing. I made a mistake just as much as you did."

"What did you think?"

"It's not important anymore." Sonja went into the bedroom and looked around to see if she'd forgotten anything.

"But for me ... for me, it is important," Kim said softly. "Please, tell me. I ..." She raised a hand, helplessly. "It can't do any more harm."

"Harm?" Sonja grimaced. "No, the harm is already done, you're right about that. A confession won't change anything." She went to the apartment door. "I thought ... well ... that it was very nice of you. I expected something else, that's all." She opened the door.

"Expected something else?" Kim frowned. "What did you expect?"

"I'm sure you can imagine what," Sonja replied, annoyed. "Don't ask stupid questions."

"You thought I was just luring you to my apartment for sex, was that it?" Kim asked. "Even though I told you it wasn't like that."

"Obviously, what you say isn't always a hundred percent reliable. And yes, of course I thought that, what else?"

"Yeah, what else." Kim looked at her. "And it wasn't entirely off-base. I really had to control myself."

"Then at least you managed it once. Congratulations."

"Sonja ... I ..." Kim took a step toward Sonja and stood in front of her. "Now that I've broken so many promises, I don't have to keep this one, either." She took a deep breath. "I love you, Sonja. I don't know whether you can still believe that, but I truly love you. I love you like I've never loved another woman in my entire life. I know that won't do any good anymore, but I hope you'll believe me. Maybe I showed my love for you in the wrong way – I'm quite sure that's true – but that doesn't change the fact that I'll never love another woman the way I love you." Kim swallowed. "You're my absolute dream woman. The one and only."

"Kim." Sonja sighed. "What was the point of all that?" She sounded bored. "Don't overdo it."

"I know ..." Kim ran a hand through her hair. "You don't want to hear anything about love, and perhaps ... perhaps you're right, if that's supposed to be love, what –"

"Love is just a word that is carelessly used and doesn't mean anything. So don't give me that. I don't believe in it, and it's a good thing, too, because then the disappointment would be even worse – every time."

"Every time?" Kim looked at her. A different expression had crept onto Sonja's face. It no longer appeared dismissive, but rather ... yearning, Kim thought. Yes, Sonja yearned for something that she wasn't getting, and she tried to protect herself from disappointment by pretending that she didn't want it in the first place.

"Every time, just like this time. What's the point? Another name on the long list. Isn't that so? I'm no more than that for you – nor are you for me."

"There is no list. At least none that you're on. Where I stand on yours, of course, I don't know." *Oh, Sonja,* Kim thought. *What have I done to you? I'm so sorry.*

"The sex was good," Sonja said prosaically. "As far as I can judge. I don't have any experience with women, of course. As far as that's concerned, I would've wished for things to last a little longer."

"Only as far as that's concerned?"

"Beyond that ..." Sonja waved a hand vaguely, "... there isn't much else ... to an affair," she added.

"Because that's how you define it," Kim said.

"Because that's how *everyone* defines it," Sonja corrected. "It would be ridiculous to expect something else."

"Well, then, I'm ridiculous. Because I expected something different, and I define it differently."

"Your behavior doesn't indicate that."

"My behavior proves how ridiculous I am." Kim made a helpless gesture.

"Stop that! You're not ridiculous!" Sonja insisted angrily.

"Thanks. But in relation to you, I clearly am. Since the very first time I saw you ..." Kim sighed. "I fell head over heels for you from the start. That's never changed."

"Head over heels? You mean you wanted to sleep with me." Sonja's voice sounded dry.

"It would make absolutely no sense for me to deny that." Kim sighed. "But . . ." She leaned against the wall. She felt a certain weakness inside. "As you so aptly remarked, I've known a number of women before . . . closely, I mean . . . and I have never . . . Oh, well, at first, I thought it was the same with you, but it isn't. It's more. So much more."

"But it can never be more. It never could have been more," Sonja corrected herself. "Now, of course, it's out of the question in any case."

"Yes, unfortunately. And it's my fault."

Sonja seemed indecisive. "I can't trust you anymore," she said rather sadly. "The situation wouldn't change, you'd get jealous again, and then –"

"And then try to . . . rape you?" Kim asked, profoundly ashamed. "Never. I'd never do anything like that again. But that doesn't sound very believable, I can see that."

"No, it doesn't sound very believable," Sonja repeated. "I . . ." She took a deep breath. "I just don't want any problems, do you understand? I have enough going on. I don't need –" She broke off.

"You don't need me causing you problems, too," Kim said sorrowfully. "I understand that perfectly well."

"Kim, I . . ." Sonja slammed the door shut with a loud bang. "Ah, damn it!"

Kim raised her head. What was it now, all of a sudden?

Sonja started to walk towards the kitchen, but then she spun around. "Why can't we simply be friends, completely innocently?" she asked, breathing heavily.

Kim looked at her and tried to ignore how seductively her breasts heaved with every breath. "We can't," she said. "At least, I can't."

Sonja turned away. "Neither can I, that's the hell of it," she murmured.

"What did you say?"

"I . . ." Sonja turned around and looked at her once more. "I . . . I don't want it to end like this, and I don't want it to go on like this. I don't want to have to be wary of you all the time. I just want –"

Maybe love after all? Kim thought. "Sex?" she asked.

Sonja hesitated. "Yes," she said then. "Consensual, if possible."

"If possible?" Kim suddenly had to smirk. She tried to put that feeling away fast, though; she knew that Sonja had a point.

"I never wanted anything else. That would put us right back at the beginning."

"Yes." Kim nodded reflectively. "But you said you couldn't trust me anymore."

"And you said you'd never do it again," Sonja countered.

"You'd give me another chance?" Kim could hardly believe it.

"Your last. This is really the last one. The very last. And then I'm completely out of fresh starts."

"That . . . Sonja . . ." Kim swallowed. "Do you really mean that seriously?"

"More seriously than you can imagine," Sonja said. "I don't make statements like that frivolously."

Kim looked at her. She wanted so much to hug her, to pull her close, to sink into her softness. But she didn't dare.

"What are we going to do now?" Sonja asked. "Keep standing around?"

"I . . . Sonja . . ." Kim swallowed, cleared her throat, swallowed again. "I would so much like to kiss you, but I don't know –"

Sonja came up to her. "Then do it," she said softly. "I hope you don't think you have to ask every time, now. That could get tedious."

"Yes." Kim laughed uncertainly. "It could. But I don't want to do anything wrong, either. I don't want to do anything you don't want."

"In this case, you're not." Sonja brushed one finger across Kim's cheek. "Not at all." She nipped at Kim's lips with her own, then withdrew.

Kim couldn't believe her good fortune.

"Should I go?"

Kim shook her head. She couldn't say anything. She raised a hand and stroked Sonja's hair, approaching her carefully and waiting for her reaction.

Sonja remained standing there, very calm, doing nothing. Kim caressed her hair, her cheek, her neck, and then let one finger wander up to her lips and caress them very, very gingerly.

"Ooh!" Sonja laughed. "That tickles!"

Kim smiled slightly. She leaned forward and plucked at Sonja's lips just as Sonja had done to her, caressed them very softly and gently with the tip of her tongue until Sonja opened them, waiting for more. Kim went slowly and unbuttoned Sonja's blouse, pushing it off her shoulders along with the jacket. She abandoned her mouth, kissed her neck and the soft bend on the way down toward the tops of her breasts, then wandered up along the other side back to Sonja's mouth. She kissed her so tenderly that Sonja sighed deeply.

Sonja pushed Kim away slightly so that she could look into her eyes. "Nothing is going to change," she said carefully. "Do you understand? I will come and go, but I will never stay."

"I know." Kim nodded. "And I'll never demand it again, either."

Sonja considered her for a while, holding her eyes for so long that Kim could barely stand it. "Good," she agreed. She leaned forward and kissed Kim in return, with growing passion.

Kim felt the passion overtake her, but in a different way than earlier in the evening. It was passion, yes, but there was a warm feeling of tenderness mixed with it that seemed to carry the passion on a cushion of air. Peculiar, but that's how it was.

They kissed for a long time, merging with one another, each seeking the other's mouth over and over as though nothing else existed but these lips, marrying time and again.

After what seemed an eternity, they separated, and Sonja laid her head on Kim's breast. "That was so nice," she whispered. She laughed softly. "You kiss so well."

"I'll return that compliment." Kim smiled. "I believe it was a team effort."

Sonja raised her heads. "Well, then, we're a really good team."

"We always have been. Right from the start."

"That's true," Sonja said. "It was just a little . . . different then."

"You drove me insane whenever you were near me, just like now."

"Really?" Sonja looked at Kim.

"Don't you know that?" Kim smiled. "You kept touching me, just incidentally, on the arm, on the shoulder. You weren't even aware of it. But for me, of course, it was . . . mmm . . . exciting."

"Exciting? To what degree?"

"You coquette! You know perfectly well to what degree."

"A little coquetry is in order, I think. What woman doesn't like to hear it?" Sonja's hand slid under Kim's robe. "How exciting was I to you?" she asked in a whisper. "Could I have felt it?" She pushed her hand between Kim's thighs.

Kim moaned. "You could have," she said with an effort. "Usually."

Sonja's fingers stroked across Kim's labia. "And now?" she breathed. "How exciting do you find me now?"

Kim was breathing heavily. "You can feel it." She bit her lip. "Sonja . . ." she said in a choppy whisper. "I . . . I can't do this anymore. I don't want . . . I mean, I promised you –"

Without a word, Sonja drew her over into the living room and lay down on the couch. "Come . . ."

Kim stared at her for a moment, utterly overwhelmed, then knelt down next to the couch in front of her, watched Sonja's face, caressed her hips, slid up to her breasts.

Sonja closed her eyes and laid her head back.

"Oh, Sonja . . ." Kim began to undress Sonja, and when her upper body was naked, leaned down and took a nipple between her lips.

Sonja sighed.

Kim licked the other nipple while rubbing the first one with her thumb, and Sonja began to move restlessly. Kim unzipped Sonja's skirt to slip it over her hips, and Sonja raised them to allow Kim to pull down her skirt and panties, undressing her completely.

Sonja now lay completely naked before her. Kim swallowed.

"Come lie on top of me," Sonja whispered. "Please." Kim rose and started to take off her robe, but Sonja insisted: "No, keep it on. Come like that."

So Kim pushed the robe just a bit to the side, bent over Sonja and lay on top of her.

"Yes," Sonja breathed almost inaudibly.

Kim descended into her; that intoxicating feeling took her breath away. She sought Sonja's lips, kissed them, entered her mouth and explored it bit by bit until Sonja was panting beneath her. And so was she.

"Kim ... Kim ..." Sonja whispered with arousal when the kiss ended. Her fingers sought a path between Kim's legs and entered in between Kim's wet labia.

Kim threw her head back and moaned. She felt nothing now but lust, lust, lust. Sonja's fingers moved quickly, teasing her brutally; she thrust against them, and it didn't take long before she collapsed on top of her. Her heart raced and her loins throbbed.

"Sonja ..." she whispered, spent. "Beloved ..."

Sonja caressed her, her hair, her shoulders, her back. "I made you wait a long time for that, I'm sorry."

Kim straightened up slightly. "You're sweet," she said with a smile. "So sweet." She noticed the way Sonja's lips drew her magically in; she kissed them, then slid slowly down along her body, kissed her breasts, her belly –

"No!"

Kim looked up. "You still don't trust me?"

"I ... I'm sorry, Kim, I can't ... not today. Please understand ..." Sonja's voice sounded tormented.

Kim caressed her once more, her belly, her thighs, then stood up and pulled the couch, with Sonja on top of it, outward.

"Oof!" Sonja said.

Kim grinned and lay down next to her. "I thought we could use a little more room."

Sonja smiled. "There's something to that." She considered Kim's face, seeking understanding in her eyes. "Please, don't be mad at me," she pleaded softly. "I ... I just can't do that. Not yet. I promise you –"

"You don't need to promise me anything." Kim rested a finger on Sonja's lips to interrupt her. "There are plenty of other things we can do. You shouldn't feel forced into anything. We'll only do what you really want to. Okay?"

"I ... I feel so dumb." Sonja was embarrassed. "I'd love to –" She caressed Kim's face. "I'm sorry."

"I only feel sorry for you, because it's really very nice." Kim leaned over Sonja and gently caressed first one breast, then the other.

Sonja moaned softly.

Kim kissed her and caressed her breasts anew, until her nipples felt like they were about to burst out of their skin, hard and aroused. Then she slid one hand downward and felt for Sonja's center. Sonja was very wet again, like the first time, but Kim only stroked her gently between her legs, not entering her.

Sonja murmured something incomprehensible. Her hips rose and fell, rose again. Now she moved ever more restlessly.

Kim caressed the outsides of Sonja's labia, feeling the moisture making its way out from inside. She desired Sonja terribly, but she wanted this to take a long time. As restitution for all the sins she'd committed against her.

Sonja reached for her, pulled her close, dug her nails into her back.

"Ow!" Kim said.

Sonja opened her eyes, at least halfway, and deep, dark seas came into view, dark with arousal and desire. "Sorry." She breathed heavily. Her eyes blurred.

"That's okay." Kim leaned even closer to her. "I was just startled." She kissed Sonja again, caressing her inner thighs all the way up.

Sonja's body rose with a moan. Kim recalled that she was especially sensitive there. She caressed her more, running up and down, and Sonja's moans became ever louder.

"Please," she begged. "Please . . ."

Slowly, Kim let her hand wander back between her legs; she spread the labia a little, slipped in between them, and felt like it was almost swimming in a sea. She closed her eyes because it also aroused her infinitely, to know and to feel how wet Sonja was. She would've loved to explore those depths with her mouth.

Carefully, she entered Sonja with one finger. Sonja let out a sharp cry, and a wide hollow opened itself eagerly. Kim added all the rest of her fingers to the first one; otherwise, she could never have filled Sonja up.

Gently, she began to glide in and out. Sonja's hips thrust, rolled, writhed, forced themselves against her. She became ever wilder, digging again into Kim's back. This time, Kim was prepared and bore the pain without a word.

"Oh . . . ah . . . oh . . . yes . . . yes . . . oh . . . yeah . . ." Sonja's cries of arousal sent lightning bolts through Kim's body.

She caressed Sonja's pearl, and Sonja nearly leapt off the sofa, wordless sounds bursting from her. She became ever louder. "Oh . . . oh God . . . oh my God!" She thrust into the air, held herself rigid, thrust again. "Oh . . . yeah . . . Kim . . . yeahhh!" She could no longer contain herself. "Yes! Now!" Sonja cried out, moaned, murmured nonsense, then the building tension immobilized her while it crescendoed. She crested, and then went limp. A loud sigh appeared to signal the end.

Kim withdrew her fingers, and Sonja moaned softly once more. Kim tenderly caressed the swollen lips. Sonja twitched. Kim smiled. She began to fondle the labia again from the outside.

"Oh no!" Sonja whispered, but her hips twitched again.

Kim sought her pearl, teased it, pressed it, rubbed quickly across it.

Sonja gasped and slid her bottom back and forth on the couch.

Kim caressed her some more; Sonja moaned, sighed, moaned, and climaxed again soon after. Kim didn't let that deter her, but undaunted, drove her to the next orgasm.

In the end, there were six before Sonja begged, "No, stop, please, Kim . . . I can't anymore . . ."

Kim let her hand lie still. "You can take a minute to think about it." She grinned.

"Heavens." Sonja lay there with her eyes closed and looked ravishing, in Kim's opinion. "Heavens," she repeated. She opened her eyes. "That was unbelievable." She took a deep breath.

"Unbelievably good or unbelievably awful?" Kim asked with a smile.

"Both. It was awful and great at the same time. I felt so . . . at your mercy." Sonja looked at Kim. "You could've done anything to me. I wouldn't have been able to defend myself."

"I hope I didn't do anything to you that you didn't want."

"No." Sonja looked at her with a peculiar expression in her eyes. "You didn't."

Kim didn't know what she ought to say. What did it mean that

Sonja was looking at her so oddly? "Are you hungry?" she asked, to evade that look. "I could make us something to eat. How about a little snack?"

"I am hungry." Sonja pushed herself on top of Kim. "But the kind of hunger I have isn't satisfied by food." She fell upon Kim's mouth and kissed her deeply and passionately.

The next few hours didn't satisfy anyone's hunger for food, as Kim and Sonja were occupied with other things.

At last, they lay next to one another, exhausted, and Sonja cuddled up against Kim's shoulder. They were quiet, until Sonja sighed.

"What is it?" Kim asked.

"I . . ." Sonja swallowed. "I have to go."

A block of ice rammed itself into Kim's heart. "Yeah. I know."

Sonja caressed Kim's face one more time, then stood up and went into the bathroom. Kim heard the shower.

When Sonja came back to get dressed, Kim watched her, although she would rather have run away. She wanted to hold Sonja tight, but she knew that was impossible.

"Tomorrow . . ." Sonja gazed out the window. "Tomorrow I can't. So we'll see each other on Monday. Will you come see me, to discuss the project?"

Kim took a deep breath. "Yes. When?"

"First thing in the morning," Sonja said. "Then we have to get going, out to Eichhalde. Eight o'clock?"

Kim's lips twitched slightly. "How about seven?"

Sonja looked back at her with a faint smile. "I don't want to make you get up that early."

"It's my idea. Seven, then."

"Lovely. That would even be better." Sonja considered Kim again with that indefinable look. Suddenly, she approached the sofa and leaned down over Kim. "It was wonderful," she said softly. "Thank you." She brushed a kiss onto Kim's lips and straightened up. "Until Monday, then."

"'Til Monday." Kim could barely get the words out.

Sonja turned around and left.

▫▫▫▫▫

On Sunday, after an extended back-and-forth with Jo and Jennifer, Kim allowed herself to be talked into a trip to the women's café.

"I'd say miniature golf is out for a while, the way you've been," Jennifer said.

"I'm sorry," Kim replied. "I'll work on my focus next time."

"You don't have to be sorry." Jennifer grinned. "When you lose, I win. I don't object to that."

"But then there's no challenge for you. That's boring."

Jennifer grinned even more. "Jo is my challenge," she looked lovingly into Jo's eyes. "In every respect. That never gets boring."

"When are you two getting married?" Kim asked with a chuckle.

"Oh . . . uh . . ." Jennifer glanced quickly at Jo.

Kim followed her gaze and tilted her head with curiosity. "You've really talked about it?"

"Um . . . no . . ."

"Yes," Jo contradicted her. "We have."

"Well, and . . .?" Kim was still looking inquisitive.

"Yes, we have," Jennifer admitted with a sigh. "We've talked about it."

"So – what are you waiting for?" Kim asked.

Jo groaned. "Jenny can't decide. At first, she wants to, but then –"

"I . . ." Jennifer grimaced. "I . . . The topic is just plain too new to me. I never considered that –"

"That one day, a woman might come along and shackle you in the bonds of holy matrimony?" Jo teased.

Jennifer gave her a tender look. "Yes."

"You want to be shackled, but not chained up, I can understand that," Kim said.

"Exactly." Jennifer appeared relieved. "I love Jo . . ." She turned to face Jo. "I love you, darling, but . . . maybe . . . it's just too soon."

"That doesn't matter." Jo smiled lovingly at her. "There has to be an engagement first, after all." She pulled a small box out of her pocket and held it under Jennifer's nose.

Jennifer stared at it, but didn't touch it.

"Don't you want to open it?" Jo smiled.

"Jo ... love ... that ... that ..." Jennifer's face was becoming covered with tiny red spots.

"Well, come on already," Kim said. "I want to see what's in there, too."

Jennifer reached cautiously for the box and opened it even more cautiously. A ray of light from somewhere in the café caused something inside to sparkle. She opened the little lid the rest of the way and peered inside.

"Actually, it was a nose ring for a steer." Jo grinned, "but I had it adapted to fit your finger."

Jennifer raised her head. "You *would* do something like that." She leaned forward and kissed Jo, long and deep.

Kim watched the two of them with a smile. "Can I see?" she asked after a while.

"It's nothing special," Jo said with a shrug. "I'm not rich enough to afford anything that is *really* worthy of Jennifer."

"It's wonderful." Jennifer took the ring out of the box and slipped it onto her finger. It was a narrow gold ring set with small stones cut in heart shapes.

"I know it's a little bit kitschy ..." Jo said, embarrassed.

"Would you stop it?!" Jennifer boxed her on the side. "Even if it were from a gumball machine – it's the intentions that matter."

"My intentions are the best ... the very best." Jo grinned. "My intention is to drag you to the altar."

"By the hair?" Kim laughed.

"If I have to," Jo countered. "No, of course not." She wrapped an arm around Jennifer. "But this is the woman with whom I want to spend the rest of my life, even if we had to be on a deserted island."

"A deserted island would be nice," Jennifer said softly, cuddling up to Jo.

"Sure, if we didn't have to earn a little money even to do that." Jo sighed. "Just a couple million."

"Oh, we can do that, hon, no sweat." Jennifer kissed Jo once again.

"Then I'm going to have to ask Mrs. Kantner for a raise," Jo said when Jennifer finally let go of her. She turned to Kim. "What do you think she'll say?"

Kim flinched. "Why are you asking me?"

"Well, you know, with your close relationship . . ."

"What close relationship are you talking about?" Kim crossed her arms.

"About the one that demands the shortest possible route between the mini golf course and your front door," Jo said. "We were a little startled when you left so quickly yesterday, but then Jenny thought –"

"You weren't supposed to say that!" Jennifer interrupted her.

"You've known Kim longer than I have, and . . ." Jo smirked, "more intimately, which is why I think you were probably right."

"Jo, it's none of our business. It's no one's concern but Kim's." Jennifer looked at Kim. "Unless, of course, she wants to tell us about it."

Kim rolled her eyes. "There's nothing to tell."

"Nothing?" Jo gave her a skeptical look. "She wasn't there when you got home? Or did you two meet up somewhere else? At her place?"

"Jo!" Kim tore at her own hair.

"Leave it," Jennifer said. "She doesn't want to talk about it."

Jo tried again, but Jennifer smacked her so hard on the side that Jo gasped. "All right then."

"So you really just went home to sleep yesterday, nothing else?" Jennifer asked.

Kim hated to lie to Jennifer; she was her best friend, but she didn't want to betray Sonja. "Of course."

"If she says that's how it was, then that's how it was," Jennifer said to Jo. "And besides . . ." she held up her hand with the ring on it, "we have other things to discuss right now."

Jo smiled. "What, for instance?"

"For instance, how we're going to tell my parents that we're getting married."

"Your . . . parents?" Jo stared at Jennifer.

"Well, of course," Jennifer said. "I want my family to be there for my wedding, don't you want yours?"

"Oh." Jo stared at the tabletop. "I don't think that'll work."

"Why not?" Jennifer asked.

"I . . ." Jo swallowed. "I can't talk about it right now."

Jennifer looked at her thoughtfully. "It's not just my parents," she went on. "My siblings, too, my brother and my sister – and my cousins, aunts and uncles . . ."

"My God, how large is your family?" Jo asked.

"Very large. For the wedding, we're at least going to need a ballroom."

Kim grinned at Jo's look of horror. "Do you want to take back your marriage proposal?"

Jo shook her head. "No, of course not."

"Forgive me," Jennifer said. "Maybe we should've talked a little bit more about my family before now. But we haven't known each other all that long . . ."

"Yeah, maybe we should've talked a little more," Jo replied, bewildered. Then she smiled. "But if you want a big wedding, then you're going to have a big wedding, I promise."

Jennifer flung her arms around her neck. "You're simply amazing!" She laughed. "I love you!"

"I love you, too." Jo hugged her tightly. "You should have everything you want."

"Actually, the parents of the bride are supposed to pay for the wedding," Jennifer said with a grin. "The question is, which one of us is the bride?"

"Will there be one wedding dress or two?" Kim was now imagining what Jennifer and Jo would look like in dresses, rather than their usual slacks.

"Now, me . . . no," Jo said. "A dress? No way."

"Oh . . ." Jennifer leaned back and gazed into the air as though she were looking at a picture in front of her. "I might be able to imagine it. I really liked wearing dresses when I was a kid."

"You?" Kim asked.

"Yes, for goodness sake, there are nice ones," Jennifer defended herself. "Of course, I never had anything in pink."

"Well, thank God for that." Kim chuckled.

"But since a wedding dress is white, that really isn't a problem," Jennifer mused further. "I'm sure my mother will help me pick one out."

Jo gaped at her, just as she had at the first mention of parents.

"My parents have known for a long time," Jennifer said casually. "A wedding . . . well, they won't have been expecting that, but I'll bring 'em around."

"I . . ." Jo swallowed. "I'm going to meet your parents?"

"In advance, I hope. Things will be a little hectic at the actual wedding, I would assume. But my mother will manage it. She organizes big family celebrations all the time. Everybody always goes to her for that sort of thing."

"Uh . . . Jenny . . ." Jo appeared overwhelmed. "This is all a bit sudden for me."

"Yes, sure." Jennifer looked at her tenderly. "You have to get used to it first, I can see that. But my family is . . . well, they're crazy, but really, they're all right."

"They truly are a little crazy, you'll see," Kim said. "But really nice."

"You know them?" Jo was getting more and more nervous.

"Jennifer brought me along to one of those big family celebrations once." Kim grinned. "It was very entertaining."

"But it wasn't your wedding," Jo said, shaken.

"No, it wasn't." Kim looked at her. "You need to calm down a little, Jo. This really seems to have knocked you off your feet."

"I . . . it's a little strange to me," Jo said.

"You don't have a large family?" Kim asked.

"No, I –" Jo broke off. "No, not so big."

"You'll get used to it. And besides, you won't see them every day," Jennifer said. "They live half a day's drive away."

"Hm." Jo looked relieved.

Kim looked at Jennifer and arched her eyebrows. Jennifer shrugged. After that silent dialogue, she turned back to Jo. "We're not that far along today," she said reassuringly. "And besides, I don't even know yet whether I want to marry you at all."

"You don't?" Jo seemed confused.

Jennifer pursed her lips. "Then I'd have to give the ring back, wouldn't I?" She looked at Kim.

Kim nodded earnestly. "Yes, you would."

"No." Jo shook her head. "You can keep it, no matter what you do."

"Jo ... sweetheart ..." Jennifer leaned over to Jo and looked deep into her eyes. "I'm definitely going to keep it, just as long as I keep you. And I'm never letting you go." She stroked Jo's cheek tenderly. "Never."

Jo looked like she was about to turn bright red, but she just gazed at the floor, embarrassed. "Really?"

"Yes, really," Jennifer whispered and kissed her on the nose. "For ever and ever, that's how it goes, isn't it?"

Kim smiled. Her heart warmed to see the two of them. Then the smiled vanished from her face. *I'll never have this with Sonja*, she thought. *There's not even a chance.*

"Aren't you happy for us?" Jennifer interrupted her thoughts.

"Yes, of course." Kim's head jerked up. "I'm very happy for you."

"You don't look it." Jennifer considered her observantly. "You look more like Jo just stole me away from you." She grinned. "Or maybe I stole Jo from you?"

Kim shook her head. "You know that's not true."

"Well, who knows?" Jennifer tilted her head coquettishly. "Maybe our night way back when left a more lasting impression on you than I thought."

"Not to mention our experience in the Darkroom," Jo added with a grin.

Kim raised a hand. "You can forget that right now. I'm very happy for the two of you, and I'm looking forward to your wedding – I hope I'll be invited." Now she was grinning, too. "I can still taste your mother's wonderful cake." She licked her lips appreciatively.

"Yeah, no comparison to what you show up with from time to time."

"I just can't refuse Margit, or Rolf, either," Kim apologized with a grimace.

"How's your boss doing, then?" Jo asked with interest. "Is he okay?"

"He's moving to a rehab facility next week," Kim replied. "That's the last I heard."

"That means you're still the department head," Jo said.

"Only for the interim," Kim corrected. "Officially, I'm just a team leader."

"But unofficially, everybody knows you run the show," Jo said. "And not too badly, either." The corners of her mouth twitched impishly. "What does Mrs. Kantner have to say about the fact that you're practically her equal now?"

"*Mrs. Kantner* . . ." Kim replied with emphasis, "says nothing at all about that. Why should she?"

"Well, now, I thought . . . just conversationally . . . when you see each other . . . to the extent you talk to each other . . ." Jo needled her.

"You just can't let it be, can you?" Kim said.

"Aww, allow me this one pleasure," Jo answered brightly. "After all, I haven't had much fun with my boss so far . . . compared to you."

"I really did enjoy collaborating with her, that is true."

"And it's also true that that's not what I meant," Jo said. "It's unfair for you to leave me high and dry like this – when I should be sitting right at the wellspring because of you."

"At the wellspring of what?" Kim asked.

"Of information about Sexy Sonja!" Jo cried out. "Good grief, that woman is pure dynamite! Even though she's not my type, I can feel it. She must be amazing in – *Ow!*"

Jennifer had apparently poked Jo in a sensitive spot again. "Sorry, love, but we've been there already."

"Another hard smack like that, and I'm going to have to call in sick," Jo panted. "I thought my S&M days were over."

"You used to be into S&M?" Jennifer's eyes were opened wide and innocently.

"Yeah, sure." Jo made a face again, but this time not of pain, rather amusement. "Johanna Mayrhofer's Dominatrix Studio. Ever heard of it?" She grinned from ear to ear.

"With a name like that, people must've been beating down the door," Kim teased. "It's so much more alluring than *Lady Chantal* or something like that."

"Yeah, I thought so, too. That's why I had to run away and come here. I couldn't handle the onslaught anymore." Jo tried for a serious expression, but couldn't pull it off.

"Ah, that's why you have all those whips and handcuffs in your closet," Jennifer said. "I did wonder about that."

"Yeah." Jo shrugged. "When Mrs. Kantner throws me out, I'll still have my whips, and I can open up my business again. You never know." She turned to Kim. "Or I'll sell them to her. Does she like that kind of thing?" She jumped up before Jennifer could finally break a rib.

"Ask her yourself." Kim sighed. She gave up. "I'm sure she'd be glad to tell you all about it."

"Uh-uh . . ." Jo waved a hand vaguely. "I'd rather not risk it. Then the dynamite might explode. But you know what?" She snapped her fingers. "*She* could open a studio with the name *Lady Dynamite*."

Jennifer sighed deeply. "Would you rather marry her instead of me? You seem to be very preoccupied with her."

"I see her every day, and I wonder –" Jo glanced at Jennifer before sitting back down next to her. "I wonder what's up with her."

Kim frowned. "What do you mean?"

"May I talk about this now, or am I going to get smacked again?" Jo braced herself.

"Just try not to grill Kim about . . . you know what," Jennifer said. "Then I won't hit you."

"Thank you very much, Mistress," Jo replied with a grin. A moment later her face took on a thoughtful cast. "I've told you before, she's always completely done for after her husband calls – and intolerable. I might be, too, if I had to go through that kind of hassle every day. But anyway . . . well . . . I can't always keep from hearing their phone conversations."

"You eavesdrop on them?" Kim was stunned.

"I . . . No. Normally, she always shuts the door, but one time recently, she didn't close it all the way, she just left it ajar, and although she was trying to talk quietly, I couldn't help . . . I had to hear it."

Kim sat quietly, without responding.

"You don't want to know? You're not interested?"

"Kim . . . honestly . . . if you want Jo to stop, say so," Jennifer added. "I could understand that."

Kim ran a hand through her hair. "Go ahead," she said softly. "Then I can finally get it over with."

Jennifer arched her brows, and Jo told her story. "First, she said to him, 'Never call me at work again', but it sounds like he doesn't seem to think much of that. Apparently, he really chewed her out over the phone, and then she said, in this voice – I can't even describe it – like ice that cuts: 'There are limits, Uwe ... to which you agreed. Cross them again, and I'll say what happened. I won't care anymore.'"

Kim didn't feel particularly enlightened. To the contrary, the puzzle of Sonja seemed to have grown even more complex.

"Do you have any idea what that means?" Jennifer asked.

Kim shook her head thoughtfully. "No. None. Like I said, the whole time I was working for her, her husband never called. This is all strange to me."

"And she never said anything to you ... I mean, now?" Jennifer asked. "You still talk to each other. Not even you try to keep that a secret."

"Yes, that's not a secret," Kim said absently.

She was recalling the night Sonja had cried upon her breast. Back then, she had assumed Klaus was the cause. But that no longer seemed very likely. Her husband seemed to be the root of all evil. But if that were the case – why didn't she divorce him?

That question kept coming up, over and over – and Sonja had refused to answer it.

Kim took a deep breath. "I can't say anything about that." She sighed. "And that's not me keeping a secret. I simply don't know."

"It sounds like he's up to something bad, and she could turn him in for it, but she doesn't," Jo mused. "But then why is she so worn out? If she were protecting him somehow, she'd have him wrapped around her little finger."

"That doesn't matter to her ... wouldn't matter to her," Kim said. "If it were like that."

"Most women ... straight women, I mean ... really like to have their men wrapped around their little fingers," Jo pointed out. "We all know that."

"But she's not like that," Kim flared. "She's –"

"Yes?" Jennifer and Jo leaned forward at the same time, interested.

"She's exceptionally proper," Kim finished stiffly. "She wouldn't want that sort of relationship." *And what is she doing with me, then? What kind of relationship is that?* she thought.

"She could get a divorce."

"Damn it again, that's *her* business, Jo!" Kim burst out loudly. Some of the other women present in the café turned to look at her. "It's her business," Kim repeated more quietly. "It's none of our concern."

Jennifer tilted her head to one side. "Not yours, either?"

Kim stood up. She looked down at Jennifer and Jo.

"No, not mine, either." She left.

"**D**id we have a date?" Jo looked at Kim, astonished. She still held her jacket in her hand, which she had just been about to hang up. "This early on Monday morning?"

"Ms. Mayrhofer, do you have –" Sonja came out of her office into the anteroom. She hesitated briefly. "Ah, Kim ..." she said. "You're here already."

"Seven o'clock." Kim raised her wristwatch in the air with a smile. "On the dot."

"Astounding." The corners of Sonja's mouth seemed to twitch. "Ms. Mayrhofer," she turned back to Jo. "Do you have that analysis from Friday?"

"Sure," Jo confirmed. "But I'd really like to hang up my jacket first. I just got here."

"Ah, yes ..." Kim chuckled. "Good morning ..." she turned slightly toward Sonja, "... all around."

"Good morning." Sonja seemed confused. "I'm sorry, I've been here since five. It almost feels like midday to me now."

"Good morning," Jo joined in the general greetings with a suppressed grin, then hung her jacket up in one closet and walked over to another one. She took out a folder, brought it to the desk, and opened it. She handed the page on top to Sonja. "Here. The analysis."

"Thank you." Sonja was about to disappear back into her office with the paper.

"Sonja?" Kim held her back.

Sonja half turned, looking visibly impatient.

"Are we putting off our departure?" Kim asked. "In that case, I'll go get some coffee."

"Yes . . . yes, do that." Again, Sonja turned toward her office.

"Would you like some, too?" Kim asked. "If you've been here since five already."

"No." This time, Sonja didn't turn around. "I've had enough." She went into her office.

"I want one." Jo grinned. "I'll go with you." They walked in silence until they got to the coffee vending machine. "Had a bad night, you two?" Jo inquired.

"Don't you have enough bruises already?" Kim asked in return. She pressed the button for an espresso.

While the coffee machine droned loudly into action, Jo gave Kim a searching look. "She wasn't with you last night?"

"Have I ever answered that kind of question before?" Kim retorted with another counter-question. She took the paper cup with her espresso from the vending machine.

"No. But I can always try. Maybe I'll wear you down eventually." Jo appeared to be in the best of moods. "Tell me, since when are you two on a first name basis in this work environment? Before now, it's always been *Ms. Wolff* and *Mrs. Kantner.*"

"Sonja . . . Mrs. Kantner doesn't find that necessary anymore."

"So she finds . . ." Jo hadn't expected this much amusement on a gray Monday morning. She was thrilled with the entertaining start to her week.

"Jo." Kim was getting annoyed. "Would you believe me if I promised you that she really wasn't with me last night?"

"Oh." Jo took her coffee cup likewise from the vending machine. "Sounds like it could be true."

"It doesn't just *sound* that way. And now . . . please . . . let's drop the subject."

"And I would just have loved to know –" Jo broke off. "But no, you're right. I don't want to get on your nerves any more."

"Thank you. I'm deeply indebted to you for such consideration."

"If you keep making fun of me like that, I might change my mind."

They had arrived back at the office and went inside. Jo sat down at her desk.

"It's still strange." Kim laughed. "I almost sat down at that same table. For a moment, I forgot this wasn't my office."

"It hasn't been that long, after all," Jo said.

The door to Sonja's office stood open. Kim peeked inside and saw Sonja sitting at her desk. *Like before*, she thought. *As though nothing had changed.*

Sonja lifted her head. "Come in." When Kim entered, she added: "Close the door, please."

Kim raised her eyebrows and did what Sonja asked. She shut the door behind herself and turned around to face her. "Shall we discuss the project? What kinds of tasks did you have in mind for me?"

"A lot. Probably more than you can manage with your ten or twenty percent." Sonja stood up.

Kim was about to toss her coffee cup into the trashcan when Sonja darted over to her. Her kiss came suddenly and was more than hungry. She pressed Kim against the wall.

"Since five . . ." she breathed heavily, "I've been looking at the clock every minute. Those two hours were endless."

"S-sorry." Kim was stuttering with surprise. "If I'd known, I would've come earlier."

"We had an appointment for seven, and you were punctual – surprisingly enough." Sonja grinned. "I think that's quite a compliment to me."

"I'm always punctual. Usually," Kim qualified. "But actually –"

"Yes, you're a dutiful employee." Sonja laughed softly. "I have no doubt whatsoever about that." She examined Kim's face. "It's awful, but we have to get to work now." She kissed Kim once again, her tongue promising so much more. Her hand slid down across Kim's hips to her bottom –

She tore herself away with a sudden jerk and walked quickly over to her desk. “The project.” Flushed, she brushed a lock of hair away from her cheek.

“Yes, the project.” Kim took a deep breath. Then she just couldn’t do it anymore. “Sonja, you look wonderful,” she said quietly. She went up to Sonja and took her in her arms. “You’re the most beautiful woman I know.”

“A woman who has to work,” Sonja replied with an effort. “Besides which, Ms. Mayrhofer could walk in here at any moment.”

“Jo won’t do that.” Kim laughed softly. “And even if she did see us, it would just make her happy.”

“You told her –?” Sonja pushed Kim away from her a little.

“No.” Kim shook her head. “I didn’t. But there are no limits to her imagination. Not even you can do anything about that.”

Sonja sighed. “I can’t, that’s true.” She looked at Kim. “But she won’t –?”

“She won’t.” Kim caressed Sonja’s cheek. “Don’t worry. She may be curious, but she’s not a blabbermouth. You can trust her completely.”

“I had that impression so far, too. But with things like this … sometimes you can’t count on continuing discretion.”

Kim smiled, let go of Sonja, and went to the door. She opened it and stuck her head out. “Jo? Would you please forget everything you’ve heard and seen here today? And whatever you may see or hear in the future?”

“Heard? Seen? What?” Jo’s patently amused voice asked in return. “I don’t know anything. I’m blind and deaf. They hired me through the program for people with disabilities.”

Kim shut the door and turned back to Sonja. “Did you hear?” She grinned.

“Oh my God.” Sonja sat down behind her desk, propping her arms on it and laying her face in her hands. “This is so embarrassing.”

“Not at all. “ Kim went over to her. “Believe me, you don’t need to worry about anything. I just wanted to prove it to you.”

Sonja raised her face slightly above her hands and looked at Kim. “Do you always act that way with each other? I mean, is that normal?”

"If that were normal, the two of us wouldn't be –" Kim motioned with a finger from her chest to Sonja, and back. "Jo is a good friend. And she's in a relationship with my best friend of many years, Jennifer. If you can trust anyone, it's her." She crouched next to Sonja and caressed her hair. "Is this truly so awful for you? We all know each other. That's just the way it is."

"We . . . you . . ." Sonja cleared her throat. "You mean, all women who . . . women who –" She broke off.

"– love other women," Kim finished. She knew Sonja didn't want to say it out loud. "Yes, all of us, we lesbians."

Sonja flinched. "Is it . . . I mean . . . does everyone already know –" She seemed confused.

"No." Kim laughed and caressed Sonja's shoulder. "No one knows. Only Jo and Jennifer. That was unavoidable. They practically witnessed it from the start, after all, when I didn't even know that you . . . and I . . . you know."

"Do you always tell each other everything as soon as it happens?" Sonja straightened up and sat back in her executive chair. She looked reluctantly at Kim. "Was I the topic of conversation among all the regulars at the bar?"

"No, no." Kim stood up and looked down at Sonja. "Not at all. Jennifer just happened to grill me back then, when I'd just returned from the seminar. I was . . . well . . . pretty mixed up."

"*You* were mixed up?" Sonja looked astonished. "For you that was completely normal. I mean, I . . . it wasn't for me, but you'd had some experience already."

"There are experiences and then there are experiences." Kim reached for the arms of Sonja's chair, turned her toward herself and leaned over her. "I'd had experiences with women, but not with you," she said softly, holding Sonja's gaze.

Sonja moved uneasily in her chair, trying to evade Kim's eye. "Isn't it always the same?" She stared over Kim's shoulder at the opposite wall.

"Oh, no." Kim kissed her tenderly on the cheek. "You're something very special, I've told you that before. And I felt that way about you back then, too."

"Because I'd never been with another woman before?" Sonja

asked, still not turning to face Kim's gaze.

Kim shook her head. "You weren't the first like that. I think I've indicated that before."

"Yes." Sonja cleared her throat. "I remember. But –" She gave Kim a sort of evaluating look from the side. "If it wasn't that, what was it? I still don't understand."

"*You*, Sonja!" Kim laughed. "It was *you!* What else?" She leaned down and brushed a kiss onto Sonja's lips. "You are a wonderful woman, don't you know that?" She smiled tenderly at Sonja.

"I've had my doubts lately," Sonja murmured, almost more to herself than to Kim.

"What's wrong, love?" Kim became serious. "Tell me. Something is weighing you down – it was weighing you down even then. Otherwise we might never have come together. Only because you cried –"

"I cried?" Sonja looked up at her, alarmed.

"Don't you remember? In the hotel? You had a bad dream – I think."

"A bad dream . . . yes." Sonja stared ahead in silence.

Kim straightened up. "You don't have to tell me anything if you don't want to. I did promise not to ask."

Sonja pushed her chair back and stood up. "I . . . Some things aren't so simple." She flipped through some files on her desk, although she obviously wasn't really seeing them.

"You aren't exactly happily married, are you?"

Sonja glanced briefly at Kim. "No. But I *am* married. And I have to take that into consideration."

"Your feelings don't matter?" Kim raised her eyebrows.

Sonja laughed dryly. "My feelings? Least of all!"

"That must be awful for you." Kim could see the burden in Sonja's face and felt helpless. "Can't I do anything? Help you somehow?" She raised her hands.

"Help?" A faint smile crept over Sonja's lips. "I can't be helped. I have only myself to blame." Her smile became soft and loving. "You're already helping me enough. With the project, and . . . well, in other ways, too."

"Other ways?" Kim smiled, too. She stepped up to Sonja. "What do you mean by that?"

"You know . . ." Sonja seemed embarrassed.

Kim pulled her closer and kissed her. "Is this what you mean?" she whispered against her lips.

Beep! "Mrs. Kantner?" Jo's voice squawked out of the intercom. "I don't mean to be pushy, but your meeting is in twenty minutes."

"Oh . . . yes." Sonja twisted out of Kim's arms and pressed the talk button. "Thank you, Ms. Mayrhofer. I'll be right out." She looked down at the desk, on which a great many papers lay. "And I haven't even told you what you're supposed to do on the project. You'll have to find out in the meeting. I called it especially so that we could discuss the new situation. The new concept . . . and the fact that you're involved now. That's important, too, after all."

"Nice of you to see it that way." Kim smiled. "The meeting's in the conference building?"

"Yes. And I'm not even finished with half of it." Sonja sighed. "It's all just too much."

"Explain the most critical parts to me on the way." Kim gathered up the papers. "Is this all?" She held up the packet.

Sonja nodded. Then she frowned. "One more thing . . ." She went over to one of her filing cabinets and pulled out a file folder. "We should take this with us, too. Then I think we've got everything."

"Good." Kim nodded. "Let's go."

Sonja went to the door and opened it. "I'll be unavailable for the next two hours, Ms. Mayrhofer," she said to Jo. "After that, I'll be on my cell. We'll leave directly from the conference room."

"Understood." Jo nodded in confirmation. "I'll hold the fort." She winked at Kim.

Kim shook her head in reproof. She bent over to Jo as she walked past her.

"It's not what you think," she whispered to her.

"I don't get paid to think." Jo grinned.

Kim grinned back and followed Sonja out of the room.

She could still hear when the telephone rang and Jo picked it up.

"No, Mr. Kantner, your wife isn't here," Jo greeted the caller. "She's in a meeting right now."

2

"Rolf! Am I ever glad you're back!" Kim greeted Rolf Winkelmann by embracing him heartily.

"If you want to bring on my next heart attack, just keep that up." Rolf laughed. "You're practically crushing me to death."

Kim stepped back in alarm. "I'm sorry, I didn't know – are you still feeling poorly?"

"No." Rolf winked at her. "After everything I went through with the therapists in the rehab facility, I'm as fit as a three hundred dollar gym shoe. But I still have to breathe, Kim!" He glanced over at Kim's desk. "The work hasn't let up at all, I see."

"I know. I warned you." Kim sighed. "To do this right, I really should have hired some more people, but the budget . . ."

Rolf waved her away. "I'm very familiar with that argument. Service twenty-four hours a day, seven days a week, but you don't need people for that. The leprechauns will do it."

"Yes, more or less." Kim laughed. "But first, sit down here – this is yours!" She indicated the chair from she'd jumped up from when Rolf entered the office. "I'll go back to my old office."

"It's not quite that simple." Rolf furrowed his brow and looked at her. "I'm not coming back to work full-time again, and I'm not going to keep working for much longer, either. I think you'd better just keep this office. After everything you've accomplished over the last six months, there can hardly be any doubt that you'll be my successor."

Kim stared at him. "No, Rolf, that's – I'm just your temporary stand-in, really, that's all."

"You're much more." Rolf smiled. "You have been from the beginning. You know I've always viewed you as my successor, I just hadn't thought –" He sighed. "I just hadn't thought it would happen so soon."

Kim frowned. "And if I don't agree?"

"Don't be silly, Kim. Then they'll hire someone else to replace me, and I don't want that, for the company or for you. I'm taking early retirement, one way or another. Margit is very happy about it. And actually . . . actually, so am I." Rolf took an all-encompassing look around the office. "It took my being in rehab to realize that work isn't everything. I knew that before, too, but living without work for months really made it clear to me for the first time. I didn't miss it. Not the stress, not the irritated customers, not the overwhelmed employees and clueless superiors demanding I do pointless things. That all seems so unnecessary now." He gave Kim a fatherly smile. "You're young. You still have it all in front of you. And I think it's a lot of fun for you. I enjoyed it, too, and I had a good, long run. But sooner or later, it's got to stop. Margit and I want to buy a little house in the Camargue, where we've always gone on vacation. We want to make a permanent move there."

"Then you'll both be – leaving Germany?" Kim looked stunned.

"Yes, but you should know that you can come visit us in France anytime. You're always welcome. You're practically a daughter to us."

Kim shook her head. "I never would've thought it would come to this."

"Aw, Kimmie." Rolf came up to her and took her in his arms. "You'll see, it won't be that much of a difference. After all, we haven't seen each other every day lately, either."

"But . . . but . . ." Kim swallowed. "When you and Margit are so far away . . ."

Rolf held her a little away from himself. "I'm convinced Margit will find a way to get one of her cakes to you on a regular basis." His eyes twinkled with pleasure.

That broke the spell. All of a sudden, Kim had to laugh. She let go of Rolf. "Yes, that'll maintain the relationship!"

"Absolutely." Rolf nodded. "I'm only here for a visit today, too. I have to go to personnel to set up the early retirement with them. Starting tomorrow, I'll come in half-days, just for the mornings. I don't need to teach you the ropes anymore, of course, but I'll stay as long as it takes to wrap up all the loose ends with the personnel department, including hiring your replacement. Knowing their usual pace, that could take several months."

"If it were up to me, the longer, the better. But I'll grant you your cottage in the Camargue. You've earned it fair and square. Do you have a place in mind already?"

"We do. We've looked around whenever we've been there the past few years, and I think Margit probably knows exactly what she wants. Most of the houses aren't in very good condition. So I'll have some work to do before what we buy is really habitable. But I don't want to just sit around and be lazy, either, so that suits me just fine."

"Don't overdo it." Kim looked at him with concern.

"No, no." Rolf laughed. "Working in the fresh air hardly feels like work, it's more like recreation." He reached out a hand to her, and when she gave him hers, he laid his other hand on top. "I'm glad to be able to hand everything over to you, child. This way, I know it's all in good hands."

Kim felt tears welling up inside. It sounded so final. "I'm glad that you're well again," she said, swallowing hard.

Rolf let go of her hands. "Thank you, my dear. Then I'll see you tomorrow."

"See you tomorrow." Kim watched him as he left the office.

She felt as though she'd been thrown into the deep end and now had to swim. During the last several months, she'd taken over Rolf's tasks, but had never thought of it as anything other than a temporary solution. Until Rolf came back. And now he was back, but *that* was the temporary solution. Sometime in the foreseeable future, she was going to be left entirely on her own.

She walked over to the window and looked out at the busy street. It wasn't that she felt overwhelmed by the work, but Rolf hadn't just been her boss – Rolf and Margit were like family to her. And now, her family was moving far, far away.

Out of the corner of her eye, something caught her attention. Softly flowing hair with the auburn glow of ripe chestnuts. Sonja. She was walking, energetically as always, down the street.

Where was she going? Kim frowned. Sonja was dressed unusually for a day at work. Kim had never seen her wear jeans to the office. On Saturdays, yes, when they got together, but never at work. Well, there must be a reason for it. Maybe all her suits were at the cleaners.

She would've liked to open the window and call something out to Sonja, but due to the central air conditioning the windows had no handles. So Kim just followed Sonja with her gaze, as she walked on down the street and disappeared around a corner. Her heart beat a little faster. It still did that, after all these months. *We'll see each other later, at lunch*, she thought.

And she smiled.

At the appointed time, Kim stood outside the cafeteria and waited for Sonja, who was quickly approaching. "You changed your clothes?" she asked amazed, when Sonja had reached her.

Sonja frowned. "Why would I change clothes?"

"You were wearing jeans earlier."

"Jeans?" Sonja looked at her and shook her head. "To work? I don't think so."

"Not in the office, on the street," Kim explained. "When you were on Michelbergring."

Sonja furrowed her brow even more deeply. "On Michelbergring? I wasn't on Michelbergring. I had one meeting after another all morning long. I never left the main office building."

"I was wondering what you were doing over on Michelbergring, on foot, on the street. You never even looked up." Kim laughed. "Wow. It was someone else who looked exactly like you. I could've sworn it was you."

Sonja shook her head, disbelieving. "No, that definitely wasn't me. I've been here all morning, and I haven't even looked up for a second."

"Funny. I thought you were going to walk through my office door any minute."

"Ask Ms. Mayrhofer, if you don't believe me." Sonja seemed out of sorts.

"No, no." Kim laughed once more. "I don't need to ask Jo to believe you. I should probably see an eye doctor instead." They entered the cafeteria together. "Rolf came to see me this morning."

"He's finally back?" Sonja looked at her with interest.

"Yes and no." Kim took a deep breath. "He's back, but only part-time, and not for too long, either."

"What does that mean?"

They made their way over to the table that had become their regular place in recent weeks. The bottle of spring water, that Sonja usually ordered, was already served for her.

"It means that he's taking early retirement." Kim sighed. "And until then, he's only working half days. He and Margit want to buy a house in the Camargue and spend their golden years there."

Sonja nodded. "That's always been their dream."

"Yes, I know, but –"

"It's happening so suddenly."

Kim nodded. "Rolf invited me to visit them there anytime." She looked at Sonja. "Maybe some time, we could go together –"

"The two of us?" Sonja appeared to find that extremely absurd. She stared at Kim.

"Yes, the two of us." Kim sighed. "Don't you think it's getting to be about time?"

"About time? For what?"

"For a vacation?" Kim observed Sonja's face. "The two of us?"

Sonja's expression didn't change. "That won't work. You know that."

The waitress brought Sonja's salad and gave Kim an inquiring look. "The number two special, please," Kim ordered.

With a nod of acknowledgement, the waitress disappeared.

"Vacation, Sonja," Kim said. "Do you even know what that is?"

"Of course," Sonja replied. "As soon as the reorganization is finalized, I'm taking my vacation."

"But you won't spend it with me," Kim surmised.

"Kim, please ..." Sonja waited until the waitress had set Kim's food in front of her and they were alone at the table again. "We weren't going to have this discussion anymore. Until now, that's worked quite well."

"Six months."

"That's a long time." Sonja began to eat. "And I thank you for ..." she looked up, "for being so ... patient."

"Yes." Kim sighed and leaned back in her chair. "I never would've thought that I could be so patient."

"Is your patience exhausted?" Sonja looked at her salad, not at Kim.

"Sometimes I think so. It's so hard for me –" Kim leaned forward and propped her elbows on the table. "It's so hard for me to spend every night without you," she continued quietly.

"I know." Sonja looked up, but gazed over Kim's shoulder. "Me, too."

Kim's heart skipped a beat. Sonja had never said a thing like that before. Kim had often wondered whether Sonja missed her at all when they weren't together. "You, too?"

"Yes." Sonja picked at her salad, and said no more.

"Sonja ..." Kim said. "Vacation. Only a couple of days. Just for us. A couple of days, and a couple of nights. Would that be that so difficult?"

"More difficult than you can imagine," Sonja said tiredly.

Kim gave her a pleading look. "Back then, at the seminar, it worked. I'm not asking for more than that."

"A seminar isn't the same as a vacation."

Further questions were inherently forbidden, because then Kim would have broken her promise. She sighed. "Let's talk about something else."

Sonja looked relieved. "Rolf and Margit in the Camargue ... I imagine that being quite amusing," she said. "The locals will soon have a whole new appreciation of cake in all its varieties."

"They've been there many times." Kim took up the topic. "Their future neighbors probably already know all about Margit's cakes. Who knows whether they'll even sell them a house, under those circumstances?" She laughed.

"Indeed." Sonja grinned. "The whole of Camargue will barricade itself." Her gaze wandered dreamily into the distance. "It must be beautiful there. Rolf always described it so vividly whenever he comes home from there. The landscape, the horses. The photos, too . . . it's really a dream landscape."

"My dream is to be in that landscape with you." Kim watched Sonja's face lost in its reverie. "Like Rolf and Margit. I'd even take on the burden of Margit's cakes for that."

"I couldn't ask such a great sacrifice of you." Sonja's gaze returned to Kim. "Unfortunately, I have another meeting coming up right now, so I can't stretch my lunch hour today. I'll see you in two hours, at the team meeting." She stood up.

"And this evening?" Kim asked.

"I didn't want to overtax your patience." Sonja looked down at her. "But if you want, I'd be glad to."

Kim smiled. "I want."

"Then around the usual time." Sonja smiled likewise. Very gently.

It seemed difficult for her to leave the cafeteria, but with a last glance at Kim, she managed it after all.

They couldn't even give each other an innocent little kiss in public, the way dating or married couples did when they parted after lunch. Kim missed that more and more. During the day, when Sonja and Kim were both working, it was all right. Work offered plenty of distraction, and sometimes they even worked together. But nights . . . nights were an ordeal.

As soon as Sonja left, Kim tried not to think about her anymore, or about the empty bed or her lonely apartment that still held Sonja's scent. She knew she'd see Sonja again the next morning, when they worked together, or at lunch at the latest, but first, she had to get through the night. Alone.

A person could get used to anything, of course, and she had to come to terms with what she couldn't change. Nonetheless the wish grew in her to have Sonja all to herself. At night, too.

And Sundays. Sonja was never available on Sundays; they only ever got together Monday through Saturday. Why Sundays weren't available to her, Sonja didn't say. That's just how it was.

Kim suppressed the thought that Sonja wanted to spend that one day of the week with her husband. All alone. Kim had the days, Sonja's husband had the nights – and Sunday. It was like a ménage à trois.

And yet, it wasn't that at all. Of course, they never talked about Sonja's husband, but it was clear that Sonja didn't spend all that time with him voluntarily. He was still terrorizing Sonja during the day with his phone calls, but Jo was now sheltering her from those fairly well. Sonja had never actually asked her to do that, but Jo did it anyhow. Often Sonja didn't even find out that her husband had called.

"Hey, there, lost in thought? I hear your boss is back." Jo said to Kim. They'd almost collided at the cafeteria door.

Kim was startled. Her thoughts had been miles away as she'd wandered to the exit, and she hadn't seen Jo coming. She smiled, surprised. "News travels fast."

"Always," Jo said. "I had lunch with the little cutie in your department."

Kim frowned.

"Please, don't mention it to Jenny." Jo looked contrite. "It doesn't mean anything. I just don't like to eat alone, and you usually leave me in the lurch because of Mrs. Kantner."

"I'm sorry." Kim felt guilty.

"If only you knew what torture you're abandoning me to," Jo teased. "She's already on her third boyfriend since I've known her. And every time, it's the same. Dick-obsessed, ad nauseum."

Kim chuckled. "I hope it's entertaining, at least."

"It's getting repetitive." Jo sighed. "Don't straight women ever learn?" She looked quickly at Kim. "Oh, excuse me, I didn't mean to –"

"It's fine. I'd say lesbians aren't much better, wouldn't you?"

"When I look at you, yes." Jo shook her head. "Mrs. Kantner has gotten much nicer since you've been with her, I'll admit that, but she's still married." She raised her hands when she saw Kim's expression. "I know, you don't talk about that with her, but that doesn't stop me from thinking my thoughts, does it?" She grinned. "New subject. What are you wearing to the wedding?"

Kim arched her eyebrows. "Why does that matter at all?"

"Well, we were thinking about making a sort of costume party out of it. Otherwise, it's so boring. All the lesbians will show up in the same outfit. Pants, shirts, maybe a suit here and there. So we thought – that is, Jenny's mother thought –"

"You really get along with Jennifer's parents, don't you?" Kim grinned. "You weren't so enthusiastic at first."

"They –" Jo scuffed the floor with her toes. "They're very nice."

"Are your parents coming to the wedding, too?" Kim asked.

"No." A shudder ran through Jo's body. "No, definitely not."

"You've never said anything about them. Or about your siblings or your other relatives."

"No," Jo replied tersely.

"No family at all?" Kim gave her a searching look.

"No, none at all." Jo turned away and walked back into the main office building, strangely stiff.

That behavior was so atypical for Jo that Kim watched her go, astounded. She'd known Jo for quite a while now, and still, she felt like she knew nothing about her. Perhaps she ought to ask Jennifer some time . . .

But that would be unfair. If Jo didn't want to say anything, she'd just have to accept that. Exactly like with Sonja.

She sighed. Everyone else seemed to have their little secrets; only Kim was an open book.

Or at least it seemed that way to her.

"You have no idea how much work a wedding like this is!" Jennifer threw her exhausted self into an armchair. There were only a few of them at the women's café, and they were always hotly contested, but this Sunday afternoon's coffee klatsch hadn't drawn that many women. The weather outside was too nice.

"I thought your *mother* was organizing it," Kim replied, taken aback.

"Yes. Yes, she's organizing everything. The invitations, the whole kit and caboodle, but the problem is, she's organizing me, too." Jennifer brushed the hair off her forehead with the palm of her hand. "I should've known. With my sister's wedding, it was exactly the same."

"Are you that disorganized?"

"Have you ever put together a wedding?" Jennifer asked pointedly in return. "Sorry." She lifted a hand. "I'm a little on edge."

"I can tell." Kim laughed. "Where's Jo?"

"No idea." Jennifer shrugged. "She said she'd be here later. I've been at my parents' since Friday and I just now got back."

"Jo didn't come with you?"

"No, she had to take care of something or other. She couldn't."

Kim didn't say anything, but her facial expression spoke for itself.

Jennifer reacted to Kim's expression with irritation. "We're not attached at the hip. We actually do things separately from time to time."

"That's perfectly fine," Kim said soothingly. "I've just been wondering –" She chewed hesitantly at her lower lip. "I've just been wondering what's up with Jo's family."

Jennifer leaned her head back as if that were the only way she could draw a deep breath, which she also did. "I wonder that myself."

"You don't know, either?" That wouldn't have been too surprising at first, with Jo and Jennifer having other things to do beside talk about their families. But by now they'd been together quite a while, and indeed – they were planning their wedding.

"She doesn't talk about any of it." Jennifer sighed. "I've made cautious attempts to bring up the subject from time to time, but she's always evasive."

"So she has family? Because recently she said . . ." Kim hesitated. "The topic happened to come up, and she claimed not to have any family."

"No, I think she has one. Theoretically. They just never show up." Jennifer shook her head. "I'd love to get to know her parents, just like she's gotten to know mine, but Jo acts as though they were dead, even though I don't think they are." She leaned back in the armchair and tilted her head to one side. "She definitely has a brother."

"She told you that?"

"No, she talked about him in her sleep. *But you're my brother*, she kept mumbling. *But you're my brother*. I woke her up, because she was so obviously in distress, and I asked her about this brother. She said she didn't have a brother, and that I must've imagined it."

"Hmm." Kim considered this. "I would've liked to have a brother; I wouldn't deny having a brother if I really had one."

"Something must've have happened between her and her brother. And it seems like that doesn't just apply to her brother, but to her entire family."

"Maybe the rest of her family really doesn't exist," Kim supposed. "Maybe it's just her and her brother. Orphans."

"Could be," Jennifer said. "But like I said, I don't quite believe that. Sometimes I get the feeling . . . she wants to tell me something about it, but then she doesn't."

"Maybe she just needs more time."

"Yeah." Jennifer sank into reflective silence. "I'm like Doris Day," she said then, suddenly.

"What?" Kim gave her a dumbfounded look. If there was anyone Jennifer didn't remotely resemble, it was Doris Day.

"I want to know before the wedding. That's what I mean. I think people should say everything before getting married. They shouldn't keep any secrets from each other."

"That's reasonable." Kim thought of Sonja. Her secrets didn't exactly seem to be good for their relationship, either. "When people get married, they should know everything about each other. Otherwise they really do wind up in a Doris Day kind of comedy afterwards."

"If it's even a comedy," Jennifer said. "It could be a tragedy, instead."

"That, too." Kim never would've assumed that she'd be thinking such things in connection with Jo. Jo had always seemed so certain, so self-assured, so bold and playful. But perhaps that was more illusion than reality. Perhaps she kept herself laughing to keep from crying. "You don't think there's any point in trying again to talk to her about it?"

"Why won't you talk to *me* for once?"

Jennifer's and Kim's heads shot up simultaneously. They both expected to see Jo, but it wasn't Jo.

"You're avoiding me on purpose, aren't you?" The blonde glaring at Jennifer looked very young, not even eighteen.

"Um ... I ... I haven't had time. I haven't been to the women's café much lately," Jennifer stammered, taken by surprise.

Kim watched the two of them with amusement. If she was interpreting it correctly, this girl was one of Jennifer's virgins, whom she'd initiated into the joys of love. And as young as she looked, that couldn't have been terribly long ago. Perhaps right before Jennifer met Jo. Because after that, she'd lost interest in that sort of thing.

"I wanted to see you again, but you never gave me a chance," the blonde complained.

"I'm sorry." Jennifer had apparently recovered again. "But I really didn't have time –"

"Didn't have time or didn't want to?" the other woman interrupted her. "You have the time for *her*." She was pointing at Kim.

"Kim is an old friend. We've known each other forever," Jennifer defended herself, wondering at the same time why she was bothering. Did this woman have any claims on her whatsoever?

"Do you sleep with her, too?" The woman's blue eyes flashed behind the retort.

"Hold on there ..." Jennifer looked up at her, indignant. "What business is that of yours?"

"What business is it of mine?" The girl gaped at Jennifer as though she'd just hit her. "We slept together!"

Jennifer's brow furrowed. She seemed to be having some trouble recalling that. "Um ... yeah."

"That's all you have to say for yourself?" The young woman was working herself into a frenzy; her face was covered in red splotches.

"I . . ." Jennifer raised her hands in apology. "I am really sorry . . ."

"You're sorry you slept with me?" The blonde looked like she was about to burst into tears.

"No, I –" Jennifer seemed overwhelmed.

"Calm down for a minute." Kim stood up and tried to place an arm around the shoulders of the blonde woman.

The blonde shook her off forcefully. "Don't touch me! I don't need your sympathy!" She raised one arm and pointed her finger at Jennifer. "I want her to remember me. She should say what it meant to her!"

Oh, God, Kim thought.

Jennifer looked pretty confused.

"It meant nothing to you! Nothing!" Now the tears the outraged girl had been suppressing were flowing freely. They coursed down her cheeks in long, wet streams. "You don't even remember my name, do you?"

Jennifer arched her eyebrows apologetically. Apparently, that was true. She did not, in fact, remember.

"Felicity!" the blonde girl sobbed. "You said . . . you said it was the prettiest name in the world!"

"Felicity." Jennifer repeated the name quickly. "Of course, Felicity."

Felicity wailed. "You . . . you . . . you're . . . a monster!"

Despite her protests, Kim grasped Felicity firmly by the shoulders. "Calm down, Felicity," she repeated urgently. "You need to calm down. This won't do you any good."

Felicity suddenly seemed to respond to Kim's voice. "What good is it supposed to do?" she whispered exhausted, still broken by sobs. "Nothing does any good." She tore herself from Kim's grip and ran away, out of the café.

"Phew!" Kim watched her go, then sat down again. "That was intense."

Jennifer took a deep breath. "Wait 'til one of *your* exes shows up."

"Nothing like that has ever happened to me, thank God," Kim said. "But I haven't specialized in virgins quite the way you have."

"That's not true at all. They're attracted to me, somehow," Jennifer defended herself. "But until now, they've always understood that I wasn't intending to get involved. They got that, and they went looking for someone else. I've had no quarrel with any of them." She cast another glance at the spot where Felicity had just been standing. "Definitely nothing like that."

"She's just so young. You were her first. And you know what they say . . ."

"You never forget your first, yeah, yeah." Jennifer shook her head. "It's all baloney. Do you still remember the first woman you slept with?"

"Well, yes, I do. It's been quite a while, true, but still . . ."

"Okay, sure, I remember, too." Jennifer sighed. "But I don't blame her for anything because of it."

"That girl is in love with you," Kim pointed out, "that's probably the difference."

"I was . . . in love, too," Jennifer said. "At least I thought so. At that age, you don't have any idea what that means yet."

"From the height of your hundred years of wisdom, of course it looks different." Kim laughed. "You're exactly the same age I am. And I think we're still pretty young."

"Of course we are, but a couple of years' experience makes a big difference. Don't you think?"

Kim nodded. "She'll calm down, she'll find a girl her own age, and everything will be fine again."

"Let's hope so. Otherwise I really will feel like I'm in a Doris Day movie."

"'The prettiest name in the world?'" Kim chuckled.

"Tcha . . ." Jennifer shrugged, embarrassed. "I'm not exactly the most original when it comes to compliments."

"It doesn't matter that much with virgins." Kim grinned. "They're hearing it all for the first time."

"Maybe that's why it was always so easy with them," Jennifer pondered. "You may be right about that."

"I'm not questioning your powers of seduction." Kim lifted her hands. "That's not how I meant it." She gazed into space. "We were all like that once. That naïve, I mean. We had no experience, we thought the first time would be true love . . . Time puts things in a different perspective."

"Does it?" Jennifer looked at Kim. "I think true love comes when you least expect it. By surprise." She hesitated. "Do you love Sonja? I mean really. Completely and utterly."

Kim smiled. "You and Jo, you love each other completely and utterly. Anyone can notice that. I never would've thought I'd ever see that look in your eyes." She leaned back. "Yes, I love Sonja," she confessed. "But it's difficult. If I could be with her . . . like you and Jo . . ."

"She'd have to be free, for that."

"Free. Yeah." Kim stared into space. "True love comes by surprise, you're right. And it pays no attention to little details like that."

▫▫■▫▫

"Oh-ho, so you're getting promoted again already?" A woman's murmur snaked its way into Kim's ear from behind.

Kim rolled her eyes before turning around with a friendly smile. "Only because Mr. Winkelmann is retiring unexpectedly, due to his medical condition."

"Who knows what caused that condition." This face with the hard eyes didn't fit at all with the murmuring voice, which suggested meekness. Helmke Grotenauer-Albrecht's dyed red hair was carefully coiffed and cemented in place with hairspray.

Kim arched her eyebrows. "What do you mean to imply by that?"

"Oh, everybody knows." Helmke had long been responsible for all the company's gossip and intrigue. "Older man . . . young woman . . . who works under . . . I mean, *for* him."

"I'm warning you, Helmke. If you keep spreading rumors like that, one of them might come back to bite you."

"I have nothing to hide," Helmke said confidently. "No one can do anything to me."

Yes, the skeletons in your closet are all still alive, Kim thought. *Or at least most of them.* "It isn't even definite that I'll be Mr. Winkelmann's replacement," she said.

"Oh, no? I have other information about that." Kim's words bounced off Helmke as if she were a rubber wall.

Where did she get her information? Kim wondered. Helmke seemed to know what was going on with everything and everyone, even though everyone hated her and supposedly, no one told her anything. She had her methods. Whoever hired her hadn't done the company any favors.

"If and when it's definite, it will be officially announced," Kim said calmly. "Until then, nothing's certain."

"Won't you miss him, your ... boss?" Helmke stretched out the pause so long that Kim could've practically sued her for slander.

"He'll be a great loss to the company," Kim replied, composed. "His valuable experience is irreplaceable."

"You seem to possess astounding abilities," Helmke went on. "You'd never know it to look at you. But your bosses can hardly contain their enthusiasm. Even Mrs. Kantner –"

Kim's self-control was about to run out. "Promotions are never decided by just one person. Upper management makes those decisions as a group."

"Based on a recommendation." Helmke needled her some more. "Always based on a recommendation. Which is usually made by your boss. If you have a good relationship with him. You seem to have that with all your bosses."

"I was with the company for years without being promoted once."

"Maybe you hadn't let your true talents show yet," Helmke surmised spitefully.

"Where *your* true talents lie, at least, is clear. Not in your work." Kim wondered why Helmke hadn't been fired long ago, but her special methods probably helped her in that respect.

"How can you possibly claim to have any basis for judging that?" Helmke asked. "We've never worked together."

Thank heaven, Kim thought. "You can request a transfer to my department, if that's so important to you," she remarked with a sweet smile. "When I finally am the department head, I'd be glad to consider it."

She turned around and continued on her way out of the cafeteria, where Helmke had intercepted her. Kim had eaten lunch with Rolf. Rolf had already left for home – since his heart attack, he no longer stretched out the meal by drinking coffee. Kim had remained to drain her coffee cup in peace.

Had she not done that, Helmke probably wouldn't have caught her. But you couldn't have everything.

When she reached the street, she stopped short. Hadn't Sonja said that her off-site appointments today would keep her away until well into the evening? And now she was crossing the street in front of the main building? She was heading away from Kim, who ran to catch up with her.

She tapped Sonja on the shoulder. "Got you!" she said, laughing.

Sonja turned around. "How dare you?" Her eyes flashed at Kim as though she wanted to strike her.

"Sonja." Was she mistaken again, like the last time, from the window? Kim looked at the face, so well-known to her. Sonja. Yes, it was definitely she. She couldn't be mistaken from so close. "What's the matter?"

"I would ask you the same thing, madam." Sonja frowned in her own unique manner. She was wearing a dress that Kim hadn't seen on her before, but she bought new clothes often enough. "What do you want from me?"

"What . . . what's wrong, Sonja? What did I do?"

"You're assaulting me in the middle of the day in the middle of the street. I don't know what you mean by your question, but I won't tolerate your assault." Sonja's voice hissed furiously.

Like back when, Kim thought. *At the very beginning. She was always refusing to tolerate things then, too. Have we gone back to that?* She was irritated and confused. Apologetically, she raised her hands. "If you don't want me to touch you, okay. I'll be good. I was just having lunch with Rolf," she added. "If you'd said you were going to be back sooner . . . I'll see you this evening, then."

Sonja's mood seemed to waver between fury and amusement. The corners of her lips twitched. "Is there something more you want from me?"

"So I *won't* see you?"

Sonja shook her head, turned around, and walked away.

Kim stayed behind, confused, and watched her go. Sonja sometimes went through phases when she couldn't stand having Kim touch her in public, even when it happened completely innocently. But she didn't normally become so cold and distant. She simply moved away, or asked Kim not to touch her.

That evening Kim was at home sitting in an armchair reading when the doorbell rang. She looked up. Hadn't Sonja said she *wasn't* coming? It could hardly be anyone else at this hour.

She stood up and pressed the buzzer to unlock the door. Right away she heard rapid footsteps coming up the stairs. Sonja never walked slowly; it wasn't in her nature.

Sonja's glossy mane appeared above the landing as she ran up the last few steps. She laughed in Kim's direction. "Sorry I'm so late. I'm sure you were expecting me earlier." She brushed a kiss onto Kim's cheek, then breezed past its bewildered owner into the apartment.

"I wasn't expecting you at all, actually." Kim shut the door behind her. "I thought you weren't coming."

"But . . ." Sonja turned to face Kim and frowned. "Didn't we have a date?"

"Yes. This morning, you said we'd see each other, but then at lunchtime, you'd changed your mind."

"Lunchtime?" Sonja looked at Kim as though she doubted her sanity. "Who told you that?"

"You did." Kim's confusion grew. "When we ran into each other outside the cafeteria . . ."

"Outside what cafeteria?" Sonja shook her head. "I wasn't in any cafeteria. I was out and about all day long."

Kim looked more closely at Sonja. She was wearing one of her suits, not the dress from this afternoon. There was something bizarre about the whole thing. When Sonja was supposedly out and about all day, was she, then, really out? Kim was slowly starting to doubt it.

"Would you rather I left, Kim? If I'm bothering you . . ."

"No, you're not bothering me." Kim smiled at Sonja. "I'm glad you came." She didn't dare to touch Sonja, because she was remembering the blazing eyes of this afternoon.

Sonja approached her. "If you don't kiss me immediately, I'm going to smack you." The little crinkles of a grin were forming in the corners of her eyes.

Kim drew Sonja into her arms and sought her lips. They were so soft and sweet; nothing had changed about that. Every time was a new, intoxicating experience.

Sonja pressed up against Kim while, at the same time, taking off her own jacket. "Sometimes I think these off-site meetings are going to kill me," she whispered. "Not a single word from you, not a look . . . I can't touch you . . . I need you a hundred percent of the time, not just ten." While Kim continued kissing her, Sonja pulled down the zipper on her skirt and let it drop. "Come . . ." She pulled Kim down onto the floor with her.

Kim lay on top of her and smiled down at her. "I really ought to think about putting a bed here, right next to the door. As often as we –"

"I don't need a bed." Sonja's lips reached hungrily for Kim's.

Obviously, she's fundamentally changed her mind since this afternoon, Kim thought. Whatever had been up with her then. Sonja's tongue probed Kim's mouth as though she were trying to suck sweet honey from it.

Kim moaned and forgot everything that had happened before this intoxicating moment. "Sonja . . ."

Sonja's fingers caressed Kim's breasts, and even though she was still fully dressed, Kim felt her touch as if on naked skin. She unbuttoned Sonja's blouse and sank into her breasts.

Sonja sighed and writhed beneath her. "Yes," she breathed. "Please . . . come . . ."

By now, Kim knew precisely what Sonja expected of her, and she was expecting the same in return. She slid her fingers into Sonja's panties, opened her steaming center, and brought her quickly to a climax.

Sonja stiffened only briefly and remained where she lay; her hands tugged Kim's shirt out of her pants and wandered first up her back, then down again. Her fingers felt their way under the tight waistband and massaged Kim's bottom. "I love caressing you there," she whispered hoarsely. "You're so solid and strong."

Kim bit her lip. Sonja knew what her touch unleashed in Kim – that's why she did it, after all – but Kim wanted to draw things out a little longer.

Sonja's hands pressed Kim against her, and she thrust one leg upwards. "Come . . ." Her voice was husky. "I want to have you."

"I wish I could get undressed first, for once," Kim squeaked out laboriously. Her hips were moving of their own volition, in answer to Sonja's pressure.

"How bourgeois." Sonja laughed softly. "Doesn't it feel so much more illicit this way?"

It's illicit anyway, Kim thought. *Even when we're naked.* She moaned, because Sonja hadn't let up at all, and shortly thereafter, sank down on top of Sonja, her insides still twitching.

"Was it good?" Sonja caressed her hair. "Isn't it fun to do something forbidden?"

Kim asked herself, not for the first time, whether that was the reason for this affair: that it increased the allure for Sonja to do something forbidden. She was committing adultery, every time. For Kim, there was nothing forbidden about it, but for Sonja, there was.

"At least it's more comfortable here than on our last field trip." Kim grinned. "On those old boards."

"Don't remind me. I think I still have splinters in my butt."

"It was your idea. Not mine."

"I . . ." Sonja looked into Kim's eyes. "I don't know why I have such a hard time controlling myself in your presence. It's never been so hard for me before."

It could have something to do with a certain feeling that you don't want to talk about, Kim thought. *At least, that's what I'd like it to be.* "Shall we get up?" She rose and offered Sonja her hand.

Sonja pulled herself up. Her fingers quickly and deftly opened Kim's shirt and began to caress her breasts again.

"Oh, no!" Kim moaned and leapt to the side. "First, we're going to bed. What do I have one for, anyway?"

"To sleep in. What else?"

Kim dodged away. "We've already tried out every corner of my apartment, and a great many corners in a whole lot of other places, too. After all that research, I have to be honest with you. It's most comfortable in bed." She turned toward the bedroom and went swiftly inside.

Sonja followed her, divesting herself of the last of her clothing. "On Saturday, we'll drive out into the woods. It's quite comfortable on the hood of a car, too."

"On the hood?" Kim stared at her as she undressed. "Outdoors?"

"Well, sure. Haven't you ever done that?"

"Well . . ." Kim shook her head. "No, actually. Generally I prefer indoors."

"It's more exciting outdoors." Sonja was lying down next to Kim in the bed. "To make up for your stuffy bedstead." She cuddled up to Kim and began to caress her.

"Is there any chance that you're writing a book about the most unusual places and positions?" Kim asked. "It seems like you want to try everything."

"I've already tried a few things." Sonja kissed her.

And Kim was certain that Sonja didn't just mean what the two of them had tried together.

"Helmke's really getting on my nerves." Kim sighed, as she and Jo were having lunch together. They were in the regular cafeteria, since Sonja wasn't with them. "I feel like she's following me." She cast a quick glance toward the table where Helmke sat with two other women, to all appearances interested in nothing but her conversation with them.

"I think she's a lesbian," Jo said.

"Helmke?" Kim laughed. "With the hyphenated last name?"

"She's been divorced a long time."

Kim raised her eyebrows.

"Didn't you know that?"

Kim shook her head. "I'm not interested in things like that."

"But the little cutie from your department is. She told me, in between all her other shocking little tidbits."

Kim laughed again, because Jo was grimacing painfully. "But never in her life has Babsie suspected that Helmke could be a lesbian. It would never occur to her. I'll bet she doesn't even know we exist."

"Could be. But that would explain why Helmke keeps following you like that."

"Well, she's not following me like *that*," Kim said.

"Who knows?" Jo grinned. "Maybe this is her version of courtship."

"You're pulling my leg." Kim shook her head disapprovingly.

"No, not at all. I'm serious." Jo leaned forward. "Have you ever looked into her eyes?"

"Hard as glass."

"Because she has such strangely light-colored eyes, that don't go with her hair color at all."

"Which isn't real, anyway," Kim replied, enjoying the pizza, which was a rarity on the cafeteria's menu.

"Of course, that's obvious. I'd like to know what her natural hair color is." Jo dismissed the thought. "No, I wouldn't, nobody cares about that, but her eyes aren't always so hard, that I can tell you. She likes you."

That made Kim feel quite uncomfortable. "Don't say things like that."

"I'm telling you that because I've seen it," Jo insisted. "And I think you ought to know."

"Even if it were true, it wouldn't mean anything to me," Kim said.

"Yeah, she can't hold a candle to Sonja . . . er, to Mrs. Kantner, I admit that, but you know what unrequited love can do to some people."

"To me Helmke is . . . has always been, the embodiment of heterosexuality. In all its negative aspects."

"Some people are just late bloomers," Jo pointed out. "We didn't all seduce our best friend in the sandbox."

"Helmke?" Kim shook her head once more.

"Who knows why her husband divorced her. I hardly believe she would've let him go voluntarily. Not the way she digs her claws into everyone she gets hold of."

Kim cast another cautious glance over toward Helmke's table – something she shouldn't have done, because Helmke happened to be looking directly at her. "Shoot." Kim quickly steered her gaze back to Jo. "Now that you've got me thinking along those lines, she suddenly looks very different," she said quietly, as if Helmke were near enough to hear her.

"Somehow lesbian, right?" Jo grinned. "She's watching you. Every time you go into the other cafeteria with Mrs. Kantner, you should see the look on her face."

Kim's eyes flew open in horror. "Do you think she suspects –?"

"She certainly doesn't know for sure. Otherwise you would've heard from her long ago. But I'd be careful."

"Hopefully she's leaving Sonja alone." Kim was concerned.

"She's not attracted to Mrs. Kantner, she's attracted to you," Jo said. "Just like me."

Kim's eyes opened even wider.

"That came out wrong," Jo said. "But you know I liked you from the start, whereas Mrs. Kantner is just not my type . . . which simplifies working with her enormously. I don't know what I'd do if I found her attractive and had to work with her every day."

Kim sighed. "Remember who you're talking to?"

"Must've been awful when you were still her assistant. Even if it sometimes did have its advantages." Jo winked.

"It had zero advantages. I had to pull it together all day, every day."

"That you managed that . . ." Jo tilted her head to one side. "When you think she's so hot . . ." She raised her hands apologetically. "I didn't want to say it, I'm sorry, but if you could see the looks on some men's faces when they come to her office for a meeting . . ."

Kim swallowed. "I *have* seen them. I know what you mean."

"Aren't you afraid sometimes –" Jo broke off, but Kim had already caught her meaning.

"Sure."

"Are the other ones lesbians, too?" Jo changed the subject so fast that Kim could hardly follow her, but Jo's glance toward Helmke's table enlightened her.

"To listen to you, one would think the entire company is lesbian." Kim laughed softly.

Jo laughed, too. "Except for Babsie. I would never suspect that of her!"

"Maybe she'll be just the one to surprise you." Kim batted her eyelashes mischievously. "You never know. After all, she's awfully eager to have lunch with you."

"She goes to lunch with me because I'm the only one who'll still listen to her." Jo laughed. "Even her straight coworkers have had it up to here."

"I always thought straight women loved to talk about that stuff."

"Yes, when they get to brag about their own conquests, but Babsie doesn't let anyone else get a word in edgewise." Jo shook her head. "That woman can talk nonstop."

"She's one of the best people in the Call Center." Kim nodded. "Might have something to do with it."

"I'm sure. The customers never get to say a word, and that does it for their complaint."

"No, oddly enough, the customers are satisfied. They don't usually complain any further."

"Probably because she's convinced them that they have the best gadget in the world. She claims that about her boyfriend of the moment, too." Jo grinned so broadly at this that Kim choked.

"Does she?"

"Oh, yeah." Jo nodded in feigned seriousness. "And how. In detail."

"That you can stand it . . ." Kim shook her head in disbelief.

"Well, I have ducked out on her a few times," Jo said, "but she always manages to find me again. I have to eat sometime."

"You poor thing."

"I shouldn't have been so friendly with her in the first place. She took it the wrong way."

"Hello, Kim." Helmke walked past Kim and Jo's table with her colleagues and greeted them smugly.

Kim felt the sudden need to hunch her shoulders, as if to guard herself from attack.

"Good afternoon," Jo said with a grin. "*Sweet* Helmke," she then added emphatically,

Helmke stumbled and stared at Jo in disbelief, then, high heels clacking madly, caught up with the others who'd already passed her.

"What was that about?" Kim asked, confused.

"If she knows I'm a lesbian, it doesn't matter. She's welcome to spread that around. Everyone knows. I'm going to . . . intensify our relationship a little over the next few days." Jo chuckled. "That'll divert her attention from you and Mrs. Kantner."

"You don't have to do that, Jo," Kim said, embarrassed. "I can manage alone."

"I doubt it," Jo replied. "I think she's tasted blood. For you, it wouldn't be so bad, but –" She looked at Kim.

"Yeah." Kim sighed. "I don't even know what Sonja thinks about it."

"About coming out? I can tell you that. If she hasn't done it by now, the chances are pretty slim. I mean, if –"

Kim looked to the side. "If our relationship – if you want to call it that – even lasts," she said softly. "Go ahead and say it. The thought has occurred to me before."

"I thought so. Affairs never last. I'm sorry to have to say it so harshly."

"I . . . I just can't imagine it." Kim propped her elbows up on the table and ran a hand through her hair. "Just recently she told me how much she misses me when I'm not with her. When she has appointments on her own, without me. That she wishes she had me for herself one hundred percent."

"But that doesn't mean that you can have *her* one hundred percent, does it?" It was a rhetorical question, and Jo wasn't expecting an answer. "That'll never happen."

"Never." Kim repeated the word as though it were the sword of Damocles, hanging above her, ready to fall at any time. "Why do you say that?" She gave Jo a tortured look.

"Because it's true." Jo sighed. "Do you think I don't know how it is? Why did I ask you if you had a partner before I –" She brushed the back of Kim's hand gently. "Because I know how it is," she added. "I know all too well."

"It didn't last?" Kim looked up at Jo from below.

"It *never* lasts," Jo emphasized. "Never."

A week later Kim was on her way back to Michelbergring after having lunch with Jo because Sonja was busy with off-site meetings. She was hardly surprised to see Sonja in the middle distance, striding energetically toward an unknown destination.

This time, Kim didn't speak to her. She hesitated a moment, looked up at her office window, looked back at Sonja's disappearing figure, and set herself – without really thinking about it or making a conscious decision – in motion.

She followed Sonja to an apartment building. It was just a few stories high, with several small apartments on each floor; clearly relatively modest ones. Sonja pulled a key out of her bag and went inside.

What was Sonja doing there? Was she visiting someone? Someone, indeed, whose key she possessed? Kim's jealousy was aroused.

Jo hadn't mentioned that Sonja was going to be in this neighborhood. Sonja knew that Kim was very friendly with Jo, and therefore Sonja wouldn't tell Jo all her plans. So Sonja had kept this "meeting" secret from Jo. She could leave the office any time and claim to have off-site meetings. She'd done that so often, it wouldn't occur to anyone to question it if, for once, it wasn't true.

Kim approached the building and quickly scanned the names next to the doorbells. The names told her nothing. But then, why should they? Whoever Sonja was here to grace with her presence, she wasn't intending to introduce this person to Kim.

Kim looked up, as if she could somehow determine which apartment Sonja had entered, but that was impossible. It was daytime, so no one needed to turn on a light when entering an apartment, and aside from that – Kim gritted her teeth – aside from that, two people didn't need to turn the lights on to roll around on the floor.

She glanced behind her several times as she walked away from the building, but Sonja didn't reappear. Kim would've preferred to stand outside the door until Sonja emerged, but she couldn't justify that. She had to get back to the office.

A coworker waylaid Kim with a question as soon as she walked back inside the building, and then she found a memo from Rolf on her desk that required some investigation on her part, because a device that a customer had sent in for repairs had gone missing. Thus passed the afternoon, without her really being aware of it.

It was already getting late when the telephone rang.

"You're still there," Sonja said with a gentle laugh. "Of course you are!"

Kim froze at the sound of Sonja's voice. She cleared her throat. "Where are you?"

"Take a wild guess! Or look at your caller ID," Sonja suggested.

Kim glanced at it. Sonja was calling from the phone in her office. "You're still at work?"

"Same as you." Sonja sighed. "I have to cancel our date, much as I regret it. I can't make it today. I have mountains in front of me that I still have to work my way through, and tomorrow morning I have a meeting with upper management, at which time I have to present the new numbers. No chance for anything but work this evening."

This wasn't the first time Sonja had canceled because she had too much to do, but it was the first time Kim had harbored any doubt as to the truth of that assertion. "So you're not coming?"

"Not unless you'll still be up at two in the morning. But I don't think that'd be very sensible."

Kim took a deep breath. "No, it wouldn't be."

"I'm so sorry. But you know how it is."

"Yes, I know … how it is," Kim said with an effort. It was hard for her not to ask Sonja where she'd been that afternoon, but she knew that was a question Sonja would never answer. Why else had she denied knowing Kim out on the street? It was even simpler to deny this afternoon. "Then … then 'til tomorrow. At lunch. Or will you be out and about?"

"No, not tomorrow." Sonja sighed once more. "After the meeting with upper management, I'm going to need something more substantial than just a salad. You can go ahead and order me a stiff drink." She laughed. "Then I'll collapse right there, and they'll have to find themselves a new leader for the reorganization."

"They won't. They'll just bring you right back to life. You're the best," Kim said automatically. She'd said that sort of thing so often before and had meant it, but today, it almost felt like a prerecorded answer.

"You're sweet." It seemed as though Sonja didn't quite want to hang up yet, but she didn't speak. "I'm looking at all the papers here on my desk and thinking about how often we used to do this together," she went on at last.

"I could come over there and help you," Kim offered. "If you like."

"Ah, no." Sonja sighed. "You have a pile of work yourself. I'm taking enough advantage of you on the project. Really, I should come over there and help you. But the way things look, we're both going to be sitting alone in our offices for quite a while yet. Thanks for the offer. That was nice of you."

"Maybe we should combine our offices. Then at least we could sit across from each other while we're working."

"Then we wouldn't do any work," Sonja said with a teasing laugh. "No, it's best the way it is." She made a kissing sound, said, "See you tomorrow," and hung up.

Sonja was sitting in her office. She was there, where she was supposed to be. Kim felt relieved. At least this evening she knew where Sonja was. She opened the next folder and started in on the next customer's complaint. Today, she didn't need to go home early.

When her back started to hurt a while later, she stood up and stretched. The streetlights flickered in through the window. She swung her arms – office gymnastics – and stepped up to the window to look outside.

One glance sufficed. Sonja. She was walking past, below. No, this time, Kim wouldn't be convinced that that wasn't Sonja. It clearly was.

So, she has a lot to do, Kim thought. *But not in the office.* Sonja appeared to be on her way back to that apartment.

▫▫■▫▫

"What do you do after work, when you're not meeting me?" Kim asked the next day, as she and Sonja were having lunch. She simply couldn't hold back any longer. All night, she'd lain awake, imagining Sonja going into that building. "And when you don't go home?"

"Excuse me?" Sonja stared at her, nonplussed.

"Well, yesterday evening, you canceled, but not long after that, you weren't too busy to be over on Michelbergring."

"What are you talking about?" Sonja was still staring in disbelief. "I was in the office all evening. Until well after midnight."

"You weren't in your office at nine."

"Of course I was." Sonja looked angry. "Maybe I got up for a quick cup of coffee or to use the restroom, but other than that, I never left my office."

Kim took a deep breath. "Why are you lying, Sonja? What don't you want to tell me?"

Sonja's eyebrows drew together. "What is this about?" she asked coldly. "What are you trying to imply? Are we going through all that again?" She took a deep breath. "After your last attack of jealousy, I told you I wouldn't put up with another one. Have you forgotten?"

"I'm not implying anything. I saw you with my own eyes," Kim said wearily. "Is there another woman? Or another man? Who lives on Michelbergring? Where did you go?"

"I didn't go anywhere!" Sonja raised her voice. "You've never been satisfied with our affair," she said, controlling herself with an effort. "I know you've never accepted it, even though we never discussed it again. Is this your way of ending it . . . this affair that you never wanted? Do you want to leave me? Then come out and say so. You don't need to make up stories to get rid of me. I'll go on my own." She stood up and left the cafeteria, striding briskly and not looking back.

Kim didn't even try to stop her, although she felt the impulse to; she just watched Sonja go.

Was this it? Had Sonja just been looking for an opportunity to end the affair and place the blame for it on Kim? So that she wouldn't be the guilty party?

So that she could turn her attention to someone else?

Sonja.

Kim had neither seen nor heard from her in the days following their altercation. Radio silence.

Every time the phone rang, Kim looked hopefully at the caller ID, but it was usually a customer or a colleague, sometimes Jo or Jennifer, but never Sonja.

And why should it be? She'd gotten what she wanted. She was rid of Kim.

Kim leaned back in her office chair with a sigh and stretched her arms above her head. Should she call? She remembered all too well what Sonja had said that time in Kim's apartment. That she was giving her one last chance . . . the very last chance.

But the jealousy that had caused such a rift that time had been unfounded . . . rather halfway unfounded, since Sonja was, in truth, sleeping with her husband. This time the facts were clear: Sonja possessed the key to an apartment here on Michelbergring, and she had kept it secret from Kim. Whom the apartment belonged to, why Sonja went there, why she couldn't or wouldn't tell Kim about it, how long this had been going on – Sonja told Kim none of it.

We've only been together half a year, Kim thought. *Has love flown so quickly?* She sighed. *What love was there, really?* Sonja had never claimed to love Kim; she had, in fact, denied it. She'd offered Kim a no-strings-attached affair because that didn't require love; because she, Sonja, couldn't give Kim more than that. She never lied.

Yes! Yes, she has! Kim smacked the table and stood up, looking out the window. Sonja had lied about the apartment. Lying by omission was still lying.

Kim laughed bitterly. What a cliché! The married woman and the lesbian. And in the end the wife went back to her husband – as it always was and always would be. The lesbian had no chance against the socially recognized institution of heterosexual marriage.

When Jennifer and Jo got married, they would be *partnered*, as they called it so nicely, but they were still far from being seen as married in the eyes of the law. Not like they would be if they were a man and a woman.

But would it have done any good if Kim were a man? She frowned. Sonja's problem wasn't with a new marriage, it was with the old one. She kept herself afloat with affairs, because for some reason, she couldn't dissolve her existing marriage. She didn't seem to want a divorce.

She or her husband. But even that was no longer a hindrance. A person could qualify for divorce by living apart for a year – Sonja would simply have to move out.

Had she done that, perhaps? Was the new apartment on Michelbergring *her* new apartment?

But then, why hadn't she said so to Kim? They could've met there, in the new apartment only a few minutes away from Kim's workplace. It would've been easy to spend their lunch breaks there together, to have much more time together. Unobserved.

Kim took a deep breath. Obviously, Sonja hadn't wanted that, or else she would've invited Kim.

Kim leaned her head back and closed her eyes. Whenever she did that, Sonja appeared. Sonja, smiling at her . . . Sonja, glaring at her like she'd done the last time . . . Sonja, lying in bed . . . or on the forest floor . . . naked . . .

Kim opened her eyes again. There was no sense in this. She'd never get away from Sonja this way. And if Sonja didn't want her, didn't want her *anymore*, then that's what she needed to do. She had to forget Sonja.

"Kim?" Rolf Winkelmann stood in the doorway. "Did you work on that Mr. Kurowski's complaint? I don't have it in my files."

Kim tried to pull herself together and stop thinking about Sonja. "No . . ." She cleared her throat. "Marietta took care of that, I believe."

"What's going on?" Rolf looked at her thoughtfully. "Is something bothering you? The last couple of days you've barely been approachable." He came toward her. "It doesn't have anything to do with me, does it? I'm fine; you don't have to worry about me. I'm already looking forward to the Camargue." He smiled confidently at Kim.

"No, it –" Kim swallowed. "It has nothing to do with you. I'll ask Marietta –"

She wanted to step past Rolf, but he held her back. "Don't try to kid me, Kimmie. When you started here, you were acting this same way, but back then, I didn't know you so well. I thought maybe you were having difficulty with your orientation, because this was so completely different from what you had done before. But your orientation is long over. Are you afraid of the responsibility, when I'm gone? I can't imagine that. But I know the date's getting closer, and then, of course –"

"It really has nothing to do with you, Rolf." Kim looked him directly in the eye. "I can see that you're doing well, and I know things won't change all that much when you're gone – except, of course, that I'll miss you."

"Your income will go up." Rolf grinned. "Considerably. If you had a family, I'd suggest that you might want to start thinking about buying a house."

Kim sighed. "Yes, if I had a family . . ."

"Is that what's bothering you? That you don't? You can come visit Margit and me anytime, you know that. You can spend your whole vacation with us, if you want; you can even bring people with you. We'll be happy for any company we get, since we're going to be living way off the beaten track."

"You found a house?" Kim looked at him curiously.

"Yes, I think so." Rolf smiled, as though he could see the house and the gorgeous Camargue landscape before him now. "It's half ruined, but that suits me just fine. Then I'll at least have something to do. And Margit will plant a garden, grow fruits and vegetables.

Maybe we can even keep a few animals. It'll be an honest-to-goodness farm!" He laughed. "Geese, ducks, chickens – you name it."

"Lovely." Kim couldn't concentrate on Rolf's narrative; once again, Sonja's face had appeared before her. Sonja's lips, shaped for a kiss at first, then muttering angry words. It ran like an infinite loop in her head.

"What happened between you and Sonja?"

Kim was startled. "What ... why do you think something happened?" She returned to her chair and sat there, acting as though she needed to sort through the files on her desk.

"You two used to eat together all the time, you were busy with her project half the week – but now, all of a sudden, that's stopped. Did you have an argument? What's going on with you?"

"Oh, nothing ... nothing important," Kim said quickly. "A difference of opinion on the project. She wants to continue without me."

"Hm." Rolf tipped his head to one side. "Sonja said the same thing."

Kim's head shot up; she gaped at Rolf. "You asked her?"

"I ran into her recently. Otherwise I hardly see her anymore. She's always out and about. But when I saw her, it seemed to me that her mood mirrored yours. You two seemed similar that way."

"Did we?" Kim asked sarcastically. She couldn't imagine that Sonja wasn't doing well; she was entirely free from worries – in contrast to Kim.

"Oh, yes. You always have. When she was doing well, you were, too. When you were doing poorly, she didn't look very happy, either. I know things aren't entirely smooth in her marriage, and at first, I attributed it to that, but Sonja's marriage could hardly have anything to do with you. So it has to be something between the two of you."

No, I definitely don't have anything to do with her marriage, Kim thought and almost sighed. *It's the same, with or without me.* "It's nothing. You're imagining things. The project is coming to an end, and she simply doesn't need me anymore, that's all."

"That isn't all," Rolf said, "but I'll respect the fact that you don't want to talk about it. Nor does Sonja, obviously. At least you agree on that."

"Seems that way." Kim examined her desk thoroughly.

"Whatever goes on with you women ... We men will never understand. One day, best friends; the next, you hardly say a word to each other. Doesn't that get a little tiring?"

"Yes, it does." Kim almost had to laugh. "You're right, it's nonsense, behaving this way. I'll talk to Sonja."

"Do that. I think that would be better." Rolf raised a hand in mock salute and left the office, to ask Marietta about the complaint he was looking for.

Kim became even more pensive than before.

Yes, if only it had been just that: a fight between friends.

But it wasn't.

Kim yawned and looked at the clock. Good grief, it had gotten late again. Why didn't she just set up a bed in her office?

She stood and massaged her lower back. Spending practically the whole day sitting wasn't healthy. Her spine creaked and groaned like an old woman's. She ought to get more exercise.

But when? She simply was too busy with work. How was she supposed to squeeze in the time for a trip to the gym or an hour's jog in the woods?

Woods ... crap. Yes, it had been nice in the woods ... with Sonja. Saturday was just around the corner, and it had been a Saturday when they – no, that was over. She ought not to think about it. Sonja hadn't called again, and despite what Kim had promised Rolf, she hadn't spoken to Sonja, either. When she had lunch with Jo, they went to the regular cafeteria. Kim knew how punctually Sonja's stomach announced itself, so she always made sure they'd go to lunch after Sonja would be finished with hers. So it was guaranteed that their paths would never cross.

It was over and done. Sonja didn't call, and that was a clear sign that she was making good on her threat. If she yearned for Kim, the way Kim yearned for her, she only had to pick up her telephone to tell her.

Kim's eyebrows arched of their own accord. She yearned for Sonja, and she wasn't picking up the phone either. Therefore Sonja's behavior could hardly be considered as unambiguous as she was making it out to be.

But Sonja was the one who had walked out. She made the decision, not Kim. So only she could revoke the decision.

Kim gathered up her things and shut down her PC. Enough for today. Truly, it was enough.

A few minutes later, she rode the elevator down to the ground floor. She had parked outdoors, because she'd made a quick trip to the shopping center after lunch. She left the office so late in the evenings that, even with the later hours they kept these days, all the stores were already closed.

Key in hand, she approached her car. It was quite calm at that hour. Although the Ring was heavily trafficked during the day, that changed abruptly after ten o'clock at night. As if they'd rolled up the sidewalks.

She looked around to make sure that no driver had blundered onto the uninhabited street at just the right time to run into her door when she opened it.

Sonja! Damn! She was walking along the opposite side of the street, a good distance away.

Kim hesitated for only a second, then took off running. Mindful of Sonja's reaction the last time Kim had touched her from behind, she ran around Sonja and stopped in front of her.

Sonja stopped short and glared at her.

"I'm sorry, Sonja," Kim said, abashed. She sought Sonja's eyes, which bore a very strange expression. "I didn't want this. It was wrong of me." Again, she attempted to interpret the expression in Sonja's eyes, to read them, but she couldn't. She took a deep breath. "Please, forgive me." She looked around once more. "But what are you doing here? Please, just tell me. I won't hold it against you." She gave Sonja a look that pleaded for forgiveness.

Sonja just kept looking at her as though she didn't recognize her. "I live here, if you must know," she replied sharply. "And now I'm calling the police. Honestly . . . I never would've thought I'd be the victim of a stalker. I thought that only happened to other people, celebrities and whatnot, not a little supermarket manager like me."

"Supermarket manager?" Kim stared at her, astonished. "Since when –? Sonja . . ."

"Sandra," the other woman snapped. "I really have no experience with stalkers." She laughed softly. "Now I'm even telling you my name." She examined Kim's face. "But I'm sure you already knew it."

"Sandra?" Gradually Kim was getting the feeling that perhaps she'd come across a multiple personality in Sonja. "Why . . . Sandra? Sonja . . ."

"Whoever this Sonja is, who you seem to be confusing me with, it's not me." She swept past Kim and went on.

After a moment of shock Kim caught up to her and walked beside her. "Sonja . . . you . . . you live here? Since when? Did you move out of your house?"

"Would you mind very much leaving me alone already? How long I've lived here is none of your business whatsoever." She quickened her steps.

"No, but –" Kim was extremely confused. "I thought your husband –"

"My husband?" She stopped and looked at Kim as though Kim had just escaped from a psychiatric ward. "Wherever you're getting your information, it doesn't seem to be a very reliable source. I don't have a husband."

"You don't . . . have a husband?" Kim stammered. "You're divorced?"

"Divorced?" The woman didn't quite seem to know whether she should laugh or be furious. A look of amusement overtook her face. "I don't need to bother. I've never been married." She shook her head and continued on her way.

"Never . . . married?" Kim was talking to herself, since Sonja was long gone. Once again, Kim had to run to catch up with her. "Sonja . . . I . . . I don't understand."

"It certainly seems that way. You don't understand a number of things. But that has nothing to do with me. Perhaps you should see a doctor."

"Sonja . . ."

"Damn it, stop calling me Sonja! My name is Sandra; it has been since I was born. Go look somewhere else for your Sonja." She stopped, reached inside her jacket pocket, and pulled out a key. "If you try anything else, I'll scratch up your face," she threatened, holding up the key. "I learned that in self-defense class." She considered Kim for a moment. "Although I did think I'd be using it against a man, if ever I had to do it." She let the key fall. "You're obviously confused. You should go home and get a good night's sleep." Her voice no longer sounded threatening, but soothing. "Tomorrow, I'm sure everything will look different."

Kim stared at Sonja and simply could not believe that she would be full of such denials. "Sonja, I . . . I know I hurt you, because I implied that you . . . but why didn't you just tell me that you live here now?"

"Why should I?" She laughed dryly. "Was I supposed to put a notice in the paper, or what? The people who have any business knowing about it know that I live here. It could hardly interest anyone else."

"It would've interested me a great deal," Kim said softly, "but it's clear why you didn't tell me. I just didn't want to believe it. I –" An expression of hurt was in her eyes. "I love you, Sonja, and that will never change. But from now on, I won't bother you anymore. I finally understand." Shoulders hanging, she walked past her, back down the street.

She'd walked no more than a few steps when a voice stopped her. "What . . . what's your name?"

Kim turned around. "Please, Sonja, don't do this to me. You know my name. Don't act like you don't know me. We've been sleeping together long enough."

The woman raised her eyebrows. "Sleeping together?"

Kim let out a hollow sound. "You're making fun of me. But maybe six months isn't long enough for you to remember. Maybe you can forget that from one day to the next. I can't. I never will. Please, stop treating me like a moron." She sighed. "But really, you're right. Really, I am one. I thought the two of us . . . Only a moron could think that."

"Assume I suffer from Alzheimer's, and tell me your name, please."

"You can't be serious. Alzheimer's?" Concern crept into Kim's thoughts. Was that the solution to this puzzle? Sonja was ill? And she didn't want Kim to know? "Kim," she said. "My name is Kim."

"Kim. Okay." She seemed to consider something. "Well, I don't suffer from Alzheimer's – at least, I don't know about it if I do –" She laughed softly. "Which, of course, could itself be a symptom of the disease." She became serious again. "I don't have Alzheimer's, and you – I'll assume – don't either. And if I accept the premise that you're not a stalker," she looked closely at Kim and shook her head, as if she couldn't believe that, "then you really think that I'm this Sonja."

Kim sighed. "Sonja, please . . . you don't need to keep up the act. I won't follow you anymore, and I avoid you at work anyway. I don't know whether you've noticed that."

"If I were Sonja, I probably would have noticed. If you two have slept together . . ."

Kim made an agonized face. "I'll go, Sonja. I know you have the right to treat me the way you're doing now, but I . . . I can't take it anymore. You take care of yourself." She turned around shuffled back down the street, almost like an old woman.

"Kim!" The voice that she knew as Sonja's stopped her again, and this time, the woman came after her. "Wait. I'd like to show you something." She pulled a wallet out of a small briefcase that Kim had never seen her with before. "Look at this." She held her driver's license under Kim's nose.

They were standing right under a streetlight, so Kim could read it perfectly well. "Sandra Kruschewski? Then why have you always gone by Sonja Kantner?"

Sandra rolled her eyes. "I haven't. Don't you get it? My name is Sandra Kruschewski. It always has been. This Sonja Kantner must just look really freaking similar to me."

"But . . . Sonja . . ."

"Please . . ."

"Okay, Sandra . . ." Kim no longer knew what to say. She lifted her gaze and explored Sonja's – no, Sandra's – face, searching for familiar things and differences. There were many familiar things, and she saw no differences. "I . . . I can hardly believe it. You look so much like her. As if you were twins. Is it really not you?" She frowned.

"I am me. And I don't have a twin. I'm an only child."

"I've read about people who are supposed to be as alike as twins, even though they're not related. But I never believed it."

"Now you can." Sandra laughed. Then she tilted her head to one side – exactly the way Sonja had done when she wanted to tease Kim. "She really looks like me, your Sonja?"

Kim raised her eyebrows and sighed. "She's not my Sonja. Not anymore."

"I'm sorry. And I'm also sorry that I took you for a stalker, but –"

Kim laughed dryly. "What else were you supposed to think? If you're not Sonja –" Again, she looked closely at the face that seemed so familiar to her. Wouldn't there have to be some difference? Something that differentiated Sandra from Sonja? Or was this in fact Sonja, after all? That nagging thought wouldn't leave.

"I can see you still don't believe me," Sandra said. "Maybe you ought to introduce me to this Sonja some time. When you see the two of us side by side, you'll probably realize that we don't look all that much alike, after all."

Sonja would never have made that suggestion. "You really aren't Sonja," Kim said, astonished.

"I'm really quite curious now. There's a woman walking around, right around here, who looks exactly like me? Or almost exactly?"

"Exactly. Precisely."

"That can't be." Sandra shook her head. "You must be mistaken. I just can't imagine –" She broke off and observed Kim now, almost as intensively as Kim had observed her before. "Or is this just some new kind of come-on?"

"Come-on?" Kim looked at her, confused.

"Well, you know, claiming that you had a relationship with a woman who looks exactly like me, that you even love her – that would shorten the preliminaries, wouldn't it?"

"The preliminaries?" Kim still didn't comprehend.

"Were you trying to come on to me?" Sandra arched her eyebrows.

"Um ... no ... actually ... I thought you were Sonja." Kim felt like she was on a seesaw. She swung back and forth between heaven and earth and didn't know where she belonged.

"Really." Sandra looked at her, eyebrows still raised, as if she were slowly beginning to doubt that Sonja actually existed.

"Were you serious when you suggested meeting Sonja?" Kim asked. "Then you can let your own eyes convince you how similar you look, and that I'm telling the truth."

Sandra pursed her lips and thought about it. Then she smiled. "That does sound intriguing, for some reason. Your whole life, you think you're unique, and then suddenly, you aren't."

"I'm sure you are unique." Kim gave Sandra an embarrassed look. "I didn't mean to say that . . . I'm sorry I've pestered you so much."

"That's all right," Sandra said. "Now that you've made me curious, where can I meet this Sonja? Although –" she smiled crookedly, "maybe you should warn her first, if we really look as similar as you say. I know what's waiting for me, but she . . ."

"Yes." Kim gazed thoughtfully into space. "I'll have to tell her in advance."

"Otherwise she'll pass out when I come in the door!" Sandra laughed.

Kim suddenly had to laugh, too. "Actually, I doubt that. She's used to worse."

"Oh?" Sandra shook her head. "And here, I was thinking, *sure, why not?* That sort of resemblance is possible. But now it's seeming so implausible to me again. I've never met anyone who looks remotely like me before."

"Neither has Sonja, I'm sure. I can't promise that she'll be interested, but I'll ask her."

"I think she'll be interested," Sandra said. "Or are you such . . . enemies?"

Kim flinched. "Enemies?"

"Sounds like a fairly dramatic story, the way you've acted toward me."

"Dramatic. Well . . ." Kim shrugged. "Not really. It was just a very normal affair, I assume. For Sonja, at least."

"That sounds even more dramatic." Sandra suddenly raised a hand in front of her mouth and yawned. "If it weren't the middle of the night, I would ask you in for a cup of coffee, but I'm awfully tired. I really have to go to bed."

Kim looked at her watch. "Oh, God, me, too. It's even later than I thought." She looked at Sandra and saw Sonja. "Sleep well," she said – more tenderly than she would have to a stranger. She started to turn away.

"About the meeting . . ." Sandra held her back. "Phone number?"

"Oh . . . yeah." Kim looked at her. "Do you have something to write with?"

"Sure." Sandra reached into her briefcase. "Here." She held out a notebook to Kim. "Write your number in there. I'll call you as soon as I have time."

Kim wrote down her number and gave the notebook back to Sandra. If she actually was Sonja, she wouldn't call. Even now, Kim still couldn't quite think straight.

"I'm so curious, it'll probably be sooner rather than later." Sandra laughed. "You'd better let Sonja know soon."

Kim nodded. "Good night. And again: I apologize."

"Don't worry about it. At least the mystery has been cleared up. Being accosted by a strange woman over and over was getting on my nerves . . . and being called by someone else's name, no less."

Kim grimaced with embarrassment. "It won't happen again."

"You could call Sonja Sandra a few times, to balance things out." Sandra raised a hand in farewell. "Good night." She turned around and walked toward the building into which Kim had seen her vanish once before.

Kim watched her go, feeling like she'd just encountered a mirage.

Once Sandra had disappeared completely inside the house, Kim turned around and walked back to her car.

▫ ▫ ▫ ▫ ▫

It wasn't a night for sleeping. Kim tossed and turned, and as usual, Sonja's face appeared before her, but she no longer knew whether it was really Sonja.

Sonja . . . Sandra . . . how could it be? Or was it actually one and the same person, Sonja, having a bit of fun by leading Kim on?

But why would she do that? Kim had made a mistake yet again, and Sonja had enforced its consequences, as promised. Sonja wanted no more contact with Kim, private or professional. But if Sandra was Sonja, Kim hadn't made a mistake at all, and Sonja had had no reason to –

After a while Kim's head was buzzing, almost roaring. The images of Sandra's and Sonja's faces overlapped, and there was definitely no difference. Kim had studied Sonja's face like a beloved landscape – when she had slept with her, when they had worked together; every smile, every twitch of the lips, every eyebrow hair was well known to her. It must be Sonja!

She sat up in bed. One thing, at least, differentiated Sandra from Sonja: Sandra was much more relaxed. At the beginning, Sonja had come across to Kim as relaxed; she'd laughed a lot and never regarded problems as unsolvable, but since Kim and Sonja had gotten closer, that had no longer been the case.

At first, the problem was with a certain night in a hotel room, then Kim's transfer, and then her husband's phone calls that burdened Sonja. Presumably not just his calls. After all, she went home to him in the evenings . . .

Kim lay down again and crossed her arms over her head. Was "Sandra" Sonja's evasive maneuver? The chance to be the way she really wanted to again, but couldn't? Had she managed to create in her own small apartment a refuge into which she could retreat, where neither Kim nor her husband could disturb her, where she could be completely herself and live only for herself?

Kim's mood darkened considerably. Sonja had never wanted to spend the night with her, ostensibly because she had to go home to her husband, for whatever reason, but she was actually spending the night in her own apartment. So she didn't have to go home to her husband, at least not every night. She had lied to Kim.

And if she'd lied to her about this, why not about other things as well? Had anything she said ever been true? Did she spend her Sundays there, too . . . the Sundays that were never available for a date with Kim?

All of Kim's thoughts ran in circles. Had her entire relationship with Sonja – no, *her affair*, Kim had only imagined the relationship – been one big lie? Did Sonja have that apartment all along? If it weren't for the phone calls that Jo could confirm, Kim would even have begun to doubt that Sonja had a husband at all. She was familiar with Sonja's personnel file, but who would check up on something like that?

Sandra and Sonja were the same person – everything she knew led to that conclusion. It couldn't be otherwise.

She rolled onto her side and stared out the window into the clear, starry night. The stars twinkled like little diamonds on a sheet of black velvet. Each a tiny jewel in the vastness of the universe.

Many of them had burned out long ago, but the light had been traveling so long that they still shone in the sky. And so this starry sky was nothing but a lie. You couldn't tell which of the stars still existed and which didn't.

The whole world was a lie, so what difference did a little lie like a name change make? Whether Sonja called herself Sonja or Sandra, whether she lived in a suburb or right here on the Michelbergring, whether she slept with her husband or with Kim or with anyone else – none of that had the slightest significance in the grand scheme of things.

When the star called the sun had long been extinguished, it would still shine on the other end of the galaxy, and no one would know how old those rays were.

Kim sighed deeply. Seldom had she ever felt such despair, such hopelessness. Sonja was the great love of her life, she knew that, but if Kim had been Sonja's great love, then Sonja wouldn't have behaved as she did. She would have told Kim the truth, about the apartment, about "Sandra," about everything.

Kim was only one chapter in her book – one of many. No more meaningful than all the other chapters there had been already . . . all the affairs she obviously needed to maintain her mental equilibrium.

And she apparently needed "Sandra", too. When she was "Sandra", she didn't have to accept responsibility for what she had done as Sonja. "Sandra" was a free woman, unmarried, with her own small apartment and no obligations.

Some people needed that, a sort of time out from reality, although Kim would never have guessed that Sonja was among them. She appeared to be one of the most realistic people Kim knew. But perhaps that was precisely the problem: As Sonja, she didn't allow herself to be emotional or unrealistic, but inside, she needed to. That's why she'd created "Sandra," who opened up all the possibilities that Sonja forbade herself.

What other passions was she addicted to? Gradually, Kim was starting to feel like she didn't know Sonja at all, like she'd never known her, not even superficially. The woman now taking shape in front of Kim's eyes bore no resemblance to the woman Kim had fallen in love with; she was a completely different person.

Kim began to worry. How long had Sonja been playing this game? Did she even know what she was doing anymore? Was she in control of it, or did the game have control over her? Could she let "Sandra" appear when she wanted to, or did "Sandra" simply come out at will – like Dr. Jekyll and Mr. Hyde?

A shudder ran through Kim's body. This was taking on new dimensions ...

But maybe she was just spinning herself into an unnecessary frenzy. Certainly, "Sandra" existed, there was no doubt about that, but precisely what her function was, only Sonja could explain.

Kim would have to call her tomorrow.

The telephone rang just as Kim was discussing the Kurowski case with Marietta. Absently, she reached around for it, halfway behind her back, and answered.

"Have you talked to Sonja yet?" Sonja's voice asked.

Kim was confused for a moment. She turned her gaze away from Marietta, toward the small screen on the telephone. A cell phone number – not Sonja's. "Sandra?"

"Yes, sorry, I didn't even say who it was. I'm so curious."

"Uh . . . no, I haven't spoken with . . . her" – Kim had almost said *you* – "yet. I've been too busy."

"Too bad," Sandra – or Sonja said. "I'm free around noon today. We could meet for lunch."

Kim considered. "I could call her right now. Will you hold on?" She'd see what happened when she dialed Sonja's number. Was she sitting in her office with the cell phone, and would she talk with Kim on both lines?

"You have to hang up with me, first."

"I can put you on hold and call on another line."

"I think I'd rather just call back in half an hour," Sandra said. "I just need to know, because otherwise, I'm going to eat with a colleague."

Sonja – with a colleague? Who would that be? Kim shook her head. "All right. Go ahead and call me back. Or I'll call you back on your cell. I have the number now."

"That would be fine. It might even be better. Bye, talk to you later." Sandra hung up.

Kim looked at Marietta as if she could provide an answer to all the questions swirling around in her head. "Kurowski is straightened out?" she asked. "You can authorize the account credit."

"Okay." Marietta nodded and disappeared.

Kim hesitated for a few seconds – the receiver was still in her hand – then pressed the telephone's cradle and waited for a dial tone. She dialed Sonja's number.

"Mrs. Kantner's office. Jo Mayrhofer speaking," Jo answered.

Kim hesitated. "Is Sonja there?"

"Not at the moment. But she'll be right back."

Kim was silent.

"May I take a message?" Jo asked. "Would you like her to call you back?"

"No, no." Kim answered automatically. Sonja probably wouldn't call her back anyway, even if she asked her to. "It's nothing important, I just wanted to –"

Sonja wasn't in her office. She'd sought out a corner where Jo couldn't hear her, in order to call Kim from the cell phone and pose as Sandra.

"Here she comes. Wait, I'll put you through."

The line crackled, then Sonja answered. "What do you want?"

As Sandra, her voice had sounded significantly gentler; clearly, she was differentiating the two.

"I . . . well . . . I don't know . . . Are you an only child?" Kim blurted out.

"Excuse me?" It sounded like Sonja was pulling out her chair to sit down.

"I mean, do you have a sister who looks a lot like you?"

"Are you feeling all right?" Sonja sounded extremely displeased. "Where did you come up with that idea?"

"I . . . hmm . . . do you have time for lunch with me? Then I could explain."

"I have neither the time nor the interest in eating lunch with you," Sonja said. "I thought I made that perfectly clear. Those days are over."

"Yes, fine . . . but . . . but . . . I'd like to introduce you to someone." Kim grinned. Sooner or later, Sonja would have to come out of her mouse hole. After all, she knew why Kim was calling. But of course, she couldn't admit it.

"Professionally?"

"No, more . . . personally."

"Your new girlfriend? I'll pass," Sonja said. "I don't need to put myself through that. And I'm surprised you're even suggesting it. Apparently I misjudged you. If this is a purely personal call, I'm going to hang up now."

"No, Sonja!" Kim raised her voice. "Don't hang up. It's nothing like that, I assure you."

"Then you were just looking for some pretext to call me? You should've chosen something professional instead. I won't discuss personal things with you. I gave you one last chance, and you –" Kim clearly heard Sonja take a deep breath. "That was it for me," she went on. "I'm not going to debate it."

"Do you know someone called Sandra?" Kim asked. She would have to react to that.

"Not that I know of." Sonja answered so quickly, it seemed to Kim that she'd just been waiting for the question.

"She's the one I'd like to introduce you to," Kim went on. "She looks so much like you, you could be twins." Well … well …? Where was the reaction?

"Twins?" Sonja seemed genuinely surprised.

"Yes, one would assume you were," Kim said. "But if you don't have a sister –"

"I have a sister. But she doesn't look anything like me."

"Ah. Then this isn't she."

"Are you pulling my leg?" Sonja's voice was sharp. "What's all this about? If you were hoping to beg my forgiveness: it's too late. I'm not backing down. What I said before stands. You of all people ought to know that. We've worked together long enough. I made one single exception, but it wasn't worth it, as it turned out and I will never do that again. I should've known, Kim. Jealousy is jealousy; no one can just set that aside, no matter what promises they make."

"I know." Kim felt like a scolded child. Sonja was right. "Sonja …" She swallowed. "Don't you think we ought to talk once more? I agree that I made a mistake. And I promise you, when you meet Sandra, everything will change."

Sonja would have to admit that Kim hadn't really made a mistake, she'd just misinterpreted the facts – at least, she hoped so – but what else could she have done?

Sonja laughed dryly. "You're really pulling out all the stops!" Again, Kim heard her take a deep breath. "This woman you claim looks so much like me doesn't exist. You made her up to have an excuse to call me. But you're not catching me in that trap. I'm not falling for it. And now I need you to leave me alone!"

Although Kim didn't hear the crash, she was sure that Sonja's telephone receiver had been severely mistreated in the course of hanging up.

She hung up her receiver much more gently. If she called "Sandra" right back, she could ask Jo later whether Sonja had picked up. But no, that was silly. What good would it do? If Sonja didn't want to admit that she was Sandra, she could always come up with an explanation.

She scrolled through her caller ID for Sandra's number and

pressed the button to call her back. *We'll just see what happens now.*

It rang a couple of times before Sandra picked up. "Kruschewski?"

She really had this down pat.

"Lunch at twelve o'clock?" Kim asked.

"You asked Sonja?" Sandra seemed pleased.

"Yes, I did." That, at least, wasn't a lie, but Sandra knew perfectly well that she'd refused. Why didn't she say anything? If Sandra came and Sonja didn't, the fraud would be exposed. Did she want to let it come down to that? What did she hope to achieve by that?

"Great," Sandra said. "Where should we meet?"

"Why not right in front of the cafeteria? Do you know where that is?"

Sandra claimed not to know, so Kim explained it to her as though she believed her. "Twelve o'clock sharp," Kim said. "That's important."

"Oh, no problem." Sandra laughed. "I always get hungry at that time."

Yeah, I know, Kim thought. Aloud, she said, "Then I'll see you in front of the entrance at noon."

"See you then." Sandra hung up.

Kim shook her head. Sonja really wanted to bring matters to a head. As Sonja, she refused, but as Sandra, she agreed? What was the point of that?

It wasn't quite twelve o'clock yet when Kim arrived outside the cafeteria. Neither Sonja nor Sandra – ha . . . neither! – was there. Fine, maybe Sonja wouldn't come, either as Sandra or as Sonja. She could simply sidestep the problem.

Or she could choose one of the two, then leave, and come back as the other. Everyone knew that slapstick comedy routine. Kim was curious about how Sonja would play it.

"Am I on time?"

Sonja came as Sandra? Kim hadn't actually expected that. She looked at the smiling face that wasn't supposed to be Sonja's.

"Absolutely," Kim answered. "I expected you to be on time, you've always been –" No, she couldn't say that. She knew nothing about Sandra's punctuality, only Sonja's.

Sandra looked around. "Sonja isn't here yet?"

How long was she going to keep playing this game? Kim shook her head. She knew full well that an encounter was impossible.

"Then we'll just wait." Sandra laughed. "Although my stomach is growling already! I open the supermarket every day at seven, but I have to be there by six, or sometimes even earlier, for deliveries."

"*Do* you." Kim gave her a dubious look. Sonja was constructing an entire, around-the-clock life for Sandra. Why? Kim was about to open her mouth to say something when Sandra suddenly grinned.

"Well, how about that." She was looking over Kim's shoulder. "She doesn't look quite *exactly* like me, though. I think you were exaggerating."

Kim stared at her. She couldn't be serious. Kim stood with her back to the main office building, and if she were to turn around now . . . Slowly, she turned her head, then her shoulder, so as not to lose Sandra out of the corner of her eye. Her mouth hung open. Sonja. She was wearing a business suit. Kim turned her head back. Sandra wore jeans.

Kim turned far enough to get Sonja, who was approaching, in the same view as Sandra, who stood next to her. This couldn't be true!

Sonja was looking down at the ground; she hadn't noticed Kim and Sandra yet, but the moment she looked up –

She did so, took two more hesitant steps, paused, and stood still.

Kim looked at her, pointed at Sandra, and shrugged.

Sonja shook herself and walked onward. The closer she came, the more astonished Kim felt to look at her. Again and again, she glanced back at Sandra, then turned her gaze back again, and she couldn't shut her mouth.

Sonja had reached them. It seemed like she was going to walk past Kim and Sandra, but Sandra spoke to her, smiling: "Pleased to meet you, Sonja."

Sonja didn't look at Sandra, though, but at Kim. "So, you weren't lying. How long did you search to dig her up?"

Kim gasped. This was too much at once. “I . . . I . . .”

“It was more of a coincidence,” Sandra answered in Kim’s place. She seemed mildly confused. “I only recently moved to the area.”

Sonja shifted her attention and looked at Sandra. “Who are you?” Her eyebrows knit reluctantly together.

“Sandra Kruschewski.” Sandra offered her hand. “And I’m just as surprised as you are, Sonja . . .” She laughed. “I’m sorry, but since Kim has mentioned you so often and we look so much alike, do you mind being on a first-name basis?”

Sonja ignored Sandra’s hand for several seconds. “Kruschewski?” Her brow furrowed in disbelief.

Sandra withdrew her hand. “Yes, that’s my name.”

“Coincidences happen.” Sonja looked at Kim once more. “Or is this not a coincidence at all?”

“I haven’t the faintest idea what you’re trying to insinuate.” Kim still hadn’t gotten used to the sight. Sonja, doubled. Sure, they were dressed differently, and that decreased the resemblance somewhat, but otherwise –

“You’re familiar with my personnel file,” Sonja said. “Did you base this little comedy on that?” She let out a dismissive sound. “It’s quite a nasty joke, I must say. I never would’ve thought you capable of this much viciousness.” She gave Kim a furious glare. “But apparently, I’ve been mistaken about you from the very beginning.”

“Whoa, hello!” Sandra raised her hands. “You two are awfully dramatic. Too dramatic for me.” She looked at Sonja. “I would have liked to get to know you better, Sonja, but I’m not getting involved in this fight. I might happen to look like you, but I have nothing to do with this.” She shook her head. “You really ought to talk to each other, you two. Something is obviously very wrong here. I’ll say my farewells. I think I’d rather eat at home.” She turned around and started to walk away.

“Sandra!” Kim called her name helplessly.

Sandra turned around. “Talk to each other. This is awful, the way you’re treating each other. I have no desire to get caught in the middle of that.” She left for good.

Kim turned back to face Sonja. “I . . . I have no idea what to say.”

“Respect.” The corners of Sonja’s lips curled in contempt. “You went to considerable lengths just to talk to me. But I'm not buying it. We have nothing more to say." She headed for the cafeteria's entrance.

"I'm not –" Kim ran after her. "I'm not going to great lengths, at least not in this case. I saw Sandra coincidentally on the street and I thought she was you. I still can't believe she isn't you. Until just now, I thought –"

"Please, leave me alone. At least let me eat in peace." Sonja stood still and looked at her. "I really don't have the stomach for this little game."

"Little game?" Kim shook her head. "Until a moment ago, I thought you were playing games with me. I thought you had invented Sandra."

"Invented her? Why would I do that?" Sonja kept walking.

Kim accompanied her into the managers' lunchroom. "I had no idea. I wanted to ask you today – or, that is, I thought you would have to give me an explanation, because . . . because you were one and the same person."

"One and the same person?" Sonja looked at her in disbelief. Then she shook her head. "The ideas you come up with . . ." She sat down at the table that had so often been theirs together.

"Shall we eat together?" Kim asked, still standing. "I'm just plain confused. You look so much alike, you and Sandra. But obviously you don't know each other."

Sonja looked up at her. "We really do look alike," she admitted. She sighed. "Fine, let's eat together. You can explain how you happened upon her. But I'm not discussing anything else with you."

"I accept." Kim sat down. "How I happened upon her, you already know. I saw her on the street, and because I thought she was you, I spoke to her. She thought I was stalking her." She laughed softly. Even though everything wasn't cleared up yet, at least Sonja hadn't been lying to her. She felt immensely relieved. Even though the similarity between Sandra and Sonja was still quite bewildering.

Sonja's lips curled into a hint of a smile. "I would have, too."

"Of course. Now, in hindsight –" Kim shook her head. "How must I have looked to her? And it was incomprehensible to me that she claimed not to know me." She looked at Sonja. "Well, not completely incomprehensible."

Sonja arched her eyebrows. The waitress brought her salad, and Kim ordered her own food.

"Yes, I know," Kim said, "that subject is off limits. But I saw her several times, and at some point, I figured out that she lived on Michelbergring."

"I don't live on Michelbergring." Sonja mixed her salad dressing. "You know that."

"Yes, I ..." Kim cleared her throat. "I thought you might have moved out of your place."

Sonja's fork froze in the middle of tossing her lettuce leaves. After a while, she continued the motion. It looked like a rusty machine coming back to jerky use after a long pause. She said nothing.

That's still her sore spot, Kim thought. "Now, of course, I know that it's Sandra's apartment and not yours," she went on. She looked at the door as if Sandra might come in. "When the misunderstanding was cleared up, I told her how much you resemble each other, and that that's why I confused the two of you. She was intrigued and she wanted to meet you. I told you that much over the phone."

"You did *not* tell me *that*!" Sonja protested fiercely. "I couldn't make any sense at all out of your hints and insinuations."

"Fine, okay, I get that. After all, I thought that you – it was all just nonsense, what I thought, as it turns out. I'm glad of that." Kim smiled at Sonja.

Sonja shook her head, disbelieving. "It certainly is odd how alike we look."

"Yes, you two must be related somehow," Kim said. "Very closely related. I can certainly imagine unrelated people who look similar – all the celebrity look-alikes you ever see aren't related to the celebrities, after all – but *this* similar? You really do look like twins."

"I think you're just imagining that. We probably don't really look all that much alike."

"Funny, Sandra said the same thing when she saw you approaching us." Kim observed Sonja's face. "I think you see it less clearly than someone else. Too bad Sandra is gone. If you two stood side by side in front of a mirror –"

"Anything else?" Sonja shook her head once more, but more in disapproval than disbelief this time. "This might be amusing for you, but as you can see, neither Sandra nor I have any interest in deepening our acquaintance."

"Sandra does, though," Kim said.

"Okay, it's my fault again." Sonja sighed. "As always. Really, Kim, this whole caper doesn't mean a thing, to her or to me. We're not kids anymore. To a child, it might have been entertaining, but we are grown women with grown-up lives. *Separate* lives," she added with emphasis. "What are we supposed to do about our resemblance?"

"That's true." Kim considered Sonja's face once again, trying to imagine Sandra's next to it. "If one of you were unemployed, you could share a job." She laughed.

As always, Sonja ate her salad leaf by leaf. "What does Sandra do?"

"She's a supermarket manager, she said." Kim was watching Sonja so closely, it was starting to feel a little embarrassing even to her. This story with Sandra was making her doubt her own senses. She needed to convince herself once more that her eyes weren't deceiving her.

"Supermarket manager." Sonja thought about that. "I would never have wanted to work in a supermarket. So the similarity isn't so great, after all." She went on eating.

"Well, it is a management position," Kim objected. "Maybe not as high as yours, but still, she's an executive, too."

A smirk crept into the corners of Sonja's mouth. "I try to find differences, you look for similarities. This is silly. Neither of us really knows Sandra. Or do you know her better?" It looked innocent, the way Sonja watched Kim as she asked that question, but Kim had the impression that it wasn't.

"No, I don't know her better. I've had exactly one extended conversation with her, in the middle of the night, on the street. She almost called the police." She laughed once more. "Oh, God . . . it was pitch dark except for a couple of streetlights, not a soul was on the street except for us. Most people were probably asleep already, and there weren't any cars passing on the Ring. It must've been spooky for her."

"She obviously survived unharmed," Sonja remarked dryly. "And your presence doesn't seem to make her uncomfortable, either."

"You're reading too much into it. She doesn't know me, and I don't know her. Everything she told me, she did because she wanted to prove to me that she's not you."

"And you still didn't believe it." Sonja leaned back. "What did you think? That I can split myself in two?" She looked directly at Kim.

"Well . . . no . . . uh . . ." Kim stammered a bit, because it wasn't actually clear to her what she had thought. Last night, lying in bed, unable to sleep, everything had seemed so clear and unequivocal, but now –

"You simply assumed that I was deceiving you," Sonja said. "Some of your comments finally make sense now. I truly couldn't imagine what you meant."

"I know that now." Kim was embarrassed. She glanced shyly up at Sonja. "I apologize explicitly for that once again. But what would you have done in my place?"

"I certainly wouldn't have blamed you for something you hadn't done." Sonja propped her elbows on the table and folded her hands. "Definitely not, given the fact that the jealousy issue had almost caused us to break up before."

"Yes." Kim dropped her eyes. "I know."

"But with this new information, I can now see what it was all about," Sonja said. "What happened can't be taken back. If one little nudge like that is enough for you to accuse me of infidelity –"

"One little nudge?" Kim looked up. "She looks exactly like you. *Exactly*. No matter what you two say, on the outside, you're twins. It was impossible for me to tell you apart."

"A person sees what she wants to see. You could've told the difference – if you'd wanted to."

Kim dropped her gaze again. Maybe she really could have. Sonja was right. In truth, Kim had been waiting for an event like that to happen. She couldn't have imagined that Sonja –

"I admit that my behavior fed into it," Sonja went on. "I would say we're done. I don't want to fight. We had a nice time together, and now . . . now, it's over, that's all. Let's remember the good things and forget about the bad." She looked at Kim with her eyebrows raised, as if waiting for her agreement.

How could she simply brush aside everything that had happened between them? Kim stared at her, uncomprehending. "Forget . . .?" she stammered.

"I knew it wouldn't last long. In fact, it lasted much longer than I expected. That was a surprise. Every time we met . . . or when we worked together – it was like a gift, always fresh." Sonja laughed softly. "I haven't gotten that many gifts in a long time." Her gaze caressed Kim's face. "Please, Kim . . . let's part as friends. Don't ruin what we had."

"Sonja, I . . . I don't want to part at all. Can't you see that?" Kim's eyes begged Sonja for a sign – a sign of hope.

Sonja sighed. "Yes, I can. But we blew that chance."

"I did, you mean." Kim took a deep breath. "You're probably right. It's all my fault."

"It's not a question of fault," Sonja said. "It was more a question of . . . relationships. Inescapable circumstances. Like the budget I have for the reorganization. It's got a limit, and everything has to stay within its limits. That's why I add up figures all night long – and still, I constantly have to amend things. But for human relationships, there are no amendments."

That was Sonja, as she lived and breathed. Budgets, amendments, circumstances – a world full of cut-and-dried rules. Rules to which she deferred and rules she tried to satisfy. True, it brought her success in her professional life, but in her private life, it was . . . frustrating. The cost/benefit calculation no longer worked, so the affair was over. She'd look for someone else whose numbers came out better.

"You mean to say by that, that it's not worthwhile to continue our . . . relationship," Kim stated, "because a reevaluation wouldn't produce a different result?"

"More or less." Sonja leaned forward. "As they say, new wine doesn't belong in old skins."

From that point of view . . . "It was a misunderstanding, Sonja," Kim pleaded. "Just a misunderstanding. Please, believe me, I really did confuse you with Sandra. If that hadn't happened, there would've been no reason –"

"Then you would've found another reason – eventually. Why kid ourselves about that? The problem is something else entirely."

Kim saw it the same way. "What do you think the problem is?"

Sonja tilted her head. "The subject is finished. I think our lunch is, too." She stood up.

"Could we . . ." Kim swallowed. "Could we have lunch together again sometime?"

Sonja hesitated. "Better not. But I'm glad that we could at least clear up one misunderstanding. Sandra Kruschewski – how odd." She shook her head and left.

"What is Ms. Grotenauer-Albrecht doing here?" Kim asked, after she'd watched Rolf walk Helmke to the elevator and say goodbye to her.

"She applied to be your replacement," Rolf said. "Your post has to be filled again, after all."

"She did *what*?" Kim stared at him with an expression that "horrified" didn't begin to describe.

"You know the company follows an internal hiring policy in these things," Rolf replied, mildly confused. "The position has already been advertised inside the company, but not outside yet. We'll only do that if we don't find anyone suitable in any of the departments."

"Why didn't you talk to me about it?"

"Oh, you've been so busy recently, I thought I'd take some of the load off your shoulders. Do you want to be present for every preliminary interview? If you do, I'll let you know next time."

"Well, maybe not for all of them . . . but I would've liked to be informed about this one." Kim shook her head. "I trust you completely, but given that this is about *my* replacement . . ."

"You're right. That was thoughtless of me. But she's not seriously in the running anyway, is she?" Rolf grinned.

"You think not?" Kim asked innocently.

"Please." Rolf grinned even more broadly. "Do you want to invite a tarantula like that into your nest? Everyone knows what her primary occupation consists of. I mean, it's all the same to me, I'll be gone then, but you –"

Kim chuckled. "It won't be all the same to me, you're right. Although I must admit that I'm partially responsible that she applied. I suggested it to her." She furrowed her brow guiltily.

"Seriously?" Rolf looked at her in disbelief.

"No, I wasn't serious. I just wanted to get rid of her, but apparently, she took it seriously. I'm sorry."

"Oh, it wasn't so bad. I've never conducted an interview quite like that one, but even at the end of one's career, there's always something new to learn."

"What was so unusual about your conversation?"

"In her youth, I'm sure she was once an exceptionally shrewd hussy, and rank after rank of men fell victim to her. She thinks she's still that femme fatale." Rolf rolled his eyes.

"She played the vamp?" Kim had to laugh. "I'll have to scold you double for denying me that."

"I couldn't have known. I don't know her that well. Until now, I'd only heard about her from other people's stories." Rolf chuckled. "I must admit, I was curious."

"And obviously she didn't let your curiosity down." Kim laughed once again. "Yes, somehow I can imagine that very well. She's pushy, and thinks that equates to a talent for seduction."

"She thinks she's as sexy as her underwear. Which I was given several opportunities to admire."

"Rolf ... if Margit finds out about this ..." Kim threatened him teasingly with her finger.

"It would just make her laugh." Rolf grinned. "She knows me. I'm not attracted to artificial vamps. And what would I want with another woman, when I have Margit?" He took his leave with a twinkle in his eye.

Rolf and Margit – the dream couple. Kim wandered thoughtfully back into her office. She heard the soft chime of the elevator; someone was getting out. A moment later, a shadow fell across her desk.

"I completely forgot to say hello to you," Helmke purred as she stretched provocatively against the doorframe.

Kim started. Even though she'd just been talking to Rolf about Helmke, she hadn't expected to see her so soon. She considered the – what had Rolf said? – *artificial vamp* in her doorway.

A faint smile crept across her face; she couldn't help it. Helmke's lacy black bra showed around the shamelessly low cut of her blouse, as she tried to look seductive. And she was actually wearing stockings with garters! Since she had stretched her arm above her head in a lascivious Hollywood-starlet pose, her skirt had ridden up so high that her garters were visible. Not by accident, Kim suspected.

"You applied to be my successor?" she asked in feigned earnest.

"Yes, Mr. Winkelmann thought that with my long professional experience, I'm way overdue for a promotion," Helmke spoke in a hopelessly failed breathy imitation of Marilyn Monroe.

"*Did* he." Kim could barely suppress a grin. Knowing Rolf, he'd meant that ironically, and he must have been trying gently to advise Helmke of her lack of professional competence. But Helmke had no sense of irony whatsoever.

"You offered it to me, too, after all," she breathed again, approaching Kim's desk.

Kim recalled the image of the tarantula that Rolf had used. In fact, Helmke bore a certain similarity to that spider, despite her dyed red hair.

"Um . . . yes. It's open to anyone to apply for the position."

"Couldn't you put in a good word for me?" Helmke planted herself right on top of the papers on Kim's desk. Her skirt slid up even higher, and now Kim could see not only her garters, but her bare upper thighs, as well. "I mean, then we could always work together, you as the boss, and me . . . under you." Helmke underlined her offer with a swelteringly erotic look – or at least, what might pass for one in an amateur children's puppet troupe.

Kim didn't know what to say. Helmke was scooting so close to her, she felt the urge to run screaming out of the room. But she decided to ride this devil a little longer. "You mean, we'd have the same relationship that I had with Rolf?" She arched her eyebrows as though she were anticipating nothing more eagerly than Helmke's reply.

"Yes, exactly." Helmke leaned over and placed a hand on Kim's shoulder to support herself while her lips inexorably approached Kim's. They were open slightly, and the beet red lipstick clashed garishly with her hair.

"Helmke, are you a lesbian?" Kim asked in an affectionate tone.

Helmke jerked back and sprang abruptly off of the desk. "Lesbian? Me? Where did you get that idea?" Hurriedly, she smoothed her skirt down and fussed nervously the neckline of her blouse.

"I just thought ... My sex change wasn't all that long ago, but I am a woman now." Kim gave Helmke such an innocent, naïve look, butter wouldn't have melted in her mouth.

Helmke gaped at her. "Sex change?"

"It's no problem at all these days." Kim stood up. "Don't I look almost like I was born a woman?"

Helmke's lips were no longer open slightly – her lower jaw gaped open. This lent her the facial expression appropriate to her character.

"I have no objection to a relationship," Kim said, "but there are a few sequelae to the procedures. You know, surgery can do a lot, but not everything. Eventually, you'd be faced with that; I just wanted to warn you in advance."

Helmke's mouth clapped shut with an audible *plop!* She turned around and raced to the elevator.

Kim held a hand over her mouth to keep from bursting with delight. Only once the elevator had departed did she allow herself a resounding laugh. She braced her hands on her hips, and tears ran down her cheeks until she calmed down again and sat back in her office chair.

She dialed Jo's number. When Jo picked up, she said, "Oh, by the way, if in the near future you hear the rumor that I used to be a man, do let me know."

Jo reacted with surprise. "What?"

"Helmke was just here," Kim explained as she brushed a last tear of laughter from her eye. "She wanted me to hire her; that is, she applied to be my replacement –"

Something that sounded like "oomph" came out of Jo's mouth.

"Yes, exactly. Of course, she doesn't have the slightest chance. Rolf and I will make the decision, and Rolf wasn't impressed by her seductive arts. So she tried them on me."

"I should've given her more to keep her busy," Jo said.

"Oh, nonsense." Kim laughed. "It was funny. She got pretty close to me, and then I told her that my sex change wasn't all that long ago and there are still leftovers –"

"I'm sure I would've found any of those." Jo's grin carried clearly over the phone line.

"Yes indeed." Kim grimaced slightly. "Anyway, I don't know what put her off more: my current sex, or my *former* one. She fled before she could tell me. On top of which, she vehemently denied being a lesbian."

"I believe that. But how does she reconcile that with the fact that she tried to seduce you?"

"No idea. I just wanted to warn you in advance, Jo. Given Helmke's lightning-fast news spreading abilities, it's possible the rumor could reach you as soon as today."

"Well, I hope so." Jo laughed. "Helmke really is a piece of work!"

"Yes, she is. But she doesn't know it. I feel sorry for her, somehow. But I couldn't help it. I couldn't resist."

"I can understand that," Jo said. "I've been a little busier with her the last few days, myself. I was trying to keep her away from you, actually, but obviously I didn't succeed."

"Doesn't matter. Either she'll withdraw the application herself after this revelation, or she'll be turned down. Somehow, she must have realized that the possibility existed. Otherwise she wouldn't have come on to me and asked me for my support."

"Yes, of course, fundamentally, she knows. She just doesn't understand it," Jo said. "She must have something on her current boss, or else she would've been tossed out a long time ago. Unfortunately, I haven't been able to find out what she's got on him."

"Then how do you know that's what's going on there?" Kim frowned.

"Helmke was sort of bragging about it, that he can't get rid of her because then he'd land in the stocks himself," Jo said. "But unfortunately, she didn't reveal any more than that."

"Where does she get her information?" Kim shook her head in wonder. "I mean, what I just told her was intentional, but if they're real secrets, why don't people just keep them to themselves?"

"Who knows? Men in particular tend to spill quite a bit in bed. Maybe she had a thing with him sometime in the past."

"Anything's possible." Kim sighed. "Our relationship – I mean, mine and hers – is now over, alas, before it could ever really start . . . nipped in the bud." She let out a sigh of self-denial, as though she regretted nothing more.

Jo laughed. "Yes, it's going to haunt you for the rest of your life, that you missed this big chance."

"So it is." Kim laughed as well. "Let me know when you hear something."

"Sure." Jo hung up.

Still laughing, Kim turned back to her work.

▫▫▫▫▫

"Someone named Sandra called. She wants you to call her back." Babsie handed Kim a slip of paper when she returned from a meeting with Rolf.

"Thanks." Kim took the paper and stuck it in her pocket. Sandra . . . that immediately reminded her of Sonja, and she didn't want to think about all that right now.

Her relationship with Sonja had not improved in any way. It wasn't as bad as it had been at first, when she'd felt like Sonja avoided any encounter with her at all cost – no, they saw each other, they greeted each other, they exchanged a few words, about work, about the weather, about food.

And that was it. Sonja's gaze was always pointed in another direction. Whenever Kim tried to catch her eye – she'd watch her for so long that it became embarrassing – Sonja ignored her.

When Sonja's gaze did happen in that direction, she smiled slightly, as though she had expected nothing less than that Kim would be looking at her, but her smile never grew beyond that faint beginning. It was like a reminder of earlier times, not a prospect of laughing together in the future.

However, Sonja's gaze also always contained a hint of entreaty, an expression of grief and loss.

Why won't she talk to me? Kim thought. But Sonja just wouldn't.

Kim reached for the ringing phone. So many customers, so many complaints. "Wolff."

"This is Sandra," the voice that sounded exactly like Sonja's said. "I called earlier this morning. Your secretary said she'd give you my number to call back. In case you misplaced it."

Kim had to laugh in spite of the brief fright that Sonja's – no, Sandra's – voice had triggered in her. "She's not my secretary, she's a coworker. I'm not high enough in the company hierarchy for a secretary."

"Whatever," Sandra said. "Obviously, you didn't have time to call back, but I – well, to be honest, I have to admit that I'm curious. Did you and Sonja hash things out?"

Kim swallowed. "One could say that, yes."

"Oh, that doesn't sound good," Sandra replied. "I know it's none of my business, but what awful thing came between you two? Or more precisely – since Sonja apparently feels that you've offended her – what did you do?" She laughed. "You didn't seem like that much of a monster to me, despite the fact that I thought you were a stalker."

Kim was unable to answer right away. Here was Sonja's voice speaking to her, about Sonja, but it wasn't Sonja, even though it sounded like Sonja. It was just confusing. "That's been cleared up, fortunately." She took a deep breath. "It was my fault. Sonja can't do anything about it."

"Hm." Even that little noise sounded dubious. "Sonja is . . ." Sandra cleared her throat, "a strong personality. I sensed that."

Kim sighed. "Yes, she is that. She's an exceptional leader, and she keeps everything under control."

"Not everything, apparently," Sandra contradicted. "Otherwise, she wouldn't have been so upset. I recognize that in myself. When I have things under control, I'm very relaxed, and you can have anything from me – but woe betide you if anything goes wrong. The employees in the supermarket are all afraid of me!" She laughed. "No, I don't think it's quite that bad, but you've seen how mad I can get."

"You had good reason." Kim paused for a moment. "And so did Sonja. I screwed everything up."

"So the conversation didn't accomplish anything?"

"Not much." Kim sighed. "Except now she knows that you really exist. She had considerable doubts about that before."

"It is difficult to believe," Sandra agreed. "I mean, at first I couldn't imagine it, either. Someone who looks exactly like me ... Imagine if someone tried to tell you that. A stranger. At night, on the street."

"Yeah." Kim laughed softly. "I'd suspect other motives, too. That's why it was so important for you two to meet."

"On the other hand: you're no stranger to Sonja ..." Sandra objected. "If you're not an absolutely notorious liar, she must have at least had to consider believing you." She waited, and when Kim didn't answer, she asked, "Are you a notorious liar?"

Kim shook her head, because Sandra's question made her laugh again, if sadly this time. "No, I'm not."

"Then she only didn't believe you because she didn't *want* to believe you. Because she thought you were lying in this case, even though you don't otherwise."

"Yes, I think so. Let's not talk about this anymore, there's no point, Sandra. Even your showing up didn't lead to us solving our problems. And that's not your job, now, either."

"No, but ..." Sandra seemed to think about something. "You know, since we met briefly that one time, I keep thinking about her – Sonja, I mean."

Welcome to the club, Kim thought.

"She really does look a lot like me," Sandra went on. "It's unbelievable. I've been standing in front of the mirror for days, trying to find the differences, but I haven't managed to."

"I'm sorry," Kim said. "I didn't want that to happen. It probably really is just a coincidence. Like *The Prince and the Pauper*."

"The pauper was most likely a bastard of his father, the king.

That's what I've always thought."

"Could be." Kim frowned pensively.

"I know what you're thinking now." Sandra laughed softly. "My father is indeed something of a ladies' man, so that's entirely possible. But you'd have to ask Sonja's mother about that."

"Or your father."

Now Sandra laughed out loud. "You mean, that would be easier than asking Sonja about her mother?" Her laughter came out as a rolling chortle. "Yes, that may be so, when I think back on the encounter with Sonja . . ."

"That . . . that's not really what I meant . . ." Kim felt exactly the way she had back when Sonja had made fun of her. It was . . . the same voice. And the same manner.

"Fine," Sandra said. "I'll ask him. Why not? My mother is long dead. It can't hurt her anymore."

Kim sighed. "Even if . . . Assume you were half-sisters, what good would that do? Besides, I'm fairly certain that Sonja wouldn't believe it anyway. Not without a DNA test."

"I'm sure we could get that done," Sandra replied musingly, as if her thoughts were already on another subject. "What's Sonja's last name?"

"Kantner."

"The name doesn't tell me anything." Sandra paused to think for a moment. "Could be that her mother lives in my father's neighborhood," she went on. "He still lives in the same house I grew up in."

"Then you would've had to meet as children," Kim said.

"That's true, too. If my father had had an affair with a neighbor who still lives there, then there would've been signs. Especially if the children looked so much alike."

"Some people are very discreet." Kim made a face. *Especially Sonja*, she thought.

"We won't get anywhere like this. I'll ask my father the embarrassing question." Sandra hesitated. "Ask Sonja some time where she lived as a child."

Kim let out a skeptical sound. "I don't know if she'd answer that sort of question from me."

"You can try."

In the background, a tinny announcement came on, trying to make the weekly specials sound appetizing to the customers.

"Oh no," Sandra said. "Somebody put on the wrong announcement – that one was from last week, and it's an expired offer. I have to go and get back to taking care of my supermarket." She laughed and hung up.

Kim propped her chin in her hand. Suddenly, her eyes opened wide. Her mouse found and opened a program on her computer screen. Her memory had not deceived her. Why hadn't this occurred to her long ago? Sonja had even mentioned it. But in all the excitement . . .

"Kim, do you have a second?" Rolf stood in the doorway. "We need to talk about a few more things I forgot about earlier."

"Sure." Kim stood up. "What else is there?"

"I'll show you in my office. Come with me."

Kim followed him, and in Rolf's gentle presence, forgot about her personal worries for an hour.

Jo looked like she'd just swallowed a frog. "Ms. K-K-Kantner . . ." she stammered.

Kim stifled a smile, but then couldn't hold back her grin anymore. "I don't believe Sandra answers to that name." She gestured toward a chair and looked at Sandra. "Would you like a seat?" With another gesture, she made the introduction. "This is my best friend Jennifer, and the character with the frog face is Jo, her fiancée. The two of them are about to get married."

"Pleased to meet you." Sandra sat down.

Jo was still gaping at her.

"Close your mouth," Kim said. "This isn't Sonja."

"But . . . but . . ." Jo could barely get a word out.

"I know you see her every day, but obviously you don't look too closely. Then let me make the official introduction: Sandra Kruschewski." She rested a hand on Sandra's shoulder. "Not related by blood or by marriage to Sonja Kantner."

"That can't be." Jo gasped, dumbfounded.

"But it is." Sandra smiled. "Kim thought I was Sonja, too, but I'm not."

"But you look like Sonja?" Jennifer considered Sandra with interest.

"Seems that way," Sandra said. "You don't know her?"

"No, I'm the only one here who doesn't know her. But now at least I know what she looks like." She turned to Jo with a frown. "I'm not so sure I'm okay with you keeping this job, darling."

"She's not my type," Jo replied a bit testily, "I've told you that often enough."

"Too bad." The corners of Sandra's mouth twitched with amusement. "Then I must not be, either."

Jennifer gave her a sharp look. "She's engaged." She placed her hand on Jo's arm.

Sandra laughed. "Don't worry, I'm not getting involved. It was just a comment."

"How ... how ...?" Jo stammered again. She couldn't tear her gaze away from Sandra.

"Kim found me on the street, just coincidentally," Sandra explained. "I've been living on Michelbergring for the last few weeks."

Jo now stared at Kim. "Well, that must've been a surprise."

"That it was." Kim nodded. "At first, I thought she was Sonja. To be honest, I thought so for a pretty long time, and I even tracked her down to her apartment."

"I almost called the police," Sandra added, laughing. "But then Kim introduced me to Sonja, and I saw that she really does look very similar to me."

"Similar?" Jo let her gaze wander back and forth between Sandra and Kim in disbelief. "That's quite an understatement. You could be twins."

"Yes, Kim said that, too." Sandra shook her head. "But we aren't. That'd be too improbable, anyway."

"You sure are mean." Jennifer shot a chastising look at Kim. "You kept something like this from me?"

Kim shrugged. "I was going to tell you, but then Sandra said she'd like to come along to the women's café, and so I thought, a picture is worth a thousand words." She grinned.

"I don't know Sonja in the slightest," Jennifer said. "So I'm no judge. But you could have called me. This isn't exactly an everyday story."

"Yes, that is true," Kim replied guiltily, "but I have so much going on right now. The whole transition with Rolf, there's so much that still has to be taken care of . . ."

"And Helmke's application to be your successor," Jo added with a chuckle.

"Yes, that, too." Kim laughed. "Although that was more of a one-off. She withdrew her application."

"You don't say. Why would she do that?" Jo chuckled some more.

"Sex change!" Jennifer laughed out loud. "Only you could come up with something like that!"

"It was a stopgap," Kim said, embarrassed.

"Sex change?" Sandra looked uncertainly around the group.

"You didn't tell her yet?" Jo asked.

"No, we haven't spoken in a while," Kim said. "And it wasn't that important, anyway."

"Perhaps not important. But funny." Jo's lips curled into a broad smile. "Especially to anyone who knows Helmke."

"Helmke is a coworker at the company," Kim explained to Sandra, "who's rather ... well, let's say odd. She spins webs of intrigue, and she always knows the latest on everything. Since I'm about to take over the whole department on Michelbergring because my boss is retiring, I need a replacement for my position, and she applied for the job. During which, she used somewhat," she cleared her throat, "unusual methods."

"And what does that have to do with a sex change?" Sandra asked. "Is she –"

"Oh, no, no." Jo laughed. "No, she's clearly a woman and has never been anything else. But Kim told her *she* had a sex change in her past, and at that, Helmke ran away in horror."

"But that's not nice. A sex change is a serious thing, after all." Sandra winked.

"Yeah," Kim said. "I'm going to have to apologize to all transgender people for using that particular escape, but I was truly desperate. Helmke was getting so much on my nerves –"

"You poor thing." Jo gave Kim a sympathetic look. "You really don't have it easy at the moment."

Kim sighed and said nothing to that.

"So, you haven't been in the city long?" Jennifer asked Sandra. "I've never seen you here before."

"The supermarket chain I work for just recently transferred me here," Sandra confirmed, nodding. "The supermarket here wasn't running well, and . . . well . . . I'm supposed to build up a couple of additional shops in the area, too."

"She doesn't just resemble Sonja on the outside," Jo said.

"In a certain way . . ." Kim agreed. "Yes." At the same time, she could sense a warm-heartedness exuding from Sandra, who sat next to her, that was foreign to Sonja. Sonja always seemed a little reserved; Sandra was open and friendly.

"I hope you two don't mind that I came along?" Sandra inquired with a glance at Jennifer and Jo.

"Oh, no." Jo looked at her. "Now that I'm getting used to the sight of you . . ."

"Kim told me that she wanted to go to the women's café, and since I'm new in town, I thought I'd check it out."

"No problem." Jennifer waggled a hand. "Sooner or later, you probably would've come here anyway."

"I don't know," Sandra said. "If Kim hadn't mentioned it, I wouldn't have known that this café even exists. It's pretty out-of-the-way."

Jennifer opened her mouth to say something, but before a sound came out, a blonde rushed towards her like a bolt of lightning.

"Who is this woman?" Felicity snarled, looking ready to scratch Jo's eyes out.

Jo looked at Jennifer, then at Felicity, then back again.

Jennifer slowly turned red.

"Felicity . . ." Kim had recalled her name as soon as she saw the blonde shock of hair waving wildly about.

"I'm not talking to you!" Felicity spared her a brief glance, then glared back at Jo. "I'm talking to Jen."

"Jen?" Jo turned halfway toward Jennifer.

Jennifer had turned a bright red. "It . . . I . . ." She didn't look at Felicity, or at Jo, either. She looked at the table in front of her.

"What's going on, Jenny?" Jo asked.

Jennifer turned her head slightly. She could only just glimpse at Jo from below.

"Who is this woman?" Felicity repeated her original question, even more furiously.

Finally Jennifer struggled through to an answer. "That's none of your business," she said awkwardly, looking only briefly at Felicity.

"Come on, Jenny, why aren't you telling her who I am?" Jo asked, irritated.

"She's the one you're screwing now, I can see that," Felicity said angrily. "How long? More than one night?" She directed her gaze toward Jo. "She doesn't normally give you more chances than that," she explained, as if to warn Jo. "She seduces you, screws you, and then she disappears – forever."

Jo stared at Felicity, speechless.

"I told you –" Jennifer had barely started to reply when Felicity interrupted her again.

"You said you thought I was sweet – everything about me, my lips, my breasts, my –" Felicity was almost screaming. "Even my name. But you forgot it!"

"Is there a problem here?" Susi, the owner of the café, had been standing behind the counter, and came over. She looked questioningly first at Felicity and then at the others.

"A problem?" Felicity spun around and stared at her like a bull staring at a red flag. "The problem is that this woman sitting here has no morals. She'll just sleep with you, use you, and then throw you away. That's the problem!" She turned back toward the table and fixed Jennifer with a blistering glare. "You should tape a sign on yourself: *Only for one night, please*. Then we'd know right away where we stand." She sobbed and ran past Susi toward the restroom.

Susi sighed. "That was bound to happen, Jennifer. I've been expecting something like that for a long time." She arched her eyebrows and gave Jennifer a chastising look.

Jennifer raised her hands helplessly and shrugged. "But I can't do anything about that."

"Probably not." Susi lowered her eyebrows again. "Probably none of you can." She cast a reproving look around the circle, touching on everyone seated at the table, and then went back behind the counter.

After Susi had gone, the atmosphere seemed to relax. Everyone took a deep breath.

Everyone – except Jo. "Who was that, Jenny?" she asked in the same tone of voice that Felicity had used earlier.

Kim stepped in quickly, because Jennifer still appeared to be in shock. "Don't get the wrong idea," she implored Jo. "That was long before your time."

Jo's eyebrows were almost meeting in the middle of her forehead, she was frowning so severely. "Before our time?" She looked at Jennifer.

"Yes." Jennifer exhaled heavily once more. "Back then ... well, you know ..."

Jo turned around and looked over toward the restroom, although there was nothing to see but a closed door. "You slept with her," she said slowly, and turned back around. "That was obvious from her outburst. And she's still chasing after you, even though it was that long ago?" Her voice sounded a little skeptical.

"Please, love ..." Jennifer gave Jo a pleading look. "Not you, too."

"She's acting like it happened yesterday," Jo said.

"But it didn't. It was before we met. And you know we both ..."

"Yeah." Jo looked deep into Jennifer's eyes. "I know."

Kim felt a bit awkward with Sandra next to her, witnessing all of this. She laughed, embarrassed. "It's not always like this here. I don't want you to get that idea. That kind of scene is actually pretty rare."

"Oh, I found it very interesting." Sandra smiled. "It was like a movie set. Entrance ... furious scene ... exit."

"I don't think Felicity sees it like that." Kim glanced at the restroom out of the corner of her eye. Felicity still hadn't reemerged.

"I think for her, this is reality, not a movie."

"I'm sure," Sandra said. "Poor kid."

"Kid . . . well . . ." Kim shook her head dubiously. "Not really quite a kid anymore, but yet still one in a way, and that's the problem. Old enough to have sex, but not old enough to deal with everything that comes with it." She took a deep breath. "We were all like that once. It's not exactly an easy time."

"You mean it gets better later?" Sandra arched her eyebrows, and it looked so much like Sonja that Kim had to gulp.

"Not necessarily."

"What happened between you and Sonja?" Sandra asked. "I mean, you don't have to tell me anything, of course, but I already know you slept together."

Kim felt a gentle ache in the region of her heart. "She was . . . she is . . . Jo has the job I used to have."

"That means Jo works for Sonja; I had more or less picked up on that already."

Kim nodded.

"And you used to work for her." Sandra looked thoughtfully at Kim.

Kim cleared her throat. "Did you talk to your father?"

"Yes." Sandra arched her eyebrows skeptically. "He denies the possibility."

"But you don't believe him?"

"Hm." Sandra looked even more skeptical than before. "He had this really funny look on his face."

Kim looked musingly at Sandra. "I found something out that had escaped my notice before. Sonja alluded to it earlier, but I somehow didn't catch on. Her maiden name is Kruschewski."

Sandra stared at Kim, dumbfounded. "Kruschewski?"

"Yes, amazing, isn't it?" Kim shook her head. "I looked it up in the personnel database. I knew I'd seen that name somewhere before."

"And what are you going to do now?"

"I don't know." Kim pursed her lips indecisively. "If she'd wanted to say something, she could have said it when she heard your name. But she didn't."

"Maybe it really is all just a coincidence." Sandra shook her head, though, as if she couldn't believe that. "The name Kruschewski isn't the most uncommon name anywhere."

Kim nodded. "That's right. But it's still strange. That you two look so much alike . . . and then the name, too . . ."

"Yes." Sandra frowned again. "But then, why isn't she interested in finding out more about it?"

Kim shrugged. "I don't know that either."

"You don't want to ask her?" Sandra arched her eyebrows and examined Kim's face.

"Our relationship is . . . difficult." Kim grimaced again.

"Seems that way." Sandra smiled gently. "If you don't want to ask her, I'll ask her. I just want to know, now."

Kim stared at her a bit quizzically. Uncertainly, she cleared her throat. "I can understand . . ." She sighed. "I can understand that you want to know whether you're related."

"I honestly can't imagine that we aren't." Sandra laughed. "Even if she's only a distant cousin . . . I'd still be happy about it."

"The question is whether Sonja would be happy about it, too." Kim had her doubts.

"Why shouldn't she be?" Sandra shrugged. "I'm not so awful that someone wouldn't want to be related to me." She tilted her head. "Or do you think I am?"

Kim shook her head, laughing. "It's not about you, it's about Sonja. She's a pretty closed person, very discreet. She doesn't like it when people intrude into her private sphere."

"Who does?" Sandra chuckled. Kim and she thought at the same time about the fact that Kim had unwittingly intruded into Sandra's private sphere. "But this time, she'll just have to learn to like it. It affects me, too, after all."

"Yes." Kim nodded. "You have the right to find out if you're part of the same family."

"I think so, too." Sandra laughed once again. "It can't really be all that bad to have to get used to one new family member. If Sonja is that difficult, it'll probably be more of a challenge for me than it is for her."

Kim sighed. "Sonja is always a challenge."

"You've been through a lot with her; I could tell, the first time when you spoke to me on the street." Sandra gave Kim a sympathetic look.

"No, I . . ."

"Oh, yes." Jo stepped in. "I know I'm not supposed to say anything, but I've seen enough."

"Jo . . ." Kim gave Jo a tormented look.

"She's a great manager. Mrs. Kantner, I mean." Jo laughed. "It's hard for me to use her first name. We're still fairly formal with one another." She shook her head. "She's absolutely first-class; she's miles better than all the other managers, but as a human being . . ."

"She is very nice," Kim said stubbornly.

"Oh, yes, I can't complain now, but at the beginning . . ." Jo shook her head. "I was this close to quitting my job. It was like working next to a case of dynamite that might explode at any second."

"Yes, she's got that going on." Sandra laughed. "I could sense that even in the brief moment when we all saw each other. I must admit, patience isn't among my greatest virtues, either. That's why I can't wait to solve this mystery. Either we're related somehow, or we aren't. That kind of uncertainty drives me berserk."

"You must be related. You're so similar." Jo grinned.

"Will you give me her number?" Sandra turned to Kim. "I'll call her first thing tomorrow."

When Kim hesitated, Jo said, "I can give you my office number. If you call there, I can connect you with her. She'll be in until ten o'clock tomorrow; after that she'll be out and about."

Kim shot Jo an angry glare.

"This has gone on long enough." Jo gave Kim an amiable look in return. "You can't protect her from everything forever."

"Protect?" Kim looked surprised.

"Yes, you do. You're like a helicopter mom. You want to keep everything away from her that might upset her, but that's not always possible. She's an adult. You're not her mother."

Kim felt rather strange. She'd never thought of herself as Sonja's mother. Sonja was four years older than she was. "Do I really act like that?" she asked, dismayed.

"Yes." Jo grinned even more. "You're so desperately in love with her, it's almost not pretty anymore. She can do anything she wants, and you just take it. As your friend, I'm telling you: stop it."

"Good advice." Jennifer chipped in her own two cents. "I don't know her, of course, but I can see what she's done to you since you've known each other. It definitely hasn't been pretty."

"She . . . she couldn't help it." Kim squirmed. She wanted to defend Sonja, but on the other hand, she herself didn't understand why Sonja behaved the way she did.

"A person can always help it," Sandra contradicted. "No one is forced to beat other people over the head."

"That's true," Jo said. "Beside which, Mrs. Kantner can be very diplomatic in her negotiations, you know that as well as I do." She looked at Kim. "Why doesn't she do things that way in her private life?"

"Her private life is none of your business." Kim was getting annoyed.

"Maybe not ours, but it is yours." Jennifer struck an emphatic note. "Your private life is connected to hers. Or do you deny that, too? And that makes it our business."

Kim lowered her eyes.

"Of course not," Jennifer said. "I warned you about her from the start, remember? Straight women just aren't a good choice."

Kim flinched and looked at Sandra. "I'm sorry. She doesn't mean it that way."

Jennifer's brow furrowed, uncomprehending, and Sandra laughed. "But she's right!"

Kim looked confused.

"You're a lesbian, aren't you?" Jennifer asked Sandra. "I've been assuming that this whole time."

"Rightly so." Sandra nodded.

Kim gaped at her. "You're a lesbian?"

"Yes." Sandra smiled as sweetly as Sonja had done in her most tender moments. "Of course, what did you think?"

"Um . . . to be honest . . ."

"To be honest, you thought she was just like Sonja, because she looks just like her." Jo laughed. "Me, too. I was almost going to ask

Sandra if she was married – to a man, I mean."

"That's funny, I thought she was a lesbian all along," Jennifer said. "Because, after all, she came here to the women's café with Kim. Straight women rarely do. Or if they do, it's only for one reason."

"For a little sexual adventure." Kim chuckled. "Preferably with you."

"In times past." Jennifer grinned. "Long, long past. And if they're looking for that kind of adventure, then they're not really so straight after all. So I assume there are only lesbians here."

"You just don't know Mrs. Kantner." Jo looked at Jennifer. "So you didn't really have the same kind of preconceived notions that Kim and I have, and you could just let your sensors work." She looked at Sandra. "At any rate, that's cleared up, and I'm glad things are the way they are."

"If I thought there was any doubt, I would've said something earlier," Sandra replied. "I thought it was obvious."

"You said at the beginning, you probably never would've come to the women's café without me," Kim said. "That's why I thought –"

"I don't like this sort of cafés," Sandra explained. "That's the reason. Not because I'm not lesbian."

Jo clapped her hands. "Susi, would you bring us four glasses of champagne?" She looked around the group and grinned cheerfully. "I think we have something to celebrate."

Sonja wasn't feeling well. Well, when did she ever? Anything one could call a sense of *well-being* had been almost entirely unknown to her for quite some time.

She'd gotten to the office very early in the morning; she'd hardly slept at all. It had been a long time since she felt her home was a place of peace and quiet where she could replenish the energies she used up during the day.

She missed Kim. It hurt her not to be able to see her anymore, but that had been inevitable. She knew this type of relationship all too well. Kim was an exception because she was a woman, but in the end, it was always the same, after all: jealousy destroyed everything.

Jealousy, yes. Once, she'd been a jealous person, too. A long, long time ago. That's why she had tried to ban it from her life. She seemed to have managed, since where there was jealousy, there must be love, too. And she was finished with love.

She thought about how things might have been. Her thirty-sixth birthday was right around the corner. If Kim had still been there . . .

No. She couldn't think that way. A birthday was no reason to rescind a decision . . . just because she was lonely.

She leaned back in her chair. She was lonely. Had been for a long time. She'd tried to dull the loneliness with affairs, with work, but the feeling came over her more and more. Neither affairs nor work could whitewash her growing awareness of being alone.

She liked to work long hours. It helped her to keep her thoughts in check, but it didn't solve her problems. Not the personal ones. How long had she grappled with this already? It seemed like an eternity.

Young and strong as she once was, she'd never doubted that every problem could and would be solved eventually. Now, though, she was starting to feel old. A weakness was taking hold of her of a kind she'd never before experienced.

Just a birthday. And not even a particularly important one. But with it, she would pass the middle of her thirties once and for all, on her way to forty. At forty, one was supposed to have one's life under control, right?

She took a deep breath. Under control. What was that, anyway? Could a person have something under control that was slipping farther and farther away?

That's why she loved her work: she made plans, and even when she couldn't follow through on every one of them a hundred percent, most of them went very well. And the things that weren't working so well, she could put on the right track by dint of her own personal effort. If only she could claim that about her own life.

She stood up and walked around the room. Her life certainly hadn't gone the way she'd imagined it at seventeen: a husband, two children, a little house with a yard. Honestly, she hadn't wanted any more than that. Had that been too much?

She asked herself whether the life she was leading now was all there was. Was there nothing more she could get out of it? Had she used up all her chances? It almost seemed that way.

With Kim, something had come along that she hadn't expected. Not so . . . not so deep. The first experience, and everything that had followed from it, had turned a number of things inside her upside down.

Never would she have thought – no, not *never*. When she was young . . . when she'd been fourteen . . . she suddenly remembered it now . . . and, in fact, even earlier than that . . . in grade school . . . her first teacher . . . she'd been young, young and cute. Early twenties, perhaps. Barely a grown woman. But at age six, she had seemed very grown-up to Sonja. Grown-up and beautiful. A role model for her. But not just a role model.

She laughed aloud in disbelief. No, that couldn't be. She was never . . . had never . . .

She hadn't, but she'd also blundered into the cycle of masculine desire very early on. She was attractive – she knew she was, because men told her so – and she had to cope with the consequences of that.

Her mother had never had any sympathy for that, probably because of wounds from the experiences of her own youth. She let Sonja sense that no man Sonja brought home could ever satisfy her mother.

What would she have said if I'd brought a woman home? Sonja thought, suddenly chuckling. The laugh disappeared. No, her mother was not a woman who would have tolerated such a thing. Even now, she was intolerant of any number of things.

"Mrs. Kantner?" Jo called in through the open door. "A call for you. Should I put it through?"

Sonja hesitated for a moment. Jo's presence reminded her of Kim. Not always, but sometimes. She knew that would never go away, as long as her secretary was best friends with Kim. Every glance from her showed Sonja that she knew much more about her relationship with Kim than Sonja would have liked.

Sonja went resolutely back to her desk. Work was waiting. She couldn't neglect it just because her private life was becoming more and more of a nightmare. "Yes, put it through," she said aloud.

The telephone rang, and she picked it up and answered.

"Hello Sonja, this is Sandra," said a voice that she didn't recognize as so nearly her own, so it didn't seem very familiar to her.

"Sandra?" She frowned. "I don't know any Sandra."

"You don't remember me? Well, we only met very briefly that once, outside the cafeteria ... with Kim. I'm the one who looks exactly like you." Sandra laughed softly.

Sonja froze. She had wished to avoid being reminded of that encounter, ever, but now it had happened. "I remember," she said. "We look a bit alike."

"That's what I thought at first, too," Sandra said. "But meanwhile I've determined that we resemble each other more than just a little. And our last names ... I mean, before you were married ..."

Sonja's expression hardened. "What about it?"

"Sonja ..." Sandra laughed once more. "Believe me, I can understand that you don't want to hear about it. It seemed more than improbable to me at first, too ... but the same name, the same appearance ... don't you think, too, that we could be distantly related?"

"Related?" In truth, Sonja had never considered this possibility. She figured it all for a joke of nature. "No, I don't think so."

"Do you have siblings?" Sandra asked.

"I don't know what business that is of yours," Sonja replied irritably.

"I bet you do. I don't have any, which is why I'd be so glad to meet a cousin my age. Especially if she looks so similar to me."

"Cousin?" Sonja shook her head. "This is ridiculous."

"Do you really think so?" Sandra paused for a moment. "At first, I thought you might be an extramarital daughter of my father's. But my father denies it. Perhaps you could ask your mother –"

"My mother?" Sonja's horror was clearly audible.

"Is she really such a dragon?" Sandra laughed. "Well, then, maybe better not. So you don't think that's possible? I mean, your mother was young once, too ... just like my father. It's hard to imagine, but they were teenagers once. And teenagers sometimes do things that they'd rather not remember later on. That's how it was for me, anyway. I assume for you, too."

"You assume a great deal." Sonja pressed her lips together to a knife-edge.

"If assumptions bother you so much, then let's just get to the bottom of things." Sandra wouldn't be deterred by Sonja's dismissive behavior. "It could only help us both. Either it turns out we really are related – which I think would be nice – or it turns out we're not related, and then it's all cleared up, too. You'd probably be happier with *that* solution."

"This has very little to do with happiness," Sonja said. "I am simply too busy to get involved in such flights of fancy."

"It doesn't pique your interest at all?" Sandra asked. "Really? I just can't imagine that. I could only ask my father; you're the only one who can ask your mother. Or ask her some time about other Kruschewskis, maybe she'll remember my father – not because she ever had anything going with him, but because of the family name. Maybe he's a cousin of a cousin of a cousin of hers. His first name is Harald."

"I will *not* ask her!" Sonja replied furiously. "My mother doesn't have time for this kind of nonsense and neither do I."

"Why are you being so stand-offish, Sonja? Even if we're not related, it could be fun to try to find out why we look so similar. Then those genetic tests could finally be good for something."

"Genetic tests?" Sonja's eyes opened wide. "You're crazy."

"Am I?" Sandra shook her head over such lack of understanding. "Kim said you'd refuse. She knows you much better than I do, of course. She was right."

"Kim." Sonja's jaws clenched. "She set all of this up. I suspected that from the very beginning."

"She didn't set anything up." Sandra sighed. "You really are a hard nut to crack, I must say. Kim warned me about that, too."

"She warned you about me?" Sonja had to laugh against her will, with a bitter undertone. "It's gone that far? Where is she spreading her stories? On the Internet?"

"She's not spreading anything anywhere." Sandra sighed once more. "She loves you. Don't you understand that? She loves you very much."

Sonja was speechless for a moment. "That's . . ." she stammered. "That's outrageous. What incredible cheek."

"That she loves you? Is that how you see it?" Sandra inhaled deeply. "I'd say she must have a very thick skin, because she still does love you. I don't think I could keep that up in the face of such persistent rejection. But you two would know about that. It's none of my business, after all. I'd just like to know why you and I look so much alike."

"That doesn't interest me in the slightest." It cost Sonja some effort to recover from the shock that Sandra's words had triggered.

"Oh, yes, you are interested," Sandra claimed. "And if you don't help me figure this out, I'll just keep looking into it on my own. I'm not afraid to ask my father again. He beat around the bush a little when he answered, and that makes me suspicious. Maybe your mother would react exactly the same, if you ask her."

"I will not burden my mother with this nonsense!" Sonja hissed furiously and hung up.

"I'm driving out to see my father again this weekend. I just can't let go of this mystery," Sandra announced.

"Do you really think you'll be able to find anything out?" Kim asked.

"He's keeping something secret." Sandra frowned. "I'm not used to that from him. He's the best father a girl could have. We've always been good friends. And all of a sudden –" She broke off.

"You think solving the puzzle is worth jeopardizing your friendship with your father?" Kim asked.

"I don't think I'll be jeopardizing it." Sandra chuckled. "He adores me . . . and I adore him. I don't know what could possibly come between us. Even when I told him that I'm a lesbian –" She smiled. "Lots of people would wish for such a harmonious coming out."

"And your mother? How did she take it?"

Sandra sighed. "Unfortunately, she was already dead by then. My father and I have been alone for a long time. But I think it wouldn't have bothered her, either. She was always so relaxed. Even on her deathbed."

"You picked that up? As a child?" Kim thought back on her own experiences.

"I wasn't such a small child anymore," Sandra said. "I was fifteen. Naturally, it was a shock for me ... for me and for my father ... but there was nothing we could do, of course. She always told us we needed to go on living without her. It took years. It wasn't a surprise to us. But nevertheless –" Small tears welled up in the corners of her eyes.

"I'm sorry. I shouldn't have asked." Kim stood up and went over to Sandra.

They sat together at Sandra's small dining table. Since Kim worked in the neighborhood, Sandra had invited her over for an "unspectacular supper," as she called it. It might have been unspectacular, but it had been quite delicious. Sandra was a good cook.

Kim positioned herself next to Sandra and stroked her hair soothingly. It was like Sonja's hair, soft and smooth. "My father died when I was twelve," she said softly. "Since then, my mother and I have been alone."

Sandra raised her face to Kim's. "Well, then, you understand." The tears ran down her cheeks, and she brushed them away slowly and carefully. "But they always remain in our memories, don't they?"

"Yes." Kim smiled. "My father was rarely at home, he worked so much that I hardly saw him, but when he was there, it was like fireworks on New Year's Eve. I loved him very much."

"Maybe that's why we liked each other right off the bat," Sandra said. "We've had similar life experiences."

Kim laughed. "You liked me right off the bat? I got a very different impression at the time."

"Please, Kim." Sandra grinned. "What would you have done in my place? But it's true: I liked you immediately. I have a weakness for ... how shall I say this? ... the crazy type. Unfortunately, it's not a very successful weakness." She sighed.

"I'm not actually very crazy. Sonja found me rather –" Kim broke off, but it was too late now. "... square," she concluded.

"Sonja doesn't know what she's talking about," Sandra said softly. She stood up. Her face was now right in front of Kim's. "You're not square." Sandra whispered. "You're sweet." She leaned forward, and her lips touched Kim's.

Sandra's closeness made Kim feel weak. Sandra felt like Sonja, she smelled like Sonja, she was just as seductive as Sonja.

Sandra's lips parted, and her tongue gently caressed Kim's lips so that Kim could no longer resist. She let Sandra in, and they kissed for a long time. Kim closed her eyes. She had been yearning so much for Sonja. It was a desire that had never diminished, even when she tried so hard to suppress it.

Sandra's tongue explored her mouth, and Kim followed its arousing movements. Sandra took a step forward. Her hand rested on Kim's breast and began to caress it. Her kiss deepened.

Kim wrapped her arms around Sandra and pulled her closer, right up against her. The kiss carried her away, Sandra's presence confused her, she knew this wasn't Sonja, and yet –

"No," she said all of a sudden. She pushed Sandra cautiously away. "I'm sorry, but I can't do this."

Sandra looked at her. "Sonja?"

Kim shut her eyes again and took a deep breath. "Yeah," she said when she opened her eyes again. "You're so much like her, but –"

"But I'm not her." Sandra nodded. "Unfortunately." Her mouth twisted slightly. "You want to be with her, not with me."

"Sandra, I –" Kim looked unhappy.

"It's okay." Sandra smiled. "Too bad for both of us."

"Do you . . ." Kim cleared her throat, "do you have a girlfriend?"

Sandra sighed. "I did. Until I moved here."

"She didn't come with you?" Kim was trying to defuse the excitement that Sandra's kiss had provoked in her, and that was still raging inside her.

"I . . . well . . ." Sandra stepped aside and went over to the couch. "I didn't want her to come with me."

"You didn't want her to?" Kim remained standing and looked at Sandra.

Sandra shook her head, obviously lost in her own recollections. "Can you picture anything from this description: *crazy artist*?" She looked up. "Multiply what you imagined by ten, and you have Patrizia."

"Your weakness for the crazy type?"

"Yeah." Sandra inhaled and exhaled deeply. "It just wasn't working anymore. I don't think she would have come along even if I had asked her. Her friends in the art scene were much more important to her." Again, she sighed. "She wasn't my first in that circle, as you can probably imagine. My weakness hasn't exactly brought me a great deal of success." She gazed into an unfathomable distance.

"You're so . . . down-to-earth," Kim countered, rather bemused by Sandra's preference, "if I may say so."

"You may." Sandra looked up. "And I am. That's probably why I'm so attracted to the unusual, to the eccentric. But it's not particularly healthy for my psyche to keep tripping over it and falling flat on my face."

"I'm not especially . . . eccentric," Kim said. "At least I don't think so. But you like me anyway."

"Yes." Sandra looked at her. "I like you . . . a lot."

"Perhaps I do have something eccentric about me that I just haven't discovered yet." Kim laughed. "But I don't really think so."

"Your eccentricity is your masochism," Sandra said with a smile. "Maybe that's the reason."

"Masochism?" Kim frowned.

"Please . . ." Sandra laughed. "Sonja, of course. It seems to me that a person has to be very masochistic to stick it out with her."

"You don't know her. She is –" Kim considered Sandra's face. "She's exactly as sweet as you are." She smiled tenderly.

"Too bad that smile wasn't really meant for me." Sandra surveyed Kim, seeking her eyes. "I can't talk you into staying here tonight, can I?" she asked quietly.

"I think I'd better go now." *Before I lose myself in those eyes*, Kim thought. They were Sonja's eyes, and when had she ever been able to resist those?

"Maybe it would be better that way." Sandra nodded and stood up. "I'm not sure if you –"

"Yeah." Kim looked at her. "I'm not sure about that, either."

▫▫▫▫▫

"I knew it!" Sandra burst in on the middle of a conference call that Kim was conducting with two other department heads who were in charge of customer support for two subsidiary branches.

"One moment, please." Kim muted the conference. "I'm in the middle of a conference call, Sandra!" She whispered even though she'd muted the line. Somehow, she felt like the others could still hear her.

"I'm sorry, I couldn't wait." Sandra took a deep breath. "Twins!"

"Uh . . . what?" Kim was missing some context here.

"Sonja and I are twins – not just real, true sisters, but hatched from the same egg. That's why we look so much alike." Sandra was breathing heavily and dropped into the visitor's chair in Kim's office.

Kim stared at her, then turned back to the telephone and pressed the button to reactivate the call. "Pardon me, please," she said. "We'll have to end the conference. An emergency has come up. I'll call you back." She cut the connection. "What did you just say?" Once more, she stared at Sandra.

"We're right out of *The Parent Trap*." Sandra's face beamed. "Our parents got divorced when we were both still very small, which is why we don't remember each other. My father actually wanted to keep both children – but our mother, who Sonja grew up with, was apparently quite the harridan. He couldn't keep us both, so he kept me, and Sonja stayed with her mother."

"But . . . but you said your mother was dead."

"She is. The woman I knew as my mother. My father never told me that she wasn't my birth mother; even after her death, he kept that to himself. The way my father describes my biological mother, I seem to have won the jackpot with my . . ." she hesitated, "stepmother, compared to Sonja. She was really wonderful."

Kim was still staring at Sandra in disbelief. "That . . . that . . . Sonja and you . . ."

"Twins." Sandra laughed. "Imagine: I have a twin sister! I was an only child, never had any siblings, and I always wished I had some, and now I actually have a twin!" She was terribly excited. "I have to tell Sonja right away. Will you call her, or shall I?"

"Um . . . I don't know if that's such a good idea." Kim furrowed her brow.

"I already talked to her once on the phone, I know how she is," Sandra said. "And to be honest . . . I recognize it in myself, too. Now I understand why. People often like least about other people the things they don't like about themselves – and as twins, Sonja and I naturally have a great deal in common." She tilted her head to one side.

Just like Sonja, Kim thought, and now she finally knew why.

"I think it'd be better if I call her. After all, this is about her and me. You, not so much." Sandra pulled her cell phone out of her purse. "Or I'll tell her in person. I waited to see you, too, because I wanted to tell you in person."

"In person?" The smooth skin on Kim's forehead folded into even more skeptical wrinkles than before. When Sonja felt backed into a corner, she could get mad as hell; Kim had seen that often enough already. A telephone allowed the necessary distance. And she could simply smash it to bits if she felt like it.

"I think news like this should only be delivered in person." Sandra put her cell phone away again. "I'll go see her. Her office is in the building next to the cafeteria where we met her?"

"Yes." When Sandra stood up, Kim added: "I'd better not go along. You two need to sort this out on your own. But maybe you should call Jo ahead of time and ask whether Sonja is even there. She's out on the road a lot."

"Yes, true." Sandra seemed undecided.

"I'll do it." Kim picked up her receiver and dialed Jo's number. "Jo," she said when Jo answered, "is Sonja there?"

"Should I put you through?"

"No, no." Kim answered quickly, before Jo could press the relevant button on her phone console. "Sandra's coming over. She wants to talk to Sonja. That's why she wanted to know if Sonja is there."

"Sandra?" Jo sounded blank. "You're calling for Sandra?"

"Yes," Kim replied impatiently. "So is she there, or isn't she?"

"She is. And she's not in a good mood today, just to warn you. Mondays are usually pretty bad for her."

"Can't do anything about that," Kim said, already imagining Sandra getting nailed to the wall by Sonja. "She's probably going to be in an even worse state shortly, but it's necessary. Sandra's coming over, and she'll explain everything." She hung up. Jo was probably quite bewildered now, but Sandra could worry about that when she was in her office. "You haven't picked yourself a good day," she said to Sandra. "Sonja is there, but in an exceptionally bad mood, Jo says."

"Perhaps you would like to accompany me, Helicopter Mom?" Sandra grinned.

"Actually, I would like to." Kim nodded. "But like you said, this is none of my business. Most likely, that would only make things worse, because then Sonja would accuse me again of concocting the whole thing. Or do you want me there for support?"

"I'll manage."

In that regard, too, Sandra was just like Sonja. But why shouldn't she be? She was her twin sister. Kim still couldn't quite believe it.

"It's really better if my sister and I –" Sandra fell silent. "My sister and I . . ." she repeated with an undertone of yearning. "How long have I wished I could say that?" She looked at Kim. "I always had the feeling that I wasn't alone. Sometimes it was really weird. As though I were seeing life through the eyes of another person. And when I encountered Sonja for the first time – back then, I didn't think anything of it, but it was as if I'd already known her forever. But there was so much tension between the two of you, it obliterated everything else."

"I'm sorry," Kim said guiltily.

"You don't have to be sorry." Sandra smiled. "The feeling was so different . . . I had to stop and think about it first myself. I've stood in front of the mirror so many times . . . and sometimes it was like Sonja was standing next to me. I almost saw her, as though she were there. It was a little frightening. But now . . . now I know what that was. It was the thing that connects us as twins. We're not made to be alone, but to be a pair. Sonja must have felt exactly the same way, even if she never talked about it."

"She'd never admit that," Kim said. "I think she'll dispute everything. This is going to turn her whole life upside down."

"I think her life is already pretty much upside down," Sandra replied thoughtfully. "I've felt that for a long time. Long before I saw her for the first time. There was always something . . . a threat . . . something dark. Of course, I thought it had something to do with my life. But in my life there may be a great deal of chaos, but nothing that could be described as a dark secret. There really isn't." She laughed.

"You mean, Sonja's hiding something?" Kim had always had the same feeling, but given her relationship to Sonja, she'd tended to blame it on the strange three-way configuration in which they found themselves. In truth, she had thought Sonja was hiding the fact that she loved her husband. Even though he tormented her. That sort of thing happened, after all. But Sandra had nothing to do with that, and spoke of the same sensation, so it couldn't be that.

"In any case, I felt that clearly. I've even dreamed – no," Sandra laughed sheepishly, "dreams are lies, I don't believe in that sort of thing. It was my dream, not Sonja's."

Kim didn't want to inquire. "I'm curious what Sonja will say."

"She'll probably scream." Sandra laughed in reply. "I would, in her place."

And Sonja did, in fact, scream. "Get out of my office right now, you liar!"

Jo heard this through the closed door and wondered whether she ought to intervene.

But then she heard Sandra's voice, which was loud enough to stand up against Sonja's. In truth, she couldn't have said for certain whether it was Sandra's or Sonja's voice – they both sounded the same.

"Sonja, this isn't exactly easy for me, either, but our father –"

"*Our* father?" Sonja glared at Sandra. "You dare, madam –?"

"Oh, stop that," Sandra replied. "We're sisters. Twin sisters, no less."

"There is no proof –" Sonja began.

"You know that would be easy to produce. We just need to have a

DNA test done," Sandra interrupted. "Of course, this photo here doesn't prove much." She placed a photo of two babies, lying side by side in a crib, on Sonja's desk. "Papa says that's the two of us."

Sonja was shaken to her core. She stared at the picture, and finally – after she'd jumped up in anger when Sandra had told her the news – she sank back into her chair and calmed herself down.

"I needed some time to recover from the shock myself," Sandra said. "When Papa showed me the picture, I could hardly believe it." She sat down across from Sonja in a visitor's chair. "Hello, sister. Nice to meet you." She grinned broadly.

Sonja slowly raised her eyes. "I don't believe it," she said dully.

"That's certainly your right." Sandra shrugged. "Give me a couple of your hairs, I'll add a couple of mine, and in a week, we'll know the truth."

Sonja's eyes wandered over Sandra's facial features, examining them again and again.

"We could stand in front of a mirror," Sandra said. "You don't really see it here. You just see me, and I just see you. We don't see ourselves."

"That was Kim's idea." Sonja recalled that Kim had suggested something similar – after the first encounter with Sandra.

"No, it's mine," Sandra contradicted, "but it's so logical, anyone could think of it – Kim, too, obviously."

Sonja sat there, deep in her own thoughts. She remained silent.

"Didn't you feel it?" Sandra asked. "Back then, when we met outside the cafeteria . . . I had such a strange feeling. Didn't you?"

Sonja snorted. "I had any number of strange feelings right then; that particular one must've escaped me."

"Feelings about Kim. I understand."

Sonja's head shot up. Her eyes flashed at Sandra.

Sandra smiled. "I like Kim, too."

"Why should I care about that?" Sonja turned away.

"I think you do care." Sandra watched the back of Sonja's head attentively. "We're twins, and that means we probably like the same people."

"That makes no difference to me." Sonja turned back toward Sandra in her office chair and looked at her angrily. "I don't want to hear about it." She let herself sink back into her chair and laid a finger on her cheek.

"I always do that, too, when I don't know what to say next."

Sonja's gaze, which had been directed toward the table, shot up.

"I could name a few more things that I think are the same for both of us." Sandra laughed softly. "The list is probably endless."

Sonja stood up, walked over to the window, and turned her back to Sandra.

"You can't ignore it." Sandra stood up likewise. "We're related to each other, whether you want to accept it or not." She went over to Sonja and stood behind her. "Can't you imagine anything positive coming out of this?"

Sonja didn't stir.

"I never had siblings," Sandra said. "Neither a brother nor a sister. That's probably why I'm so glad to have found you now. Aren't you happy at all?"

"What am I supposed to be happy about?" Sonja didn't turn around; she spoke to the window instead. "Even more problems?"

"I don't want to cause you any problems. That's not my intention at all," Sandra replied gently. "I'm convinced that you're my sister. That we're twins. Everything points to that." She sighed. "I was terribly excited when I found out . . . when Papa told me. He certainly took a long time getting to it." She laughed, shaking her head. "Your mother never told you anything?" Her gaze traveled along the nape of Sonja's neck, which stretched before her like a fortress wall. "*Our* mother, I mean. Since she's obviously mine, too, even though I don't know her."

Sonja laughed dryly. "I'm sure she'll be thrilled!" She turned around and gave Sandra a peculiar look. "Did you grow up without a mother?"

"No, I had a wonderful stepmother, although I always thought she was my real mother."

"Had?" Sonja arched her eyebrows.

"She's dead." Sandra squinted slightly. "A long time now."

"I had a stepfather." Sonja swallowed. "He's still alive, but he's not with my mother anymore."

Sandra laughed lightly. "That seems to be a specialty of your . . .

of our mother. Not living with one man for very long, I mean."

Sonja's eyebrows drew together.

Sandra raised her hands. "She's my mother, after all, but I don't know her. You're right. I shouldn't make that kind of comment."

"No, you shouldn't." Sonja's brows relaxed. She took a deep breath. "We ought to do this properly."

Sandra looked inquiringly at her.

"The DNA test, I mean," Sonja continued. "I set no store by speculations or conjecture, I need proof."

"Papa's word is proof enough for me," Sandra replied, "but you don't know him, so I understand that it's not enough for you."

"No, it's not enough for me." Sonja went back to her desk and sat down again. "I don't build skyscrapers on sand."

"Or on a photo." Sandra laughed once more. She waited a moment, and when Sonja said nothing, she added, "How should we proceed?"

"As you suggested." Sonja looked very ruminative. "A couple of hairs from each of us will be enough, you think?"

Sandra nodded. "Since we both have the same hair color, I assume that yours isn't dyed, either. That simplifies matters."

Sonja took a mirror out of a drawer in her desk. She studied herself for a moment, and then twined her index finger around a strand of her hair. With a decisive yank, she plucked the hairs out by their roots and handed them to Sandra. "I assume you'd like to take care of this?"

Sandra accepted the few hairs and closed her thumb and forefinger around them. "Do you have an envelope, perhaps? Then we could sign and seal it right here. I'll do the same thing with my hair sample, and then we should probably both go together to put the envelopes in the mail. Otherwise, you could just assume that I sent in two of my own samples."

"Yes, that would be best." Sonja tilted her head to one side.

Sandra grinned. "You were thinking the same thing, weren't you? Do we even need to do this test?"

"It was a logical conclusion that has nothing to do with kinship."

"You'd like it better if the obvious were not confirmed, wouldn't you?" Sandra smiled.

"Not everything that's obvious is also true," Sonja said.

"She has to accept it now!" Sandra hollered into the telephone with a laugh.

Kim didn't know right away what she was talking about, but after a second, it became clear. "The genetic test?"

"Yes." A rustle on the line indicated that Sandra was probably shaking her head. "I wouldn't have needed it, but she wanted absolute proof."

"That's typical for her," Kim said.

Sandra laughed with Sonja's voice. "For me, too, but in this case – why would my father lie to me? Of course, he kept it secret from me for all these years that I had a sister, but lie to me . . . really lie . . . he never did that."

"You're not angry with him?" Kim asked.

"In a way . . ." Sandra hesitated. "In a way, sure I am. I can't really be furious with him because I love him – and I know that he did this out of love – but I'm not a little kid anymore. He should have told me once I was old enough."

"To him, you're probably not so grown up." Kim smiled.

"Yes, he thinks I'm still his little girl." Sandra sighed. "But now it's out. I'm going to call Sonja right now. We'll see how she reacts."

"Don't expect too much," Kim replied quickly. "She's not –"

"I know." Sandra interrupted her, and there was a smile in her voice. "I know how she feels. I'm sorry to say it, but I know better than you do how she feels, because I feel the same thing. I'm just like her."

Phew. Kim ran a hand through her hair. This was going to take some getting used to. Now that it was clear that Sonja and Sandra were twins, everything had changed. Although she'd already been convinced that they were related somehow. But twins –

"I absolutely have to call now. I can't stand it anymore." Sandra giggled. "Oh, my God, I feel like a virgin before the first time. I'm so excited, like I'm about to –"

"I can tell." Kim smiled. "To be honest, I'm not doing much better."

"Do you think this might have an effect on your relationship with her?"

Kim took a deep breath. "No, I don't really think so. This has nothing to do with us, after all."

"I'm sorry," Sandra replied sympathetically. "I know how that is."

"Have you ever been in love with a twin before?" Kim asked sarcastically.

"No, but with someone who –" Sandra cleared her throat and broke off. "No. I never have."

"Don't wait any longer, call her. So the issue will finally be clear."

"Hasn't it been for a long time already?" Sandra asked somewhat ambiguously. "Okay, I'll call her now. Ciao." She hung up.

Kim thought about what would happen next. Sandra would dial, Sonja would pick up . . .

And then?

"Oh, man, today has been rough!" Jo groaned when she met Kim for lunch.

Kim raised her eyebrows inquisitively.

"You know Sandra called, don't you?" asked Jo as they went inside.

Kim nodded.

"And can you perhaps imagine that Mrs. Kantner wasn't one to tangle with after the phone call?"

Kim turned her head to the side.

"You have nothing to say?" Jo got in line for the buffet.

"I *can't* say anything about it." Kim sighed. "That's a matter between Sandra and Sonja. It's none of my business."

"Really?" Jo examined the salads on display and walked on past them. "You like both of them, isn't that so?"

"They are . . . I mean, until very recently, I didn't know that there were two of them." Kim grimaced uncomfortably.

"Nobody knew" Jo pointed at a large aluminum pan full of goulash. "I'll have that, please," she said to the server behind the counter. "Except their parents, of course," she added. "Why didn't they ever tell them?"

"No idea." Kim shrugged. "I'll have the same," she said to the woman in the white apron, who was handing Jo a full plate, and the woman nodded.

"They must've been pretty serious enemies, if the children didn't even know about each other." Jo pushed her plate along the shelf in front of the counter, in the direction of the cash register.

"Apparently." Kim followed her with her own tray. "I know absolutely nothing about it."

"Sandra didn't tell you anything, either? I mean, that Mrs. Kantner isn't saying anything, I get that, she doesn't talk about things like that, but Sandra must be much more open about it." Jo looked at the display on the register, pulled some money out of her pants pocket, and handed it to the cashier.

"It's amazing that she is. Now that we know that they're twins."

"You always said that Mrs. Kantner was more open at some point." Jo scanned the cafeteria for an open table.

"Yes, she –" Kim swallowed. "But not about personal things."

They sat down together at the same table. "Oh, no, Helmke!" Jo whispered.

Kim looked up and saw Helmke coming in; she was alone – and had already spotted Kim and Jo. Downright elated, she stormed across the room, high heels clacking, right to their table.

"I can sit with you two, can't I?" She didn't even wait for an answer.

That ends any personal conversation, Kim thought.

"I'm sorry I reacted like that last time," Helmke said, and both Jo and Kim regarded her with surprise. Had it ever happened, even once, that Helmke had apologized for anything? "It is – a little unusual, you have to admit that."

Kim didn't know what to say. Should she disabuse Helmke of the false impression that Kim herself had given her, or let her go on thinking that her present shape wasn't the one she'd been born with?

"Jo told me that you – well, that you prefer not to talk about it."

"Ah, did she?" Kim looked at Jo. Jo made a face. "And what else did she say?" Kim turned back to Helmke.

"Nothing, unfortunately." Helmke sighed. "She's much too secretive, I find. We're all friends, after all. There shouldn't be any secrets between us."

Kim doubted that anyone was actually friends with Helmke. "Now that you know my biggest secret . . . I can rely on your discretion, can't I?"

Jo had to work awfully hard to conceal her smirk. She was going to snort any second.

"But of course!" Helmke replied with utter conviction. "You know me!"

Exactly, Kim thought. She only hoped that Helmke had picked up on her subtle hint that what she had already told her was Kim's greatest secret, and wouldn't steer the conversation around to Sonja.

"How is Mrs. Kantner doing?" Helmke asked. "She seems a little nervous to me lately."

Jo gasped for air in order to stifle the laugh that was trying to burst out of her. "She works a lot, and very hard. She probably doesn't get enough sleep because of it. People get nervous easily under those conditions. But really, I haven't noticed that about her. She's the same as always."

"Are you sure?" Helmke asked. "I get the impression she's kind of shaky."

Kim was about to say something, but Jo shot her a warning glance. "She's a dynamic leader," Jo said. "They're always tightly wound. Just look at Suderdorf."

"Suderdorf." The name seemed to set a machine in Helmke's brain in motion, searching for information. "Yes, he has reason to be nervous," she said a moment later. The database had provided her with the necessary information.

"Why?" Jo asked.

Now Kim gave her a look, one of astonishment.

"I'm as silent as the grave. No one will find out anything from me," Helmke said. "I have nothing to do with firings."

"He's going to be fired?" Kim asked surprised. She immediately bit her tongue. What was she doing asking about gossip and scandal?

"I didn't say that," Helmke replied smugly. "But in this company, morals are still worth something, I'm telling you. One can't just – well, men are just like that, we all know that, but if you're going to open your fly, you'd better not do it in the presence of your own – female – boss."

"What?" Kim's food almost fell out of her mouth.

"They had a thing together, and now she's tired of him and she's dumping him." Helmke shrugged. "Apparently he didn't hedge his bets."

"Hedge his bets? What do you mean by that?" Jo asked innocently.

"Well, there are things a person can do, for insurance," Helmke remarked confidentially. "Then nobody can throw you out on the street."

"I'm sure the idea would never cross your boss's mind." Jo batted her eyelashes.

"He knows better than that," Helmke replied. "I'm much too valuable to him."

Kim thought about Sonja. There had been a time when she had been valuable to Sonja, too, first as a coworker, and then – she would've sighed loudly, if Helmke hadn't been there.

She yearned for Sonja. When she'd held Sandra in her arms, she'd realized just how much she missed Sonja. If only she could have imagined that Sandra was Sonja, she wouldn't have gone home.

Sandra appealed to her in a certain way. Her similarity to Sonja made it impossible for Kim not to develop feelings for her, not to look at her and see Sonja there.

When she saw Sandra laughing, she saw Sonja's laugh before her, back then, when she'd laughed so much and so heartily, in the office, when they were only boss and employee.

Sandra had never lost that laugh, but Sonja had. And she didn't say why.

Maybe I ought to ask Sandra what it could be, Kim thought. *She said they feel the same things, so maybe she knows, after all.*

Thinking about Sandra triggered a peculiar mood in her. In many ways, Sandra was what Kim had always wished for in Sonja. Sandra was free and unattached, didn't keep burdening herself with all these enigmatic, insoluble problems – and she was unequivocally lesbian. On top of that, she liked Kim and showed it clearly. Yes, and the most important thing: she looked exactly like Sonja, talked like her, moved like her, arched her eyebrows like her – one almost might think there was no difference at all.

Why don't I just get together with Sandra? Kim thought. *That would be the simplest thing.*

She shrank from the thought. The solution was being served to her on a silver platter, and yet, she couldn't accept it. It was impossible. Because as much as Sandra and Sonja did resemble one another, they were different. They had lived different lives. They were not the same person, not remotely.

She stood up. Jo and Helmke interrupted their conversation and looked at her in surprise. "I ... I have an appointment." Kim cleared her throat. "I almost entirely forgot."

Jo looked skeptical, as though she wanted to say something, but in Helmke's presence, that wasn't possible.

"Excuse me, please." Kim quickly distanced herself from the table. She glanced briefly into the executive lunchroom, then walked on into the main building. As she crossed the foyer, she nodded to the young woman currently on duty at the reception desk. Kim knew that she'd recently gotten married to an equally young colleague from IT. The two of them whispered sweet nothings to each other whenever they met.

Kim and Sonja couldn't even do that – she balled her fist in her pocket. This state of affairs was completely untenable. She imagined touching Sonja, kissing her, caressing her, cuddling her – but Sonja wasn't there.

Kim quickly left the corridor leading to her former workplace. She assumed that Jo would leave her a little bit of time before she came back. Perhaps she was using the opportunity to extract from Helmke the secret of why she couldn't be fired. Although Kim wasn't really very interested in that at the moment.

She crossed the outer office and entered Sonja's office. Sonja sat at her desk, deep in thought. She wasn't working.

Kim stopped a couple of steps in from the door. "Sonja."

Sonja's head jerked up. Apparently she hadn't heard Kim coming. Her face drew closed. "What do you want?"

"I know what Sandra told you –" Kim began.

Sonja interrupted her with a dry laugh. "Who doesn't?" She turned away. "Why don't I just put out a weekly bulletin?"

"I can imagine that all of this isn't easy for you," Kim said gently, approaching her desk. "I wanted to offer you my support. If you want it, of course."

"Support?" Sonja turned back to face Kim. "For what? Learning to feel like a twin? Do you have any experience with that?"

"Isn't it nice, not to be alone?" Kim asked.

"I'm not alone. I have a brother and a sister; I don't need Sandra. The whole family circus has never appealed to me, anyhow." Sonja stood up and distanced herself from Kim, as if she were trying to prevent her from getting too close.

"Is that why you don't have any children?" As she said it, Kim wondered why she was asking. Maybe it had been the "not yet" from Sonja's initial introduction in the conference that had put the idea into her head that Sonja wanted children. They'd never discussed it.

Sonja froze. She seemed to have retreated inside herself, as she had at the beginning. After a while she said quietly and hesitantly, "I had an accident." She spoke as though an internal pressure were compelling her to say something she didn't want to say. "I was pregnant then. The accident caused a miscarriage. Afterward, the doctor said I couldn't have children."

Kim would have liked to take Sonja in her arms and comfort her, since she appeared to need it, but she didn't look like she would accept that kind of offer. Kim stepped around the desk and approached Sonja. "I'm so sorry. Why didn't you ever say anything?"

Sonja first looked at her for several long seconds. "When would we have talked about that?" she asked, mildly amused. "Between the orgasm in the bed and the one in the shower?" She shook her head. "It had nothing to do with us, not in the slightest. It was years ago."

"We didn't just sleep together, Sonja," Kim said gently. "I know, you only wanted an affair, but that's not what it was. For me, it never was only that, and I don't think it was for you, either."

"Not *that* subject again. We're done with that." Sonja went around Kim back to her desk and sat down. "I need to work," she added in a very terse tone. "Please leave."

"I didn't come here to annoy you. Nor did I come as your former lover." Kim stepped behind Sonja's executive chair and considered the back of her neck from above, as it peeked out from beneath the soft cascade of chestnut brown hair. How dearly she would have liked to kiss it. "I'm here as your . . . friend. I think you could use one. The situation with Sandra has upset you more than you want to admit. And I'd like to help you."

"The situation with Sandra . . ." Sonja hesitated, ". . . is harmless," she went on. "I simply have to learn to get used to the idea. That's all. It's not so bad."

"You don't have to be afraid. I won't spread any rumors, no matter what you tell me. Trust me." Without thinking about it, Kim rested her hands on Sonja's shoulders.

Sonja went rigid under Kim's loosely placed fingers. "Please . . . don't . . ." she whispered.

Kim felt Sonja trembling, more and more. "Sonja," she whispered hoarsely. She bent down and did what she'd wanted to do all along: She laid her lips against Sonja's quaking neck and kissed it.

"Kim . . . I . . . no . . ." Sonja breathed, but she didn't stir.

"I've been yearning for you," Kim whispered. "So much . . ." Her lips wandered around toward the front of Sonja's neck, and her hands slid down over Sonja's breasts.

Sonja let herself sink back into her chair. "We . . . This can't be . . ." she whispered. "You have to understand . . ."

Kim felt Sonja's heart pounding firmly beneath her hand. The soft breasts made her fingers tingle. She wanted to touch them, kiss them, sink down into them. She unbuttoned Sonja's blouse and slipped her hand inside Sonja's bra, touching the erect nipple.

Sonja moaned.

"I can certainly ask Mrs. Kantner." Jo's voice carried through the outer office. Apparently she was speaking to someone in the corridor.

Sonja straightened up frantically and grabbed at the buttons on her blouse; Kim's head was flung upwards by the commotion in the chair, so that she automatically straightened up as well. The sudden shift made her dizzy, and she was still breathing heavily. She steadied herself against the back of Sonja's chair.

"Mrs. Kantner, Mr. Gerlach would like to know –" Jo appeared in the doorway and fell silent. She glanced at Kim and then at Sonja. "I'll come back later," she said quickly, turned around, and disappeared into her own office.

"Oh my God," Sonja groaned. "How embarrassing." She turned red.

"Not at all." Kim laughed. "You know Jo won't say anything." She stroked Sonja's hair, soothing her tenderly. "Don't worry about it."

"That's not the issue." Forcefully Sonja pushed her chair back and stood up. "I'm her boss. She comes in here, unsuspecting, and I'm … sitting here with my blouse half undone. She'll never respect me again. After everything else she already knows …" She looked at Kim. "I would assume."

"She doesn't know anywhere near as much as you assume. And she has tremendous respect for you, you can rely on that. That isn't going to change, either. Not because of a trifle like this."

"Trifle?" Sonja flared. Her eyes glinted.

Kim smiled. "You're right, it wasn't a trifle. It was much nicer than that."

"I … Kim …" Nervously, Sonja brushed the hair out of her face. She went to the door and shut it. Then she turned to face Kim. "I can't …" she said hesitantly. She took a deep breath. "I can't do this. You must understand that I –" She broke off and looked into Kim's eyes for a long moment. "Oh my God, Kim …" she whispered. She swayed.

Kim rushed over to steady her. When Sonja didn't fend her off, she wrapped her arms around her and pulled her close. "What's wrong, love?" she whispered, kissing her hair.

"This can't work." Sonja's weak voice disappeared into Kim's shoulder. "It just can't work."

"I won't demand anything of you," Kim said softly. "I accept that you …" she swallowed, "that you don't want to be with me anymore. It's my own fault. But how could I have imagined that Sandra –"

"You don't understand," Sonja whispered. "That's not how it is."

Kim shut her eyes. Feeling Sonja, holding her in her arms again, almost overwhelmed her; she could've fallen to the floor and listened to her from her knees. "I love you, Sonja," she murmured roughly. Her voice no longer obeyed her. "I love you, and I'll always love you. But I know that I can't demand the same of you, and I'm not. I just want to be a good friend to you . . . if you'll let me. I –"

"Kim." Sonja interrupted her, lifted her face and looked at her. "You're going in the wrong direction."

"The wrong . . . direction?" Kim frowned. Sonja had always been able to do that very well: to confuse her. She didn't understand a word.

"I don't want you to be my good friend."

"Oh." Kim let go of her and took a step back. *Not even that?* She felt disappointment rise up in her. She should have known. Sonja was logical and systematic, and friendship meant nothing to her. She probably had enough friends already. Male ones.

"Look at my blouse."

Perplexed, Kim did what Sonja asked. Sonja hadn't had time to button the blouse up completely before Jo came in, and her breasts shone forth, soft and seductive, covered only by the bra. Kim swallowed.

"My blouse is still half open," Sonja said. "I did nothing to try to stop you from opening it. If Jo hadn't come back –"

"I . . . I apologize," Kim stuttered. "I shouldn't have done that, I know, but you . . . you were so – I've longed for you so much, Sonja. It was my fault, all my fault. I didn't want to force you into anything –"

Sonja's mouth twitched. "You still don't understand. You don't need to apologize for anything. I wasn't prepared for it, and my head wanted to stop me, but I liked it. I –" Her head fell. "I've longed for you, too. Terribly," she whispered to the floor.

Kim stared at her. She couldn't say a word.

"Don't just leave me standing here like this," Sonja continued softly. “Please, hold me in your arms.”

“But . . . you . . .” Kim felt paralyzed. But then she reached one hand out toward Sonja, touched her, stepped toward her and embraced her again, more gently this time, because she could hardly believe that this wasn’t all just a dream.

Sonja allowed herself to go limp in her embrace, so that Kim almost had to catch her. “I don’t want to fight this anymore. If you’re jealous, well, then you’re jealous. Maybe I should even take it as a compliment. But . . . please . . .” she lifted her face, “not another twin. That’s really hard.”

Kim had to laugh. “Twins, I believe, only come in two-packs. Unless, of course, your parents kept the secret that you were triplets or quadruplets. Then there could be another surprise or two.”

“I hope not.” Sonja sighed. “The one is enough for me.”

“You don’t like Sandra?” Kim looked at her rather unhappily.

“Oh, no, I do.” Sonja shook her head. “I just still can’t quite believe it. But the first time I saw her . . . I knew it was true. I’ve always known. I sensed that something was missing in my life, something that ought to be there. But I could never explain what it was.”

“I think Sandra felt exactly the same way.”

“Probably.” Sonja sighed again. “I haven’t treated her well. I need to apologize to her. I just couldn’t – I mean, she’s like me. Until now, I’d always thought there was only one of me.”

“And there is.” Kim brushed a kiss across Sonja’s lips. “You are unique, and so is Sandra. But nevertheless, you’re twins, and you have a number of things in common. Don’t you think it would be exciting to find out what?”

“I don’t quite know. It’s really very . . . strange.” Sonja took a deep breath. “Sandra thinks it’s funny. She recognized several of my gestures as her own, and it didn’t seem to bother her. But I’m not so sure.” She looked at Kim. “Imagine if someone suddenly walked through the door who looks exactly like you. Who talks like you, moves like you, even has your same idiosyncrasies – wouldn’t you find that a little bit – confusing?”

Kim had to laugh. “When you put it like that . . . sure.”

Sonja sighed. “Now, what are we going to do about Jo? What she saw –”

"She'll keep to herself," Kim concluded.

"But –" Sonja made an uncomfortable face. "I simply can't face her now . . ."

Kim raised her eyebrows. "You're going to have to."

"I can't." Sonja broke away from Kim and went over to her desk.

"Sonja, if there's one thing you're not, it's cowardly." Kim followed her. "And Jo – it was no surprise to her."

"But it looked like it was." Sonja sat down.

"Well . . ." Kim's face wrinkled like a dachshund's. "I just came from having lunch with her. She still thought that we . . . you and I . . . that we weren't –"

"Presumably, we all thought so at that point," Sonja remarked somewhat ironically. She looked at Kim. "Even you. Or didn't you?"

Kim raised her hands. "I wasn't planning – I hope you don't think that."

"To be honest, I don't know what to think."

"Should I talk to Jo?" Kim asked. "I'm not embarrassed by what happened."

"That won't do me any good, though." Sonja sighed. "You're not her boss." She hesitated briefly. "I'm just going to have to bite the bullet." She stood up.

Kim smiled. "May I ask you something?"

"Hmm?" Sonja walked slowly toward the door.

"Are we back together now?"

Sonja stopped. She turned toward Kim and looked at her. "Do you still have any doubts about that?"

"The wedding is going to be horrible! Just horrible!"

"Aw, sweetheart, we'll manage." Jo looked confidently at Jennifer.

"I will never understand why people get married," Sandra said.

"Your sister got married, too," Jennifer responded sourly.

"This proves that we're not completely alike." Sandra shrugged.

"You'd never get married?" Kim asked. "Under any circumstances?"

Sandra looked at her. "Up 'til now, I thought so," she replied reflectively. "But if the right woman came along . . ."

Kim cleared her throat and put a little distance between herself and the small group that had gathered in Jennifer's apartment to accomplish the final wedding preparations – or, truth be told, to prevent Jennifer from collapsing into utter hysteria.

"I know why I never wasted a thought on getting married," Jennifer went on. "I just can't do it. I'm not built for it. A wedding like this is putting one foot in the grave."

"Now, really, love . . ." Jo looked at her, aghast.

Jennifer threw her arms around Jo's neck and kissed her frantically. "If it weren't for you . . ." she gasped as though she were drawing her last breath, "I'd never do this to myself."

"That's quite a big compliment for me." Jo laughed.

"The biggest." Jennifer let her go. "You're the one. The one and only. No one else." Her eyes gleamed so tenderly at Jo; the whole room filled with warmth.

Kim's cell phone started to vibrate. She glanced at the number and answered. "Yes?"

"I tried you at home, but it just rang and rang," Sonja said. "You're out someplace?"

"I'm at Jennifer's," Kim explained. "She's a little nervous about the wedding next weekend."

"Ah. The wedding. Is it next weekend already?"

"Yes. And it's a good thing that it'll finally be over then. Jennifer's driving all of us crazy." Kim laughed softly and winked at Jennifer. Jennifer stuck her tongue out at her.

"All of us?" Sonja asked.

"Well, Jo and Sandra and me. We're here together."

"Sounds like you weren't planning to go home anytime soon," Sonja said.

"Are you still at the office?" Kim asked.

"Where else?" Sonja sighed. "The Saturdays I spend here keep getting longer. And I thought the longer this project went on, the easier it would get. But now, at the last minute, they had to come up with a whole bunch of things they could've told me about months ago. Then I would've planned for them from the start, and they would've been long since taken care of. Now the project is almost finished, and time is pressing. It's nearly impossible to accommodate anything new."

"Always the same story. Poor Sonja. You're going to stay in the office for a while yet?"

"Actually, I didn't want to. But if you're not home yet . . ."

"If you're done working, then come join us," Kim said. "Jennifer would be happy for more support. Beside which, you're the only one who –" She broke off sheepishly.

"The only one who has any experience with getting married," Sonja finished dryly. "I know."

"I'm sorry," Kim said. "I didn't mean to mention that. It just sort of slipped out."

"I'd be glad to lend Jennifer my support. But I don't even know her. She wouldn't want a virtual stranger there today."

"Let me ask her." Kim held the phone away from her ear. "Jennifer? Would you object if Sonja were to come over?"

"Sonja?" Jennifer arched her eyebrows.

Jo turned to face Kim, astonished.

"No, of course not," Jennifer said. "If she'd like to."

"Did you hear?" Kim asked, the phone back to her ear again. "Everyone would be glad to have you come."

"I'm sure Jo wouldn't." Sonja laughed. "I don't think this is such a good idea."

"She's invited!" Jennifer called over to Kim. "Tell her she's invited to my wedding –" She looked questioningly at Jo. Jo nodded, taken by surprise, "to *our* wedding. She's totally welcome."

"Oh, yes, Sonja!" Sandra clapped enthusiastically. "Join us!"

"Sounds like a great party you've got going there." Sonja sounded indecisive. Apparently the thought of coming over appealed to her, but she couldn't quite set aside her doubts.

Sandra stepped quickly over to Kim and took the cell phone out of her hand. "Come on already, sis! Let's start making up for lost time." She listened briefly to what Sonja was saying, then laughed.

"Yes, exactly. Wouldn't that be great? Come over and we'll figure it all out." She listened for another second, said "okay," gave Jennifer's address, and hung up. She handed the phone back to Kim. "Sorry, I hung up automatically, but she'll be here soon anyway, and then you can talk to her some more."

"She's coming?" Kim looked at her, amazed. Even though she had made the suggestion to Sonja, she hadn't expected her to accept it.

"Yes, she's coming." Sandra went back to Jennifer and Jo.

"Oh, God!" Jo groaned. "Did any of you stop to think about me for one second? She's my boss!"

"Which is precisely why it's high time I met her. I already know what she looks like, of course," Jennifer glanced at Sandra, "but I'd like to have a look at her in person. At the two of you together." She winked at Jo.

"You can't be thinking –?" Jo stared at her, dumbfounded.

"She's already done it with one of her secretaries." Jennifer kept a straight face. "You never know."

Sandra laughed out loud. "She's not serious, Jo!" She turned around. "And I think Kim would probably object." She tilted her head in that way she and Sonja had, so that one couldn't be sure what she was thinking.

"It wasn't her fault, Jennifer, you know that," Kim said.

"No, of course not, just yours," Jennifer said mockingly. "You raped her. Excuse me, but it takes two to tango – at least, to the best of my knowledge." She caressed Jo's cheek affectionately. "I was just playing, sweetheart. You know I trust you. Like you trust me."

"It's not quite that simple." Jo smiled uneasily. "What will I call her? 'Mrs. Kantner?' You're all on a first-name basis with her, but I can't do that to her face."

"I'm sure we'll find a solution." Jennifer turned around. "What do you guys think? This material or that one?" She held up several fabric swatches. "For all of you bridesmaids."

"You're nuts," Kim said. "I'm not wearing a dress."

Sandra took the fabric into her hand. "It feels wonderful. Why not?"

"You can do whatever you want," Kim said. "I'm coming in a suit."

"A simple suit won't do", Jennifer protested. "Pick something fancy! It's a costume party, after all. Come as Robin Hood for all I care, but it has to be something dressy."

"In tights?" Kim's eyes flew open. "Let me see that fabric again."

There was so much more to discuss, the time flew. Suddenly, the doorbell rang.

Jo raised her eyes and hesitated.

"I'll go." Jennifer trotted to the door and opened it. "So you're Sonja." She offered her hand. "Jennifer."

"Hello." Sonja shook Jennifer's hand and entered somewhat hesitantly.

"You know everybody," Jennifer said, "including Jo, my fiancée. "I suggest we all act like friends and forget the professional relationship while we're here. Otherwise it'll just get silly."

Sonja appeared just as taken aback as Jo had earlier. She said nothing.

"You two really are as alike as two peas in a pod," Jennifer determined as she let her gaze swing from Sonja to Sandra. "I'd only heard it secondhand before."

"We're gradually getting used to it," Sandra said. "Right, Sonja?"

"Yes, gradually," Sonja replied slowly. She had other things to get used to right then. The twin problem had retreated into the background for the moment.

"You have experience with this," Jennifer said. "What do you think? The fabrics for the bridesmaids. We can't agree." She drew Sonja over to the table where the fabric swatches lay.

Sandra stepped up to the table next to Sonja, and Kim observed them from behind. The same hair color, the same figure – it was unbelievable. If they weren't dressed differently, no one could have told them apart.

Sonja looked around for Kim, a bit lost.

Kim went quickly over to the table. "I'm not wearing a dress," she said decisively. "You can forget about that."

Sonja looked at her and chuckled. "Aw, it might not be so bad."

"I think so, too." Sandra backed her sister with a wink.

Kim looked into the two identical faces watching her. She'd never seen Sonja and Sandra this close together before, except the one time at the cafeteria, and that had been so brief, she could barely remember it. The uproar had displaced the memory. But now –

"That's unfair," she said. "There are always two of you. And with Jennifer, three. I don't have a chance against that."

"You can still think about it," Jennifer said. "This, or … the tights." She grinned.

"Tights?" Sonja asked.

"Robin Hood. Kim wants to come as Robin Hood," Jo explained.

"Ah, yes." Sonja turned to Kim. "You did say it was going to be a costume party."

"It has to be," Jennifer said. "Otherwise, my mother will have a fit. Women as far as the eye can see, and not a bright color among them, or anything like that. A costume is at least a bit decorative. She's gotten quite a few costumes ready, and anyone who comes without wearing proper clothing will get put in one of those."

"Seriously? She's taking it that far?" Jo asked, surprised. Apparently, she hadn't heard about that before.

"That doesn't apply to you, of course, darling," Jennifer said with a tender smile. "You're getting a wonderful wedding suit."

"I wish I could trade with you." Kim grimaced.

"There are wonderful costumes," Jennifer said. "Even ones without tights. But as a bridesmai-"

Kim groaned. "If only I hadn't agreed to that!"

"You should've thought of that earlier." Jennifer smirked some more.

"I couldn't refuse my best friend on something like that." Kim looked miserable.

"I wouldn't think so." Jennifer turned to Sonja. "Did you have this kind of problem with your bridesmaids?"

"Um … actually … actually, no." Sonja looked more than taken by surprise. "My sister –" She looked at Sandra. "Not Sandra … I mean, my other one –"

"Of course," Jennifer interrupted. "You didn't even know Sandra then."

"I would choose this fabric." Sonja focused on her task once more.

"I liked that one best, too." Sandra nodded.

"Is anyone surprised that you agree?" Jennifer looked from one of them to the other. "You're twins."

"We definitely don't always agree about everything." Sandra glanced briefly at Sonja. "We might have, if we'd grown up together."

"I don't think we would have then, either." Sonja put down the fabric. "But you'd have to ask some real twins about that."

"Well, we're not exactly fake twins," Sandra objected with a gentle laugh. "We are real ones. But we still have to get used to it."

"Quite a funny situation. Sandra and ... Mrs. Kantner –" Jo broke off.

"Sonja," her boss corrected. "I think it's about time. In the office it's still a bit –"

"Yes." Jo looked at her. "I think it's going to take me a while to get used to it."

"Then we'll both just have to practice." Sonja smiled. "I feel exactly the same way."

Jo ran over to Kim and whispered in her ear. "Good grief! I've never seen her smile like that. Now I understand why you –" She broke off and grinned at Kim.

Kim looked at Sonja and smiled also. "Yes. It's easy to understand."

"I think we'd better go." Kim turned to Sonja.

"Already?" Sonja sighed.

"I'm afraid so." Kim rolled to one side and brushed a finger affectionately across Sonja's cheek. "The wedding is in an hour. Really, we're already late."

Kim and Sonja had spent the night in a hotel, since it was too far to drive to the wedding on the same day. It was the first time they'd woken up together since the seminar.

Kim could hardly believe it when she awoke and there was Sonja, lying next to her. She'd simply looked at her, disbelieving, marveling at her beauty, her symmetrical features that had become so familiar to her again over the last few weeks.

"Why can't we just lie here a while longer?" Sonja sighed deeply.

"We could." Kim laughed. "But Jennifer would never speak to me again. Nor Jo to you."

"It's dreadful, how dependent a boss is on her employees." Sonja sighed again.

"Yeah, it's not easy being the boss." Kim bent over Sonja and brushed a kiss across her lips.

Sonja's lips wouldn't let her go with just a peck; they captured Kim's and caressed them.

Kim felt her belly getting warm, and not for the first time that morning. She and Sonja had spent the past several hours in one tender embrace after another. The hotel bed had surely experienced its share of sex before, but Kim doubted it had ever been so sustained. She freed herself forcefully from Sonja's mouth. "We have to go," she repeated in a whisper.

"Just one more time." Sonja pulled her down again and kissed her passionately.

Kim caressed Sonja's breast and let her hand wander between Sonja's thighs. "Sweetness," she whispered. She felt her arousal take hold of her and sweep all her doubts away. "You're the hottest woman in the northern hemisphere – and probably the southern one, too." She entered Sonja, and Sonja moaned.

Her hand sought a path between Kim's legs, too, and Kim didn't know what to concentrate on first: Sonja's growing excitement, or her own.

Suddenly, Sonja leaned forward, and her lips rested on Kim's breast, suckling at the nipple. Kim felt weakness overtake her. Lightning shot from her breast through her insides, leaving them aglow; she felt her labia swelling even more.

Sonja's wetness let Kim's hand slip out of her easily, and Sonja sat down on top of her. She pushed Kim's fingers back inside herself and rode her, wilder and wilder. Her hair flew up and down around her head, like fluttering birds.

"Oh, God!" Sonja gasped and cried out, her thighs clamping down around Kim's hips. Their vise grew ever tighter; Sonja convulsed around Kim's fingers and hips, riding her ever more violently, stiffened, collapsed.

But it wasn't long before she slid down Kim's body and dove inside her with her tongue.

Kim thrust her hips upwards; it shot through her like an electric shock, her nipples nearly bursting with the tension. She moaned loudly.

Sonja's tongue began to dance wildly inside her, just as wildly as she'd ridden atop her before. Kim's pearl became the center of the action; she spurred her to ever greater heights with her lips and tongue. Suddenly, she thrust several fingers inside Kim while the tip of her tongue beat a drum roll on Kim's pearl that drove it to the very peak of sensation.

Kim felt her breath catch as her womb exploded. She convulsed, unable to breathe or move, paralyzed until the spasm finally let her go. "Oh my God, Sonja ..." she gasped, her lungs struggling fervently for air.

Sonja slid on top of her and smiled. "I'm afraid that was the last one for the next few hours – who knows when we'll get another chance?"

"Please, don't even think about it," Kim moaned. "Forget all the secluded corners and closets you're imagining right now."

"I'm not imagining anything," Sonja said with a soft laugh, standing up. "In any case, we're going to have to take turns in the shower, or else we'll never get anywhere today."

"I think so, too." Kim smiled, crossed her arms behind her head, and watched Sonja as she walked into the attached bathroom. She was so happy. She had Sonja with her, had finally spent an entire night with her after such a long time, and she'd had a – well, yes, a strenuous morning.

Right up until the last minute, she hadn't believed that Sonja would really come. Not until she was standing at the door, picking Kim up. It was like déjà vu – like the time they'd driven to the seminar together in Sonja's car. Sonja sat in the driver's seat, Kim next to her, contemplating her beautiful face and listening to her.

Only this time, she was able to show how much she liked her.

"Your turn." Sonja stepped out of the shower and gestured behind herself. She wore a hotel bathrobe and looked even more seductive than usual in it.

"Can't you ever wear anything that doesn't immediately make all my hormones surge?" Kim asked with a laugh.

Sonja arched her eyebrows. "A bathrobe isn't exactly an evening gown." She laughed as well.

Kim went over and kissed her. "Since you'd be inside either one, there's no difference," she whispered. She sighed, tore herself away from Sonja, and went into the bathroom.

Shortly thereafter, they were both fully dressed. "Is there any point in having breakfast here in the hotel?" Sonja said. "I'm sure there'll be plenty to eat at the wedding."

"And Sandra?" Kim asked.

"Oh, right, we were going to meet up in the breakfast room." Sonja nodded. "Why, really? We could've just met at the wedding."

"No idea." Kim shrugged. "She said she'd come up this morning by car. Maybe she didn't want to go alone. Or maybe she wanted to have some coffee first."

"Are you ready?" Sonja looked at Kim.

"I think so. I can go to the registry office without a costume, anyhow. What comes after . . ." Kim grimaced.

Sonja laughed. "We'll just see what we get."

They left the room and went downstairs to the breakfast room.

When they arrived, they saw Sandra alone at a table. She smiled when she saw Sonja and Kim come in. "You two took your time."

Kim looked rather sheepish. Sonja cleared her throat. "Shall we go, then?" she asked.

"In a minute." Sandra stood up. She looked at Sonja. "Sonja, may I introduce your father?" She indicated an elegant older gentleman who was just coming in the door.

He stopped abruptly and stared at Sonja, then at Sandra again, then back at Sonja.

"Here she is, Pops." Sandra smiled. "Your other daughter."

Sonja stood there like a statue, not moving. "How could you –?" She glared furiously at Sandra. "Without asking me?"

"Would you have said yes?" Sandra smiled again. "I know you like I know myself, don't forget. I'd be furious in your place, too, but I couldn't do this to Pops any longer. Ever since he's known about you, that we met each other, he's wanted nothing other than to see you. Please – don't be mad. Or if you are, be mad at me. He's our father, *your* father."

Harald Kruschewski came closer. "Sonja," he whispered. "My little girl . . ."

Sonja stared at him.

"I know this is awful for you," he said. "What we did to you two –"

"What kind of a father are you?" Sonja asked coldly. "For thirty-five years –"

"You're right," he said guiltily. "But have you ever asked your mother that question?" He looked at Sandra. "How similar you two look," he said, overwhelmed. "I would hardly have known which one was you, and which one was she." He turned back to Sonja. "I'll go away again immediately. I just wanted to see you. By no means do I wish to burden you with my presence."

"But Pops . . ." Sandra linked arms with him and gave him a tender look. "Just let her calm down a little. I don't know what I would do –" she swallowed, "if I were to see our mother. I'd probably react exactly the same way."

"You haven't met her yet?" her father asked.

"No." Sandra shook her head. "Sonja hasn't introduced me yet."

"Is she –" Harald Kruschewski looked at Sonja. "How is she?"

"What business is it of yours? She hasn't interested you for thirty-five years, any more than I did." Sonja acted as cold as an iceberg.

"This is too much for you, I understand that." Harald Kruschewski smiled at Sandra. "I'd really better go now, child. You meant well, but Sonja really isn't as enthusiastic as you expected," he turned to face Sonja, "and as I had hoped. That really doesn't surprise me. You're both like your mother that way. She doesn't like surprises any more than you do."

"That's true." Sonja looked at him in amazement.

He smiled wistfully. "I was married to her. And we had you two. Even though it was a long time ago, I still remember what she was like." He looked at both of his daughters. "You're so much like her. She was a beautiful woman, just like the two of you."

"She's still –" Sonja cleared her throat. "I'm sorry. I'm . . . I know how my mother can be."

"I believe that!" He smiled, but then became serious again. "I shouldn't have done this to you. I should never have let her blackmail me."

"Blackmail?" Sonja stared at him.

"The laws were different then than they are now. The children always stayed with their mother. The father had practically no rights. But I didn't want that. I would only have gotten custody of the children if she had committed adultery. But she didn't do that." He laughed somewhat bitterly. "No, she didn't go that far. She had other methods."

"I don't believe it!" Sonja gasped, spun on her heel, and stalked out of the room at a rapid clip.

Sandra restrained Kim, who was already jumping up to follow Sonja. "She'll calm down again, believe me. But for the moment – go easy on her. I'll take care of my father."

Kim ran after Sonja, who was already unlocking the car door. Kim reached her just as she was about to get in.

"I'm driving back. I don't feel much like a wedding anymore. I'm sure Sandra will be happy to give you a ride home."

"Sonja . . ." Kim looked at her. "I know that was a shock for you, but he is your father – yours and Sandra's."

"For thirty-five years, he forgot that," Sonja said bitterly.

"It doesn't seem that way to me."

"You blame my mother, too?" Sonja hissed at her.

Kim had to smile. If Sonja's mother were like Sonja – which, indeed, her father had claimed – things couldn't be easy with her, either. "I don't know your mother. But I see that your father –"

"Don't call him that!" Sonja's voice rose.

"All right," Kim said. "Let's not talk about this right now. Stay here, please. None of this has anything to do with the wedding. We promised Jennifer and Jo."

Sonja looked down at the ground and took a deep breath. "You're right. But Sandra –" She raised a wrathful gaze. "I'm going to kill her!"

Kim laughed. "No, you aren't. Twins don't do that sort of thing. She's like another part of you. That's why you're so furious with her. You'll be able to sort this out once the storm has passed. Don't you think?"

Sonja tilted her head in the manner that was so characteristic of her. "You know, a while ago, I thought I had problems – serious problems. But when I look around at all this ... my whole life is in chaos. One giant mound of chaos ... a catastrophe. And I don't see any possibility –" She broke off in despair.

"Don't think about that." Kim wrapped an arm around Sonja. "I love you. Never forget that. Promise me that?" She looked at Sonja, trying to catch her gaze. "Do you promise?"

"I hate disorder. And I'm constantly confronted with it now." Sonja looked at Kim. "You're the only constant. You ... you've never abandoned me. I ..." she swallowed, "I don't know what I did to deserve that."

"You *do* deserve that." Kim drew Sonja into her arms. "Never doubt that you deserve it. My life would be pointless without you. If for no other reason, you deserve it. What would I do without you?"

Sonja laughed rather miserably. "You'd find someone else."

Kim looked at her earnestly. "Love isn't like a sweater that you can just exchange for a new one."

Sonja's mouth twitched indecisively. She seemed to be vacillating between crying and laughing. "You're wearing me out."

"I thought I already did that this morning," Kim answered wittily. Sonja seemed to have recovered herself, which reassured her, and the wedding mood returned.

"If you think that was all, just wait until tonight," Sonja said.

The corners of her mouth had made their decision.

Amused, they pointed upward.

The bridal couple's deep kiss seemed like it would never end. The registrar smiled and cleared her throat.

Jo and Jennifer appeared to wake as if from a dream. They gave each other one more tender look.

"You still need to sign here," the registrar said. The signatures were accomplished, and the official handed over the certificate. "Good luck," she said, and it sounded like she meant it.

Sonja looked reflective as they left the wedding chamber. Kim wondered whether she was remembering her own wedding day, and whether she'd had such an intimate relationship with her husband back then as Jo and Jennifer had today. At the same time, she wished she might one day have the chance to stand in such a wedding chamber – with Sonja as her bride. But that was out of the question. "Are you all right?" she asked.

Sonja lifted her gaze slowly, absent-mindedly. "Oh . . . yes."

"Doesn't it just make you want to bawl?" Jennifer's mother looked at Kim and dabbed a tear from the corner of her eye with a miniscule handkerchief. "I'm glad this is almost over. Only Axel is left, and then they'll all be married."

"That's not going to happen any time soon, Mama." Jennifer's brother Axel grinned at his mother.

Jennifer's mother turned around. "I used to think that about Jennifer, too; she was always so set against it."

"I was, too, until I met you," Jennifer's father laughed, walking over to them. "She gets that from me. But then, when the right woman comes along –" He laughed once more, took his wife's hand, and kissed it.

"Yes. Jo is all right." Jennifer's mother nodded. "I've had my share of worries, but I think Jennifer's in good hands with her."

"Now she can see for herself how it is," Jennifer's sister Kathrin chuckled. "She was always making jokes about Jens and me."

"Avoidance tactics," Axel said, from all the exalted wisdom of his twenty-two years. "She was really just jealous."

"I could tell!" Kathrin's husband Jens laughed.

Jennifer's mother looked around at Jo and Jennifer. "You'll be all right on your own, won't you? I'm going on ahead . . . to take care of the buffet."

"Yes, sure." Her husband nodded. "There are plenty of cars here."

Jennifer's mother disappeared quickly toward the exit.

"Where did my mother go?" Jennifer asked a minute later. "She was just here."

"The buffet . . ." Sonja said.

"Ah." Jennifer took a deep breath. She hung on Jo's arm, seeming like she never wanted to let go of her again. "Now we have all that behind us."

Jo smiled at her. "Are you happy?"

"At the moment, I think I'm still too worked up to be happy," Jennifer replied. "Ask me again when everyone else is gone."

"I'm sure I will." Jo grinned. "But I'm already happy. I hope that doesn't bother you."

Jennifer looked at her. "No, that doesn't bother me." She threw her arms around Jo, and once more, the two of them sank deep into a kiss.

Kim glanced at Sonja, and again, she thought Sonja seemed very reflective.

"Sonja, I'm sorry." Sandra approached them. "I didn't mean to catch you off-guard like that, but I felt so sorry for Pops . . ."

"It's all right. It had to happen sometime."

"Are you still mad at me?" Sandra gave her sister a guilt-ridden look, and it appeared as though Sonja were looking at herself, as if the two of them were the same person in a mirror. Kim still found this confusing.

Sonja – was she the person in the mirror, or the real one? – considered Sandra for a while. "No, I don't think so," she said then, to Kim's great relief. Kim had been feeling the tension between them almost physically. "I was very angry –"

"Understandably," Sandra said. "I knew you would be. I would've been, too. But Pops –"

"Is he still here?" Sonja asked.

"Yes." Sandra nodded.

"Why doesn't he just come with us to the wedding reception, then? We could talk there," Sonja suggested.

"Really?" Sandra looked at her in amazement. "So much for twin-sense. I wasn't expecting that."

"I'm glad I could surprise you." Sonja chuckled. "Doesn't it feel strange to you, too, to feel like someone else knows what you're thinking before you do? I don't like it too much."

"Neither do I, you're right." Sandra laughed. "And once again, we're in agreement. Apparently we can't avoid that entirely."

"Hardly." Sonja smiled. "We'll just have to live with it."

"Can we drive to the reception together?" Sandra asked. "I'd really like to discuss one more thing with you. Alone."

Sonja looked rather surprised, but handed Kim her keys. "Will you bring my car over? I don't think you can park that long here in front of City Hall."

Kim was just as amazed as Sonja, but she took the keys and nodded.

"Could you do me a big favor?" Sandra asked. "Drive over to the hotel and pick up my . . . our father. Bring him to the wedding reception. So he and Sonja can get to know each other."

Kim was a bit taken aback, but Sandra and Sonja were already leaving the building, and there was nothing else for her to do but to drive to the hotel.

"Have you known my daughter long?" Mr. Kruschewski asked after he got into the passenger seat, as Kim tried to find her way back to Jennifer's parents' house.

"Sandra? Not very long," she answered absently, because she had to concentrate on the road so closely.

"No, Sonja." Harald Kruschewski laughed softly. "I'd never dared to hope that I'd ever see her again. But I know so little about her. Nothing, really. She looks like Sandra, but I've known Sandra since she was a little girl. I raised her; Sonja is like a stranger to me, but I look into her face, and she seems so familiar. A peculiar situation." He looked sideways at Kim. "You probably can't relate to that. As a father, I suppose I'm a bit sentimental."

"Not at all," Kim said. "I can relate perfectly well. The first time I saw Sandra, I thought she was Sonja."

"It's tricky with twins." Harald Kruschewski shook his head. "They were still so tiny then, and at that age, all babies look pretty much alike. Seeing her again as an adult . . . it's unsettling. I knew that Sandra is a twin, but over the course of the years, I'd almost forgotten. I always had just her."

"Why did you – I'm sorry, that's none of my business." Kim turned to follow a curve.

"Why did we get divorced?" Mr. Kruschewski sighed. "Do you

know Sonja's and Sandra's mother?"

"No." Kim shook her head.

"Be glad," he said.

It occurred to Kim that Sonja had never talked about her family. Not about her husband, of course; Kim could understand that. She wouldn't have wanted to talk about him, either, but neither did Sonja talk about her birth family. "Sonja has a brother and a sister," she said. "They aren't your children, though?"

"No." Harald Kruschewski cast an interested glance at Kim. "Those must be half-siblings."

"Probably." Kim had never given much thought to Sonja's family. This was probably also because she herself was an only child. Her mother had emigrated to Australia years ago. She didn't have any other relations nearby, so she'd concentrated more on friendships.

"Yes, Elli was a beautiful woman." Harald Kruschewski sighed. "Lots of men were interested in her. She was quite . . . striking. I'm not surprised that she remarried." He looked curiously at Kim. "Has that marriage lasted?"

"I . . . I don't know," Kim replied, stunned. Harald Kruschewski was quizzing her as if she must know everything about Sonja and her family, but meanwhile, she was feeling more so than usual that the opposite was true. "Sonja . . . Sonja did mention that her . . . stepfather no longer lives with her mother."

"That doesn't surprise me, either. I'm glad that although Sandra looks like her mother, she didn't inherit her character. At least not entirely. She can be very stubborn." He laughed.

"Sonja, too." Kim laughed as well.

"Are you friends?" Harald Kruschewski asked.

"Um . . . yes." Kim felt warm. It was quite clear that Sonja wouldn't appreciate it, if Kim were to divulge any secrets to the man who, while he might be Sonja's biological father, was such a cipher to her.

"That means you like Sonja," Harald Kruschewski determined. "I'm glad. Then she must be more like Sandra than her mother."

"I can't judge that. Sonja and I . . . we work for the same company."

"Ah, so you're more like colleagues."

Kim was perfectly happy to have him think so. That was safe territory. "Yes," she confirmed. "She used to be my boss, but I'm in a different department now."

"Boss . . . yes. They both get that from their mother." Harald Kruschewski laughed. "Sandra is very ambitious, too. It wouldn't surprise me if she were to take over the whole supermarket chain soon."

Kim looked surprised. Until now, she'd never really thought of Sandra as such a career woman. She managed a supermarket, sure, but that wasn't exactly – "Really?" she asked, astounded.

"Maybe not quite." He laughed again. "But I've never been as ambitious as she is. She works hard."

"Like Sonja. They are twins, after all."

Harald Kruschewski lapsed into silence. "Do you know why Sonja doesn't have any children?" he asked after some time. "It's clear enough why Sandra doesn't, but Sandra told me Sonja's married."

"She . . . she – please, Mr. Kruschewski, ask her yourself. I can't say anything about that."

"Forgive me. These are the thoughts of an old man. I have two daughters, but no grandchildren. One just tends to wish for things to carry on – that the family survives. To a young person like you, that probably just seems silly."

Kim turned down the street where Jennifer's parents lived. The curbs on both sides were crammed with parked cars, some of which were even double-parked. There wasn't a single space left. Jennifer's large family had monopolized the entire town. "No. That doesn't seem silly to me at all." Kim pulled up in front of the entrance. "I'll drop you off here and find a place to park Sonja's car."

"This is Sonja's car?" He looked around appreciatively. "Boy, oh boy."

"She's a department head and in charge of a very important project, the most important one in the company at the moment. She'll probably be promoted to a senior executive position as soon as the project is finished."

"Oh," Harald Kruschewski said. "And I thought Sandra was ambitious."

"Looks good on you." Jennifer grinned.

"Happily, your mother thought of everything. You could've said something earlier, you know," Kim replied. "I have no objection to this kind of costume."

She wore a gentleman's suit from the period around 1815, with knee breeches and a few ruffles, which were typical for men back then, but no skirt. The wide jacket clung comfortably to her hips, and the color shimmered between blue and yellow – she felt like a member of the Congress of Vienna, but it wasn't an uncomfortable feeling. In one of the typical women's dresses of that time, she would barely have been able to move, and she was glad to have dodged that privilege.

"Anyway, I let you wear a suit as my bridesmaid," Jennifer said.

"Because otherwise, you wouldn't have had a bridesmaid!"

"There you are." Sonja suddenly appeared next to her. She wore a dress that was much less elaborate than Kim's costume. She didn't need another thing, however. She looked breathtaking in her bare-shouldered dress. Kim gulped at the vision.

"It took a while to pick out the costume." Kim could hardly tear her eyes away from Sonja. She'd seen her naked often enough, but these uncovered shoulders were far more seductive than that.

"I think everyone's here now." Jennifer looked at Jo. "We should open the festivities."

Jo turned rather red.

"You'll manage," Jennifer said encouragingly. "We practiced long enough."

Jo didn't seem convinced, but Jennifer pulled her onto the dance floor. Until then, the stereo had been playing soft background music. Someone turned it off, and the live band struck up a waltz.

Jo and Jennifer stood in the middle of the dance floor, completely alone. After two beats, Jo began to spin Jennifer in three-quarter time. Their steps became ever jauntier, and a few seconds later, they were flying around the room like a pair of professional dancers. The ample skirt on Jennifer's wedding gown floated like a cloud over the parquet floor.

"My goodness!" Kim couldn't hold back, it looked so impressive. Jo and Jennifer made a gorgeous couple.

"Magnificent!" Kathrin clapped her hands and laughed.

"Please, come dance!" Jennifer called. "Don't leave us all alone like this!"

Kim looked at Sonja. "May I?" She smiled.

Sonja smiled back. She said nothing.

Kim encircled her waist and danced with her out to the middle of the floor. Kathrin followed her with Jens, and shortly thereafter, Jennifer's parents joined in, too. The dance floor filled.

Sonja nestled into Kim's arms and danced with her, as she'd never done before. It would never have occurred to Kim to ask Sonja to go dancing with her. She would've turned it down, anyway. Suddenly, though, nothing seemed to please her more than to move through the room with Kim.

Kim would've liked to close her eyes to enjoy this moment, but she had to lead. All of a sudden, she thought she was seeing double. Sandra stood at the edge of the dance floor, and she was wearing the same dress as Sonja. It would've been impossible to tell them apart.

Kim opened her mouth to say something, when she noticed that Sonja was now leading instead of following. Sonja waltzed over toward Sandra.

"Would you like to cut in?" she asked when they'd reached Sandra.

Kim looked at her, taken aback.

"Not necessarily," Sandra said, and suddenly a light went on in Kim's head.

"You're not Sonja!" She stared at the woman on her arm.

"Didn't take you long to notice!" Sandra laughed and remained where she was. "I think the two of you ought to dance. I'll go over to my father, so he won't be so alone." She separated from Kim. "Have fun. And thank you for the dance." She smiled, turned around, and left.

"It was Sandra's idea," Sonja said. "I think she just wanted to dance with you."

"I . . . I'm sorry . . . I thought you –" Kim felt like she was inside a top that was spinning much too fast.

"Really?" The corners of Sonja's mouth began to twitch, then she grinned. "Sandra brought the two dresses with her. She wants to enjoy being a twin. For today, at least."

"You have a lot to catch up on. Ordinarily, you two would've played all sorts of tricks on people when you were kids, because no one could've told you apart."

"Apparently, that's even harder to do today. It's certainly a peculiar feeling. When I saw you dancing with Sandra, I almost thought it was me, even though I was standing here."

"Would you like to dance?" Kim asked.

Sonja hesitated.

"You don't have to. I was just asking."

"Whatever Sandra can do, I ought to be able to do, too, right?" Sonja asked a bit doubtfully. "I mean, I can dance, but –"

Kim looked at her. She knew what Sonja was trying to get at: she'd never danced with a woman before. "It's your choice."

"Can you lead?" Sonja asked.

"You saw me," Kim said.

Sonja lifted her arms. "Well, then – please."

"But you really are Sonja, now, right? You're not pulling my leg twice."

Sonja laughed softly. "I really am. I'm quite sure."

Once again Kim wrapped her arm around Sonja's waist. That is, the first time, it had been Sandra's. She led Sonja onto the dance floor. The band had clearly taken a fancy to waltzes and was now playing another one. Of course, Jennifer's mother might have been the one who chose the program. She loved waltzes.

The swaying rhythm took hold of her, and Kim took the first step. As much as they looked alike, she noticed now that Sonja was not Sandra. She wasn't used to dancing with a woman, certainly not in public like this. She didn't nestle into Kim's arm as Sandra had done, for whom this was normal; Sonja felt stiff and rigid.

Kim leaned forward. "Let yourself fall into me," she whispered in Sonja's ear. "I'll catch you. You don't need to be afraid. Just close your eyes."

Sonja looked into her face, seemed to ask herself a few questions that Kim couldn't guess at, but then she actually did close her eyes.

That very moment, she felt softer. Kim danced with her to the end of the waltz, and the longer they danced, the more Sonja nestled into Kim's arms, exactly as Sandra had done.

After a while, she opened her eyes again. "This is nice," she said softly. "You're an excellent dancer."

"It's wonderful to dance with you." Kim smiled at her. "We ought to do this more often."

Sonja arched her eyebrows.

"All right, it's wasn't a serious suggestion. Forget about it."

Sonja sighed. "I think it was a serious suggestion."

"Perhaps, but I know perfectly well that it isn't doable. Let's just enjoy the moment, our time today. This won't come again soon."

"No. It will never come again." For the moment Sonja seemed to forget where she was and laid her head on Kim's shoulder.

Kim very much enjoyed holding Sonja in her arms to dance, and she swung Sonja's huggable, supple body through the room, as if immersed in a dream. She knew that this wasn't reality, not her reality with Sonja, but for today, at this wedding, she suppressed all thoughts of reality. It was like a real-life fairy tale.

Sonja and Sandra led several more people into their twin trap over the next hour, amusing themselves royally.

"You two are just mean," Harald Kruschewski complained, "luring people in like that. That's not nice." But the corners of his eyes showed plenty of little laugh wrinkles, and he beheld his two beautiful daughters with fatherly pride and the same admiration. "You aren't little kids anymore, after all."

Sonja chuckled. "You're right. But it was fun anyway. Sometimes it's nice to be a kid again." She looked at Sandra. "I'm going to change clothes now and finally rescue the poor people."

"Aw, do you really mean that?" Sandra asked, disappointed.

"That was enough fun for one day," Sonja said. "I haven't had so much fun in years. It's overtaxing me."

"Understood." Sandra gave her sister a strange look.

"Where's Sonja's husband, then?" Harald Kruschewski asked.

"Didn't he want to come?"

Kim froze, and Sandra said quickly, "He doesn't much care for weddings, I think."

"I'd like to meet my son-in-law some time, you know," Mr. Kruschewski said. "You won't be blessing me with one of those, after all." He looked at Sandra.

"But maybe with a daughter-in-law." Sandra laughed. "You never know." She looked around. "A wedding like this puts funny ideas in a person's head."

"I wouldn't object," Harald Kruschewski said. "Do you have someone in mind?"

"Yes." Sandra looked at Kim. "But I'm afraid she's otherwise engaged."

"It doesn't do to interfere with existing relationships," Harald Kruschewski said, who hadn't caught Sandra's look. He was watching the dancers in the middle of the room with interest. "That only brings unhappiness." His gaze turned back to Sandra. "There are a lot of single women here."

Sandra laughed. "What am I supposed to do? Just ask all of them?"

"I don't think most of them would turn you down," Kim said. "An attractive woman like you –"

"Thanks." Sandra studied Kim's face. "But I have something else in mind."

"They're not crazy enough for you." Harald Kruschewski sighed. "That one you brought over once –" He shook his head. "My God, you could have anyone, the way you look, and then something like that."

"He means Patrizia," Sandra explained to Kim. "I once made the mistake of bringing her with me, and she was truly – well, like I said, it was a mistake."

"You don't need that, child," her father said. "Maybe you ought to ask Sonja how she did it. She didn't just get married yesterday, after all, so she seems to have found the right one."

Kim stiffened, then spun around and walked rapidly across the room, until she'd reached the far end. She took a glass of punch to try to calm herself, but her hand shook.

"What's wrong?" Sonja spoke to her from one side. She was now wearing a different dress than Sandra, which made it significantly easier to tell them apart.

Kim tried to suppress the shaking in her hands, but she couldn't. She set her punch glass down again. "Your father would like to get to know your husband."

"What?" Sonja stared at her.

"Ask him yourself. I –" Kim broke off and leaned against the table.

"What did he say?" Sonja asked.

"Well –" Kim took a deep breath. "Since Sandra isn't married, your . . . husband is his only son-in-law. It's certainly understandable that he wants to meet him. Now that he's found his daughter again, he wants to have the entire family around him."

Sonja made a dismissive sound. "Surely not." She looked at Kim and rested a hand on her shoulder. "Please, don't be upset. He doesn't know –"

"No, he doesn't know. And it would probably surprise him quite a bit, too," Kim replied forcefully. "After all, he still thinks at least one of his daughters is straight."

"Kim . . ." Sonja wrung her hands.

"You are, too, aren't you?" Kim asked. All her frustration rose up in her once more. She'd held it down because she'd been so happy to have Sonja back, but now, again, she became aware of how precarious that happiness was. They existed on borrowed time, and how long that time would be, she couldn't even guess. Nor did she want to. "Why shouldn't he meet his son-in-law, then?" she asked bitterly. "Knowing me doesn't do him any good, after all."

"Please, Kim . . ." Sonja turned away. "I was so glad that at least you –"

"That at least I heel like a good little doggie?" Kim asked. "Yes, apparently I did. But at some point –" She took a deep breath. "I love you, Sonja. I love you so much, I can't imagine how it will be when –"

"It won't –" Sonja faced her and examined her face slowly, questioningly, from top to bottom and back again, holding her gaze. "It won't end," she said softly. "I'm working on that. Really."

"You're getting a divorce?"

"I – I can't do that," Sonja said wearily. "But – but . . . maybe –"

"I'm sorry about what my father said." Sandra came up to them. She looked from Kim to Sonja and back. "It appears you've already discussed it."

"Yeah." Kim's lips were pinched.

"Sonja, what is it with your husband?" Sandra asked. "Something's not right. I can feel it. You're not happy. And if things were good in your marriage, you wouldn't be with Kim. And your husband would be here."

"Why don't you ask him, if you all are so interested in him!" Sonja snarled and ran out the door.

Sandra turned to look at Kim. "How do you stand this? Why –?"

"Why don't I just take you?" Kim said. "I've asked myself that many times already."

"There's nothing I'd wish for more," Sandra said.

"I know." Kim looked at her. "And it would be the simplest solution. Nothing much would change. From the outside, no one would see any difference. You look just like her. You're like her in so many ways –"

"But not completely." Sandra sighed. "For example, I've never been heterosexual. I don't understand why she is. She's my twin sister, after all. But I don't think she's straight, she's bi. And you know how it is with bi women. We all do."

"Yes."

"Do you know him? Her husband, I mean?"

"Oh, no!" Kim laughed dryly. "How would I? I'm just her –"

"Oh, come on, Kim, you're not that." Sandra came up and hugged her. "You know you aren't. She – she feels the same about you as I do, you can be sure of that."

"Sandra . . . we . . . we can't do this," Kim whispered.

"It's not easy for me, either." Sandra swallowed. "This morning . . . when you two came into the hotel breakfast room . . . I saw your eyes. You had just –"

"I –" Kim swallowed. "What am I supposed to say to that?"

"Nothing." Sandra sighed. "It's just – not easy." She let go of Kim. "You're right. We can't do this. I can't do it to Sonja, not to my own sister, even though theoretically, I hardly know her. And you certainly can't."

"No, I can't," Kim said.

"Ah, you two found each other?" Sonja came back in. "Well then, I can go." She tried to walk past Kim to the exit.

"Don't, Sonja." Sandra held her there. "It's not what it looks like. Or yes – it is. From my end. You know it is. We like the same people, we *love* the same – it can't be any other way. We're going to have to come to terms with that. But you also know I would never do that to you. Or would you do it?"

Sonja looked at her, her eyes flying over the face that was her own. "No."

"So please . . ." Sandra said. "Make up with each other. There's no reason to spoil the wedding. It's been so nice up to now." She grinned. "We could put one over on a few more people. We could switch dresses again."

"Please, no!" Kim groaned.

"Fine, then. For your sake, we won't do it. But I'm keeping the option open. For another occasion." Sandra looked at her sister.

Sonja's mouth curled upwards. "Certain occasions are out of the question. Even though you still like Kim so much."

"Do you think we should go outside and shoot each other?" Sandra suggested.

"Will you stop it already?" Kim interrupted her.

The two of them turned to face her simultaneously, in complete synchrony, and arched their eyebrows in the same gesture.

Kim groaned again. "I can't take this anymore!"

A young man, someone Kim hadn't seen before but who nevertheless looked oddly familiar, approached them cautiously. "Pardon me?" He looked at each of them in turn, as if he didn't know whom to address.

When neither Sandra nor Sonja answered, Kim took pity on him. "Yes?"

"I'm looking for –" He swallowed. "I'm looking for Johnny. Johnny Mayrhofer."

"Johnny?" Kim repeated, confused. "Mayrhofer?"

"My . . . my sister," he said.

All three stared at him.

"You . . . you're her brother?" Kim suddenly recalled what Jennifer had told her about Jo's dream. "What do you want with her?" She wasn't sure whether or not it was a good idea to tell this young man where his sister was, although he looked utterly harmless.

"She . . . this is her wedding, isn't it?" He swallowed once more. "A Mrs. Hermann called me. She said she was . . . her daughter was –"

"Jennifer," Kim said. "Jennifer Hermann. My best friend. She got married today."

"Then is she –" He looked around, unsure of himself. "Where is she? Where's Johnny?"

Kim didn't know what to do. Jennifer's mother had called Jo's brother? How did she even know that he existed, or where he was? Not even Jennifer had known that.

"Wait here a minute." She didn't see Jo and Jennifer. Maybe they were off making out in a quiet corner somewhere. Or they were otherwise occupied. In any case, it would probably be better not to let this strange brother go looking for them; that could go very badly.

She looked at Sandra and Sonja. "Could you two take care of this young man for a minute? I have to find Jennifer."

Both of them nodded in unison. Kim refrained from imagining how that was going to work out; instead, she concentrated on the task before her.

She went to Jennifer's mother, who was eyeing the buffet skeptically. She was probably thinking it wouldn't be enough. "Jo's brother is here," Kim said. "You called him?"

"Oh . . . yes." Mrs. Hermann didn't seem to have her mind wholly on the subject. The buffet interested her much more than Kim's question.

"Why?" Kim asked. "What are we supposed to do now? What if Jo doesn't want to see him? Does Jennifer know about this?"

"No." Mrs. Hermann now turned her full attention to Kim. "It was supposed to be a surprise."

"We don't know what happened between Jo and her brother. Jo has nightmares about him. Was it a good idea to call him?"

"He's her brother. And Jennifer gets the impression that Jo – that she misses her brother. And so I thought –"

"Hopefully, that wasn't the wrong thing to do," Kim said. "Have you seen Jennifer?"

"She's upstairs," Mrs. Hermann said. "Changing."

Kim nodded and ran up one flight of stairs to Jennifer's room. She knocked.

From inside she heard Jennifer's voice. "Yes?"

"Can I come in? It's me, Kim."

"Yes, come in."

Kim opened the door. She'd been afraid that Jo would be in there too, but she was in luck. Jennifer was alone. She'd taken off her wedding dress and now stood there in just her underwear. "Brides keep getting hotter and hotter," Kim said with a grin.

"Don't you dare. I'm a married woman now." Jennifer grinned back. "Oh, sorry," she added quickly.

"Forget it." Kim waved it away. "We have other worries at the moment. Jo's brother is here."

"What?" Jennifer gaped at her.

"Your mother called him, and now he's standing downstairs; Sonja and Sandra are loading him up with punch," Kim explained.

"My mother did what?" Jennifer looked stunned.

"How did she even get his number?" Kim wondered.

"She knew Jo's last name and where she's from. There probably aren't that many Mayrhofers in the city," Jennifer mused. She sighed. "This is so typical of her. She couldn't bear not to have Jo's family here. Without them, the wedding wouldn't be complete."

"Yeah, and what are we going to do now?" Kim looked inquiringly at Jennifer.

"Find Jo." Jennifer reached for a pair of jeans that lay on a chair and pulled them on. "I hope she hasn't run into him already." Quickly, she slipped into a T-shirt, and they left the room together.

They met Jo on the stairs. She was just coming up. "You look normal again." She grinned at Jennifer. It didn't look as though she'd seen her brother already; she seemed completely relaxed.

Jennifer inhaled. "Sweetheart, I have to tell you something," she began.

"Already? We only just got married." Jo grinned again. "I thought it'd be a while before you hit me with the rolling pin."

"No rolling pin," Jennifer said. "Unfortunately, it's not that simple."

Jo realized that they were talking about something serious. "What's wrong?"

Jennifer folded her hands. "I don't know how to say this, but there's someone –"

"Someone?" Jo frowned deeply.

"What's the story with your brother?" Kim burst out. "Are you enemies? Did he do something to you?"

"My . . . brother?" Jo stared at her and swayed a little.

"My mother called him," Jennifer explained. "I don't know where she got that idea, but now – he's here."

"My brother." Jo sank down onto a step.

"So you're not denying his existence anymore?" Jennifer asked.

Jo swallowed. Her breathing was heavy, as though it required a great effort. "No . . . I . . . no, I don't deny it," she whispered weakly.

"Should I . . . should we send him away?" Kim asked. "Do you want to not see him?"

Jo looked up. "He . . . if he's here now . . ."

"You don't have to see him if you don't want to, darling," Jennifer said gently, sitting down next to Jo on the stairs. "I have a thing or two to tell my mother!"

"No . . . I . . . if . . . I'd like to talk to him," Jo breathed in an unsteady voice.

"Really?" Jennifer looked worried. She clearly recalled more than one night in which Jo had woken from nightmares.

"Yes." Jo braced herself against the banister and rose slowly. "Where is he?" She looked at Kim.

"It might be better not to do this in front of all those people –" Kim suggested.

"Bring him up to my room," Jennifer said. "We'll be in there." She took Jo's arm and led her up the stairs.

Slowly Kim walked back downstairs. She considered whether she really ought to get Jo's brother. How would Jo react? Did she really mean what she said? What would he do when he saw her?

There are three of us, she thought. *He's alone. And not a particularly muscular fellow, actually fairly small and delicate for a man. We ought to be able to handle it.* She quickened her steps and headed toward the punchbowl.

Sandra and Sonja were still standing side by side, annoying people. Some still hadn't gotten used to the sight. Jo's brother did indeed have a glass of punch in his hand, but he didn't appear to have drunk any of it; it was still full to the brim.

"Your sister is upstairs," Kim told him when she'd reached him. "In Jennifer's room. I'll take you there."

"She –" He had violet-blue eyes, which looked at Kim in disbelief. "She really wants to see me?"

Kim nodded. "Yes. She's waiting for you."

He looked at Sandra and Sonja. "Thanks." He set the glass of punch on the table. "When you start seeing double even without any alcohol, it's probably time to leave the party."

"They *are* double," Kim said. "It's not a question of the alcohol."

"I know." He smiled, and now Kim realized what had seemed so familiar about him. The family resemblance to Jo was unmistakable. They weren't twins, but definitely related.

"I'll be right back," she said to Sandra and Sonja. "I'm taking him to Jennifer and Jo."

"I suggest we go join Pops." Sandra glanced at her sister. "Or would you rather not?"

Sonja shook her head. "No, that's fine."

"Good," Sandra said. "See you later."

Kim nodded and pointed toward the door. "Come on, it's this way."

Jo's brother followed her up the stairs. Jennifer's door stood open. Jo sat on the bed, Jennifer next to her.

Kim tried to keep herself between Jo and her brother, in case anything were to happen.

"Johnny ..." Jo's brother whispered tonelessly, stopping two steps inside the door. "Forgive me. I was so dumb. I'm so horribly sorry."

Jo raised her head, which she'd held low. She stood up, took a step, and stopped. "Frankie," she whispered. "You came ..."

"Johnny ..." Frankie breathed, once again weak.

Jo leapt forward and crashed into him, throwing her arms around his neck. Tears coursed down her cheeks. “Frankie,” she whispered. “Frankie . . .”

Jennifer and Kim stood in the room, rather helpless; they didn’t know what to do.

Jo turned around, her face flooded with tears. “This is my brother,” she said, sobbing. “Frankie.”

“Or just Frank,” her brother added. He looked likewise deeply shaken, and his eyes shone wetly. “But most people call me Frankie.”

Kim and Jennifer breathed simultaneous sighs of relief. It didn’t seem as though Jo and her brother still had a problem with each other. On the contrary.

“Jo . . . darling . . .” Jennifer looked at Jo, uncomprehending. “Why . . . why did you . . .?”

“I . . . Frankie . . .” Jo staggered to the bed and let herself drop. “He . . . you . . .” She gulped heavily and looked at her brother. “Do Mama and Papa know –?”

Frank Mayrhofer shook his head. “No. I’m here alone.”

Jo’s head sank to her chest. Frank went over and sat down next to her. “They’ll never understand it,” he said gently. “Not about you, and – not about me, either.”

“About . . . you?” Jo raised her head and looked at him, dumbfounded.

“Yes. I fought it, I didn’t want to accept it, and everything I hated about myself, I saw in you. That’s why . . . that’s why – My God, Johnny, I am so sorry!” A tear loosed itself from the corner of his eye and ran down his cheek.

Jo lifted her hand to wipe away the tear. “But . . . but . . . you . . .”

“Yes, I know.” He laughed softly. “All those women I slept with . . .” He shook his head. “But it was never any fun. I never told anybody that.” He looked at his sister and smiled. “You probably wouldn’t understand it, either.”

“No.” Jo started to smile as well. “I don’t understand that. It’s plenty of fun for me.” She looked up at Jennifer. “May I introduce my wife, Frankie? This is Jennifer.” She raised an arm. Jennifer grasped her hand and stood beside her. Jo smiled even more and sought Jennifer's eyes. "The sweetest woman in the world," she said tenderly.

Frank stood up. "Nice to meet you, Jennifer."

"Likewise, brother-in-law," Jennifer replied with a grin. She sat down next to Jo. "I'm so happy for you, sweetheart. I thought . . . I never expected your brother to be so . . . nice." She looked apologetically up at Frank. "I'm sorry, but Jo has nightmares, and she sometimes says your name. So naturally, I thought –"

"You had every right to think that," Frank said. "Oh, Johnny . . ." He moaned. "What have I done to you?"

Jo looked at him. "It's all better now. But Mama . . . Papa . . ."

"If they throw me out, too, then they won't have any children left," Frank said. "They'll stop and think before they do that. Mama needs to finally get it through her head that her effing church and the effing neighbors aren't all that matters. And Papa – ah, it's all the same to him anyway. He only does what Mama tells him to, always has. If she changed her mind, he would, too."

"She's not going to change her mind," Jo said sadly.

"Just wait. When she sees that she's all alone . . . At any rate, I'm not just going to let it lie anymore. I've done that far too long. I don't even know what I can do to make it up to you." He looked at her guiltily.

"A couple of weeks ago, I was –" Jo swallowed. "I was home. I stood outside the door, all weekend. I wanted to invite all of you to the wedding, but –"

"I understand," Frank said. "I probably couldn't have brought myself to do it, either, if it weren't for –" He laughed out loud. "You won't believe this, but it was actually the pastor who read me the whole of Leviticus. He's gay. And recently had his coming-out in church. A couple of people left, of course, but most of them applauded when he announced it from the chancel. Good thing we're not Catholic; then he probably wouldn't have gotten away with it."

"No, probably not." Jo looked bemused. "The pastor . . . Mama's pastor . . . is gay?"

"Yeah, and now of course the whole rumor mill is starting up, about what people are saying he might have done with the boys in confirmation class and all that. But he's totally cool. I don't think you know him at all. He first came after you ... were gone." He dropped his gaze. "Man, I was such a –"

"You couldn't help it." Jo looked at Jennifer. "I think a glass of champagne wouldn't hurt about now, don't you? Today is turning out to be a day of celebration for me in more than one respect. First, you chose me ... and now, my brother, too ... I would never have dared to hope for all that."

"Champagne is a good idea," Frank agreed. His whole face beamed. Then he went over to his sister and hugged her once more. "And you can be certain that this won't be the last time we drink champagne together. Next time, we'll drink it with Mama."

Jo laughed dryly. "I still can't see that!"

"But I can. I see it before me, quite clearly. Even if I have to handcuff her first." Frank laughed out loud. "She already thinks we perverts do that kind of thing anyway! So she shouldn't be surprised."

Jo stood up. "Frankie, you're still a little boy," she scolded. "That's not how you act around grown-ups."

"Oh, my big, big sister ..." Frankie teased her.

Jennifer stood up as well. "What a weight this is off my chest. I didn't know what was pressing down on Jo. I couldn't get it out of her."

"I'm sorry," Jo said. "You and your storybook family ... everything seems so simple with you guys. Everyone accepts everyone else, you're all happy and love each other ... I couldn't keep up with that."

"Sure you can. At least as far as your brother is concerned." Jennifer grinned. "Nonetheless, I'm going to give my mother an earful. She could've kept me in the loop on this one. As long as we're on the subject of *great family*."

"She is great," Jo insisted. "I wish my mother were here, to see that there's another way." Again a tear stole into her eye.

"Don't think about that anymore, love." Jennifer kissed the tear away. "We're a family now, you and I."

Frank raised his hand, as if asking to be called on in school. "May I belong to your family, too?" he asked shyly.

"Sure!" Jennifer laughed. "Has Jo told you yet how big my family is? There are a couple of neighbors in the crowd downstairs, but most of them are family – and Jo married into that. So if you want to belong, you're going to have to be ready to put up with many, many family celebrations like this one."

"I'll do my best." Frank laughed.

As they went down the stairs, Kim let her gaze roam around the room, searching for Sonja. Jo's problems were solved, at least partially, but her own were far from over.

Kim saw that Sandra and Sonja were standing and conversing with their father. Anyone seeing that image would've taken it for the perfect family photo, two gorgeous daughters with their still-handsome father.

Looking more closely, however, an observer would realize that Sandra was standing closer to her father and touching him often, while Sonja stood to one side, more like a spectator who wasn't involved in the scene.

Sonja looked in her direction as Kim approached the small group. "Is something not right between Jo and her brother?" she asked.

"No." Kim smiled. "Everything is fine now." She turned around and looked at Jennifer, Jo, and Frank, who were already toasting each other with champagne.

"That was kind of weird," Sandra said. "The boy was absolutely flustered, kept interrogating us about Jo the whole time, as if we must know her inside and out. When he's the one who's related to her, not us."

Kim nodded. "Yes, apparently he was really a bit of a mess. But now," she smiled once more, "everyone's doing great."

"What was the problem?" Sandra asked. "Did they have a fight?"

"Yes ... I think ... something like that." Kim looked at Sonja. "Can I talk to you for a minute?" Sonja raised her eyebrows, Sandra likewise. Kim groaned. "And could you two please stop that?" Sandra and Sonja grinned in unison. "I guess there's no point." Kim sighed deeply.

"I'd like a glass of champagne, too," Sonja said. "Shall we go get some?"

Kim nodded, and they took themselves off to the buffet. "I'm sorry," Kim said. "Your father's question rattled me so badly –"

"I know," Sonja said. "Me, too." They stopped in front of the buffet and each took a glass. "In fact, it's still rattling me that he *is* my father." She raised her glass. "Let's make a toast. To fathers, mothers ... families ... the nicest thing there is." She clinked against Kim's glass and drank. Her words had sounded bitter.

"Your father and Sandra ... they're a part of your family. And they're nice." Kim observed Sonja's withdrawn expression.

"Yes, they are nice. I'm sure I'll get used to it."

Kim laughed in surprise. "That they're nice?"

"I did mention that I don't care for this whole family circus," Sonja replied irritably.

"My family –" Kim raised a hand, "is as good as nonexistent. That's probably why it's hard for me not to envy other people their families."

"You envy me my family?" Sonja raised her brows in astonishment. Fortunately, Sandra wasn't there to double the effect.

"The part of it that I know, yes. I like Sandra, and if she were my sister –"

"You'd be a twin, and on top of that, you couldn't make out with her," Sonja said. "I don't think you'd like that so much."

"We haven't –" Kim sighed. "She looks like you." Her mouth twitched. "Are you jealous?"

"Jealous?" Sonja looked at her as though that were an absurd idea.

"It bothered you, admit it. You were absolutely furious."

"Was I." Sonja looked at Kim coolly.

"Would it reassure you if I were to tell you that Sandra and I have decided that we can't – and don't want to – do that to you?"

"Have you." Sonja was still acting quite composed, but Kim could've sworn that she was seething inside. "How nice of you."

That's what it was, Kim thought. *She hasn't been jealous all along. She knew she had no competition. Now she's not so sure anymore.* She grinned internally. "Yes, I think so, too."

Sonja's eyebrows knit together in a way that Kim hadn't seen in a long time.

"I love *you*," Kim said. "You truly don't need to be jealous. Sandra confuses me, because she looks like you, and I like her, because in many ways she *is* like you – but that's all."

"I'm not jealous." Sonja turned around and set down her glass. "That would be completely pointless. Jealousy accomplishes nothing – except trouble."

"Why don't you want to admit it?" Kim asked. "What would be wrong with that? It just shows that –"

"It shows nothing at all," Sonja interrupted her. "Jealousy is a destructive force that never does any good."

Kim frowned. "Are you still mad at me because I –?"

Sonja shook her head. "That has nothing to do with you."

"I understand," Kim said. If it was true that it had nothing to do with her, it could only be connected with Sonja's husband. He was jealous, and made her life a living hell.

"I hardly think so." Sonja looked at Kim. "All right, fine, I'll admit it. This whole twin affair is driving me half crazy. It's fun to pull people's legs, but when I saw Sandra dancing with you – well, you suit each other so well. And Sandra . . . is free.. It would only be logical –"

"Feelings aren't logical," Kim interrupted her gently. She examined Sonja's face. "*Love* isn't logical. And as much as you two resemble one another . . . you're not the same. On the dance floor, it might've looked that way – on the outside, you two are impossible to tell apart – but a human being doesn't just consist of genes. Her experiences are important, too. You know that as well as I do. And your experiences couldn't be more different."

"Probably." Sonja took a deep breath. "I wish I could change that."

"You'd rather have had her experiences?"

Sonja looked over at Sandra and her father, who still stood next to each other. "She's so . . . cheerful."

"You were, too – in the beginning, when I met you, when you first joined the company." Kim looked at her. "What happened? What changed you so much?"

Sonja didn't answer.

"Was it my fault?" Kim asked. "Did it turn your life so upside down that you were suddenly involved with a woman –"

"If only it were just that . . ." Sonja ran a hand through her hair. "That would be simple."

Kim looked at her, astonished. "Simple?" She certainly wouldn't have thought that.

"That Sandra has always –" Sonja sighed. "We're twins. It's impossible for us to be completely different in such a fundamental way."

"But you had never –"

"No." Sonja shook her head thoughtfully. "That's the experience story again. She grew up completely differently than I did. My mother would never have –"

"I don't think Sandra would've let that stop her." Kim looked back over toward Sandra. Sandra happened to be looking in her direction just then and arched an eyebrow inquisitively. Kim smiled gently. Sandra did, too. It was so natural, as if they'd known each other forever. And yet –

"You don't know my mother," Sonja said.

"So she is like your father said?" Just recently, Sonja had still denied that.

Sonja sighed anew. "Oh, yes, that she is."

"I don't understand –" Kim shook her head. "I don't understand how a mother could separate her children … twins. She never mentioned Sandra?"

"Of course not. Or else I would've known about her."

"Yeah." Kim simply couldn't grasp it. "She just forgot about her?"

"Hardly. After all, she did give birth to her. But my mother can be very … systematic. If she decides that something doesn't exist, then it doesn't exist."

"Even her own daughter?"

"She has three other children," Sonja said.

"But the fourth one didn't matter to her." Kim shook her head once more.

"The other three didn't, either," Sonja said. "In a way."

Kim's astonishment grew. Her face was one big question mark.

"She didn't have us because she loves children," Sonja added.

Kim was shocked. This didn't sound much like a happy childhood.

"Daughters aren't really important, in any case," Sonja continued. "The only one who counts is my brother, her son. After he came along, she stopped having children. Her task had been fulfilled."

"Sonja … I –" Kim was speechless.

"And her son-in-law, of course." Sonja's voice now sounded even bitterer than it had before. "My husband."

"Well, then, she must've been very proud of you when you got married." Kim swallowed. If Sonja had grown up like that, how could Kim, a woman, ever compete with her husband – or with any man?

"Of me?" Sonja laughed dryly. "Of herself! It was *her* achievement. I only fulfilled my obligation, the task she had set for me. And I was supposed to go on fulfilling it. Have children. Sons, in particular. Since I can no longer do that, she's lost all interest in me."

Sonja stood there, like a fortified tower behind a high wall meant to remind everyone that it was unconquerable.

Nonetheless, Kim stepped forward and took her into her arms. "Beloved . . ." she whispered.

Sonja jerked. She had kept her composure until now, but all of a sudden, she seemed to lose control. "It was a girl," she whispered. "The baby I lost, it was a girl." A quiet sob caught in her throat, as though she didn't want to permit herself to cry. "It wouldn't have been good enough, anyway."

"Oh, my God, my sweet darling," Kim whispered, stroking her. "What have you been through?" Her heart pounded with sympathy. Sonja had always seemed so strong, so unshakable, but that was all just a façade. She was strong, yes, otherwise she never would've survived all this, but she had to fight for that strength every single day – against such obstacles.

Sandra came over to them. "What's wrong?" she asked, concerned.

"She's not feeling well," Kim said. "Maybe I'd better take her back to the hotel."

"No, I –" Sonja straightened up and brushed back her hair. "It's all right now. It's over."

"You don't have to –"

Sandra interrupted Kim. "Let her be," she said gently. She rested a hand on Sonja's shoulder. "It's over – like she says." She glanced at Sonja's face, which still bore traces of the effort. "Everything okay?"

"Yes." Sonja nodded.

"Isn't there anything I can do?" Kim asked.

It wasn't Sonja who answered, but Sandra. "No. She just needs to go to the bathroom and wash her face."

Kim was confused. Sandra was acting as though she were Sonja's mother. Or not ... After everything she'd heard about Sonja's mother ...

Sonja nodded again.

"I'll go with you," Sandra said.

Sonja didn't argue, and the two of them disappeared upstairs.

Kim stayed behind, rather puzzled.

"What's wrong with Sonja?" Jennifer had switched from champagne to punch in the meantime. "Why does she look so upset?"

Kim sighed. "Jo isn't the only one whose mother... takes some getting used to."

"Oh." Jennifer looked around until she spotted her mother in the crowd. "I guess I really shouldn't give mine too much of a hard time."

"No, you shouldn't. Be glad you have her," Kim said. "And I'm going to call my mother today. Even if she is in Australia, having a mother like her is a great bit of luck. I've never been so aware of that before."

"Sonja's mother is that bad?" Jennifer asked, interested.

"Seems that way. This is the first time she's ever talked about her."

"She's very closed," Jennifer said. "I've noticed that. Sandra's completely different. Funny how twins can be so dissimilar. I could never mix them up." She laughed. "Except when they do it on purpose!"

"Yes, the exterior certainly plays its part. It's deceptive at first." Kim took a deep breath. "Anyway, this is a wedding I'm not going to forget any time soon ..."

"Neither will I." Jennifer looked over at Jo and Frank, who were standing there happily and conversing animatedly. "Even if it weren't my own, I wouldn't."

Soft music floated pleasantly through the room. Kim stood at the window and looked out. A week had passed since the wedding, Jennifer and Jo were still on their honeymoon, and Kim was – as usual on Sundays – alone. It was a beautiful day, and she was considering a walk in the nearby castle grounds.

The prior week had proceeded without upset. Sonja and Kim had seen each other every day, but they hadn't talked about what had happened at the wedding. The memory seemed to have sunk into obscurity.

The telephone rang. Kim turned around. It couldn't be Sonja, she didn't call on Sundays; Jo and Jennifer were in the Caribbean; and it was the wrong time for her mother in Australia to be calling. She went to the phone and picked it up.

"Don't you think it's much too pretty a day to sit inside?"

As usual, she had to think about it for a moment, but since Sonja was out of the question as a Sunday caller, it had to be Sandra. The voice was the same.

"Yes," Kim agreed. "I was just thinking about going for a walk."

"Good idea," Sandra said. "I'll join you. It's pretty bleak in the city, in spite of the nice weather. There's a park near you."

"That's what I was thinking, too," Kim said.

"I'll come over. Don't go without me." Sandra laughed.

"I won't." Kim laughed, too. "I'll be glad to have the company." She hung up.

She and Sandra hadn't seen each other since the wedding. *How practical*, she thought, rather mischievously. *Sonja during the week, and Sandra on Sundays, that's convenient*. Even though she chided herself for having such thoughts, they were somehow always close to the surface.

There wasn't much traffic on Sundays, so Sandra wasn't likely to take much longer than a quarter of an hour. Kim picked up a book and sat down to wait.

The quarter of an hour wasn't quite past when the doorbell rang. Kim walked to the foyer and pressed the button. Then she put on her shoes. Perhaps Sandra wouldn't even come up, but would be waiting down below.

Then she heard footsteps on the stairs. So she was coming up, after all. Kim opened the door. "That was quick!" A moment later, she stopped short. "Sonja?" she asked, astonished.

Sonja smiled. "I know you weren't expecting me."

"No . . . uh . . . it's Sunday." Kim let Sonja in.

She'd barely shut the door when the bell rang again.

Sonja looked inquiringly at Kim.

"That's Sandra," Kim explained, an embarrassed flush creeping across her face. This annoyed her. There was no reason to be embarrassed, after all. "We were planning on taking a walk."

"Oh," Sonja said. "Apparently I've come at a bad time. I should've called first."

"If you'd come a few minutes later, you probably would've missed me altogether, because we'd have left already," Kim said, to forestall the possibility of any strange thoughts. "It's Sunday," she repeated rather helplessly. "You've never been here on a Sunday before."

"Which is why you obviously make other plans for your Sundays."

The doorbell rang again.

"Sandra's getting impatient." Sonja pursed her lips disdainfully.

Kim was taken aback. Sonja leaned over and pressed the buzzer. "We can't just leave her standing outside like that."

"Kim, are you coming down, or should I come up?" Sandra's voice echoed up through the stairwell.

Sonja arched her eyebrows. Only now did she believe that Kim and Sandra had actually been planning to go for a walk, and not something else; that was obvious. A walk for starters . . .

"Sandra . . . Sandra is not –" Kim saw Sonja's expression and knew what it meant. "I haven't seen her all week," she ended the sentence.

"I actually believe you." Sonja heard Sandra's footsteps coming up the stairs. "But Sandra . . ." She swallowed. "She feels the same –" She broke off.

"You've discussed it?" Kim asked.

"We don't have to."

The door swung open. Sandra looked at Sonja and Kim, who were standing right behind it. "Sonja?" She smiled slightly. "I could've bet you were here. I just had a feeling."

"Sonja only just got here." Kim suddenly felt the need to justify herself to Sandra as she'd done to Sonja before. This could get interesting . . .

"To go for a walk?" Sandra asked with the same mocking smile as Sonja.

"Actually, no." Sonja's expression was serious, not mocking. "I wanted to discuss something with Kim."

Sandra grimaced. She didn't believe Sonja actually meant *discuss*. "Then I might as well go."

"You can stay, too," Sonja said. "That might even be better."

Kim looked from one to the other. The same face, one serious, one questioning.

"I –" Sonja raised her hands. "Today is Sunday."

Despite all her twin-sense, Sandra didn't know what to make of that. "Yes?"

"Sonja has . . ." Kim cleared her throat. "Sonja has never been with me on a Sunday; she's always had other . . . appointments."

"Not appointments," Sonja said. "Obligations."

"Sounds like a long story," Sandra surmised. "Shouldn't we sit down?"

"Yes, come into the kitchen." Kim nodded. "I'll make coffee."

"Good idea," Sonja and Sandra answered in unison. Both of them laughed suddenly and looked at each other. The atmosphere had lost a great deal of its tension.

All three of them headed into the kitchen. Kim filled the coffeemaker and turned it on. She sat down at the table with Sandra and Sonja. Sandra and she looked expectantly at Sonja.

It seemed as if the tension that had dissipated just a moment ago was now returning to Sonja's body. "I . . . I don't know where to start."

Sandra tilted her head to one side. "Something bad happened," she said. "Something very bad. I dreamed about it."

"You?" Sonja looked at her, perplexed. "Yes, of course," she said then. "You can feel it."

Sandra nodded. “It’s been going on for years, hasn’t it?”

Sonja took a deep breath. “Yes,” she said quietly. “Years.”

The coffeemaker started to bubble. All three of them automatically looked at it.

“Maybe we’d better wait until the coffee is ready,” Sandra suggested.

“No.” Sonja took another deep breath. “It’s all right.” She stood up, went over to the window, and looked out. “I’m a criminal,” she said.

Kim and Sandra gasped simultaneously, as if *they* were the twins.

“You?” Kim stood up as well. She went over to Sonja. “I can’t imagine anything less likely.”

“And yet it’s true.” Sonja turned around and examined Kim’s face, as though she were searching there for an explanation.

Sandra arched her eyebrows in deep skepticism. “Excuse me, please, but if you are, then I would have to be, too.”

Sonja sighed. “That’s not necessarily so. We grew up completely differently.”

“You don’t mean to claim that your . . . our mother raised you to be a gangster’s moll. Or that she’s one herself.” Now Sandra stood up, too.

“Her? No. But I am.” Sonja laughed sadly. “Although gangster’s moll is the wrong phrase. Murderess would be more accurate.”

It was deathly still in the room. Only the coffeemaker still hissed out its last puffs of steam.

“It was years ago . . .” Sonja repeated, staring pensively into space, lost in the past . . .

“I won’t marry him,” a younger Sonja stated firmly. “Absolutely not!”

“You’re pregnant by him.” Her mother pressed her lips together.

“Those two things have nothing to do with each other,” Sonja replied. “Uwe is . . . not a man to marry.”

“But he’s all right to fornicate with?” Her mother’s lips were still a single straight line. “My daughter – a slut . . . a whore.”

Sonja flinched.

“What did I do to deserve this?” her mother continued. “Is this why I brought you up, gave you food to eat and a roof over your head, let you go to college?” She laughed dryly. “College! A girl!”

“Business administration isn’t exactly a long course of study,” Sonja said. “And on top of that, I graduated with honors, in the shortest possible time.”

“That was the least you could do!” Her mother eyed her disparagingly. “After all, you were only there to bide your time until you got married. It would’ve been outrageous for you to draw it out any longer.”

“I know.” Sonja’s hands clenched.

“You’re altogether much too involved with your job. You don’t have any time to look for a husband. If I hadn’t introduced you to Uwe Kantner –” She broke off. Apparently, it was now occurring to her that the baby Sonja carried was the result of this introduction. “Well,” she finished quickly. “I think he’s a good man, he has a career ahead of him –”

“I have that, too,” Sonja said.

“For how much longer?” Her mother looked at her. “When the baby comes, of course you’ll quit working.”

“I wasn’t actually planning to.”

“And how are you going to take care of your husband then?” her mother asked. “Is he supposed to clean and cook for himself, or what?”

“Why not?” Sonja asked in return. “Beside which, I’m not going to marry him. Like I already said. He is –” She broke off, seeming to remember something. Her gaze turned inward.

“I think he’s very nice,” her mother said. “And besides, it doesn’t matter. You’re having his baby, so you have to marry him. No other man will take a pregnant woman – or a woman who already has another man’s baby.”

“You married for a second time when you already had me.”

“That was hard enough. I would’ve had a great many more opportunities if you hadn’t been there,” her mother said. “So I just had to –” She broke off. “Beside which, that was completely different. You were born to parents who were legally married." Her face contorted with a shudder. "A single mother! Is that what you want to be? What will people think?"

"That times have changed." Sonja sighed. "Mother, don't you understand? I can't spend the rest of my life with a man I don't love."

"Love!" Her mother practically spat out the word. "As if that had anything whatsoever to do with it."

"It does for me."

"You're young." Her mother looked at her with her head cocked to one side, as though she were a vase she was thinking of purchasing. "You'll soon learn that love is just a word, nothing more. It has nothing to do with marriage."

"I can't, mother." Sonja took a deep breath. "You don't know –"

"Don't you dare bring me a bastard," her mother interrupted coldly. "If you have a child out of wedlock, then you're responsible for it. I won't lift a finger for the brat. My door is locked and barred, to you and to your –"

Sonja looked at her. Not a muscle moved in her face. "You are making yourself quite clear."

"Why are you doing this to me?" her mother asked. "You should be grateful for everything I've done for you. If you knew –" She sighed deeply. "But that's how children are … especially daughters. What else did I expect?"

"Mother …" Sonja went over to her mother. "Can't you understand me at all? I … I …" She swallowed. "I love you. I couldn't bear to disobey you, but I can't –"

"Of course you can. You just don't want to! Just to make my life more difficult. That's all you want. You've always done that. You're just like your father."

Sonja shut her eyes. That was always her mother's final argument. She never spoke of Sonja's father except in that context. "I don't know him," she said softly. "I've never seen him. How can I be like him?"

"You are," her mother insisted. "Just look at your siblings. They do what they're told."

"I always have, too," Sonja whispered. She felt tears rising in her throat. She had to hold them back. If she cried, she'd have lost. Her mother would take it as a victory. And she would accuse Sonja of using the tears intentionally, as leverage, to blackmail her mother. As if her mother had ever reacted to tears . . . They only made her tougher.

"I can't, mother," she repeated in desperation. "It's *my* life."

"Then go live *your* life," her mother hissed furiously. "But on your own. Without me." She left the room.

Sonja stayed behind and felt that she could no longer hold back the tears. She cried, tears running down her cheeks, whose hot tracks she could follow on her face.

She wiped away the tears as they cooled and drew herself up. There was no sense in crying. It wouldn't soften her mother, and she didn't get anything out of it, either. It didn't even offer her any relief, because it didn't solve the problem. She was pregnant, and it was too late to get an abortion.

She had thought about that, but it didn't seem to her to be the way she wanted to go. Children hadn't previously been part of her plan for her life; she wanted to devote herself first to her career, which was so much fun for her. She'd only just gotten a promotion.

She knew that her career would be affected by the child, whether she wanted it or not, but she'd manage.

This child ought to have a good life.

Not like Sonja's.

The car skidded around the corner, out of control. The man standing on the sidewalk was struck by it, hurled around, and run over. The sounds were hideous. A woman's scream echoed through the night.

"I hereby pronounce you husband and wife." The registrar bowed to the bridegroom with a smile. "You may now kiss the bride."

"Sonja?"

The voice came up to her from below. She didn't want to hear it, but she couldn't ignore it. She bent down, intending to brush a fleeting kiss across his cheek, but he pulled her down and thrust into her mouth, taking almost violent possession of her.

She tried to get away from him and managed; she straightened up. She mustn't let her disgust show. He was her husband. They were married now. She tried to smile. She took a step behind him and pushed his wheelchair out of the bridal chamber.

"Now you're a respectable woman. Just in time." Her mother glanced at Sonja's slightly swollen belly, which clearly showed under the tight, white dress.

"Yes." Sonja's lips were tight. "You got what you wanted."

"And so did I." A hand reached for her, a strong, masculine hand. Uwe smiled at her. "You're my wife. I've always wanted that."

"Not too long ago, you didn't want to get married," Sonja said. "As I recall."

"Yes, this kind of accident changes your life," Uwe Kantner replied, giving her a peculiar look.

Sonja seemed to stiffen even more. "We're finished here. We should go."

Sonja hung the house key on a hook behind the door.

"Unfortunately, I can't carry you over the threshold," Uwe said.

"Don't make a fool of yourself. No one expects that." Sonja seemed irritated.

"A little while ago, I still could have."

"Please ... Uwe ..." Sonja clenched her hands together. "I did what you and Mother wanted. We're married, and we live together. Isn't that enough?"

"You had no other choice," he said. "Did you?"

"No." Her voice was very quiet.

"Come here," he said.

She closed her eyes and didn't move.

"Come here," he repeated more insistently.

She opened her eyes again and walked slowly over to him.

"Kiss me," he ordered.

"Uwe . . . please . . ." Sonja stood next to him, but still at a slight distance.

"I want to sleep with you." He looked her up and down. "It's just not as easy as it was before, when we put that little thing in your belly." He stared at her belly. "I hope you don't get too fat. It's ugly enough already."

Sonja seemed to tremble. "The doctor said you shouldn't overexert yourself yet," she said wearily.

He grinned. "The doctor said, if my wife does all the work, it's no problem."

"We . . . Uwe . . . please . . . not today . . ."

"It's our wedding night. Did you forget that, my . . . treasure?" he asked spitefully.

"That means nothing to you," Sonja said. "I mean nothing to you. I've never meant anything to you. Our marriage hasn't changed that."

"What does that have to do with anything?" He didn't dispute her statements. "I want to sleep with you. I don't have to like you for that."

"But I do," Sonja said. "It won't work."

"Must I remind you why you married me?" He watched her keenly, waiting for her reaction.

She hesitated, then walked over to him.

He reached for her, pulled her onto his lap, pressed his lips hard against hers, and ran his hand up under her dress.

"And I've been happily married ever since," Sonja concluded bitterly. "Today makes five years, three months, and one day."

Kim and Sandra gaped at her, speechless.

"But . . . but why did you marry him if you don't love him?" Kim stammered at last.

Sonja looked at her. Her eyes seemed empty. "I . . . I'm responsible for his condition," she said flatly. "I ran over him. He's been in a wheelchair ever since."

"You . . . you ran over him?" Sandra frowned.

"I . . . I was drunk. I can't remember anything. I was at my mother's, we had a fight – we had frequent fights then, because I didn't want to get married. At any rate, we were both drinking, and at some point, I stormed out of the house and got in my car. I must've driven to Uwe's. He was right there on the street, he said; he was about to come see me. My car went into a skid, it hit him – he almost didn't survive." She threw her hands over her face. "I almost killed him. If he hadn't been rescued by the doctors' arts, I'd be a murderer." She looked up. "I am, because that's what I wanted."

"You wanted to free yourself from him, because your ... mother," Sandra paused. She was talking about her own mother, but she could hardly believe it, "wanted to force you to marry him," she said. "Psychologically explicable, but –" She gazed into the air. "Somehow ... I don't know ..." She looked at Sonja. "What I dreamed was something else. It was threatening, but ... different."

"You weren't there," Sonja said. "A dream is not reality."

Kim took a deep breath. "So that's it. You can't leave him because of your guilt." At last, she had an explanation for Sonja's peculiar behavior.

Sonja laughed dryly. "I would've left him a long time ago if that were it! At first, that was true, yes, the guilt was overwhelming. I took away his ..." She swallowed. "... his life, as he knew it. But after a while ... no, after a while, even that wouldn't have been enough. I've atoned for my guilt – every day. He's made sure of that."

"Why, then?" Sandra asked.

Sonja stared blankly into space. "He threatened to report me to the police. He was critically injured, and I committed a hit-and-run while drunk. You can get quite a bit of jail time for that," she said. "He enjoyed destroying my life, the way I'd destroyed his. But he got the most pleasure out of threatening me ... with the fact that he had me in his power, that I couldn't get away, that I had to do everything he said."

Sandra shook her head. "Wouldn't jail be better than being at his mercy like that?"

Sonja took a deep breath. "If only it were just jail ..." she said. "I could get through that. But afterwards ... what comes next? Do you believe that anyone would ever put me in a position of responsibility again, that any company would ever hire me? I'd have a criminal record. How would I support myself?"

She took a couple of steps.

"I worked like a crazy woman. I'd only go home to sleep. He ... he insists that I come home at night," she added softly. "That's part of our agreement. As long as I do that, he won't turn me in." She looked at Kim. "Sometimes, I've sat in my car outside your door for a long time," she said tenderly. "Wanting never to drive away. I wished so much I could stay."

Kim could barely comprehend all of this. "And Sundays?" she swallowed. "Sundays, he also demands –"

Sonja laughed bitterly again. "Oh, no! On Sundays, we go to my mother's and play the perfect family. *She* demands that. She knows about the accident. She followed me in her car and found Uwe on the street. She brought me home, so that the police –"

"I thought your mother was supposed to be so moral?" Kim asked, astonished.

"Not in *that* respect," Sonja said. "The family's reputation is more important than anything the police might be concerned with."

Sandra shook her head. "I don't get the feeling that I really want to meet my mother."

"You don't have to," Sonja said. "I don't even know how she'd react. She still doesn't know –"

"You haven't told her anything about me?" Sandra looked at Sonja.

Sonja shook her head likewise. "I'm sorry. I know I should have."

"Under *those* circumstances ..." Sandra said. "Introducing you to our father was vastly easier. I knew that he's a good person."

"Mother is also –" Sonja protested.

"She is not," Sandra interrupted her. "I find it awful to have to say that about my own mother, but what I've heard from you doesn't prejudice me in her favor, and I'm glad that I didn't have to grow up with her."

"She's been through a lot," Sonja said quietly.

"I can't judge that," Sandra said, "but the fact is, Pops is the most tolerant person on the planet. She must've gone to considerable lengths to motivate him to get a divorce."

"Don't fight," Kim interjected. "None of us knows what really happened between your father and your mother. That's in the past." She went to Sonja and touched her gently on the arm. "I am so sorry," she said. "If I'd known . . ."

"You wouldn't have been able to change any of it." Sonja sighed. "Not you, and not anybody else, either. Why should I have burdened you with it?"

"What about the baby?" Sandra asked. "Where is it?"

Sonja closed her eyes. "I lost it." She opened her eyes again and looked at Sandra. "A couple of weeks after the wedding, I had an accident. I had a green light and drove into the intersection, and some idiot ran the red light. My car was totaled, but because of the airbags, I wasn't seriously injured. But the seatbelt . . . the baby . . ." She swallowed.

Sandra came over to her and Kim. "I'm sorry." She hugged Sonja, while Kim stood back.

"Why did you come today?" Kim asked. "On a Sunday?"

Sonja looked up. Sandra still held her in an embrace. "I . . . I suddenly felt like I had to talk to you. I wanted to explain everything to you. Jo and Jennifer's wedding reminded me of so many things . . ."

"You just left?" Sandra asked.

"Yes, I –" Sonja made a face. "I'm going to pay for that, I know, but I couldn't help it. I felt so . . . alone. My sister was there, and my brother, but –"

"I understand," Sandra said. "Are they still there now?"

"Oh, yes." Sonja nodded forcefully. "Mother doesn't let anyone leave until late in the evening."

"Then I could meet all of them." Sandra's eyes flashed with mischief.

Sonja stared at her twin sister. "That . . . no . . . you really want . . .?"

"Well, sure. After all, it's my family, too. Don't I have the right?"

"Yes . . . um . . ." Sonja seemed fairly overwhelmed.

"I know now what's waiting for me," Sandra said. "It won't surprise me. I have no more illusions with respect to my mother. Aside from which, I don't know her. She's a stranger to me. She doesn't have me in her grip like she does you. She can't blackmail me."

Sonja's face contorted in agony again. "You ... you really don't know what's waiting for you. You'd better let me go alone. I know what I'm doing. This isn't the first time I've had to eat crow. I'll survive it this time, too. I always have."

"Sonja." Sandra looked at her earnestly. "You're not alone anymore. Don't you realize that yet? I'm your sister, your twin sister. I'll always stand by you, no matter what. We're practically one person. And Kim –" She turned around. "Kim won't leave you hanging, either." She smiled gently.

Kim stepped toward them again and embraced them both. "No, I won't." She gave Sandra an apologetic look.

"All right." Sandra looked at Sonja. "Let's go, before I change my mind."

"I . . ." Sonja looked at Kim.

"Go already." Kim smiled encouragingly. "You're never here on a Sunday anyway."

Sonja let go of Sandra and hugged Kim. She pulled her close and kissed her, long and deep.

"Aw, is that necessary?" Sandra said. "Can't you two do that when you're alone?"

Sonja broke away from Kim. "I'm sorry." She smiled rather shrewdly at Sandra. "You got yours, too, I believe."

"One single kiss." Sandra sighed. "And she was thinking about you the whole time."

"I'll ask my mother whether I might have a twin sister, after all," Kim replied, sighing. "Maybe there's one hiding somewhere. Anything seems possible after seeing you two."

"I'm afraid I'm not that lucky." Sandra looked invitingly at Sonja. "Get in bed with her, or get in the car with me, but make up your mind."

Sonja chuckled. "I would've said the same thing in your place." She brushed a quick kiss across Kim's lips. "I'll be back," she said. "If I have the right measure of Sandra, the Sunday-free times are over for you."

"If I'd known that . . ." Sandra grinned. "I would've come here on Sundays and pretended to be you."

"I would've noticed the difference," Kim said.

"Like when we were dancing?" Sonja teased.

Embarrassed, Kim looked at the floor. "Identical twins ought to be prohibited."

"This is where you grew up?" Sandra asked.

"Yes." Sonja looked at the house they were standing in front of. Her hands trembled slightly.

"Don't be afraid." Sandra smiled. "I'm here with you."

Sonja smiled, too, but still looked a little uncertain. "But you aren't me. Not even if you look like me."

Sandra tilted her head to one side. "Give me your jacket."

"Oh, Sandra, not again!" Sonja groaned.

"What'll happen if she sees you first?" Sandra asked. "She'll tear into you, right?"

Sonja nodded unhappily.

"So . . .?" Sandra gave her an inviting look.

"Sonja! How dare you just walk out like that?" Sonja's mother snarled wrathfully at her daughter.

"Mother . . ." Sandra was more shaken than she wanted to admit. After all, this was the first time she'd seen her mother.

She noticed the family resemblance her father had mentioned. *So that's what I'll look like in twenty years*, she thought. Her mother must've really looked like her daughters in the past. She still did.

"Unbelievable!" her mother hissed. "What unbelievable insolence. Just wait and see what that gets you."

"Where were you . . . darling?"

Sandra turned her head in the direction from which she had been addressed. That must be her brother-in-law, Sonja's husband. After everything she'd heard, she had pictured him differently. He looked pleasant and harmless.

Except for his eyes. She examined them more closely. His eyes were hard and merciless. *Every word Sonja said is true*, Sandra thought. *He doesn't love her. No man who loved a woman would look at her like that.*

"Getting a little fresh air," she answered the man in the wheelchair, whose predatory eyes were still watching her very closely.

"Think twice about how much fresh air you need – next time," he said, smiling. It was a wolfish smile without a trace of warmth.

"Is this necessary, Sonja?" A younger man's voice addressed her from the side. "Do you always have to act like this?"

My brother, Sandra thought. *I have a brother.* She was gradually starting to wonder whether this had been such a good idea, switching places with Sonja. She felt outnumbered by her new family and tried to collect herself. "Is going for a walk forbidden now?"

"Stop fighting." A young woman, who didn't resemble Sonja much except for the color of her hair, but who must be her other sister, entered the room through a door on the other side. "You always have to squabble about something. That's no fun."

"It is to me." Her brother grinned. "I love you, sister, you know that." He kissed Sandra on the cheek.

So this is the rest of my family, Sandra thought. *And Sonja has to put up with this every single Sunday*. She felt renewed sympathy for her sister.

"What do you have to offer as an excuse?" her mother asked sharply.

Sandra looked at her once again. Her eyes, too, were hard. *Poor Sonja*, Sandra thought. *If only you'd stayed with Pops and me.* Seldom in her life had she ever seen such hard eyes – other than those of Uwe Kantner. Mother-in-law and son-in-law clearly had a lot in common.

"Does a person need an excuse to breathe?" Sandra asked.

Her mother gasped. "I don't know what's gotten into you," she huffed indignantly after she'd recovered from the initial shock. "I thought you would've learned how to behave by now." She looked at Uwe.

"I don't know what you think is wrong with my behavior," Sandra said. "I'm not a twelve-year-old who has to account for her every move."

"Oh-ho, sister – I haven't heard that tone out of you for a long time." Her brother burst out laughing. "I didn't think you had the guts anymore. Are you sure you can pull that off?" He looked at his mother.

"Apologize, Sonja, please . . ." Her sister gave her a pleading look. "Please, apologize, for heaven's sake."

What's going on here? Sandra wondered. *This just isn't normal.* "What for?" she asked. "I haven't done anything."

"You can discuss that with your husband this evening," her mother said coldly, looking first at Uwe and then back at Sandra.

Uwe showed his wolfish grin once more. "Yes, we'll have plenty to discuss tonight . . . darling," he said in a sweet-threatening tone that sent cold shivers down Sandra's back. *Oh my God,* she thought. *Sonja.*

"Fine, then," she said. "I apologize. For whatever."

Her sister appeared to exhale.

"Even your apology is an insult," her mother said. "If you think you're going to get away with that . . ."

"The way you got away with having only one daughter, even though you gave birth to twins?" Sonja stepped into the room behind Sandra and stood next to her.

Their mother fainted.

"What . . . What . . .?" Sonja's and Sandra's half-sister knelt next to their mother on the floor, fanning her. She looked up at the twins, bewildered.

Sonja wanted to go to her mother. Sandra held her back. "Leave her," she said. "She asked for this. It's her fault, after all. Stop feeling sorry for her. She doesn't deserve it." Even still, the cold look with which her mother had placed her in Uwe's hands sent shivers down her spine.

"Sandra . . . I . . ." Sonja looked at her helplessly.

"I know how you feel," Sandra said gently. "But this has to stop. I don't know how you've endured it for so long."

"Sandra?" Her brother stared at the twins in just as much confusion as his sister. "Who is Sandra?"

"I am." Sandra looked at him. "And if you were my brother –" She broke off and laughed. "Ha, well, you are. You're my half-brother, just like you are Sonja's. The fact that Sonja and I are twins really ought to be clear to everyone by now."

Uwe Kantner had not yet said a word. He had gaped at the doubling of his wife just as the others had, but he seemed to have recovered quickly, since his voice sounded very self-assured when he said, "Come to me, Sonja."

Sonja flinched, and Sandra noticed that she had started to tremble. "No," Sandra said.

"Sonja . . . come to me," Uwe repeated threateningly.

Sonja took a step. Once again, Sandra held her back. "Stay here. He has no right to order you."

Sonja shut her eyes briefly, seeming to collect herself. "You're right," she said. "It's over."

Uwe hesitated for a moment, then laughed. "Twins. How cute." He looked past Sandra at Sonja. "Why didn't you ever tell me? You didn't have to keep your sister hidden like that."

"I didn't know –" Sonja began, but Sandra interrupted her.

"You don't owe him an explanation," she said. "This is up to . . ." she looked at the floor, "*her* to explain."

Her mother slowly began to stir. She looked at her youngest daughter, who still sat next to her. "What happened?"

"Sonja . . ." Sonja's half-sister looked up helplessly.

"Sonja . . ." Her mother repeated the name grimly. "What an evil trick –" She turned her own gaze upwards and froze.

"This is most definitely not a trick," Sandra said. "Mother . . ." she added dismissively. "Although you certainly haven't earned that designation. If anyone here has played an evil trick, it was you. On me and Sonja. Especially on Sonja. I had Pops, after all."

"Sandra . . ." her mother whispered.

"You still remember my name? Astounding. After so many years."

"Sandra, please . . . don't." Sonja rested a hand on her arm.

"Now I know how you felt when you saw Pops for the first time," Sandra looked at her twin. "But Pops didn't deserve it, I can assure you. You're going to get along great."

Their mother allowed herself to be helped up by her third daughter, who was still casting concerned glances at her like a hovering nurse. "You met your father?" their mother asked. Her eyes wandered back and forth between Sonja and Sandra.

"Yes," Sonja said. "Just recently."

"It's about time, isn't it?" Sandra added angrily.

Their mother examined Sandra's face curiously. "You look like Sonja," she said. "Truly."

"Hardly a surprise – with twins," Sandra replied, examining her mother's face just as intensely. "Even though we knew nothing about each other."

"This is really – unbelievable." Their brother peeled himself out of his armchair. He stepped forward and studied the faces of his sisters as well.

"Leave her, Martin." The third sister stood next to him.

"Oh, Inge . . ." Martin laughed. "We're all siblings, don't you get it? Now we have one more sister, a second Sonja."

"Oh, no!" Sandra let out a dry sound. "Not a second Sonja. Not another victim for your cruelties. From now on, that's over. Sonja and I will no longer allow it." Sandra glanced at Sonja by her side.

"What cruelties?" Martin asked. "Sonja's the oldest, that's why she's always to blame. That's normal." He laughed further. "And you're exactly as old as she is, so –"

"You can get that right out of your head." Sandra smiled sweetly in his cheeky face. "I'm not the kind of older sister who'll take responsibility for all of her younger siblings' misdeeds. I grew up alone." She turned to face her mother. "Your mother made sure of that."

"That was Harald's fault," her mother replied immediately. "Your . . . your father."

"I don't believe that for one second," Sandra said. "Pops wanted both of us, but you wouldn't allow it."

"Children belong to their mother," said Elli, Harald Kruschewski's ex-wife.

"If she *is* a mother . . ." Sandra retorted angrily. "What you did to Sonja –"

"Please, Sandra, stop." Sonja put a hand to her forehead. "There's no point to any of this."

"What did I do to her, then?" their mother asked sanctimoniously. "Brought her up to be a decent and respectable human being?" She gave Sonja a disparaging look. "That was hard enough."

"You're right, there is no point." Sandra looked at Sonja. "Let's go. There's nothing else to say."

Inge placed her hand on Sandra's arm. "Please, Sonja . . ."

Sandra pursed her lips. "I'm not Sonja."

Inge examined Sandra's face again, especially her eyes. "No, you're not Sonja," she said then, with an expression of astonishment.

Sandra smiled. "I've always wished for siblings. If you're interested, we could certainly get to know each other better. But I'm not Sonja, so behave yourselves. Because I hit back."

Uwe suddenly laughed out loud. "We should definitely invite your sister over, darling." He looked at Sonja. "We could go home together right now, in fact."

"For a threesome with twins?" Sandra asked scornfully. "That's what you have in mind, isn't it . . . brother-in-law?"

"Married life is pretty boring after five years," he replied nonchalantly. "It could stand a little freshening up. My wife used to be more like you, but these days –"

Sonja spun on her heel and left. The door fell shut behind her.

"My dear Uwe." Sandra had a friendly smile on her lips, but not in her eyes. She bent down to him. "She's not going to let you blackmail her any more, I'll make sure of that. I'm sorry you're sitting in a wheelchair, but that doesn't give you the right to torture Sonja until the end of time. Those days are over."

He looked into her face, seeing his wife, but not seeing her. "You know what that means," he said. "And she knows it, too. She'll never take that risk."

"It's better to have an end with horror rather than to have horror without end," Sandra said. "A solution can always be found." She straightened up and looked at her mother. "And that goes for you, too. Sonja will not have to suffer under you for the rest of her life, or else you're going to get to know me, but in a way you never dreamed of. Think about this: I'm your daughter, and you haven't beaten me down like you have Sonja. Anything you're capable of, I am, too."

"You . . . you . . . how dare you . . .?" Her mother gasped for air again.

"The same way you do." Sandra looked her mother up and down once more. "I'm glad I had a real mother, even if she wasn't my biological mother. Too bad Sonja couldn't experience that. But from now on, she's spending her Sundays with me – or with Pops. And her nights –" she looked at Uwe, "wherever she wants."

"She wouldn't dare," her brother-in-law replied.

"She will. She's strong. And there are two of us." Sandra and Uwe fought a duel of glares, their eyes snaring each other's, no one giving in, until at last they finally sought other targets. "Don't underestimate her," Sandra added. "You can only dip the pitcher in the well so many times before it breaks."

"She'll have to suffer the consequences," he said.

"One can always mend a pitcher," Sandra replied, "or buy a new one. I have a thing or two to show Sonja." She drew her lips back into an appreciative grin.

"You'd do better to remind her of what she has to lose," Uwe said.

"I think she has more to gain," Sandra countered. She smiled at everyone once more, turned around, and went to the front door. When she'd almost gotten there, something else occurred to her, and she went back.

She heard voices coming from the kitchen, next to the living room. They were Uwe's and her mother's.

"What'll happen if Sonja really takes the gloves off?" Uwe asked.

"She knows nothing," her mother replied.

"And if it comes out?" he asked.

"How would it come out? The only ones who know the truth are the two of us. I'm sure you can keep your mouth shut. It's in your own interest, after all."

"More in yours," he said. "You were driving the car. I'm the one in a wheelchair." All of a sudden, his voice sounded bitter and discontented.

"It was your idea," Elli said. "How was I supposed to know you'd be standing in the middle of the street?"

"I just wanted control over her, but you wanted a respectable daughter," he said. "Who could've known it would turn out this way? No one can ever give me my legs back."

"Then you go to the police," she sneered. "I've gathered up all the evidence. Not just the picture from the traffic camera, where I'm wearing the wig that made me look like Sonja, but the things that apply to you, too."

"If she ever finds out that she wasn't driving the car, that you got her drunk and then took her home, that you ran me over to fake an accident and things went wrong, then we're done for," Uwe said. "She can never find out. Otherwise we're the ones who'll go to jail, not her."

Sandra retreated and went back to the front door. Sonja was sitting in her car across the street, probably still suffering from all the humiliations. What had she said? Her mother wasn't a gangster's moll? Yes, she was – that, and much, much worse.

Sandra got in. Sonja sat on the driver's side, leaning against the steering wheel. Her eyes were red.

"How do you know that you . . . ran over Uwe?" Sandra asked.

"Mother showed me a photo. From a speed trap. I'm sitting at the steering wheel," Sonja replied wearily. "The camera box is on Uwe's street. It was exactly the same time as the accident."

"Hmm," Sandra said. "Our mother looks quite a bit like us, don't you think?"

"What –" Sonja turned and stared at her. "What are you trying to say?"

"I'd say we ought to drive to Kim's first," Sandra remarked. "You need to recover a little." She smiled. "I'd gladly offer my place for you to spend the night, but I think you'd prefer Kim's apartment. You're not going back to yours again, is that clear?"

Sonja grimaced. "I –"

"Believe me, it's not a problem. Nothing is going to happen. I'm absolutely certain about that."

Sonja stared at Sandra in disbelieve.

"Scoot over," Sandra said. "Let me drive. You look a little overwhelmed. I'd like us to get to Kim's in one piece."

▫▫▪▫▫

"That's what I heard," Sandra concluded. "If I understand correctly, it happened like this: Mother got Sonja plastered, then she put on a wig and made herself up to look like Sonja. The speed trap might have been a coincidence, or it might have been done intentionally, but at any rate, she acquired the photo as proof that Sonja was driving. In the picture, no one could see the difference between her and Sonja, and she would definitely have driven Sonja's car."

"She wanted to run Uwe over so that Sonja would feel guilty and marry him. Of course, they didn't intend for him to be so gravely injured; it was all supposed to be a kind of farce. But then, something went wrong. Sonja's mother lost control of the car and nearly killed Uwe. She called an ambulance, took Sonja home, and convinced her that she'd run him over. That's it. For the last five years, that was enough." She took Sonja's hand and smiled encouragingly at her. "But not anymore."

"But . . . but . . ." Sonja couldn't fathom this. "But I have –"

"What do you have?" Sandra asked. "Some sort of real proof? You believed what your mother told you. But it was all lies."

"That . . . that can't be," Sonja whispered, shaken. "All these years . . ."

"It's true," Sandra said, "believe me. And now I also understand a dream that I had. Of course, I never dreamed about an accident, because you had nothing to do with that, you weren't even there, but I dreamed about a threat. Like a sword of Damocles, hanging over me. But it wasn't me, it was you."

"I feel like it just dropped," Sonja said.

"It evaporated." Kim smiled and pulled Sonja into her arms. "Forever. You're free."

"Free." Sonja repeated it, uncomprehending, as though the meaning of the word were utterly unknown to her.

"It'll probably be a while before she really grasps it." Sandra shook her head. "How could a mother be so gruesome? Uwe Kantner is a pig, but . . . well, he just is, but our mother . . ." She observed Sonja, who sat next to Kim, entirely lost inside herself. "She gave birth to us, she had Sonja with her every day, took care of her, watched her grow up . . . and then she did this to her? To her own child?"

"I don't understand it, either," Kim said.

"We'll probably never understand it." Sandra shrugged. "I'm going to take Sonja to visit our father, as soon as she wants to, and then she'll see what it means to have a parent who loves her."

"That your mother could just walk away and leave you with your father back then, that alone shows what she's like," Kim said.

"I think she would rather have left both of us with him," Sandra said. "Then she would've had a better chance of finding a new husband, which clearly meant a lot to her. But then, Pops would've been happy about that, he would've been glad to have both of us, and she couldn't allow that. She kept Sonja on principle, not out of love." She shuddered. "It could've been me."

Sonja looked up. "Love really is just a word to her," she said quietly. "She never felt it. At least, that's what I believe now."

Kim looked at her.

"I know." Sonja sighed. "I told you the same thing. But . . . I just didn't want to get your hopes up." She sighed again. "Or mine, either."

"The whole situation must've felt like you had no way out," Sandra said. "I can understand that."

"I . . . I kept searching for a way out. My first infidelity –" Sonja broke off and laughed aloud. "Now it seems silly to me to even call it that. I was never really properly married, so there can't have been any infidelities. Anyway . . . well . . . I was searching for something . . . something different. I just couldn't endure it . . . nothing but . . ."

Kim pulled her close and caressed her. "It's all right," she said softly. "Don't think about it anymore."

"It wasn't what you think," Sonja said. "After the . . . wedding night, we never slept together again. He . . . Uwe got nothing out of it. That's why he got even angrier. And he took that out on me. He . . . tormented me, demeaned me, berated me. He blamed me again and again for what he said I'd done to him. We never even slept in the same room. I'd often leave early in the morning when he was still asleep, and I didn't come home at night until he was already in bed. But that was bad enough. If I'd gone home during the day . . ."

Kim recalled Sonja's expression of horror the time she had suggested taking her home, on the day she'd slept in Kim's apartment.

"Often, of course, he slept during the day – he was always home, after all – so he could stay awake at night and keep me up. He particularly enjoyed that." Sonja shivered. "Sleep deprivation is the worst form of torture. I didn't think I could take it anymore." She looked at Kim. "At the beginning, when I first joined the company, he wasn't there for a while. He had gone to a rehabilitation clinic for treatment."

"That's why you used to laugh so much then," Kim said.

"Yes." Sonja swallowed. "It was like a vacation. A marvelous . . . vacation."

"It will always be like that now." Kim looked affectionately at her.

"I think I'd better go." Sandra stood up and glanced at the two of them. "I need to think about my new family some more, too."

"Sandra . . ." Sonja looked at her, pleading for forgiveness. "I am so sorry. I –"

"You couldn't help it," Sandra said. "It's both of our family, and we can't choose our family." She smiled. "Look forward to Pops. He won't disappoint you."

"I am looking forward to that." A cautious smile crept across Sonja's face.

"Have a good one, you two." Sandra sighed expressively. "If you ever go on vacation, Sonja, will you let me borrow Kim?"

Sonja arched her eyebrows.

Sandra waved it off and laughed. "Just asking . . ." She left the kitchen.

The apartment door fell shut, and Sonja looked at Kim. "I feel kind of funny," she said. "I keep thinking I'll have to go any minute now."

"You can . . . if you want," Kim said. "Sandra is there for you, too."

"She did offer." Sonja nodded. "I'm homeless." She took a deep breath. "I could spend the night with Sandra, but it's not my apartment. And at my mother's –"

"I should hope that's not even up for debate," Kim interjected, appalled.

Sonja exhaled again. "No, it isn't."

"Is that awful for you?"

Sonja didn't answer right away. Then she stood up and went over to the window. "She is my mother."

"She didn't treat you that way," Kim objected.

"Unfortunately, that doesn't change my feelings toward her. She is and remains my mother. I've had her around me almost every day of my entire life."

"But you aren't responsible for her. Certainly not for what she put you through."

"The Big Sister Syndrome." Sonja let out a hollow sound. "I'm responsible for everything."

"No, you're not." Kim approached her. "Only for yourself. For your own acts. And you haven't done anything wrong, even if she tried to convince you that you did."

"I still can't believe it," Sonja said softly. "That I didn't do it, I mean. That it was all just –" Her face contorted. She tried to control herself.

"You're welcome to cry. You have reason enough." Kim embraced Sonja, pulled her close, and stroked her back. "It's okay," she whispered. "Everything will be fine now."

Sonja rested her head on Kim's shoulder. "It's going to take me a while to get my head around that. And then . . . I won't have a family anymore."

"You have us," Kim said. "Sandra and your father and me and . . . well, the lesbian family. It's pretty big." She laughed softly. "You saw that at Jo and Jennifer's wedding."

"The lesbian family . . ." Sonja repeated thoughtfully.

A sharp pain stabbed into Kim. That was a subject she shouldn't have brought up, it seemed to her. "It's . . . I mean . . . I didn't mean to imply . . ."

"Yes, you did." Sonja looked at Kim and smiled. "To you, every woman is a lesbian until proven otherwise, right?"

"Well, now . . ." Kim didn't know what to say. "Ninety percent of all women are straight – statistically speaking," she rescued herself.

"And I'm one of them." Sonja pulled away from Kim. "At least, I used to think so."

Kim took a deep breath. She had to ask the question. "Do you still think so?"

"I don't know," Sonja said.

Kim had a mild feeling of vertigo. Of course, Sonja had sought some sort of escape, she had had affairs with men – exclusively with men – and one single one with a woman. What did that say about her?

"My life has run completely off the rails," Sonja continued. "I think I need to get a number of things back on track first." She rubbed her forehead. "It would be better if I went to Sandra's."

Kim swallowed. "If you think so," she said with an effort.

"I would insanely love to sleep with you right now," Sonja said quietly, watching Kim's face, "but I have to ask myself whether that's just another kind of escape – like it was all along. Things always got worse, the more closed in I felt."

Kim swallowed again. "I've noticed." She folded her hands. She felt hot. Her own wish to sleep with Sonja grew ever stronger, and now the two of them were standing there, philosophizing over whether or not they ought to. Nothing like this had ever happened to her before. She ran a hand through her hair. "I . . . Sonja . . . please, go to Sandra's if that's what you want, otherwise –"

"Otherwise?" Sonja looked at her. Then, suddenly, she leaned forward, found Kim's lips, and thrust inside them before Kim even knew what was happening. "It's impossible," she whispered hoarsely. "I can't – I don't have to decide what I am. I don't need a label." She pulled Kim's T-shirt up over her head and kissed her breasts.

Kim moaned. "Do you want to go to Sandra's afterward?" she asked with an effort, while hot lightning shot through her nipples and down between her legs. Sonja's supple lips drove her crazy.

"I don't think so," Sonja whispered. "Sandra's just going to have to wait a while." She unfastened Kim's pants and slipped one hand inside.

Kim moaned anew. She caressed Sonja's breasts, hugged Sonja, kissed her. She felt the tips of their tongues meet; the pleasure was so strong, she sighed in Sonja's mouth. Tiny flames wound their way up into her lips; Sonja's tongue called them back and sent them forth again; they spread out, encompassing skin and hair, leaving everything tingling. "Oh, Sonja . . ." Kim whispered

"I need you so much," Sonja breathed.

Slowly she slipped down Kim's body . . .

▫▫■▫▫

Kim heard a sound and awoke. Or had she woken up first and then heard the sound? She didn't know.

She opened her eyes. Her bed was empty, as it always was in the morning, except of course for herself.

She sighed and stretched, yawning.

"Oh, I'm sorry, did I wake you?" Sonja stood in the doorway, dressed, and smiled at her. She came in, bent down over the bed, and kissed Kim gently on the lips. "Good morning." Still smiling, she straightened up.

Kim gazed at her, as if she were dreaming.

"I always go to work this early, you know that . . ." Sonja said. "The early bird catches the worm."

"Um . . . Yes, I know." Kim pulled herself together.

"You're welcome to go back to sleep. I don't want to disturb your rhythm." Sonja smiled again.

"If you . . ." Kim cleared her throat. "If you wait five minutes, we can go to work together."

Sonja arched her eyebrows. "I could even wait longer than five minutes."

"We could have breakfast together, too." Kim swung her legs out of bed. "Although I don't actually know whether I have much here for breakfast. I don't normally eat breakfast."

"You don't have to go to so much trouble." Sonja seemed to chuckle.

"This is a little unfamiliar. It's the first time that you ... that you're here in the morning," Kim apologized, embarrassed, and stood up.

"I know." Sonja looked at her earnestly. "Maybe it's best if I go now. Then I won't disturb you, and you can do what you always do – in peace."

"I'm not peaceful," Kim said. "If only because you're here. You confuse me."

"I'm sorry. It's all a little confusing for me, too."

"Then perhaps we should have breakfast together first," Kim suggested. "To relieve the confusion."

"If you put something on ..." Sonja grinned, eyeing Kim's naked body from head to toe. "Otherwise my confusion is only going to grow."

"Oh ... excuse me ..." Kim stammered, taken aback.

"I'll go to the kitchen and make coffee. I think I figured out how the coffeemaker works." Sonja turned around and went across the hall.

Kim watched her go and marveled for a moment that such a beautiful woman should be in her apartment in the morning. She took a few things out of the closet, put them on, and followed Sonja into the kitchen.

Sonja had set the coffeemaker in motion and was standing in front of the kitchen cupboards, taking out cups and plates to set the table.

Kim watched her. It was an unfamiliar sight, and it produced a very peculiar feeling in her. "You know, you've never done that before ... in my ... in my kitchen." She went to the refrigerator and took out the butter.

"Of course not. We've never had an everyday life." Sonja looked around. "Where are the teaspoons?"

"In this drawer." Kim pulled open the drawer.

Sonja came over and eyed the silverware. "Is this all you have?" She selected two spoons and two knives and took them out.

"Yes ... I guess I'll have to wait for my wedding to get the hundred-and-twenty-four-piece silver set." Kim bit her tongue. "Sorry. Didn't mean it like that."

"It's true, though," Sonja said, remarkably calm. "I got a number of things like that for my wedding. It's just customary." She laid the knives next to the breakfast plates and the spoons on the saucers. "What's missing?"

"Fresh breakfast rolls." Kim shrugged. "A problem at this hour." It was still dark outside.

"I always freeze them." Sonja looked inquisitively at Kim.

"I'm not that good of a housewife." Kim felt like she was on display. A display of her incompetence.

"Why doesn't that surprise me?" Sonja chuckled.

"I could scramble an egg – I do have some eggs," Kim said unhappily.

"I prefer mine boiled." Sonja chuckled even more. "Do you have orange juice, by chance?"

"Yes." Kim was relieved that she at least had something. She took the orange juice out of the refrigerator. "Ah, there is some bread in here. I didn't remember that I still had any."

Sonja raised her eyebrows in deep skepticism.

"No, that doesn't mean anything," Kim assured her frantically. "I immediately forget about it when I put it in the fridge. I'm sure it's not moldy."

"Glad to hear it." Sonja took off her jacket. "Are the eggs in the refrigerator, too?"

Kim nodded.

Sonja opened the refrigerator and peeked inside. "Three," she said. "And are they still fresh?"

"I eat eggs a lot. I bought those on Saturday."

"Good." Sonja took out the eggs. "I'll just have one. Should I make the other two for you? In the frying pan?" She looked around. "If you tell me where it is."

"Sonja, you don't have to –" Kim suddenly felt rather superfluous in her own kitchen.

"A frying pan and a saucepan are all I need." Sonja looked questioningly at Kim.

Kim hurried to bring her what she wanted.

Sonja ran water into the saucepan, set it on the range, and put the frying pan next to it. She switched on both burners. Then she took the butter from the table and dropped a small piece of it in the pan.

Suddenly, she laughed and looked down at herself. “I’m perfectly dressed for the kitchen!” She had worn the rather fancy dress suit to her mother’s the day before. “Do you have an apron?”

“Uh . . . no.”

“A kitchen towel would do, too.” Sonja knew how to fend for herself in the kitchen as well as the office.

Kim took a towel out of the cupboard and gave it to her.

Sonja tied it around herself.

Kim watched her with an affectionate gaze. She felt warm and full of tenderness. Everyday life. Yes, that’s what it was. Today, for the first time, they were living like a couple, sharing their everyday life. They were going to eat breakfast together, they were going to work together, and they knew that they’d see each other again in the evening, maybe sit on the couch . . .

“Are you dreaming?” Sonja stood in front of Kim. “We should eat breakfast, before it gets too late.” She slid the eggs out of the frying pan onto Kim’s plate. “Egg cup?”

Kim wished she could melt into the floor. “I don’t have that, either.”

Sonja smiled crookedly. “I think I’m going to have to take you shopping. If I’m going to eat breakfast here often – or cook here . . .”

“You really don’t have to do that,” Kim said. “I’ll manage.”

Sonja took off the improvised apron and sat down. “I’m not so sure.” She smiled at Kim. “I have no objection to cooking. Sometimes I like it.”

“Sonja . . . I . . .” Kim felt her mouth going dry.

“You don’t have to worry. I’m not planning to move in and impose myself on you. I’ll find myself an apartment.” Sonja looked inquiringly at Kim as she cracked her egg. “But for a couple of days . . . or should I go stay with Sandra? If I’m bothering you . . .”

“You . . . you can stay here as long as you want,” Kim replied laboriously. *Preferably forever*, she thought. She felt like a dream was coming true. But she didn’t know – still didn’t know – whether Sonja saw it the same way. “You aren’t going home again?”

“It was never my home.” Sonja appeared to hesitate. “But . . . I do have my things there." Her expression changed. "I'll have to get them."

She's afraid, Kim thought. *She doesn't want to go back there. I can certainly understand that.* "Sandra and I could do that," she suggested. "If you give me the key . . ."

Sonja looked at her, astonished. "I can't ask that of you." She swallowed. "Uwe will be there."

"Exactly. You can't go there. But Sandra and I can. He won't do anything to us. Beside which, there'll be two of us."

"You haven't asked Sandra yet," Sonja pointed out.

"She's your sister. Wouldn't you do the same for her?"

Sonja looked at her in renewed astonishment. "Yes."

"And she'll do it for you, just as gladly," Kim said. "Without a doubt."

"You should still ask her first. Or I should. I'll call her later."

"I'll take care of it. Just give me the key."

Sonja grimaced. "Thank you."

"Don't mention it," Kim replied.

Sonja glanced at the clock. "We have to get going. Otherwise I won't get through my agenda for today." She glanced at the table. "We can do the dishes this evening."

We. We can do the dishes this evening. Kim felt like she was going to float to the ceiling in sheer happiness.

She'd never looked forward to something as ordinary as dishwashing with so much pleasure.

"Sandra packed up everything that looked important to her," Kim said. "Some of it is in her apartment. I hope this will be enough for tomorrow." She indicated Sonja's clothing as well as a number of other things that lay on the bed.

"Yes, that'll do." Sonja looked oddly stiff.

"Nothing happened," Kim reassured her. "Everything went very smoothly."

"Uwe –"

Kim laughed a little. "At first, he thought Sandra was you. But she chased that idea out of his head pretty quick. After that, he left us alone."

"This isn't over," Sonja said dully. "I just don't believe it."

"Don't think about it anymore." Kim wrapped an arm around her. "I bought a few things. Tomorrow morning, we'll have rolls – that is, if you want to spend the night here. Of course, you can always go to Sandra's –"

Sonja looked at her and smiled a little. "Are you trying to get rid of me? So soon?"

Kim swallowed. "I just don't want you to feel trapped." *She's had enough of that.*

"I don't feel trapped. After all, I can go at any time." Sonja held a hand in front of her mouth and yawned. "Although I do feel a little tired."

"Do you want to go to sleep?"

Sonja looked at her. "Will you be mad at me if I don't?" She made a slightly embarrassed face. "I hardly dare to ask, but ... do you have a television?"

"Television? You want to watch television?"

"I know I'm falling in your esteem because of it, but sometimes I find television very relaxing."

Kim smiled. "Me, too. Do you like Campari? I just bought some. Campari Orange?"

Sonja nodded.

"Go sit on the couch," Kim continued. "Make yourself comfortable. I'll bring the Campari right in. Chips?"

Sonja made a face. "I was hoping to wait a little while before I got to the next dress size."

"You don't have to eat them. I want some." Kim let her gaze wander over Sonja's perfect figure. "And as far as dress size is concerned ... Too small isn't good, either. I think the anorexic skeletons that are running around these days are just awful."

Sonja chuckled. "Fine, then, bring the chips. I might eat one or two."

"I'll be right back." Kim went to the kitchen and got the Campari and orange juice out of the refrigerator. She mixed two glasses, positioned the bag of chips under her arm, and returned to the living room. "I see you've found the remote," she said with a smile.

Sonja sat on the couch, having pulled up her legs and turned on the TV. "*Desperate Housewives*? Unless you find it too silly."

"I don't think that at all. Susan's clumsiness always puts me in a good mood. She manages to put her foot in it at every turn, even the ones you don't see coming." Kim set the Campari glasses on the table, tore open the bag of chips, and shook some of them out onto a plate. She sat down next to Sonja.

It was a little like déjà-vu. Back then, the evening at the seminar, they'd done the same thing. They had sat in bed and watched television, nibbling on chips and laughing. She glanced at Sonja. She looked tired, like she'd had a hard day at the office, and she certainly couldn't have finished processing everything that had happened the day before, but at the same time, she already seemed a little more relaxed than she had lately. "Do you feel all right?" Kim asked softly.

Sonja turned to face her. "Oh . . . yes. A gentle smile transformed her features. The strict boss was gone. "Very good."

Kim leaned forward, picked up the Campari glasses, and handed one of them to Sonja. "Shall we make a toast?" she asked. "To a pleasant evening of television."

Desperate Housewives granted them an entertaining hour. Sonja ate more than two chips and was annoyed that they tasted so good, and Kim laughed at her. In the end, Sonja lay in Kim's arms, snuggling with her, almost asleep.

"Do you want to sleep on the couch?" Kim asked softly. "Or should we go to bed?"

"If you'll carry me over . . ." Sonja murmured, her eyes closed.

Kim brushed a gentle finger across Sonja's face. "I can try it." She smiled. "But I think walking would be easier."

"I can't walk anymore," Sonja mumbled sleepily.

She is so sweet, Kim thought. *How can a woman be this sweet?* "I'll cover you up, then you can sleep here." She let Sonja's head sink to the couch and slipped carefully out from underneath her.

Sonja opened one eye halfway. "Don't you want to take me with you?" She yawned and sat up slowly.

Kim smiled and reached her a hand. "I thought you might want to be alone."

Sonja allowed herself to be half pulled upright and stood up. "I've been alone for long enough." Her eyes were already falling shut again.

Kim wrapped an arm around her waist. "Come on," she said softly, leading her to the bedroom.

In bed, Sonja snuggled right up to Kim, and immediately fell asleep.

Kim lay there, smiling, holding Sonja in her arms, listening to the even rise and fall of her breath, and enjoying the feeling of knowing that Sonja wasn't going to get up and leave in an hour or two.

It was wonderful to have Sonja with her, today, tomorrow, the day after tomorrow, day and night.

Kim wished it would never end.

Kim sat at her desk, daydreaming. The telephone rang. She glanced at the caller ID number, smiled, and picked up. "Hello, sweetheart," she said softly.

Sonja seemed taken aback, since she didn't speak right away. "Uh . . . yes," she said then. In the office, private things like that apparently embarrassed her. "Do you have some time? I need your help. But only if you're available. Otherwise, I'll just have to figure out a different solution."

"For you, I'm always available," Kim said. "Especially since I'm responsible for the fact that you got to work later than usual this morning and lost time because of it."

"Hm." Again, Sonja seemed confused. "I'm at least equally responsible for that."

Kim felt warm. She remembered this morning. Only too well. It wasn't all that long ago, after all. "Yes, it took two," she said with a grin. "But I started it."

"I didn't have to join in." Sonja cleared her throat. "Could we perhaps get back to the subject? I'd really like to have you here for a meeting in half an hour."

"At your service. I'll be there."

"Pardon me," Sonja replied. "I'm so stressed. Of course, I'm not ordering you to do anything."

"I'd have no objection to that." Kim grinned. "Under certain circumstances . . ."

"Please . . ." Sonja sighed. "Let's concentrate on work."

"That's not easy for me," Kim said, "but I will. Half an hour."

"See you then. Kim?"

"Hm?"

"It was nice this morning," Sonja said quickly, then hung up.

Kim smiled. Sonja's passion had not decreased, even though she no longer had to have sex as if at gunpoint in order to distract herself from her tightly constrained existence.

Kim crossed her arms behind her head and leaned back in her chair. She closed her eyes. She envisioned Sonja before her, this morning, the way she'd lain beneath her, the way she'd moaned –

"Well, this is it. I'm saying farewell."

Kim opened her eyes. She swallowed, still feeling the touch of Sonja's hands on her skin. "Rolf."

"My last day," Rolf said, coming in. "Now you're the boss. On your own, once and for all."

Kim swallowed again, but for a different reason this time. She stood up. "Rolf . . ." she repeated unhappily.

Rolf laughed. "Come now, don't look so downtrodden. Instead, tell me when you're coming to visit us. Then we'll have a date to look forward to."

"As soon as possible." Kim smiled. "I promise you."

"Lovely." Rolf stepped over to her and gave her his hand. "Then I wish you all the best and success as my successor. You'll manage it." He looked at her, and his eyes seemed to be getting moist. "Oh, come here!" He pulled her to himself, hugged her fiercely, and let her go again. "Don't let it be too long before you visit," he said, giving her one last fatherly look before he left.

Kim sat back down. She was still rather shaken by Rolf's final departure, after all. All along, it had felt like he was standing behind her and held his hands out protectively over her, but now that was finished.

She felt confident that she knew the work inside and out, but it was still different now to be the lone boss all of a sudden. She took a deep breath. A new era.

And it coincided with a new era in her private life – hers and Sonja's. At least she hoped so; she still didn't know for certain. It was much too soon to ask Sonja what she was planning for the future, and there was still the whole new situation with her being a twin, with her father, with everything else.

Sonja had a lot to handle, and *she* had to set the agenda. It was *her* life.

Kim looked at the clock. She needed to get going, if she wanted to keep her appointment with Sonja.

Kim walked past Jo's abandoned desk, which would remain unoccupied all week, to Sonja's office and knocked on the door, although it was standing open.

Sonja looked up from her own desk and smiled. "Come in."

Kim went to her, glancing back once more at the open door to make sure they were still alone, and brushed a kiss across Sonja's lips. "Nice to see you again."

Sonja smiled again. "It hasn't been all that long."

"Every minute is like an eternity." Kim looked at Sonja's files. "You have a problem?"

"Yes." Sonja stood up. "A technical problem."

"I'm no technician," Kim said.

"No, but you have more to do with the technical side through customer support. I feel like I can never really make myself understood with the technicians. I tell them what I want them to do, but then they always do something entirely different. That costs time and money. That's why I'd really like to ask you to take care of this."

"Sure," Kim said. "What is the issue, more specifically?"

"Have a look at this." Sonja indicated her conference table, on which lay a giant sheet of paper that looked like a blueprint. She and Kim walked over to look at it, and Sonja pointed to part of the drawing. "I've now incorporated the manufacturing hall as well. But of course, there's no usable wiring in there."

"I see," Kim said.

"My ideas might simply be too bold. After all, I'm approaching this more from an organizational perspective than a technical one. The technical people probably don't understand that. For them, the technical aspects are always in the foreground."

Kim recalled a conversation or two she'd had with the repair team. "Yes, I know." She, too, always had to convince the team to please think about the customers who weren't technicians.

"It takes an enormous amount of work to oversee all of this," Sonja said. "It was all supposed to be finished some time ago."

Kim nodded. "I'll take care of it." She looked at the name of the person responsible for the blueprint. "Oh."

"What?" Sonja looked inquisitively at her.

"Oh, nothing." Kim rolled up the blueprint. "I'll take this with me. Is that all right with you?"

"What is it?" Sonja tilted her head to the side.

"Do you know Helmke Grotenauer-Albrecht?" Kim asked.

"She's a secretary –" Sonja indicated the plans, "his secretary."

"Exactly." Kim sighed.

Sonja arched her eyebrows questioningly.

"Oh, no, no!" Kim spread her hands in horrified defense. "Not that. I never had anything with –"

Sonja made an amused face. "That's none of my business."

"It would be your business if that were the case. But it isn't. Helmke's not even –" Kim broke off. "At least, so she says. But it doesn't matter. She's just absolutely caustic. But I'm sure I can manage to get her to give me an appointment with her boss."

"You don't have to if you don't want to," Sonja said. "I don't want to ask too much –"

"Oh, nonsense!" Kim interrupted her with a laugh. "You're not asking too much. I promised to help you, and I will. Helmke won't stop me from that. Is this the last stage of the reorganization?"

"Yes. After this, I'm finished."

"Then you could take a vacation," Kim suggested.

Sonja nodded reflectively. "Yes, then I could take a vacation."

"Rolf –" Kim swallowed. She had to suppress the feelings surging inside her again. "Rolf left today, once and for all. I promised to visit him as soon as possible."

"In the Camargue," Sonja said.

"Yes, in the Camargue." Kim hesitated.

"Well, ask already." Sonja smiled.

"I already asked you once."

"And now you know why I couldn't say yes back then."

"That was the only reason?" Kim asked.

Sonja gave her a serious look. "Yes, that was the only reason. I'd love to go with you to see Rolf and Margit in the Camargue."

Kim had been so resigned to the rejection she was expecting, that she didn't grasp right away what Sonja had said.

"You're not happy?" Sonja looked uneasy.

"Yes, of course I'm happy." Kim cleared her throat. "I'm sorry, I'm a little confused."

"We don't have to go to the Camargue." Sonja went back to her desk and sat down. "It was just a suggestion."

"This is all so new to me," Kim said. "I make a suggestion, you accept it . . . without ifs, ands, or buts. I'm not used to that."

"I've done it quite often, accepted your suggestions," Sonja said. "It was because they were so good that I nominated you for a promotion."

"Yes. Professionally. That's true, but –"

"Privately, I couldn't." Sonja sighed. "Can we talk about this tonight? I have to go. Executive board meeting."

"We don't have to talk about it at all," Kim said. "You don't have to justify yourself. It wasn't your fault, after all."

"Maybe it was." Sonja collected a few things from her desk and stood up. "Will you let me know where you get with the blueprints?"

"Yes, sure." Kim watched Sonja as she walked past her and out of the office with a stack of files under her arm.

A second later, she returned. "I knew I'd forgotten something." She rushed over to Kim and gave her a soft, tender kiss. "The most important thing." She smiled, turned around, and left the office for the second time.

"I love you," Kim said softly, although Sonja was already gone, and smiled as well.

The telephone on Sonja's desk rang. Kim considered whether or not to answer it; it wasn't really her responsibility, but she had been Sonja's assistant long enough, and Jo wasn't there, so she picked up the phone. "Mrs. Kantner's office, Wolff speaking," she answered.

"This is Mr. Kantner. Will you give me my wife, please?"

Kim froze. She pictured Uwe Kantner before her, the way he'd stared at Sandra with angry eyes because he mistook her for Sonja, the way he'd dogged their footsteps as they'd packed up Sonja's things.

"Hello? Are you still there?" Uwe Kantner seemed irritated.

"Yes, I . . . She isn't here. She's in a meeting." Kim swallowed.

"As always," he said, sounding cynical. "How many meetings does she have, then?"

"She's in charge of the company's most important project," Kim said. He must know that. Or had he never been interested to find out? "That means meetings are the order of the day."

"But of course. What a successful wife I have." The degree of malice in his voice increased. "I'm so proud of her, you know."

"You certainly haven't done anything to contribute to it." Kim could no longer restrain herself. "On the contrary."

He hesitated. "You're not her secretary."

"Not anymore," Kim said. "I used to be. Her secretary is on vacation at the moment."

"Please inform my wife that she should call me – it's in her own best interest." His voice now sounded like he was already relishing the prospect of this telephone call with Sonja.

"I won't do that." *Here it goes*, Kim thought.

He laughed a little. "Female solidarity, eh? What did she tell you?"

"Enough," Kim said. "Enough to protect her from you."

He laughed some more. "Remind her that we're still married. And that's not going to change any time soon."

"What's that supposed to mean?" Kim asked. "Sonja can do what she wants. She's a grown woman."

"She is my wife," he said pointedly. "And what I have, I don't let go of so easily. Regardless of who she's whoring around with right now, she belongs to me. You tell her that!" He hung up.

Kim shook her head in consternation. Sonja was right. It wasn't over yet. Kim was glad she'd taken the call, and not Sonja. Even though she couldn't imagine that what Uwe Kantner had spewed forth was anything but empty threats.

If he'd known to whom he was speaking . . .

But he would never suspect that. He suspected a man.

Kim sighed. *That* sword of Damocles was still hanging over her.

The telephone rang once again. It couldn't be! He was calling again?

Kim grabbed the receiver. "She's not here, I told you!"

"Uh . . . Kim? I was actually looking for Sonja." Sonja's, no, Sandra's voice.

Kim took a deep breath. "Sandra. I'm sorry. Uwe just called."

"Oh. My charming brother-in-law."

"Yes, exactly. And he –" Kim ran her hand through her hair. "He threatened that he wasn't going to let Sonja go just like that."

"That was pretty predictable," Sandra said. "The way I size him up. When I think of the way he looked at me . . . And that was meant for Sonja."

"He doesn't have any more leverage," Kim said.

"You don't need leverage for hate."

Kim went cold. "Do you think . . . you think he'll do something to her?"

"We probably ought to keep a close eye on her for a while," Sandra said. "Even though he's in a wheelchair, there are still plenty of possibilities."

"Yes." Kim felt even colder.

"There's one place where we wouldn't have to watch out for her so much," Sandra said. "Where no men are allowed."

"The women's café?" Kim asked.

"I'd like to go dancing again sometime. And it's so boring to go alone."

"That's why you wanted to talk to Sonja?" Kim asked. "Sonja has never been –"

"Yes, that's what I figured." Sandra laughed softly. "Don't you think it's about time?"

"Phew." Kim rolled her eyes to the ceiling. "She's had an awful lot to deal with lately. Another new thing on top of that . . ."

"It's not really that new," Sandra said. "You two danced together at the wedding. At least, it looked like dancing."

"But not –"

"Not in the women's café, not in a room chock full of lesbians; there were a few straight people at the wedding, too, I know," Sandra said. "But she's going to have to get used to it. I'd also like to know if she –"

Kim sighed. "So would I."

"So it's in our common interest, then."

"I'll suggest it to her." Kim arched her eyebrows skeptically. "This evening. At home." She fell silent abruptly. *This evening, at home*, echoed in her head. How that sounded. As if Sonja and she . . . were a real couple.

"Do that," Sandra said. "Friday. As usual, or so I've been told."

"Yes. As usual." Only one thing wouldn't be usual about it: Sonja. If she even came at all.

"I know, I'm terrible," Sonja said with an apologetic grimace. "Bringing paperwork home with me . . . But I didn't want –" She looked at Kim with an embarrassed smile. "I didn't want to come home so late."

Kim didn't know how to respond. Affection caught in her throat. Sonja was telling her with a flower that she'd missed her, that she yearned for her, that she wanted to be with her. And that her "home" was with Kim . . .

"That bad?" Sonja asked.

Kim smiled slowly. "Not bad. I'm glad you're here, even if I do have to share you with your paperwork."

"I'm really sorry." Sonja sighed. "The closer it gets to the end, the more there is still to be done. I promise, I'll finish this as fast as I can."

"You don't have to hurry." Kim glanced toward the kitchen. "Would you like something to drink – or to eat? To go with your work?" She chuckled softly.

"Oh, dinner," Sonja said. "You were expecting us to eat together."

"I was hoping we would. But if you have to work . . ."

"I'm not used to such a regular life," Sonja said. "Especially not in the evenings. That's why I routinely eat lunch at noon, when I can. Otherwise food would probably fall by the wayside more often than not."

"No wonder you're so thin," Kim said. "But I can make you something. I hadn't planned anything special, just something cold, bread, cheese, salami . . ."

"It's pretty hard to integrate everyday life into my work sometimes. That never really occurred to me before."

Because you had no everyday life, Kim thought. "I can make you a sandwich," she suggested. "And maybe some tea to go with it. We always used to drink tea with dinner at home, and I've kept that up."

"Good idea," Sonja said. "I'll have to sit at the kitchen table to work, right? You don't have another one."

"Yes, come on into the kitchen." Kim led the way.

"You think I'm too thin?" Sonja asked suddenly.

"I think we've discussed it before. I wouldn't mind a few more ounces on you." Kim turned around, smiling. "But it's up to you."

"Well . . ." Sonja hesitated, put her files down on the table, and looked up at Kim, who was putting on water for tea. "If you don't like it . . ."

"I like it fine." Kim came over, took her in her arms, and kissed her softly on the mouth. "You are gorgeous. And I wouldn't want to be responsible for you no longer fitting into your seductive, skin-tight suits." She laughed softly.

"They're not skin-tight," Sonja contradicted, looking down at herself. "They're completely ordinary business suits."

"Well, maybe it's not the suit that's so seductive – the alluring part is what's inside." Kim drew Sonja into her arms once more and kissed her a bit more intensely.

"I need to work," Sonja panted as she disentangled herself. "Really."

"I know," Kim said regretfully, turning her attention back to the tea water.

"Maybe I should've stayed at the office after all. Concentrating on work now is twice as hard."

"I'll make you a sandwich and some tea, and then I'll disappear," Kim countered. "I'll find myself a book and read." She smiled affectionately at Sonja. "Although it will be just as difficult for me to concentrate on that."

Sonja rolled her eyes. "We're certainly a couple of specialists . . ."

"Apropos of that," Kim said. "Did Sandra reach you on the phone?"

Sonja raised her eyebrows. "No?"

"She called today when I was still in your office, after you'd left for the board meeting . . ." Who else had called just then, Kim kept quiet. "She wants to go dancing and she finds it too boring to go alone."

"Go dancing? With me?" Sonja asked, baffled.

"You see that with twins all the time." Kim grinned. "Yes, she wanted to ask you, and because I picked up, she asked me."

"That sounds more likely," Sonja said.

"No, she wanted to talk to you," Kim contradicted. "But since she had me on the line . . . Friday is dance night at the women's café. We could all go."

"All of us?" Sonja looked startled.

"The three of us. Jo and Jennifer aren't back from their honeymoon yet, not until next week."

"The three of us," Sonja repeated, as though she hadn't yet quite grasped what they were talking about.

"It's only a suggestion, of course," Kim said. "I'm sure Sandra will have no problem finding a woman to dance with, once she's there. She won't really be bored."

"A woman to dance with," Sonja repeated again.

"Ah . . . love . . . this is going to be a very one-sided conversation, if all you do is repeat what I say." Kim picked up the kettle and poured Sonja some tea, watching Sonja as she did so.

"Yes, I . . ." Sonja sat down at the kitchen table. "Honestly, I'm a little overwhelmed."

"I can see that." Kim set the tea on the table in front of Sonja. "You can think about it for a while. For Sandra and me, it's normal . . . being among women like that, but for you –"

"It ought to be normal for me, too, by and by," Sonja interrupted her. "It's just . . . I was hoping for a little rest amid all the excitement."

"That's what I said to Sandra, too. You've been through so much lately. It must be getting too much for you. Sandra should go by herself. Like I said, I'm sure she won't have to be alone for long."

Sonja opened the uppermost of the files she'd stacked on the table, hesitated for a moment, and took a sip of tea.

"Sausage or cheese?" Kim asked. "For your sandwich, I mean."

"Cheese. Thanks."

Kim put the sandwich together and brought it to Sonja at the table. "Don't work too long." She kissed Sonja on the cheek and went into the living room.

She sat down. She didn't want to turn on the TV, because that might disturb Sonja's work; a book lay on the little coffee table, but she knew she wouldn't understand a single word if she tried to read. Sonja was sitting in the next room, working at the kitchen table. Not long ago, Kim couldn't have imagined that, not in her wildest dreams.

She smiled. So many things had happened that she still couldn't comprehend. The dreadful things she'd learned had been done to Sonja, especially Uwe Kantner's threats today – those made her worry awfully, but on the other hand: Sonja was with her, she seemed to feel well, she'd come home early just to be with Kim . . . all that was so wonderful, the feeling almost overwhelmed her. She could never have put her emotions into words.

She sat there daydreaming, and because her day at the office had also been a long one, she fell asleep.

"Well, I could've kept working a while longer, since you're already sleeping." She heard Sonja's voice from a distance.

Kim opened her eyes. Sonja stood in the doorframe and smiled – like a vision from *1001 Nights*. Her silhouette seemed blurred, as if she were wearing a veil.

She came and sat down beside Kim on the couch. "Enough for today." She smiled at Kim even more. "It was good, your sandwich, and the tea, too. Next time, I won't be so unpleasant, and we'll eat together."

"Maybe we ought to make an appointment for that in advance," Kim said, but she was smiling.

Sonja snuggled against her and drew up her legs. "I am wiped out . . ." she sighed. "When this project is finally done, we won't need to make any appointments; hopefully, I'll have more time then."

"If you believe that . . ." Kim said. "You're a workaholic."

Sonja took a deep breath. "First, I have to get used to the idea that I . . . that I can look forward to going home," she said quietly.

"I'm sorry," Kim replied. "I didn't mean to blame you for anything."

"You're not." Sonja grabbed Kim's arm and pulled her close, as though she never wanted to let go of her. "About Friday . . . I gave it some thought."

Kim waited silently for her decision.

"What's it like in the women's café? I've never been there."

"I know," Kim said. "What's it like there? Quite cozy, actually. A couple of armchairs, a few chairs, a few tables . . ."

"You know what I mean. Is it . . . I mean, there are just women there?"

"That's why it's called the women's café," Kim confirmed, grinning.

"And the women dance with each other," Sonja continued, thoughtful.

"You don't have to go to the women's café if the idea makes you uncomfortable. It won't be a problem if you say no."

"When you and I . . . I mean, when we danced together, at the wedding – that was nice."

"I thought so, too," Kim agreed.

"Sandra . . ." Sonja hesitated. "Sandra is well-known, at the café?"

"She's only been there once, with me," Kim said. "You could hardly call that well-known. She said she doesn't much care for that sort of institution. But if you want to go dancing . . ."

"Among women," Sonja said.

"Yes, among women." Kim sighed. "Let's not talk about it anymore right now. Sandra can go alone, too, that doesn't depend on us. If you don't want to . . ."

"You're terrible," Sonja said. "Can I just let myself get used to the idea first?"

"I thought you'd already thought about it." Kim was surprised. "I'm sorry if I misunderstood."

"You didn't misunderstand, it's just that thinking about it isn't the same as making a decision. I thought you might be able to help me with that part."

"You don't usually need any help making decisions," Kim said.

"In the office," Sonja replied pointedly. "But this has nothing to do with the office."

"But it doesn't have anything to do with me, either," Kim said seriously. "Only with you."

Sonja rested her head on the back of the sofa. "Yes, that's probably the problem." She turned her head to look at Kim. "When Sandra told you that she . . . is like you, and after you knew that we're twins . . . what did you think?"

Kim grimaced, but she didn't answer.

The corners of Sonja's mouth twitched. "You thought it was impossible for me not to be like her, right? Like you and she are."

"I . . . I wished that . . ." Kim gave her an unhappy look. "Do we have to have this conversation now?"

"Sometime or other, we have to. I've been dodging it for a long time."

"You . . . you don't have to decide. Not this soon. I know you have a lot of other things to think about first. There are so many more important things –"

"Really?" Sonja asked. "Don't you think clarity ought to prevail for once?" She looked at Kim. "You're afraid of what kind of clarity it will be." She sighed. "Me, too."

"I understand." Kim felt awful.

"No, I don't think you do. You've only ever been with women, you don't know what it's like –" Sonja's eyes examined Kim's face. "What it's like to feel so right with a woman, and to know the difference. To be afraid of losing it again. To wonder what will happen then."

Kim stared at her, trying to comprehend what she was telling her. "You're afraid that I might leave you if you choose me once and for all?" That thought had never occurred to Kim. She'd only ever imagined that Sonja could leave her.

Sonja closed her eyes. "Horribly afraid. It's only been a few days since I –"

"I know," Kim said with empathy. "That's why I'm not demanding that you –"

"But you can demand it of me." Sonja opened her eyes again. "In fact, you have to."

"I don't have to." Kim leaned over Sonja and brushed a kiss onto her lips. "I have time. And I have patience."

"You've had those for a long time already."

"I can be patient for much longer than this . . . if you're with me." Kim ran a gentle finger down Sonja's face. "You are with me. That's all that matters."

"I have so little to offer you . . . Even now." Sonja looked at her unhappily.

"You give me so much." Kim bent down over Sonja and kissed her. The kiss was like a melding. Proof for both of them that they belonged together.

Sonja's tongue snaked in between Kim's lips, ever farther inside, as though she wanted to thrust deep inside Kim and never let that melding dissolve. Suddenly, she broke away. "I want to be with you, to stay with you . . . I don't want to think about what tomorrow will bring."

Maybe it's better that way, Kim thought. She suddenly remembered Uwe's call. Good thing Sonja didn't know about that. "Tomorrow isn't Friday yet, of course, but how about dancing?" she asked. "You don't have to think while you're dancing."

"Yes, that's true." Sonja smiled. "Why not?"

"Sandra will be happy." Kim smiled, too.

"Sandra will probably have a thousand twin-tricks in store again." Sonja grimaced. "She loves that."

"You don't?"

"I'll never get used to it," Sonja said.

"Ha! Wasn't that fun?" Sandra laughed, beaming.

"Because no one knows who's who anymore?" Sonja's face didn't show the same enthusiasm as Sandra's.

"I bet you're the older of the two of us," Sandra said. "You're the natural big sister."

"I had to be," Sonja said. "But we'll probably never find out which one of us is older."

"All right, you jokers, what do you want to drink?" Susi asked from behind the bar. "Now that you've completely confused everybody . . ."

"Twins don't come around here that often, do they?" Kim asked, amused, sliding onto a barstool. "Give me a beer, please." She laid a hand on Sonja's shoulder. "What would you like?"

"Mineral water," Sonja said. "I'm confused enough already."

"One of you two has been here before." Susi looked from one twin to the other, trying to figure out which was which.

"Guess who." Sandra shot her a cheeky grin.

"You," Susi said. "You already feel right at home here."

"I've only been here once before," Sandra said.

"So it was you." Susi grinned, too.

"Clever woman. You caught me."

"I know what's what," Susi said, "twins or not." She slid the beer across the counter toward Kim. "And for you?" she asked Sandra.

"Hm." Sandra looked at her.

"I'm not on the menu," Susi said. "Not for anyone here. I ought to put up a sign."

"Maybe you should." Kim laughed. "That many offers?"

"Millions." Susi rolled her eyes and sighed. "In movies, the barmaid is always easy to get. That confuses some people here."

Kim looked at Sonja. "I think the same thing happens in other establishments." She was trying to draw her into the conversation, since Sonja seemed very quiet.

"I'll drink something later," Sandra said. "First, I'm going to dance. I've been looking forward to it for days." She glanced at Kim. "I assume I can't talk you into it?" She let her gaze wander over to Sonja. "Or you?"

"If we dance together on top of everything else, no one will know which way is up," Sonja said. "Better not."

Sandra laughed and strolled off toward the dance floor.

"Have a seat." Kim indicated the stool next to her. "We can always dance later. And if you don't want to, that's not so bad, either." She watched Sonja with some concern. "Or would you rather leave right now?" Sonja really seemed extraordinarily quiet.

Slowly, she shook her head. "No. All of this is just knocking the wind out of me a little. It's a lot like it was at the wedding, but –"

"But it's different." Kim laughed. At the wedding, everyone had behaved fairly conservatively, but here in the women's café, things were different. It was more of a meat market. "I'm sorry. I hope it's not too shocking for you. You'll get used to it. When I came into a place like this for the first time . . ." She sighed deeply. "It was pretty bad."

"Why?" Sonja asked. "After all, everyone here is supposedly –"

"Interested in the same thing," Kim finished her sentence. "Or ought to be. It just doesn't always feel that way. Pretty rarely, unfortunately."

Sonja shook her head, uncomprehending. "They're like men," she said, observing a group dressed in leather, sitting together at a table. "But they're not. Why do they act like that?"

"I don't know, either." Kim shrugged. "We just aren't that feminine."

Sonja looked at her. "I didn't mean you. You're . . . different."

Kim smiled and looked Sonja up and down for a moment. "But not as different as you are."

A woman approached Sonja and leaned in very close to her face. "Want to dance?"

Sonja shrank back slightly. “Um . . . no, thanks.”

“Sure?” The other woman didn’t seem to want to give up that easily. “You just were dancing.” She looked toward the dance floor, apparently confused. Then she grinned at Sonja again. “Looked good,” she added suggestively. “You’ve got some hot moves.”

“That . . . ah . . . was my sister,” Sonja said.

“Oh.” The woman tried to spot Sandra on the dance floor, but there was too much going on. “Then maybe I oughta go try her,” she said, departing.

Kim laughed.

“Apparently, people don’t care which twin they dance with,” Sonja remarked, rather irritated.

“Looks that way.” Kim looked at Sonja. “But I care.”

“They probably don’t play waltzes here,” Sonja said.

“You like to waltz?”

“It was nice at the wedding.”

“Wait a minute.” Kim slid off her stool and went over to the DJane. Shortly thereafter, she returned, and she’d barely reached Sonja when the first notes of the *Blue Danube* sounded. Kim bowed before Sonja. “May I have this dance?”

Sonja’s lips twisted. “I haven’t been invited so gallantly in a very long time.”

“That just goes with a waltz,” Kim said.

Sonja smiled, linked arms with Kim, and went with her to the dance floor. “This waltz is awfully long. I don’t know if I have the endurance for it.”

“We’ll see,” Kim said.

It was too crowded to fly across the dance floor as Kim would’ve wished, but it was wonderful to dance with Sonja. Right from the start, she closed her eyes and went soft in Kim’s arms. The initial problems they’d had at the wedding were absent.

“Hey.” Sandra appeared next to them with a woman who wasn’t the one previously speculating about a dance with her. “Did you two request the waltz?”

Sonja opened her eyes when she heard Sandra’s voice. “I’m crazy about waltzes.”

“Me, too,” Sandra replied with a chuckle. “What a surprise.”

"Yeah, really." Sonja laughed.

The woman who was dancing with Sandra looked at Sonja, then back at Sandra. "Is this some kind of joke?" she asked.

"No, twins," Sandra said. "You'd better learn to tell us apart. Because I get very jealous."

The woman seemed quite taken aback, but didn't say anything.

"You're mean, Sandra." Kim chuckled. "No one can tell you two apart if you don't want them to."

Sandra laughed and danced away with the still-baffled woman.

When the waltz ended, Kim and Sonja went back to the bar remarkably quickly. Kim finished her beer in one go, and Sonja did the same with her water.

"Awfully long," Kim gasped. "Like you said."

"Yes." Sonja's breathing was similarly heavy. "Wonderful." Her face had lost its serious expression. She was now beaming just like Sandra. "I thought I was going to blast off when you spun me around like that at the end."

Kim looked at her. "I thought I was in heaven, with the woman of my dreams in my arms," she said tenderly.

Sonja leaned into her. "We could do that again right now."

Kim laughed. "I don't think everyone else wants to dance waltzes exclusively."

"I can dance to other things, but the waltz is, of course, the jewel in the crown."

Kim embraced Sonja and danced a few steps with her along the bar. "We'll just have to make our own waltz."

Sonja laughed. She stood still and looked at Kim. Kim felt like she was being pulled into a vortex, into Sonja's eyes, into Sonja's deep soul. She sank into an intimate kiss.

"It's so wonderful with you," Kim whispered when she resurfaced after the kiss.

Sonja's eyes sought Kim's face, but she didn't say a word.

"Well, you two? This isn't a waltz." Hours later, Sandra was dancing next to them again. In the meantime, they'd hardly seen each other, since Sandra kept disappearing again and again, with a different woman every time.

This time, Kim knew the woman Sandra was dancing with. She looked at Sandra in astonishment.

Sandra gave her a peculiar look in return.

Kim smiled. She observed that through the next few dances, Sandra no longer switched partners. She was dancing exclusively with Felicity.

Sonja noticed too, but said nothing until they were standing at the edge of the dance floor. "Do you know the woman Sandra was dancing with?"

Kim laughed. "That would be overstating it, but I know her name, at any rate. It's Felicity. She's one of Jennifer's . . . uh . . . she was with Jennifer once."

"She looks so young," Sonja said.

"She is." Kim tried to catch a glimpse of Sandra and Felicity, who had kept dancing when Kim and Sonja had stopped. "Very young."

"And I get the feeling that Sandra likes her," Sonja added.

Kim chuckled. "I get that feeling, too."

A while later, Sandra came up to them.

Kim grinned at her. "Where's Felicity?"

"She's coming. She just wanted to get a drink."

"She seems to be a good dancer," Kim said innocently.

"Oh . . . uh . . . yeah . . . well, she's okay," Sandra replied indecisively.

"So that's not why you've been dancing with her," Kim stated. "For some time, without interruption . . ."

"Um . . . no," Sandra said.

Kim grinned.

"Yes, fine, I like her," Sandra admitted rather grudgingly.

Kim gave her an inquisitive look. There was something else here . . .

"She told me she's attracted to older women." Sandra rolled her eyes.

"Older women?" Sonja gaped at her in disbelief.

"Yes, sister . . ." Sandra smiled, composed. "To people under twenty, that's what we are."

"Oh my God." Sonja looked utterly appalled.

"Can't be helped." Sandra sighed once again. "But she's not just attracted to older women, she paints, too."

Kim chuckled. "And she's slightly nuts," she added. "So she's exactly your type."

Sandra took a deep breath. "I'm afraid so."

"That was a wonderful evening," Sonja said as they arrived back home. "I haven't done anything like that in such a long time." She looked reflectively at Kim. "Maybe never."

"I'm glad you enjoyed it. I did have a few reservations." Kim hung up her jacket.

"Yes, it was definitely strange," Sonja said. "The atmosphere really . . . takes some getting used to."

"I don't even notice anymore," Kim said. "I've been there so many times."

"Have you met all of your . . . acquaintances there?" Sonja sounded conspicuously uninterested.

"My girlfriends, you mean?" Kim smiled slightly. "A few. But not exclusively."

"Does everyone go there for just that reason? I got the impression that some people were there as couples, but a lot –"

"Yes, a lot of them are looking for a woman when they go out dancing. There aren't that many opportunities to do so – in public like that."

"Presumably," Sonja said, pensive again.

"You're used to something different." Kim nodded. "I know."

"Well, yes, but somehow . . . I'm not. Granted, I've never –" Sonja laughed. "I've never been hit on by so many men in one evening as I was by women today."

"I think that was mostly Sandra's fault." Kim grinned. "She tore through the scene like a whirlwind. And of course, some people couldn't tell who was who anymore. And then, when they saw you, they thought you were Sandra and they wanted to grab their opportunity."

"Quite seriously, in some cases." Sonja sighed. "I'm really going to have to have a talk with Sandra. Either that, or not go out with her anymore."

"I suspect that issue has resolved itself for the moment. Felicity isn't exactly the sharing type."

"But she only just met her today." Sonja went into the living room and sat down on the couch. "It can't be that serious already."

"With Felicity?" Kim shook her head. "With her, it's serious from the very first minute, if I'm any judge. But Sandra should know that. She witnessed Felicity's scene with Jennifer."

"She made a scene with Jennifer?" Sonja asked.

"Not just one. And after they'd only once – I mean, they hadn't known each other very long."

"And you really think Sandra is interested in that?"

"You tell me. You're her twin."

Sonja seemed to think about it. "I couldn't say," she decided after a while.

"You can't, or you don't want to? I know that you – I mean, I don't want to step on your toes." Kim broke off, embarrassed. Why did she always have to meddle in such nonsense?

Sonja looked at her. "You're wondering whether what Sandra did today might also be my usual M.O.? When I'm traveling alone?"

"I … no …" Kim squirmed uncomfortably. "That's not what I meant."

"Yes, you did. To you, Sandra is my mirror image. Which she is, of course, on the outside. And then –" Sonja sighed, "you remembered a thing or two, besides."

"I … Sonja … that was all such a long time ago …" Kim slumped with increasing unhappiness. She wanted certainty – but then again, she didn't. Depending on how the certainty was going to turn out.

"Not that long ago," Sonja said. "And you witnessed things that … that I now wish you hadn't seen." She took a deep breath. "And that I wish I hadn't done."

"That … that was none of my business then, and it isn't now," Kim said. "What Sandra does is her concern. And it doesn't justify any inferences about your behavior. That's clear."

"To you, maybe, but not to me. Sandra is in fact my … alter ego.

She brings things home to me that I hadn't been aware of before."

What things? Kim thought, but she didn't say it out loud.

"Yes, that, too." Sonja twisted her mouth slightly. "That above all."

"Sonja . . . I . . . I don't demand anything of you, you know that." Kim sat on the couch next to Sonja and looked at her. "Please, don't feel obligated . . . or forced . . . into anything. I can wait . . . and I will wait, as long as you need. All of this must be horribly confusing for you, and I understand if you want to clear up other things first. Sandra, your father . . ."

The corners of Sonja's mouth twitched. "And you should come last? One of these days? After everything else has been sorted out?"

"I . . ." Kim laid her head in her hands, then ran her hands through her hair. "I'm afraid, Sonja, terribly afraid. I love you so much," she whispered.

"Oh, Kim." Sonja rested a warm hand on Kim's shoulder. Her hand slipped down and caressed Kim's back. Sonja leaned over and kissed Kim's throat, pushing her gently down onto the sofa. "We can't just be afraid all the time," she whispered, sliding on top of Kim and kissing her.

Kim closed her eyes. She felt Sonja's weight on top of her, that light, intoxicating weight, that wonderful feeling of being together with her. Sonja's hair caressed her face; Sonja's scent caressed her nostrils and spread its beguiling effects. "Sonja . . ." she whispered.

Sonja rested her face on Kim's shoulder. "If you only knew how I feel when I'm with you," she said softly. "Especially now that I . . . live here. I know it won't be forever, but I feel so at home here . . . as if I'd always lived here. Everything is so natural. I come home from work, we eat together . . ." She laughed. ". . . or not. We sit on the couch and watch television; sometimes we just look at each other and know what the other is thinking. We don't have to say anything. As if . . . as if . . . I don't know . . . as if we were living in a cocoon that protects us. From everything bad that comes from the outside."

"I would like so much to protect you from everything bad," Kim whispered, embracing Sonja and squeezing her tight. "So that no one could ever hurt you."

"You don't need to protect me. You just have to –" Sonja let her hand slide up and down Kim's thigh and kissed her once more.

Kim's heart began to beat faster. Sonja's hand left warm trails on her thigh that wouldn't cool down again. Sonja's kiss caused hot flames to flare up inside Kim, from the tip of her tongue all the way down into her belly. "Sonja . . ."

Sonja abandoned Kim's mouth to nibble at her earlobe, then let her lips glide back across Kim's cheek to her mouth. "Kiss me," she whispered when she'd arrived there. "Kiss me hard. I need you."

Kim slowly rolled with Sonja until she lay beneath her. She looked down into Sonja's eyes. They were flickering slightly, as though Sonja were waiting for something she couldn't predict. "Don't be afraid, love," Kim murmured, sinking her lips gently onto Sonja's and kissing her tenderly. "I'm here with you."

"Yes, I know." Sonja searched Kim's face, as if she needed to find something there that had long lain hidden.

Kim sought Sonja's mouth once more, and closed her eyes. She pressed slowly in between Sonja's lips and tried to let herself be led by feelings alone.

Sonja's tongue entwined with hers; she sighed in Kim's mouth. "Yes . . ."

Kim's hand felt its way to Sonja's breast and caressed it. Sonja sighed more strongly in her mouth. Kim sensed her own arousal increasing, while Sonja's rock-hard nipple stabbed her palm even through the layers of clothing. She brushed across it, again and again, and Sonja moaned. Her fingers dug into Kim's back, and her thighs spread apart.

Kim let her hand wander down to Sonja's crotch, where she rubbed lightly back and forth. Sonja's moaning grew louder. Kim's hand went higher and opened the zipper on Sonja's jeans.

Sonja moaned in anticipation.

"Shall we go to bed?" Kim whispered.

"Later." Sonja pressed her hips against Kim and let out a labored gasp. "I . . . I . . ."

Kim laughed. "I understand." Her hand slipped inside Sonja's pants and sought entry to her panties.

Sonja let herself fall back onto the couch and placed her hands on

Kim's head, so that she had to look at her. "I love you," she whispered, her eyes searching Kim's. "I love you so much."

Kim froze. "Sonja ..." she replied, stunned. Her voice sounded raw.

"I've wanted to tell you that for a long time," Sonja went on softly, "but ... but I couldn't." Her gaze pleaded for understanding. It appeared embarrassed and guilty. "I have this whole time ... It was so hard."

"I know." Kim swallowed. "I know all that, my darling." She kissed Sonja and slipped farther into her panties. Her fingers got wet.

"Not like that." Sonja moaned. "Undress me, please."

"Don't you first want to –?"

"No. Please ..." Sonja's lips pressed together intensely. "First ..."

Kim straightened up and pulled pants and panties together down off her hips. She began to unbutton Sonja's blouse, her gaze remaining on her face. It looked a little tense. "Are you all right?"

Sonja bit her lip. "You drive me insane," she said with an effort.

Kim smiled. "Well, if that's all ..." She pushed Sonja's blouse from her shoulders, slid around to her back, unhooked her bra, and tossed it aside. Sonja lay naked before her. "Satisfied?" She leaned down and kissed Sonja's trembling lips. They really were trembling a lot. "What is it, love?" Kim was confused. Sonja was behaving as though she were terribly afraid, but there was nothing here for her to fear. "Do you not want to do this? You just have to say so."

"No, I ... want to." Sonja looked at her, and her eyes flickered even more. "I want you to –" She turned her head to one side. "Please, kiss me ... down there." Her voice was no more than a breath.

Kim felt every hair stand up on her body, from top to bottom. Sonja had never allowed her to touch her between her legs with her mouth; that had always been taboo, although nothing else ever had been. This was the one thing she'd held back. Even more so than her *I love you*. Today, all the walls she'd constructed around herself were falling down.

No, she was *tearing* them down. They were collapsing as though struck by lightning. She didn't want to be hemmed in by them anymore, as she had for her entire previous life.

“Sweetheart . . . my sweetest . . .” Kim had to swallow. “Do you really want that?”

Sonja turned her head back. “Ask me again, and I’ll say no.” She smiled, but looked uncertain. “Please . . .” she whispered. “Don’t ask anymore . . .” She placed her hands on Kim’s head and slowly pushed it down along her body.

Kim kissed her way down Sonja’s body, and Sonja writhed beneath her. The nearer Kim came to the place between her legs, the more Sonja’s body stiffened, went hard. “You don’t have to,” Kim said softly. “You don’t have to force yourself.” She looked up.

“Yes, I do.” Sonja’s breathing was shallow. “I want you to know how much –” Her hands dug into the sofa. “How much I love you,” she went on in a whisper.

“You told me that already,” Kim replied. “You don’t have to prove it.”

“But I want to.” Sonja’s voice became firmer, but at the same time, she was still trembling. “It’s silly that I’ve never done it before. I’m not a kid anymore.”

“Beloved . . .” Kim laughed gently. “That’s no reason. There aren’t any rules about . . . about things like this.”

Sonja raised her head and gave Kim a serious look. “I want to experience it,” she said tremulously. “Don’t you understand? You told me that it’s the most enjoyable thing two women can do together. And I’ve never done it. I’ve deprived you of the most enjoyable thing.” She sank back, exhausted.

“Mostly, you deprived yourself. But that doesn’t mean you have to –”

“Please . . .” Sonja whispered. “Don’t talk anymore. I can’t. This is awful.”

“I’m sorry.” Kim didn’t know why she was hesitating. Sonja’s previous refusal must still be feeling much too present to her, and she didn’t want to contravene Sonja’s wishes, which had always been so important to her. She leaned down and carefully spread Sonja’s thighs farther apart. Overwhelmed, she paused there.

It wasn’t the first time she’d seen Sonja down there, that had never been forbidden, but it was the first time she knew she would be permitted to touch her, not just with her hand – but with her lips, her tongue, her mouth.

She swallowed. Her mouth felt dry. Sonja's chestnut-brown fleece shimmered just as seductively as the hair on her head when it shone in the sun. It was the moisture that generated tiny reflections of light on the hairs, with assistance from the warm glow of the lamp.

Kim let her hand float above it cautiously, without pressing into the hairs; she only tickled their surface gently.

Sonja sighed, and her hips arched upwards. "Please . . ." she whispered anew.

Kim slowly let herself sink down, considering once again the dense jungle guarding Sonja's entrance, which gave a reddish glow from the depths of the forest.

She knew that she could barely hold back her tongue any longer; it was already thrusting against the insides of Kim's lips, trying to open them.

Kim embraced Sonja's trembling thighs and took possession of that swollen paradise, engulfing it with her mouth, stroking the bulging labia with her tongue. She thrust in between them, and the fleshy fruit opened itself wide.

Sonja stiffened, but at the same time, she moaned out loud, with what sounded like relief.

Kim let her tongue thrust in as far as it could, feeling the small rough raised area inside the entrance, and began to caress it with the tip of her tongue.

Sonja's moans became louder. Her thighs twitched, her bottom thrust itself in Kim's direction, as if she wanted to be even closer to her than she already was.

Kim felt Sonja's pearl pulsating as it grew harder and more swollen. She tried to envelope clit and labia all at once, to suck in everything between her own lips. Sonja tasted wonderful.

Sonja laid her hands on Kim's head, caressing the soft shock of hair. "Kim . . ." she whispered. "Kim . . ." Her hips began thrusting against Kim, in the same rhythm with which Kim was thrusting her tongue inside her. "Oh . . . oh . . . oh . . ." She sighed and moaned alternately.

Kim licked Sonja's labia with the appreciation of a connoisseur, savoring the sweet nectar that had been off limits to her until now. She entered Sonja with one finger, stroking her from the inside now as she continued to flick her tongue across Sonja's pearl.

Sonja jerked upwards, moaned loudly, fell back.

Kim's finger no longer thrust inside her, but merely caressed her while she encouraged Sonja's pearl to grow ever larger with her tongue and lips, until it seemed ready to burst.

Sonja's moans sounded tortured. "Oh ... oh my God ..." she whispered. "Oh yes ... oh yes ... yes ..." She jerked upwards once again. Kim held tight to her thighs, so that she could not escape her reach, and redoubled her efforts with tongue, lips, and fingers.

"Oh God ... oh God!" Sonja screamed.

Kim felt how Sonja clenched around her fingers, how her pearl rivaled a pebble in hardness and nearly leapt from its sheath, how Sonja's belly fluttered and then became so solid one could've bounced a ball on it.

Sonja stopped breathing. Her body arched, and suddenly, a scream burst forth from her, a mix of a moan and a cry for help; her hands dug deep into the back and seat of the couch; she was stiff as a board, her entire body an elegantly bowed bridge.

She stayed in the air like this for several seconds, then collapsed and began breathing again, gasping heavily.

Kim didn't worry about that; she went on caressing her.

"Are you ... insane?" Sonja's gasps turned into a horror-stricken question.

"That wasn't all, not by a long shot." Kim grinned. "You know that."

"Help," Sonja breathed.

"Gladly." Kim's lips tenderly encircled Sonja's pearl. Once more, the tip of her tongue performed a delicate dance upon it, and Sonja could no longer release her clenched fingers from the sofa.

"Please ... please don't ..." Sonja gasped for air. "That was at least twenty." Quite some time had passed, and Sonja's skin glowed red, as if she had been lying in the sun too long, although she'd only been on the couch the whole time, hardly changing position at all.

"Oh, come on, not even." Kim chuckled. "Ten at the most."

"It feels more like a hundred to me." Sonja took a deep breath, but still could not breathe evenly afterward. "They are so intense. Please, please, no more. I can't do it anymore. Mercy . . ."

Kim rested her face against Sonja's soft thigh. "One minute's rest," she said with a smile.

"An hour. At least." Sonja freed her fingers from the sofa and placed them upon Kim's hair, caressing it. "Come to me, please," she asked softly.

Kim lifted her head and looked at her, then slid slowly up her body. "Was it nice?" she asked tenderly.

"No, I was just faking all that," Sonja replied. She recovered quickly. She grinned. "How can you even ask me that?"

"I just wanted to be sure." Kim nuzzled her head against Sonja's breast. "You never know."

Sonja's breathing calmed. She lay there, still, stroking Kim's hair, winding one strand after another around her fingers. "I was so stupid," she said after a while.

"Stupid? Why?" Kim raised her head.

"That I waited so long for that. I don't know why."

"You don't know?"

"Well, yes, I do." Sonja grimaced. "But . . . I needn't have. With you." She sighed. "I'm sorry."

"It can be nice to save some things for later. Anticipation can be the best part."

"I wasn't really . . . looking forward to it. I just thought, you wanted it so much, so . . ."

"Because of me?" Kim gaped at her. "You only did it because of me?"

"It was about time," Sonja said. "I wanted to give you something that I . . . that I'd never given anyone else."

"Never? But you said –"

"Yes . . . well . . . I – It was never enjoyable for me. I only acted like it so that . . . so that we could get on with things. Whenever I could, I avoided it. My mother said that . . . respectable women don't do that sort of thing, only –"

"Your mother." Kim gritted her teeth.

"Yes, I know, you don't understand it, but –" Sonja gave her an unhappy look. "It was always a battle inside me. I had very different needs than my mother would ever have permitted, and then . . . I always felt somehow . . . depraved."

Kim smiled. "I remember. You said that to me once. I thought it was a joke. I mean, as passionate as you are . . . I've rarely encountered a woman more passionate than you are."

"Yes, that's the worst part."

Kim bent over her. "Is it . . . better now?" she asked gently. "Or do you still feel that way?"

"With you, it's been different from the start." Sonja gave her a searching look, as if she were trying to take in the image. "Perhaps because it was *so* different. Which muddled everything."

Kim sighed. "Indeed."

"I am so sorry," Sonja said. "But . . . but after we came back from the seminar, everything was much more complicated than it was in the first place. I didn't know what to do."

"That's over. It's not important anymore."

"I'm constantly feeling the need to apologize to you. But I couldn't act any other way." Sonja looked even unhappier.

"I know. It was just so confusing for me back then."

"I can imagine," Sonja said. "Especially now that I've experienced the way you . . . interact with each other. Jo and Jennifer . . . and Sandra. If I had been Sandra, things would've been so simple for you."

"Maybe. But then, maybe not." Kim laughed. "I don't think I'm enough of a crazy artist for Sandra. That probably would've caused problems."

Sonja shook her head. "That is something I don't understand in the slightest. That is one way that the two of us are completely different."

"You have no idea how glad I am about that," Kim said softly, bending down over Sonja.

Sonja wrapped her arms around Kim's neck and pulled her close. "Me, too." She propped one leg up and made Kim moan, because she was pressing against her center. "I think the hour is over," Sonja said with a smile. Her eyes became hooded. "I want you to come on me, take me, do everything to me that you can think of. There are no more taboos, and I want to feel that." Her voice sounded hoarse.

Hot lightning bolts shot through Kim's belly. Her arousal had only been taking a little nap. Now, its eyes were open and it was wide awake. Kim began to move on top of Sonja. She could tell that this was going to go quickly, because everything inside her yearned for Sonja. Her movements grew fiercer. Sonja moaned beneath her. "Come, yes, come . . ."

She spread her wetness across Sonja's thigh, sliding back and forth ever faster, thrusting her hips into Sonja's as if she meant to penetrate her. The volcano inside her boiled higher and higher; she paused and let it sink back into its crater once more. Sonja waited, breathing heavily beneath her.

Kim pressed her thighs so tight that Sonja moaned aloud, because she was squeezing hers so hard between them. She began again to give free rein to her arousal, this time without interruption. The crater broke loose, and her insides overflowed with streams of boiling lava, with jets convulsing violently, until she collapsed on top of Sonja.

Sonja only let her rest for a moment before starting to tantalize her again. "Revenge is sweet." She smiled, looking like butter wouldn't melt in her mouth.

Kim couldn't answer because the next volcano was already about to erupt; she could barely get enough air to survive the explosion. "I didn't do such horrible things to you," she defended herself with great effort between two gasps.

"Much worse," Sonja asserted. "Beside which: horrible? You call this horrible? Then you don't know what you're in for." She immediately let Kim feel what she meant, encompassing Kim's nipple with her lips at the same time that her hand wandered between her legs.

"You devil woman." Kim moaned in agony.

"Always happy to be of service." Sonja chuckled.

Kim let the orgasm wash over her like a tidal wave, which still didn't quench the volcano inside her. An idea occurred to her. "Now we can finally do something we never could before," she said with a naughty wink. The next moment, she had spun around and landed upside-down between Sonja's legs.

She felt Sonja grasp her buttocks as she dove back inside Sonja's jungle. Sonja's tongue thrust inside her at the same time. They both moaned, Kim's lower belly trembling against Sonja's face.

Although it was already the middle of the night, tiredness couldn't begin to stop them.

They didn't fall asleep until morning.

Kim awoke on the couch, although without Sonja. Every one of her limbs let her know that the couch was not the ideal place to spend the night, and she moaned as she rose.

She staggered into the kitchen. "You can't be serious!" she burst out when she saw Sonja, clad only in a bathrobe, sitting at the kitchen table, bent over her file folders.

Sonja looked up with a guilty expression on her face. "I won't go to the office, even though it's Saturday. But –"

"All right, fine." Kim waved it away. Her next stop was the coffeemaker. "I'll have to get used to this sooner or later."

"I have a few things to get used to, too," Sonja said. "Don't I get a kiss?"

Now Kim looked guilty. "Pardon me." She went over to Sonja and kissed her gently.

"We're already like an old married couple. After fifty years, I mean."

"Oh, no." Kim laughed. "It's not that bad." She brushed another kiss across Sonja's lips. "It was just a... hmm ... long, hard night." She cast a mischievous glance at Sonja. "And you weren't entirely blameless, either." She looked down at the files and shook her head. "How can you get back to work again so fast?"

"It's not that I can, it's that I have to." Sonja sighed deeply and leaned back. "May I ask you something?"

"Of course." Kim went to the coffeemaker and got herself a mug from the shelf.

"Do you want to keep living here?" Sonja asked.

Kim spun around in surprise. "Uh, yes, actually, I was planning to. The apartment is enough for me. And I like it, too. I find it rather cozy. I like penthouse apartments."

"Me, too." Sonja nodded. "It's just that working at the kitchen table like this isn't exactly my ideal."

"I've always kept my work confined to the office before. I've never had that problem." Kim gave Sonja another scolding look.

"Fine, fine, it's my problem." Sonja raised her hands. "I just thought – But if you want to go on living here, that settles it." She turned back to her paperwork.

Kim's brow knit. "What would happen if I didn't want to keep living here?" She poured a cup of coffee for herself and one for Sonja, picked up both mugs, and carried them to the table, although there wasn't much room for them, Sonja having covered it with files.

Sonja pushed a file folder to one side so that Kim could set her coffee cup next to it. "You don't want to. It was just a question."

"Please, Sonja . . ." Kim sat across the table from her, holding her own coffee cup, because there really wasn't any space for it on the table. "You don't just toss out pointless questions. That's not remotely your style."

"How well you know me." Sonja looked up and smiled.

"In *that* regard, yes." Kim sipped at her coffee, but it was still too hot. "You were always like that when you were my boss."

"You make more money now. You could afford a better apartment."

"Just because I'm making more money doesn't mean I have to change apartments," Kim responded, confused. "Especially since I like this one."

"No, you don't have to." Sonja paged through a file some more and looked up a moment later. "Then I'll just have to move on my own." She laughed softly. "I really need an office at home, I'm sorry."

"You said you were going to find yourself an apartment." That was nothing new to Kim; even though she'd prefer to keep Sonja here with her, this apartment probably really was too small for two people in the long run. At least it was if one of them wanted to work there, too.

"Yes, I said that." Sonja closed one file and picked up the next.

"What is it, Sonja? Don't be so secretive." Kim checked again to see whether her coffee had cooled down enough.

"I'm not being secretive, I just thought – well, I had my eye on an apartment, but for me alone . . . I'll keep looking, it doesn't matter." The file was subjected to an intensive examination.

Had Kim not been so worn out by the previous night that she felt like a wrung-out towel, the coffee probably would've taken effect sooner and spurred her brain cells to action. So it took her a while. "You want to move in with me officially?" she asked, stunned.

Sonja raised her head. "I'm already living with you."

"For a few days. In the interim. I hadn't figured that you –" Kim took a large swallow of coffee. Eventually, she had to wake up. "That you . . . really, properly . . ."

"I have to find an apartment, one way or the other. So I thought maybe the two of us – but if you love your apartment, I certainly don't want to force you out of it."

"Well, if that's what this is about, what I love, then *you* are most definitely head and shoulders above anything else." Kim smiled. "Why didn't you say so in the first place?"

"I thought I had." Sonja looked at her, astonished.

"The things you think . . ." Kim stood up and kissed her on the cheek. "I would be happy to move in with you, woman of my dreams," she said, smiling. "If you've been doing so much thinking, you might've thought of that, too."

"I would've understood if you –" Sonja was playing nervously with her pen. "I mean, my living here with you wasn't planned. And it was only supposed to be for a little while. It wasn't a decision about the future."

"No, it wasn't, but it has apparently escaped you how I've enjoyed every second of your being here." Kim smiled. "Falling asleep together, waking up together, having breakfast together; coming home to an empty apartment after work, true, but knowing that it's not going to stay empty, or else coming home with you after work – that's a wonderful feeling."

"Some people find so much closeness intimidating."

"If anyone, then I would've thought that would be you," Kim replied.

Sonja inhaled and exhaled quickly. "Yeah, me, too. I wouldn't have thought that I . . . that I would ever – these last few years, I've so often wished that I could finally be alone, that I could shut the door behind me and no one else would be there . . ."

"Of course." Kim leaned over her and embraced her shoulders. "I understand that. Which is why I also thought you'd want to enjoy your own space for a while."

"I'm married," Sonja said.

Kim jerked up with a start.

"And yet, I never felt that way." Sonja looked at her. "But since I've been here – with you – I have felt that way."

Kim had been staring at her all along, and now that rigid stare definitely didn't want to let go. "With me?" she asked in disbelief.

"It's so different," Sonja continued. "So relaxed. So natural. There's so much peace here. When I imagined being alone in a new apartment, I suddenly felt sad. It wasn't what I wanted anymore."

"You can stay here and work at the kitchen table, too." Kim smiled.

Sonja laughed. "I don't exactly want that either. Don't be mad at me, but – that really isn't the way to go."

"All right, maybe not." Kim caressed Sonja's cheek affectionately. "I want you to get your home office as soon as possible." She straightened up and looked around. "Although it will be hard for me to leave this. I've always felt content here."

"Alone . . . in your bed . . . after I'd left?" Sonja asked.

Kim looked at her. "No, not then," she replied seriously. "Not remotely." She smiled again. "Where is the apartment you like so much? How big is it? Tell me about it."

A hesitant smile slowly overtook Sonja's face. "You want to move there with me?"

"I can't answer that until I've seen it. But since I know your good taste, I assume that I would want to, yes."

"It really is big enough for the two of us. Each of us can have an office and a bedroom –"

"Separate bedrooms?" Kim gave Sonja an astonished look.

"Well, that would have its advantages," Sonja said. "When I come home late from work and you're already asleep . . ."

"I want you to wake me in any case," Kim said. "But if you insist on separate bedrooms . . . Then we might as well keep separate apartments."

"I don't insist. I just thought it would be more practical."

"Have I ever mentioned that you think too much?"

"I think I vaguely recall something like that," Sonja replied with a chuckle. "Fine, then, just one bedroom, I have nothing against that. But I don't want to hear you complain when I interrupt your sweet dreams at night."

"The sweetest dream doesn't start until you get there." Kim leaned down and pressed her cheek against Sonja's. "Every day. That'll be wonderful."

"I'll have to ask you about that again in a couple of years," Sonja said, "after you've become haggard from too many nights without enough sleep."

"I'm sure there will be plenty of nights without enough sleep," Kim countered with a grin, "but both of us will be haggard from those."

"I'll have to think about those separate bedrooms again." Sonja looked sidelong at Kim.

"You're one to talk." Kim grinned again.

"Caught me." Sonja sighed. "You could see the apartment next week, if you want. Then you can decide. The realtor told me I could have until Wednesday to decide."

"Good." Kim straightened. "I'll go take a shower, so you can work in peace. But I hope to get a few minutes of your Saturday, as well."

"We need to go shopping," Sonja said. "I'll grant you those few minutes. I can't live without egg cups any longer."

"When is Sonja coming?"

"I'm not making any concrete predictions about that." Kim sighed and looked at Sandra. "They've completely missed the mark too many times before."

"Why does that sound familiar to me?" Felicity looked at Sandra, too.

"Yes, I know." Sandra looked contrite. "But there's always so much to get done . . ."

"The supermarket closes at the same time every day," Felicity pointed out.

"But that's when the real work starts," Sandra defended herself. "During the day, there's no time, and on top of that, I have the second store now, too."

"If you wanted to build a company, you might've told me earlier," Felicity commented.

"When?" Sandra looked deep into her eyes.

Kim laughed. "If you two want to fight, go home. Don't do it at our housewarming party."

"Who's fighting?" Felicity batted her eyelashes innocently.

"I really like this apartment a lot." Sandra let her eyes roam over what she could see from there. "I could imagine living here, too."

"No wonder. Sonja picked it out," Kim said. "You have the same taste."

"But you seem to like it, too." Sandra picked up a glass and a tiny sandwich from the buffet table. "I'll toast to your new apartment now, then. If Sonja's not coming –"

"Who says I'm not coming?" Sonja stepped from the entryway into the living room.

"Your work, sister dear," Sandra replied with a grin. "I really wasn't expecting you."

"You're here, too, so our work is just going to have to get along without us today." Sonja came over to them.

Jennifer and Jo returned from their walk-through. "Fabulous," Jennifer said. "Really nice."

"We like it." Kim smiled at Sonja and handed her a glass. "So, now we can make a toast. Nice of all of you to come." There were several other people there as well, who all now joined them with their glasses.

There was a general peal of laughter when the glasses clinked each other, since each one sounded different, almost like a melody.

"You are my sunshine," Kim said. "Did you hear it?" Her affectionate smile prompted Sonja to smile back.

"With a great deal of imagination," she said.

"I have enough imagination for that anytime." Kim's eyes sank so deep into Sonja's, they lost sight of the world around them.

"Best of luck in your new home," said Susi, coming over to them. "You have plenty of bread and salt, after all." Housewarming presents were piled up on top of the coffee table.

Kim tore herself away from Sonja's eyes. "Perhaps I should've mentioned that excessive salt consumption is bad for you." She smiled.

"And that bread makes you fat," Sonja added, linking arms with her. "The next thing we'll have to buy is a freezer, to freeze all that bread." She looked at Kim. "You see, I was right."

"Of course, darling, as always." Kim sighed. "Sonja wanted a freezer from the start, but I said we didn't need one for just two people. It's not necessary."

"They're always practical," Jennifer said. "We have one now, too."

"You got it as a wedding present," Kim replied. "That's different."

"You're just stingy," Jennifer said. "Admit it. And you two really have no reason to complain about money."

"Just because a person has more money than before, doesn't mean she has to spend it right away," Kim said. "I'm just thrifty."

"Stingy," Jennifer repeated, grinning.

"I'll buy a freezer tomorrow, then it'll be settled." Sonja shot Kim a twinkling look. "I haven't been shopping for kitchen appliances in ages, anyway."

Kim rolled her eyes. "If I'd known you loved the shopping for the kitchen that much –" She looked at Jennifer. "Usually, she has no time, but she can spend hours looking at kitchen wares."

"I'll go with you," Sandra said. "I need a few things for the kitchen, too."

"Good, you two go. Then at least I don't have to go along." Kim exhaled with relief.

"She hates the kitchen department." Sonja chuckled. "She can barely tell a pot from a pan."

"Hey, now, that's definitely an exaggeration." Kim contradicted her indignantly.

"When I moved in with you, I had to eat my eggs without an egg cup," Sonja said, with a reproving look.

Kim looked at the floor, embarrassed.

Jo laughed. "Sounds like us, doesn't it?" She looked at Jennifer.

Jennifer nodded. "A bit."

"You two brought your honeymoon videos, didn't you," Kim said. "Can we watch them now?"

The television was turned on, and a moment later, the blue waters of the Caribbean shimmered on the screen. The video was barely finished when everyone started talking about vacations, and Kim switched on the stereo for those who wanted to dance.

She danced all evening with Sonja, and the apartment felt like a ballroom in paradise. She didn't want to be anywhere else, not as long as she could look into Sonja's loving eyes.

Hours later, Kim and Sonja collapsed into bed, exhausted. "If you still want sex now, you're going to have to help yourself," Sonja murmured sleepily. "You know where everything is."

Kim laughed softly. "Let's put it off 'til morning," she said, snuggling up with Sonja; soon, both of them had fallen asleep.

Rolf and Margit came out of the house at the same time as Kim and Sonja drove up. "It's so lovely that you could come visit us."

Kim laughed after they'd exchanged greetings. "You two look thoroughly healthy. All tan, like you've just come back from vacation."

"We're on vacation every day now." Rolf grinned.

"You, maybe, but not me." Margit nodded to Rolf. "No, he isn't, either. Hauling stones around all day – which he isn't really supposed to do, his doctor said. But we've determined that it doesn't hurt him – it's like a good workout. And since there's no gym in the neighborhood, we exercise out in the open countryside."

"There's no better way to have it," Sonja said.

"We think so, too." Rolf beamed. "And now both of you are here, too."

"You look ten years younger," Kim remarked, amazed. "You could come right back to work."

"Not that!" Rolf waved that idea away. "No, no, those days are over."

"If he ever dared to do that, I would get a divorce, even after our golden wedding anniversary." Margit's eyes twinkled with amusement. She knew Rolf would never do that to her.

"Didn't you say the house was half ruined?" Sonja asked, amazed, since the house really didn't look that way at all.

"It was, when we got here." Margit gestured toward a small outbuilding. "Like that one there." The outbuilding had a very makeshift roof, no windows, and extremely wobbly-looking walls.

"And you made this out of that?" Kim looked just as amazed as Sonja at the rather solid-appearing main house.

"Yes, the two of us old folks." Rolf laughed. "With a little help from the village. There are always a few people who want to earn a little extra. Young fellows who can't find much work here in the area."

"Do the horses belong to you?" Sonja had spotted a couple of horses not far from the house.

"Camargue horses don't belong to anyone," Rolf explained. "But I think the horses believe that we belong to them. Because there are always such delicious things to eat around here." He looked at Margit.

"I don't get around to baking cakes much anymore," Margit said – Kim exhaled in silent relief –, "but I do it for the horses from time to time."

"They eat your cakes?" Anyone looking closely would've seen that Sonja was having to fight off a laughing attack, but she controlled herself and tried not to be too obvious about it.

"They love them," Margit said. "Although I have changed the ingredients a little. Too much sugar isn't good for horses."

It's not good for humans, either, Kim thought, trying to suppress a grin. That had never bothered Margit.

"Now that you're finally keeping your promise," Rolf said, beaming at Kim even more. "And you even brought Sonja with you . . ." He placed a hand on Sonja's shoulder, directed Kim with the other, and pushed both of them into the house. "There's coffee to start with, French coffee. If you're not used to it, it'll scrub your taste buds right off, but you get used to it."

"I thought you weren't supposed to drink coffee anymore," Kim said.

"I like the aroma. And besides, I only drink decaf. But it tastes just as bitter as the other kind." Rolf laughed.

For the next few hours, they sat over coffee and cake and told stories, and in fact, Margit's horse cake was palatable, so that Kim and Sonja were able to eat theirs without too much effort.

"You two have a long drive behind you," Margit said afterwards. "I'm sure you'll want a rest. I'm afraid there's only one room for the two of you. The other one isn't finished yet. We don't get that many visitors."

Kim and Sonja looked at each other, both thinking the same thing. They followed Margit through the house, which grew darker the farther inside they went. As was the custom in hot countries, people tried to leave the light and the warmth outdoors.

Once Margit had left them alone, Kim and Sonja sank together into the depths of the French bed. It was different from the ones they were used to in Germany. Here in the Camargue they both kept rolling into the middle. A person could only lie near the edge if she were the only one in the bed; as soon as there were two of them, the bed slanted inward.

"This is definitely not a bed for singles who want to sleep apart." Kim lay next to Sonja, as close as the bed demanded, and laughed.

"Good thing that's not what we are." Sonja kissed Kim briefly, then rolled back to the side, against the will of the bed, and stood up. "But I don't actually want to sleep right now. I'd rather have a look at the countryside. I've been looking forward to that the whole time."

"We saw quite a bit of it during the drive," Kim said.

"Oh, only through the car windows," Sonja complained. "A boring point of view. No, I want to really explore the area. It's already clear to me what attracted Rolf and Margit here, but I'd like to have a better look at it from up close."

"I have no objections," Kim said. "May I come along?"

Sonja gave her a mocking look. "No," she said. "I drove here with you to be alone. You're getting on my nerves every day at home."

"Then I'll stay here." Kim folded her arms behind her head as if she were taking what Sonja said seriously. "I have no desire to disturb your solitude."

Sonja pounced on her with one leap, and the bed did the rest: they rolled right on top of each other into the middle. Ultimately, Sonja lay beneath Kim, unable to move.

"I like *this* point of view better, too." Kim grinned, bending down to Sonja and kissing her.

"Kim . . ." Sonja whispered. "We can't . . . Rolf and Margit . . ."

"I could ask them if they object," Kim said.

"Please . . . Kim . . . don't do that to me," Sonja whispered. "Rolf was my dearest colleague . . ."

"Mine, too. And my boss. But what does any of that have to do with us?"

"I can't," Sonja said, still quiet. "Please . . . understand . . ." She turned her face away.

"I do understand." Kim struggled to her feet.

"No, you don't understand." Sonja had to downright scrabble her way out of the pit in the middle of the bed. "You think it's because you're a woman. But I wouldn't do it if you were a man, either. That's how my mother raised me. It has nothing to do with the gender of my partner."

"Really?"

"Yes, really." Sonja sighed. "Now I've outed myself as a really uptight person. Would you have thought that?"

"No." Kim grinned. "But you tackled me, not the other way around."

"Somehow, just coincidentally, you made sure I was on the bottom at the end. You seem to manage that pretty frequently."

"That really was pure coincidence."

"Our bed at home doesn't have this kind of a pit in the middle." Sonja arched her eyebrows.

"Sonja ..." Kim gaped at her, flabbergasted. "Surely, you don't mean to allege ..."

"I'm not alleging anything, I'm just stating the facts," Sonja remarked, grinning crookedly.

"You're just trying to tease me," Kim decided. "Because it's not true at all."

"Oh, yes, it is." Sonja smiled. "But it doesn't bother me. Otherwise I would've done something about it a long time ago."

"I should hope so," Kim said, half relieved, but also mildly out of sorts. "Don't come down on me too hard. We're on vacation."

"Yes." Sonja gazed out the window. "Our first vacation. We shouldn't spoil it. We can fight at home." She took a pair of shoes from her suitcase, since during the drive, she'd worn only lightweight summer sandals, and they seemed unsuitable for the rough terrain outside.

"We don't fight." Kim was taken aback. "Or do you think we do?" She looked a bit flummoxed. "Just because I objected to the tenth frying pan you wanted to buy?"

"We don't have anywhere near ten frying pans," Sonja said definitely. "Six at the most."

"It seems like ten to me. And I don't know what anyone needs six different frying pans for, either."

"That's because you don't cook." Sonja laced up her shoes. "You can't use an omelette pan for meat."

"That makes two." Kim grinned.

"You need different sizes, too," Sonja said. "You don't know a thing about it."

"I admit that." Kim had also put on sturdy shoes. "I've never done as much cooking at home as I have since we've lived together."

"You cook? That's news to me."

"When I stand next to you at the stove, I always feel like I'm just getting in your way," Kim said sheepishly. "Like you'd rather just kick me out of the kitchen."

"That's true sometimes." Sonja walked to the door. "You're always standing right in my way, in front of the herbs, the refrigerator . . ."

"I don't know what you're going to need next when you're cooking." Kim defended herself as they left the house.

"Exactly. That's what I mean." Sonja linked arms with Kim as they strode onto the meadow where the horses stood, chewing contentedly. "You don't have to help me cook." She smiled at Kim. "Cooking relaxes me. It doesn't bother me at all to cook for you either."

"Cooking relaxes you?" Kim couldn't remotely imagine that. She found cooking extremely stressful.

"Yes," Sonja said. "It's the opposite of my work in the office. I can be creative with cooking. At work, that's generally undesirable."

"You're constantly being praised for your creative ideas about the reorganization," Kim remarked, astonished.

"That's a different kind of creativity. In fact, it isn't even really that. It's just drawing logical conclusions. Cooking is different."

Kim sighed. "I'll never understand it."

"You don't need to." Sonja stood still and looked around. "Isn't this gorgeous?"

It was already evening, since they'd spent all day driving, and on the horizon they could see the sun beginning its descent into sleep.

"Whenever Rolf told me about this, I tried to imagine it for myself," Sonja went on softly, as if she didn't want to disturb Nature's preparations for its nightly rest. "And I did imagine it, and I'd seen pictures, but in reality, it's much, much prettier."

"That's true." Kim wrapped one arm around her. "It's like a fairyland." All of a sudden, she felt something soft and warm plucking at her hand. She looked around. A horse had apparently confused her with Margit and was looking for a piece of cake in Kim's hand. Its muzzle was like velvet. "I don't have anything," Kim said. "I'm sorry."

"What?" Sonja only now realized that Kim wasn't talking to her. She turned around in her arm, leaned into Kim, and watched the horse with a smile. "Who would've thought that Margit's cake could generate that kind of enthusiasm?"

"I don't think that's enthusiasm, I think it's love," Kim said. "Look at her eyes. The cake is only a pretext."

Sonja reached out a careful hand, and the horse snuffled at it. It snorted softly. Then it licked Sonja's palm with its long tongue. "That tickles!" Sonja laughed softly, so that she wouldn't frighten the horse.

"Hey," Kim told the horse, but equally softly, and with a smile. "That's *my* woman!"

The horse turned its head and nudged Kim, as if to say: *I didn't mean it that way*. Its friendly eyes left no doubt that it harbored no evil thoughts whatsoever.

"I should hope so." Kim petted the horse's muzzle gently. "You don't mind if we stay here on your meadow for a while, do you?"

The horse shook its head, as if it had understood Kim. Its mane settled sleekly back around its neck.

"What gorgeous animals," Sonja said, overwhelmed by the beauty of the view.

"Gorgeous animals, yes." Kim looked at Sonja. "If you weren't here, a person could think there was nothing more beautiful on the face of the earth."

"Don't exaggerate." Sonja laughed softly. "Beside which, there are two of me, so you'd have to include Sandra in that description, too."

"There aren't two of you. No way. You are unique, and you always will be."

The shadows behind the horse grew longer, and Kim and Sonja turned around to send one final greeting toward the sun.

The horse appeared to have the same thing in mind, because it stayed with them, and so the three of them stood there together and watched the sun as it kissed the horizon with red lips before setting at last.

Two women who loved each other, and one horse that loved them, too, in the vastness of the Camargue.

THE END